DRAWING DEAD

GRANT McCREA

DRAWING DEAD

a Rick Redman mystery

RANDOM HOUSE CANADA

Library and Archives Canada Cataloguing in Publication

McCrea, Grant
Drawing dead / Grant McCrea.

ISBN 978-0-679-31400-4

I. Title.
PS8625.C74D73 2009   C813'.6   C2008-905153-X

Jacket and text design: Kelly Hill

Printed and bound in the Unitied States of America

10 9 8 7 6 5 4 3 2 1

To Annie Nocenti,
without whom this book would not be
half as good as however good it is,
however-good that may be.

1.

HE HAD AN ODD EXPRESSION ON HIS FACE. Half smile, half grimace. Part puzzlement. That may add up to more than a whole. But death does strange things to people.

He was lying face up. His right arm was twisted behind his back. He clutched something in his left hand. I couldn't make out what it was.

He was in black tie. Tuxedo. White ruffled shirt. Bow tie. Bare feet. Clean, though. As though recently shod.

Oh, Brendan, I whispered. What have you done?

A guy in a lumpy brown suit waved me back.

Hey, I said. That's my friend.

Sure, he said. And I'm J. Edgar Hoover.

Who's in charge here? I asked.

Who wants to know?

I told you. He's my friend.

And I told you. I'm J. Edgar Hoover.

I wasn't getting any respect.

Maybe it was the squid-shaped wine stain on the front of my shirt. My bleary eyes. The two days' growth of intermittent beard.

J. Edgar, on the other hand, presented a more imposing figure. Sagging belly. Stick legs. That lumpy brown suit. And a gun.

There was no way around that last bit. I had to go over his head.

I stepped back. Unholstered my cell phone. Called my buddy, Butch Hardiman. New York cop. Shaved head. Mammoth shoulders. Not a bad poker player. He'd probably say he was better than me. I'd disagree.

Butch, I said.

Rick, he said in his big baritone voice.

Brendan's dead.

You're fucking with me, he said, his voice suddenly smaller, far away.

No, I'm not. I wish I were. I'm at the casino. They won't let me near him. Can you pull some rank?

I'll pull whatever rank I have down here. Which isn't much.

Do your best.

Have I ever done less?

No, I had to admit. He hadn't.

He called some friends who called some friends. It's a small world, law enforcement. Butch could almost always find someone. Someone who knew someone who could call someone who could call in a favor, real or imagined. Even in Vegas. Especially if the favor was a minor one. Like letting him and his buddy past a bit of crime scene tape.

I waited for him at a long bar studded with the usual array of electronic keno and poker machines. You barely had room to put down your glass. Why waste a moment of drinking time when you could be losing some more money to the house? I stared at the plasma screen behind the bar. Some goddamn horse race. Never understood that horse race thing. Lack of empathy, I guess. But it seemed like only the most degenerate gamblers played the horses.

I couldn't identify.

I drank a scotch. I drank another one.

A hand on my shoulder. I turned around. Butch.

What the fuck? he said.

I don't know, I said. I don't know anything. He's over there.

Butch strode over. Asked for Detective Warren. The stick-leg guy. Butch introduced himself. Mentioned a name. The name did it.

Call me Earl, J. Edgar said, extending a hand to Butch.

Guy had a lot of names.

Rick Redman, I said, extending my own hand.

J. Edgar ignored it.

He lifted up the yellow tape. We ducked under it. Walked towards the huddle of uniforms. The well-dressed remains of my former brother-in-law.

I hung back a bit. I didn't want to get too close. See too much. I'd never get it out of my dreams. There were enough dead bodies in there already.

Butch went right up. Nudged a couple of blue shirts aside. Knelt down. I felt stupid, hanging back. So I followed, blank.

I looked. I didn't want to look.

The technicians were doing their technician thing. Butch wasn't there to interfere. He wasn't there to help, either. He wanted to see the scene for himself. Do what I couldn't. File it away. Every scratch mark and dust mote. Every stain on the elaborately tiled lobby floor. What Brendan had in his hand.

The hell is that? I asked. A chopstick?

It's a knitting needle, said Butch.

I leaned in to get a look. A technician bagging evidence looked up, nodded.

Jesus, I said. The hell does that mean?

Butch shrugged.

I wandered over to the lobby's central grotesquerie. Concrete fishes and small boys were respectively spouting and pissing into a green pool. Generating little fountains of splash. One of which was slowly soaking the jacket of an old guy sitting on the low retaining wall. Old and spotted and hunched forward. The Universal Loser.

A couple of cops wandered over, poked him with a stick. He looked up. Calm. Resigned. Too far gone to be startled.

The cops asked questions. How long had he been there? What was his name? Had he seen anything unusual?

Unusual? I stared blankly at the concrete fish, the pissing boys. I guessed it was a matter of context.

I heard Butch's voice. Rick, he said. I turned around. Saw his extra-wide smile. Trying to be reassuring. Succeeding, a bit.

Come on, he said. Let's go home.

Home. The Dusty Angel Motel.

I felt his arm around my shoulder.

I suppose, I said, as Brendan's closest known relative, even if by defunct marriage, I should hang around. Find out what they're planning to do with him.

They have my cell number. They'll call.

Okay, I shrugged.

I'd seen a morgue or two before. There'd be time for the formalities later.

We flagged a cab. It smelled of sardines and sweat.

2.

BUTCH ALWAYS KNEW WHAT WAS RIGHT. Well, most of the time he did. More often than me, for sure. Which isn't saying much. He had a temper on him, though. On a guy that big, the temper could be a problem. Once in a while it came in handy.

When serious shit happens, it brings you together. Butch had been with me through a lot of serious shit. The Case of the Red Car Door. That had been good shit. We solved a crime. Butch found the photos. Somebody had hidden them away. The witnesses said the car was all black. The pictures showed a red driver's-side door. Prosecutorial misconduct, we convinced the judge. Got some innocent kids off. Got some good press.

Then there was the FitzGibbon case. Foisted on me by my unlamented former boss, the über-pompous Warwick. FitzGibbon was a major client of our firm, back then. He had a wayward kid. Turned out they were both big-time nut jobs, FitzGibbon and the kid, but the kid was worse. And his adoptive brothers put them both to shame. Twins. Wheels within wheels. Daddy got dead. So did the kid. The twins got life without. So Butch and I solved another crime. But not before a bunch of people got dead. It was hard to call that one a victory.

I wasn't a detective, a cop. I'd never even been a prosecutor. Hell, I was just an ordinary litigator who got caught up in some criminal shit once in a while, and tried to do the best for my client. Who usually wasn't paying. So, I could never have played detective without Butch to do the real work. Get access, get the phone records, run the license plates. Find the photos, think in a straight line. Pack the gun. Most important, go in first. I had a thing about going in first. Wouldn't do it. Scared the shit out of me.

And Brendan. Dear, fucked-up Brendan.

I hadn't quite known what to do with Brendan. Being as he was my former brother-in-law, or maybe still my brother-in-law—had he retained the status after Melissa died? anyway, he felt like family—it was like I owed him something, somehow. Which I didn't, really. But one thing for sure, I was all the family he had. And he had a certain naïve charm, and played a mean game of poker.

There was a Friday at the bar, a couple months before. The Wolf's Lair. My hang. My home. My commiseration. Thom behind the bar.

The cool brass rail. The warm mahogany. The endlessly various New York crowd. A serious bar. Two blocks from home, even better.

I was telling Thom about my new outfit. I called it The Outfit. So far it consisted of me. I'd quit my day job as a litigator to pursue my overstuffed dreams of poker grandeur. I felt I needed a cover. Just in case later I'd need another gig. Didn't look good on the resumé: failed poker player. Actually, it was a little more complicated than that. Something about a woman. Dorita. A tall babe with a killer set of legs and an attitude to match. Maybe we'd get to that later.

A woman sat down to my right. The sad-sack barfly type. Downcast eyes and a world of long lonely days hanging from her shoulders like the ancient Laura Ashley dress she wore, drifting to the floor, and had worn, it looked like, on every one of those days. She had a big, pouting mouth. On a girl with good bone structure it would have been striking. But it just accentuated the homeliness of her soft oval face. The freckles were cute, though. Cute enough to draw my attention for a second longer than mere curiosity required. That and her air of depressed and vulnerable sensuality.

I noticed that she was wearing only one shoe. I noticed how red it was. The shoe.

It was on her left foot.

On her right was a yellow bandage. Her toenails were painted with small piglet faces.

Five tiny snouts.

She noticed me looking. Turned to me.

I was up all night, she said. Hydrating my cat.

Well, this was a promising entrée, but just at that moment Butch showed up, and I had to excuse myself from the Piglet Lady.

Butch started bitching right away. He'd had another run-in with Inspector Nose.

Fucking guy, Butch said. Suspended Ritchie for throwing away a perfectly good paper clip. Wasting police property. I gotta get out of there.

I wasn't sure I believed the story. Not literally, anyway. But The Nose—I could never remember his real name, but the schnozz was unforgettable: long, lean, hooked, barely restraining a serious case of out-of-control nasal hair—was a tight-ass kind of a guy.

Mostly Butch and The Nose had managed to stay out of each other's way over the years, but Butch had got promoted, thanks to the

FitzGibbon case, and had to spend a lot more time in the precinct. Funny how it works. One day you're about to be fired for doing shit you weren't supposed to. Like babysitting a stupid lawyer named Rick Redman, in way over his head. Next day, the bad guys get caught, it's all over the *Daily News*. You're a fucking hero. You're a big shot.

But Butch wasn't happy about the promotion. He was a real cop. A street guy. A hustle guy. Now he had to lord it over a bunch of newbie geeks. Check on their paperwork. Tell them how to wear the blue shirt.

He hated it.

It's like the Peter Principle, he said. But I didn't get promoted to my level of incompetence. I got promoted to where I just want to get the hell out of there.

Maybe it's the same thing.

Maybe, he said, swirling the ice in his double scotch.

Come on, I said. You telling me you never wanted to be a big shot? Everybody wants to be a big shot.

Not me, man, said Butch, shaking his head slowly. Really. I never cared about that shit. Never. I like the job. The real job. Catching bad guys. That stuff. I don't know. There's got to be a better way.

To make a living? There's no good way to make a living. Marry rich, live high. That's the only ticket.

Yeah, but then you have to put up with her.

There's that. I've never given up the dream, though.

A couple of scotches later, Brendan showed up. Took a stool. Said sorry for being late. Told us some story that had to do with ginger ale, enemas and prosthetic devices. I smiled politely. It was probably a funny story, but Brendan told it all wrong. He was a terrible storyteller. Butch gave him the big baritone chuckle. Butch is a nicer guy than me.

We took a corner table to eat. Butch in the center seat. He liked to have command of the room. That authority thing. Brendan took the corner, back to the wall. Something about abject insecurity. I took what was left. Something about my life.

So guys, I said. You know I quit the firm . . .

Tell us something we don't know, said Butch.

You did? said Brendan.

I did, I repeated for Brendan's benefit.

Apparently he'd missed the news. Been living in some fetid cave off the Polynesian coast for the last few months, or something.

Does Polynesia have a coast? I asked.

They were used to my non sequiturs. So we considered that question for a while. We decided the answer was yes, and no.

I had to quit, I said, getting back on message. Jesus, the place was going down the tubes anyway. FitzGibbon was the firm's best client. And he just got pitched off a thirty-third-story balcony. And his heirs are all in jail, or dead.

And it was all your fault, said Butch.

About as much as yours, buddy, I replied. No, it wasn't all our fault. Just some of it. But that was more than enough for Warwick. So I decided to preempt him. Told him to go fuck himself.

Got to tell the Man to fuck off once in a while, said Butch.

Easy for you to say, I said.

Yeah, he said. I have no responsibilities.

You don't have a child to support, I said. And an ex-wife's grave to maintain.

Brendan cringed. It was his sister's grave, too.

Sorry, man, I said to him. That's just me. Humor to cover up the pain and all, you know.

It's okay, said Brendan.

It was always okay with Brendan. That was part of his problem.

A life of endless trauma will do things to you. It made me feel bad. But I didn't know what I could do about it. I didn't even know if it was my job to do anything about it. I mean, was I my ex-brother-in-law's keeper? He ain't heavy, he's my ex-brother-in-law? Didn't really have that ring to it.

Damn. Where was my shrink when I needed her?

So, I said, trying to head off the impending gloom, what're we gonna do?

We? said Butch.

Yeah, I said. We. Me, you, Brendan. I thought we were a team.

Damn it, Redman, said Butch, you are a presumptuous motherfucker.

That's why you love me, I said.

Brendan laughed. It wasn't that funny a line. But that was Brendan, too. When he laughed, it always seemed like he was laughing at something else. Something far away. Out of reach.

So, I said. I have an idea.

Shoot, said Butch.

You guys can join my outfit.

Outfit? said Butch.

Outfit, I said. It's called The Outfit.

What the fuck are you talking about?

Listen, just think about it. No, forget thinking. Just listen. I'm a lawyer. I've done some criminal stuff. Some sick divorces. All sorts of shit. I have some skills. Some contacts.

Sure, said Butch.

Sure, said Brendan.

Butch, you're a cop.

Detective, to you.

Better yet. You're a detective. You know the ropes. The technical shit. You have your own connections.

I see where you're going.

Brendan was sinking into his chair.

And Brendan, I said, with perhaps a touch too much obvious cheer. You're the perfect undercover guy.

He straightened up a bit.

Sure, I said. Nobody would ever think you're a cop or anything. You're an actor. A carpenter. You've been around. Lived in different places. You can be anybody, any time.

Sure, he said. Yeah. I can do that.

So. It'll be our outfit. Investigations, enforcement. Whatever comes along. Once we get it going, Butch, you can quit your job. Brendan and me, we don't have anything to quit. We can start right away.

Rick, said Butch, it's not that simple. You got to establish some credibility, get a client base. And it'll cost more than a shingle and a pole to hang it on. You got to set up an office, make it look nice. Get a receptionist. And you got to have a license to do some of that shit.

So, we'll call it something else, until we get a license. Hey, I'm still a lawyer. It'll be a law firm, to start. And the thing of it is, we can go to the World Series of Poker. Qualify in satellites. Win big in the Main Event. Use the proceeds to set up shop.

Vegas, said Brendan. I'm there.

You gotta be kidding me, said Butch. There were eight thousand players in the Main Event last year. More this year, probably. And about eight hundred of them are probably better players than any of us.

Brendan lost his smile.

Okay, okay. We're not going to win the Main Event. Probably. But there's three of us. Any one of us could go deep. Get to the serious money. We'll make a pool of ourselves. If we lose, we lose. If we win, it's a bonus. And anyway, how can we lose in the cash games? The place'll be rank with tourists.

You got a point there, anyway.

I know I do. I've thought this through. Is it a deal?

Rick, said Butch.

Yes, Detective?

I know what you're doing.

You do?

Sure. And so do you.

Just what might that be, Detective Butch?

You're going to play poker. And use this outfit shit to pretend you're doing something productive.

Damn, Butch, I said. Now I know why they promoted you.

He gave me a small bow.

So anyway, I said. Say that's true. Anything wrong with it?

Nope.

So is it a deal?

Butch put his elbows on his knees. Lowered his head. I watched his scalp twitch.

Well? I said.

I got some vacation coming, he said, his head still down.

That's a yes, I said.

Yeah, that's a yes, he said, lifting his head and smiling his big Butch smile. You crazy bastard.

Deal, Brendan?

For sure, he said.

It was a deal.

3.

I CALLED MY SHRINK. I needed her permission for the Vegas trip.

She was sitting on her recliner, as always. I sprawled facing her on the matching leather couch, also as always. She was wearing some kind of loose neo-hippie pantaloon item. Clunky sandals. And a billowy blouse thing of indeterminate but definite ethnicity. Her hair was graying, in that nice Upper East Side way. Made you feel comfortable.

What she lacked in style, she made up in compassion.

Which is what I was paying for.

Sheila, I said.

I liked to call her by her first name. I knew it bugged her. She liked to keep the proverbial professional distance. It was the only liberty I took with her, though. She was the best. And I needed all the help I could get. I couldn't afford to alienate her.

Yes? she said without a trace of disapprobation.

I'm going to Vegas.

You're going to Vegas.

Yes. I need your permission.

You don't need my permission.

Yes I do.

You don't. You're an adult. You don't need anyone's permission.

My daughter's?

Kelley? She's in college. You don't need her permission.

Maybe not. But I need yours.

No, you do not.

Yes I do, I insisted. I mean, do you think it's all right?

Is what all right?

I explained The Outfit thing. My new life. The World Series of Poker.

I do have some concerns, she admitted.

That's more like it, I said.

I thought we were making some progress.

I agree.

How long will you be gone?

Just a week or two. Maybe. It depends. We need to qualify for the Main Event first. The entry fee is ten thousand bucks. Ridiculous. But they have these mini-tournaments, satellites, they're called. You can buy in small, a hundred bucks. Work your way up to a thousand-dollar table. Win that one, you have your entry fee. Or they have these mega-satellites. Small buy-in, huge field. You go there early, before all the pros get there. It's all tourists. Easy. I did it last year.

Perhaps we can talk by phone while you're there.

Sure. I like that. You can't see me twitch.

She laughed softly.

But, she said.

But.

But the obvious. We've made some progress. You've been moderating some of your self-destructive behavior. You know the drill. You're supposed to avoid temptation. New stresses. Big changes. It sounds like this is all of those.

I can handle it, I said. It's only a couple of weeks, probably. Listen, I'm different, you know. I can do anything I put my mind to. I can do this.

Of course you can. Everything is possible. I don't want to deny you that. But why take the chance?

Because I love to take chances?

You're doing it again.

Yes, I know, I know. Using humor to evade dealing with the real issues. With reality. Yes. Of course. But I really can do this.

You're an adult, Rick, she said.

I knew that wasn't true.

But I took it as permission anyway.

If she was going to call me an adult, she'd just have to live with the consequences.

4.

TWO WEEKS BEFORE VEGAS. We decided to bone up, play the toughest games in town. Brendan and I went to Fast Vinnie's. Vinnie—that wasn't his real name, of course—was a short, scrawny guy with a thick accent of some indeterminate kind, a pockmarked face, greasy receding hair. Always in motion. He talked up a streak. Half the time you couldn't understand a thing. That's why they called him Fast.

The game was in a two-story apartment in a brownstone on the Upper East Side. The place was pretty nice, as illegal poker joints go. There were only two tables, one downstairs and one up. And they weren't the usual cheesy articles that guys who run games in New York City always seem to have—shaky aluminum-tube things with felt that comes off in clumps under your fingernails. They were good solid oak tables. And Vinnie always had a couple hot ladies there to serve drinks, order in food or run to the corner store for smokes. And good dealers. Fast and efficient.

The only problem with Vinnie's game was there was usually a bunch of Russians there. Now, I've got nothing against Russians in general. But these guys, I don't know. You hear about the Russian mafia. If these guys weren't the Russian mafia, there isn't any Russian mafia.

There was Vitaly. Mr. Dumpling. Razor-cut hair with a bald spot, shaved up too far in the back, every part of his face—nose, chin, cheeks, ears—looking like another pair of chubby ass-cheeks. Never saw the guy smile, or say a word in English other than raise, check, fold. This was the guy, you figured, did the dirty work. And there were these two guys, Anatoly and Andrei. Always seemed to be there. Anatoly was tall and thin. Wore leather vests and a soul patch. Andrei was short and round. Smoked small cigars. His fingernails bitten to the bone. They were always sitting next to each other at the table, nudging and mugging and talking in Russian between hands.

You wanted to complain about it, but you couldn't. An English-only rule applies when you're involved in a hand. Standard practice, to prevent collusion. But when you're not in the hand, you can speak Esperanto if you want.

Of course, guys don't have to talk to each other to cheat. You can spot it, sometimes, when it's badly done. Hand signals: place your fingers on the left side of your face, you have an Ace in your hand, like that. Or series of coded signals. Like the baseball manager signaling the third-base coach to signal the hitter. But that kind of stuff's not easy to get away with, in a good game. Good players, they're always watching you for the slightest tell, the smallest change in your regular pattern. More effective, you can shuffle your chips in a certain way, place them on your cards in precoded patterns. Upper left, you've got a pocket pair. Lower right, you've got rags. Whatever. Endless variations.

There are those who say that two guys colluding once in a while at a full table can't really change your results that much. But tell that to the guy who gets soaked out of a couple grand when his big bluff doesn't work, because Anatoly knows from Andrei that the scare card the guy's representing—the Ace of hearts on a four-heart board, say—was in Andrei's since-mucked hand. It doesn't have to happen that often to put a serious dent in your profit rate. Not to mention your mood.

I watched Anatoly and Andrei, behind my wraparound shades. But if they were doing something, they were doing it well. There was nothing I could pin on them. They just had that air about them. They found each other very amusing. But only in Russian. In English they were stone-faced.

They bugged my ass.

Brendan got along fine with the Russkies, though. Brendan got along fine with everybody. That innocent air of his made everybody want to like him. It helped that it also made them think he couldn't play poker.

The savvy guys figured out soon enough he could play pretty damn good. But the fish would put it down to luck. And you want to be nice to the fish. Don't tap the aquarium.

Evgeny was another Russian guy in the game. A different kind of Russian. Evgeny was a fish. And he wasn't just another fish, another guppy or goldfish. Not even a tuna. Evgeny was a big, special kind of fish. The biggest, best kind of fish. A whale. A fish with a lot of money. Dead money, you called it. You could latch on to a whale, buddy up to him, get him to play your table regular, you could live off the guy for years.

Everybody loves a whale. The casinos have a whole troupe of whale handlers. Guys paid to make the whales feel comfortable, wanted, loved, respected. Keep them coming back.

Evgeny embodied the role. He weighed maybe four hundred pounds. Had to extend his arms straight out over his belly to reach his chips. Drank vodka ostentatiously from a silver flask that never seemed to be empty. Loved to splash his chips around. Talked with a magnificent Yiddish-Russian accent.

Loveable, really. He was a loveable Yiddish-Russian fat rogue whale kind of guy.

So Brendan and I sit down. Brendan's in the four seat, four to the left of the dealer, next to Anatoly and Andrei in two and three. I'm in seven. I like the seven seat. It's right where the table curves back around to form the short side. You get a good view of all the players, but you're not right in the center of things. You can lay low there, without missing any of the action.

First hand, Vinnie makes a huge raise preflop. Evgeny re-raises five times Vinnie's bet. Vinnie laughs, tosses in three stacks of black chips. Six thousand dollars.

The flop comes Queen, Eight, Three rainbow—three different suits, widely spaced; no need to worry about flush draws. No open-ended straight draws out there either.

Evgeny instantly announces a pot-sized bet, gets up from his chair. Which is not as simple as it sounds. His arms barely reaching beyond his belly, he can only push his chair back a few inches. Then he executes a practiced wriggle or two to get back far enough to release the rest of his paunch from beneath the table. Once he's up, he teeters there for a second or two. Like a lot of fat men, he has small feet. Or maybe they just looked small at the bottom of those tree stump legs. There's that small dick thing, too, isn't there? Fat man, small dick? But maybe it's just a perceptual thing. A camel looks tiny next to a mastodon. I'm guessing. Never seen that.

All in, says Vinnie, without pausing a second. Evgeny leans over, braces himself against the table, says Call, and turns over Seven, Three off suit, with a big cheerful laugh. Nothing but a pair of Threes. Vinnie looks at him, mouth open, slowly turns over a Jack, Nine off suit for . . . nothing. No pair. Not even a draw. But a Jack hits the turn, and Vinnie suddenly has a better pair than Evgeny's. Vinnie leaps, turns a circle, cackling. Evgeny smiles in his good-natured way, shrugs his massive shoulders. A Seven hits the river. Oops. Two pair for Evgeny. Vinnie stops, stares, looks at Evgeny, who's laughing so hard we're all worried he's going to bust open like a split fish.

I can't believe you did that, says Vinnie.

Me? You got to be kiddink, Veenie, says Evgeny as the dealer pushes the massive mound of chips his way. I know you, Evgeny says. You can so every time have nothink.

That's it, says Vinnie, throwing up his arms. I'm giving up poker. I mean it. Forget it. That's my last hand, ever.

The dealer starts shuffling for the next hand. Vinnie looks around. Sees nobody's paying attention to him. He sits down, looks at the two cards he's been dealt.

Chips! he yells out.

How much? calls Internet Mike from the kitchen.

Internet Mike ran chips for Vinnie. He was called Internet Mike because he used to have a job in the Internet, back before it became the Internet. He didn't have a job anymore. The technology had outrun his cerebral capacity. He had a crack habit for a while. His hair fell out.

His teeth rotted. But he could still count to a thousand. Ten thousand. Fifty, in a pinch. So he ran chips for Vinnie.

There were worse lives.

Ten thousand, Vinnie calls back. Jesus Christ, he says, turning back to Evgeny, you are a sick bastard.

Sure, Vinnie, smiles Evgeny. But I know how to haff a good time.

Evgeny could afford to be a whale and laugh it off. Rumor was he was in the phony passport business, stuff like that. He never ran out of cash. Loved to take your money, but just as easily gave it away.

About two hours in, Brendan and I are limping along, not winning any big pots, not losing any. I'm second from the big blind. I still have about the amount I bought in for. I look down at Ace, Queen of diamonds. I just call. Unlike a lot of donkeys out there, I don't think Ace, Queen is that good of a hand in early position. It's a very vulnerable hand. Like Mike Tyson: looks strong, usually loses.

There are a couple of other callers, including Brendan and Evgeny, and the flop comes with a Queen and two rag diamonds. Nice for me. I have a pair of Queens, with the top kicker, the Ace.

The guy to my right is Won Ton John, a middle-aged guy who reportedly owns a Chinese restaurant. If he does, he must have a cousin running it for him, Sesame Noodle Sam or somebody, because nobody ever sees Won Ton do anything but play poker. He has the shades and a wispy Fu Manchu, and he'll bet Nine, Four off suit from any position, if he's in the mood. You have to watch out for him.

Won Ton puts his chin in his hands and thinks a bit. I'm not fooled. The last time Won Ton John thought about an action before committing it was in the Nixon administration. Anyway, after a little of the Hollywood he bets out $120, and I flat call. Everyone else folds to Evgeny, who calls. So there are three guys in the hand, $485 in the pot. The turn comes a lovely diamond Ten. I have the nut flush, and the board isn't scary at all. Not only that, I'm in a hand with two maniacs. So I check, figuring one of them to bet for sure. But Won Ton checks, and Evgeny checks behind him. Shit. But hey, that's poker. You can't be right all the time.

The dealer lays out the last card, the river. A blank. A nothing card. A card that can only have helped them improve to a good-enough hand to put some more money in the pot for me. Not one that can beat me. I know I'm good. I bet $400. Nonchalantly. I want it to look like I'm trying to steal the pot.

Won Ton John raises it to $1,200. Oh Lord in heaven, I say to myself. Does it get any better than this? Please, Evgeny, do your Evgeny thing. Go all in.

Which is exactly what he does. It takes him a long time. He thinks. He ponders. He riffles his chips. He looks at Won Ton John. He looks at me. He has a mammoth pile of chips. Slowly, ever so slowly, he slides them two inches forward. Which is about as far as his stubby arms will allow.

Call, I say immediately.

Won Ton John folds.

Evgeny doesn't look happy.

As the last aggressor, Evgeny has to show his cards first. He turns over two small pair, laughing. He knows he's beat.

That's when I make a mistake. An elementary mistake. But a big fucking mistake. The worst kind of mistake. Way worse than bluffing a fool. Or calling a Shark on the river with top pair and a medium kicker. Far worse than that.

No, I make the mistake of disrespecting Evgeny.

You lose! I call out in my excitement, turning over my flush and slamming the cards to the table.

Right away I knew I'd blown it. A guy who's just lost a huge pot is not a happy guy, good loser or not. He can see the goddamn cards. Evgeny didn't even need to see the damn cards. He knew he was beat as soon as I called his all in. He didn't need me telling him the result. And he certainly didn't need me doing it with a slam and a bang.

His laugh froze. It was replaced by a Look. Narrowed eyes. Cheeks deflated. He tucked his chin into his chins. It was a Look I hadn't seen from him before. He pushed his chips ever so slowly an inch to the left, towards me, with his pudgy pink hands.

I noticed the French manicure.

Hey, Evgeny, I said, trying to salvage the moment. Sorry. I didn't mean it that way.

Is okay, he said quietly. Is okay.

He didn't mean that, either.

I couldn't stay in the game after that. The table got cold. No more crazy betting with mediocre hands. No more joking and banter. I'd chilled out the whole joint. I felt like a total jerk. I took Brendan aside. Talked him into leaving early.

It wasn't easy. At the poker table, Brendan was in his element. His insecurity didn't count. The game had rules. There was always something to anticipate: your next two cards. There was always banter of some sort. Even if you weren't included, you could listen, laugh, make a remark from time to time. It didn't strain your social abilities. And like I said, he could play the game. There wasn't anything else in life he could do as well.

So I waited awhile, until Brendan got his jones fixed. He got up a few grand. I talked to the waitress. Tara said she was a refugee from Vietnam. She looked too young for that. Hell, she was too good-looking. You're a refugee, you're supposed to look, I don't know, lost or something. Tara looked like she was rented from some modeling agency. So I wasn't sure I believed her.

But it didn't matter.

5.

WE FLAGGED A CAB AROUND MIDNIGHT.

It smelled of cabbages and mold.

Hey, I said to the cabbie, Ukraine?

Yeah, he said. How you know?

I don't know, I said. Just a vibe I got.

I was about to get into the proper pronunciation of 'pierogies'—I had a Ukrainian girlfriend once who told me it was 'pair-eh-heh,' but nobody ever believed me—when Brendan interrupted.

They invited me to the Brighton Beach game, he said.

Who invited you?

Anatoly and Andrei.

You're not going, are you?

Of course, man. That's a great game.

That's a great place to get your kneecaps busted. Come on. The stakes are too high for you. And those guys are ruthless bastards. Didn't you hear about MIT Dave?

I'm not MIT Dave.

Well, that much was true. MIT Dave was an arrogant little prick who hung out at the big games in town. He got the moniker because he was reputed to once have audited a class at MIT. If he had, it wasn't in hygiene. He was a weedy little guy with thick glasses and a smell of desperation.

Wore an ancient Red Sox cap. Said he got it from his father, that he used to have a father, and didn't any more. The cap reminding him of the days at Fenway. Popcorn and hot dogs and Carl Yastrzemski. Okay, maybe Carl was before his time. Anyway, he always had the cap.

MIT Dave only had enough money to play once in a while. He'd hang around the games, run errands for guys. A few months before, he'd gone on a little rush in the smaller games, built up a bankroll. Got himself invited to the Brighton Beach game. And, they said, his rush continued. He took a couple, ten grand, maybe more, off the Russkies. And then, little shit that he was, got arrogant with them about it. Started trash-talking. Not the usual funny trash we all talked. This was bitter, you-guys-can-suck-my-balls kind of trash.

Or so the story went.

Nobody'd seen him since.

And anyway, said Brendan, he started it, right?

Come on, Brendan. Maybe he did, but all you have to do to start something with those guys is take too much of their money. Look at somebody the wrong way. Say no to a shot of vodka when you're ahead.

I saw the driver's unibrow in the rearview. Oops. Generally, Ukrainians not of Russian descent aren't too fond of Russians. But there lots of Russian Ukranians. I hadn't confirmed our chauffeur's patrimony. I told Brendan to tone it down. Just in case.

You're the one getting loud, he said.

Okay, okay, I said in a whisper, nodding towards the front seat. *Mea culpa.* But let's keep it quiet.

You and Butch come, too, Brendan whispered back. They're not going to do shit with Butch there.

Thanks for the vote of confidence. But they didn't invite us. They invited you. Something tells me they won't exactly welcome Butch. I think his occupation is a matter of public knowledge.

I'll ask Tolya. I'm sure it'll be okay.

Tolya?

Anatoly.

My, I said. Tolya. On the diminutives already. You guys move fast.

Can't you ever give me a little respect?

All right. You ask Tolya. But if you go there by yourself, you're on your own.

So, what you're trying to say is, if I'm alone I'm on my own?

Something like that.

Anyway, could be we could get some business.

I looked out the window. There was a large brown dog taking a very big shit on the sidewalk. There was nobody with the dog. The shit was going to stay there.

What do you mean, business? I said.

I told them we did investigations and shit. Tolya seemed really interested.

I'll bet he did. Jesus, man, you need to be a little more circumspect.

What's wrong with doing a little advertising?

Nothing, I guess. It's just that I can't imagine anything good coming out of getting involved with those guys.

Oh, man. You're really paranoid. They're good guys.

Oh, man. You're really naïve.

Tolya said he would keep an eye out, Brendan said, ignoring me. Might have a job for us.

You can't be serious. What, dump a body in the Meadowlands?

He didn't say anything specific. Said we could talk about it at the game.

Jesus. All right. Talk to Anatoly at the game. But Butch and I better be there. I'm not letting you go alone.

You just said if I'm alone I'm alone.

But I'm not going to let you go alone.

Change your mind?

Something like that.

Damn it, Rick, when did you get elected to be my father?

I appointed myself. And you should be very happy about it.

Sure, he said.

He looked at his knees. Like a sheepish child.

What's wrong?

Nothing.

Oh, the father thing. Sorry.

I looked out the window. There was a guy on the corner with an orange cap. The cap said *Burt's Bait & Tackle, Garrison, Mich.* The guy appeared to be urinating.

Don't be sorry, Brendan said.

Okay, I'm not sorry. So what else did you talk about, you and the Russkies?

I don't know, he mumbled, not lifting his head. Talked some poker. The World Series. Everybody wants to go. I asked him what they did.

What they did?

For a living. You know.

Really? I'm curious to hear the answer.

They said they take care of people.

You serious? I laughed. They said they take care of people? Wow. Take care of them real good, I hear.

Oh fuck off, said Brendan.

But he knew I was right.

6.

At ten in the morning, the phone rang.

Go away, I said.

I turned over. Put the pillow over my head.

The phone kept ringing.

It stopped.

It started again.

Shit, I said. I opened an eye. Quickly closed it again. I didn't need to see the pizza cartons. Empty bottles. Full ashtrays. Three weeks of dirty clothes, six weeks of damp and wrinkled *New York Times.*

And that was just the bed.

The phone kept ringing.

It wasn't going to go away.

I was going to have to find it.

I shuffled some detritus around. I found a copy of a Pete Dexter anthology I'd been looking for. This made me happy. Under it I found the phone. I wasn't sure how that made me feel. I picked it up.

Redman, I said.

Rick, it's John.

John?

John Kennedy.

Jack!

Oh, shut up.

Okay.

After twenty years the joke was growing a little stale.

Listen, Kennedy said. I might have a bit of business for you.

Business?

Yes, Rick. A job. Some work. A paying gig.

Really? I said.

I'd printed up some nice business cards. *The Outfit* in gold-embossed letters. Wrote up a fancy note, announcing my latest prestigious project. Mailed them out to everybody on my list. Old clients. Old colleagues. Kennedy was always first on my list. He was a good guy. And an excellent trusts and estates lawyer. But T & E guys hate messes. They have a good, quiet life. Going to lunch with nice, eccentric, wealthy old ladies. Holding their hands. Writing their wills. Setting up financial plans. So when something nasty came up, something requiring litigation, say, or criminal defense, or dealing with the ugly side of the press—in other words, when the real world intruded—Kennedy called me up. To return the favor, whenever I had some boring shit involving little old ladies, I'd call him. As a matter of fact, I'd referred to Kennedy the late unlamented FitzGibbon, who wasn't a little old lady, and was involved in enough nastiness to fill several bad novels. But I didn't know that at the time. He just needed some help with some trusts and such, FitzGibbon had said.

In the end, that whole thing hadn't turned out too well. Pesky dead bodies. All over the joint.

But Kennedy got paid. And in the law business, that's what matters.

Work? I said. Are you serious?

Sure. One good turn deserves another.

One? I queried. Seems to me it's about fifteen to three, right about now.

I could count on you to say that.

Consistency is the hobgoblin of my middle name, I replied, trying to remember my middle name.

Jesus, said Kennedy, you're in even worse shape than usual this morning.

I won't deny it. I was out with a bunch of Russians last night.

It doesn't get worse than that. I hear.

You hear correct. Okay, wait a minute. I'm going to stick my head under a cold faucet.

Don't forget to turn the water on.

Right.

I put down the phone. I administered to my face a good dose of the ice-cold, while my mind roamed free. Cockroaches and mold. That's all I could think about. Don't ask me why. Probably the old pizza. I'll talk about it with Sheila, I thought.

Okay, I said when I had the phone back in my hand. This better not involve homicidal adopted twin brothers.

I can't promise anything, said Kennedy. I have a client. Her name is Louise.

So far so good.

Can you shut up for just two minutes?

I'll do my best.

Okay, listen up. She's a paying customer. Big time. A regular at Sotheby's. You know the type.

I do. Vintage brooches. Gucci handbags. Prada shoes. Though I'm sure I'm not up-to-date with the brands.

No, you're not. She's a widow. Inherited some nuts and bolts fortune. Got some ultra-secret issue to deal with. Wouldn't even share it with me. Criminal overtones.

Great, I said, looking around for a shirt I had worn fewer than four times since the last laundry episode. Criminals are my favorite clients.

She's not the criminal, Rick.

That you know of.

I suppose. Anyway, there's something snaky involved. I talked you up. Your new outfit.

You're a prince, I said.

I neglected to let him know that I'd soon be spending long stretches of time out of town playing in the World Series of Poker, likely rendering me highly unlikely to be useful to my, our, new client. Why ruin the mood?

She's going to call you. She's very anxious.

Perfect. That's what I need. Another anxious woman.

Chandler, he said.

What?

Chandler. Her name's Louise Chandler.

Wow, I said. That's so cool.

You're welcome, said Kennedy.

He hung up.

The problem is, I thought, even before Vegas I'm supposed to be playing poker all day and night. Getting ready for the Series. I didn't have time for actual work.

There was always one answer to those kinds of problems.

Delegation.

I called a meeting of my putative partners. Told them to meet me at the Wolf's Lair. Butch said he was at work.

Fuck work, I said. This is more important.

I'll see what I can do, he said.

I knew that meant yes.

I found a shirt. The pizza stain wasn't too obvious. I put it on. Went to the Wolf's Lair, ordered a fine glass of breakfast scotch.

Out of respect for the early hour, I made it a single.

Looks like we may have a case, I said, once the team had assembled.

What kind of case? asked Butch.

I don't know, I said.

A case of Molson? said Brendan.

A case of naked ambition? said Butch.

A case of the clams? said Brendan.

The clams? I said. What the hell is a case of the clams?

I don't know, said Brendan. It sounded good.

Yeah, I said. Sounds great. Anyway . . .

I described the call with Kennedy.

Well, said Butch, I have only one thing to say.

Which is?

You don't have time.

Yeah, I said. I know. That's why you guys are here. I need your help.

Whoa, said Butch. Slow down, cowboy. What makes you think we have any more time than you do?

Between the three of us we can handle it.

How do you know that? You don't even know what it's about yet.

You got a point, my man. You got a very good point.

Well, shit, said Butch. We'll see when it happens.

I looked around at the team.

Butch shrugged.

Brendan involved himself with his sausage and eggs.

It looked like the beginning of a good relationship.

7.

KELLEY WAS COMING TO VISIT. My light. My anchor. My reason for living. My daughter. With whom I'd shared—and only with her had I shared—the awful, subversive, slow-motion, ugly, paralyzing disintegration and death of Melissa. Her mother. My wife.

Melissa had been a mysterious soul, beautiful and brilliant and tortured and sad. It had killed her, at the end. Or, the causal skein extending infinitely backwards, to the scandals of her childhood, accusations of incest, refusal to conform, whatever, had started it. From there it was a common-enough tale. The pills of many colors, the booze of many varieties. She had slowly lost interest in life. She'd lived on the couch in the living room. Slept there, sometimes for days at a time. There were endless, enervating trips to the clinic in Westchester. Hope. Violence. Betrayal. Hope again. Hope sucked dry. And a dead body in the living room. Nicely displayed, there for Kelley to find.

Nice touch, Melissa. Thanks for that. Nice final touch.

Ugly endings are ugly each in their own way.

But we lived through all of that, and more, Kelley and I. She was my flesh and bones. She had a sense of humor—dry, outrageous, deadpan—and a passion for words. She was a beautiful girl—got that from her mother—but she hid it from the world. Almond eyes behind outrageous frames. The generous heart behind jokes of many hues.

She showed up with Peter, her fat, funny, operatic best friend. A chain-smoking, scenery-chewing film encyclopedia. We met at the Cracked Claw, a cheesy clam joint in Hoboken. Peter was pontificating about some dissolute actress's latest exploits.

You're such a hypocrite, Kelley interjected.

Of course I am, he admitted proudly. But hypocrites get a bad name in this country.

I started a new business, I said.

You're right, said Kelley. Hypocrites are people, too. They have rights, just like everybody else.

It's called The Outfit, I said.

They should be able to organize, said Peter.

By God, I'm going to do it, said Kelley. I'm going to quit my job and organize the hypocrites.

With Brendan and Butch, I said. And you don't have a job.

Yeah, I mean, medical benefits, said Peter.

Exactly, said Kelley.

We're going to do investigations and stuff, I said. A little legal work if it comes along. Of course, we'll need a little capital to start it up.

Why should auto workers get a pension, and not hypocrites? said Peter.

It's a shame, said Kelley.

An outrage, Peter said.

A national tragedy.

Waiter, I said, another double please.

Daddy, said Kelley, you're not fooling anybody. This Outfit thing is just a front.

A front?

You're just looking for an excuse to play poker all the time.

Damn, I said. I can't get away with anything around here.

But hey, said Peter, why not do it for real? Hire me. I *love* peeping in windows.

Looking for filthy things in people's closets, said Kelley.

It's not like that, I said.

What *is* it like? asked Peter, leaning forward, chin cupped in hands, eyes wide.

I don't know, I said. I haven't done it. Yet.

Yet, Kelley snorted.

Then how do you know it's not seamy and dirty and nasty and . . . you know, fun? said Peter.

I guess I don't.

Then we want to join, said Peter. Believe me, if *we're* involved, it's going to be fun.

Okay, I said. I'll take it up at the next board meeting.

We stuffed ourselves with oysters Rockefeller, king crab legs, steamed clams and all the other seawater clutter they serve in joints like the Cracked Claw, drenched in butter and lemon, slick and evil and fabulous in your mouth.

I ran into Denise yesterday, said Peter.

I Used To Be Forty-Five Pounds Lighter Denise? Kelley asked.

Her.

Who's Denise? I asked.

I don't know, said Peter. She works at the video store. How would you describe her, Kelley?

She's fabulous, said Kelley. If by fabulous I mean flagrantly depressive and seriously overweight.

Every time she meets someone, said Peter, she says, I used to be forty-five pounds lighter; I used to be an actress, I don't know how this happened.

So, said Kelley, when we introduce her to people, we say, this is Denise. She used to be forty-five pounds lighter.

You're kidding, I said.

Would we kid you about a thing like that?

And she puts up with it?

Puts up with it? said Peter. She loves it. She doesn't have to wait for an opening. To bring it up herself.

She can go into the whole story right away, said Kelley.

Which is?

The story of her life, said Peter.

Her life story, said Kelley.

Yes, said Peter, it's kind of her life as a formerly slim actress down on her luck and saddled with a probably-autistic little monster of a child whose father's long loped off to the abundantly greener pastures offered by just about anyone else on the planet kind of story.

Sounds kind of sad, actually, I said.

Of course, said Peter. It's incredibly sad. That's what makes it so funny.

I broached a new business idea: We could rent Peter out. As a party favor. He could tell stories for tips.

I'd rather rent out my ass, he said.

It's too late, said Kelley, it's already all over the Internet.

Oh, that, said Peter. The real thing is so much better.

Speaking of the real thing, Daddy, said Kelley, what happened to Dorita?

What's that got to do with the real thing? I asked.

Oh, come on, Daddy, said Peter. Legs from here to the moon? Breasts from the Pillow Shop?

I don't know, I said. It just didn't work out. I'm sorry. I know you liked her.

She was sweet, said Kelley, a little sadly.

I know, I said. But . . . I don't know. I can't talk to my children about this kind of stuff.

They both laughed. Come on, Daddy, said Kelley, we all know you're a womanizer.

I laughed. I proposed a toast. I wondered what she meant. I wondered if she really meant it. If it wasn't a joke. Damn. Fatherhood was hard.

I'd thought Dorita was the answer to everything. My rescuing angel, descended from the clouds, to fix all that was broken, after Melissa. I'd loved her. Loved her endless legs, her acid humor, the way she held a cigarette, lit it with a platinum lighter, the blue flame two feet high. We'd been partners. Worked the FitzGibbon case together. She'd had as much to do with cracking it as I did.

And the kids had loved her, too.

But I should have come up short, slapped myself in the face. There aren't any answers to anything, really, still less to everything. Damn. I'd put her up there, in the pantheon. Sheila had warned me. And Sheila'd been right. Dorita had turned out to be human. Despite the legs, the breasts, and all. She had needs. We had fights. It didn't seem right, my rescuing angel calling me a selfish prick.

I couldn't handle it.

I told her to go away.

Fine, she said. Walked out the door. Slammed it behind her.

I let her go.

And, like so many others before, I'd never know if it had been the right decision.

I never saw her again.

Peter rescued me from the morbid remains of the recent past with a discourse about men.

My ideal man, you ask? he began, unbidden. Biceps bigger than my head, a moderately hairy chest, Russian. Bulgarian's even better. Oh God, I've got to lower my standards. Okay, no mustaches. But I'm magnetically attracted to muscles. I'll jump on his back and say, You're going to have to get me off.

I groaned. We all laughed. And so the conversation went. No more dangerous asides into Daddy's suspect psyche. And in the end, thoroughly sated, we staggered out, complaining bitterly about the abysmal quality of the several pounds of food we'd just finished avidly scarfing down.

We flagged a cab back to the house.

The taxi smelled of sweat and shawarma.

It got us home.

I was exhausted. I went straight to bed.

On the way, I passed Melissa.

Ten, twenty times a day I passed her. Long legs curled beneath her. Long black hair. Green eyes. Beautiful. Alone.

I wasn't hallucinating. But I couldn't shake the feeling that Melissa was still there. I'd get a glimpse, out of the corner of my eye. She's alive. On the couch. Just like always. I hadn't moved anything in the living room since she died. It was almost like a religious thing. It was as though if I disturbed anything, it would kill her. Again. Kill her ghost. Whatever. I don't know. I wouldn't let anyone go in there. It was like a shrine, maybe. Something like that. So we lived in the kitchen. Me, when I was alone, which was most of the time. Kelley and Peter and me, when they were in town from college, Peter attached to Kelley like a lizard on a rock. A gaudy lizard that never stopped talking.

Those were still the best times. When Kelley was there, I didn't need anything else.

And then she'd be gone again. Gone too long. Longer, it seemed, each time.

She had to be, of course. She had to go to college. Make a life.

She used to say, when she was young, that she never wanted to grow up.

Now I understood what she'd meant.

8.

I MET BUTCH FOR DRINKS AFTER WORK. His work. I didn't have any work. Which was how I liked it.

Butch had brought me a present.

He'd never given me a present before.

Here, he said, I brought you a present.

He handed me a leather box. It was an old leather box. Dark brown, distressed. Brass hinges. There was a crest embossed on it. It looked like a double-headed eagle, with something in its claws. I couldn't make out what it was, the thing in the claws. The box was old. The crest was worn. It looked to be in the art deco style.

I'm touched, I said. A leather box.

Open it, stupid, he said.

I opened it.

Inside, encased in faded purple velvet, was . . . a gun.

You've got to be kidding me, I said.

Why would I be kidding you?

I've never used a gun in my life. I'm anti-gun. Guns kill people. People don't kill people. Guns kill people. I've never even held a gun in my hand.

It's never too late to start.

I wouldn't even know which way to point the thing, I said.

Don't worry about it. You'll learn. I'll take you to the range. Show you everything you need to know. Where the trigger is. All that.

Jesus, I said. I don't know about this.

Rick, you've got a client now.

We've got a client.

We've got a client. So, we start getting serious.

For all I know it's a peeping case, Butch. Take a few snaps of Daddy Bigbucks porking the housekeeper. Who'm I going to shoot? With a gun.

Daddy points a shotgun at you, Rick. What're you going to do?

Run like hell, I said. Bob and weave. Call 911.

Yeah, that's probably the best. But there are other situations.

Name one.

I don't have to. Use your imagination.

I can't take this, Butch. I mean, the gun I can't take. Okay, I'll take it. But I'll put it up on the mantle. Admire it.

It's a nice piece of work.

I wouldn't know. But it looks pretty.

It's a Mauser P-38 Eagle. German police issue. Original case. Military blue finish. Prized in certain circles.

Not my circles.

Listen, Rick, this is a very special thing I'm giving you.

I appreciate it, Butch. I really do. It's a beautiful thing. But . . . I'm not going to use it.

Yes, you are. You're going to do it for me.

For you?

Yes, for me. Remember when we went to the FitzGibbon kid's loft? What did you do?

I stood guard at the door.

You cowered at the door. You pretended to guard it. But what you really did was cower behind the door. While I, and your girlfriend, went in.

Okay, I cowered. But I cowered really well.

It was a fine bit of cowering. But what if next time the kid hasn't sawed himself up with a ninja sword? He's standing there with Daddy Bigbucks' shotgun that he stole the night before? He blows off my kneecap? What happens then?

I run. Bob and weave. Call 911.

The fuck you do.

All right. I don't. I scramble upstairs after you. I draw my gun. I twirl it around my index finger. Three times for luck. I shoot from the hip. Hit the kid right between the eyes.

Now you got it. Get dressed. We're going to the range.

9.

I DIDN'T THINK THERE WERE ANY GUN RANGES IN MANHATTAN. Turned out I was wrong. There are gun ranges in Manhattan. But Butch didn't want to be seen in any of them. Cops hung out at gun ranges. And giving civilians shooting lessons wasn't a part of his job description.

We went to Hoboken. The west end of Hoboken. Out where the condos hadn't gotten yet. A bleak little street of potholes and bad memories. A couple scrap Dodge Darts, circa 1975, rims on the sidewalk. A stack of rusting fifty-five-gallon drums, sitting in a vacant yard in a pool of something reddish-brown and with that greenish rainbow sheen that tells you it's probably best not to inhale in the general vicinity.

And a one-story building constructed of slowly dissolving red brick, the windows covered in tar paper. A hand-lettered sign that once may have been yellow. *Gun Range and Tackle Shop*, it said.

Let's buy some worms, I said. Go fishing.

Get out of the car, said Butch.

I got out of the car. We went up to the front door. Fading green wood and rusting steel.

The front door was locked.

Closed, I said. Let's go home.

It's not closed, said Butch. Let's go around back.

It's closed, Butch, I said, walking towards the car.

Get the fuck over here, he said.

I got the fuck over there. It was against my better judgement. But I did it.

The building was narrow from the street, but stretched at least fifty yards back. At the rear was a tamped-down dirt lot, a wooden slat fence, gray from the years, fallen down in several places. More steel drums. Three shiny new police cars, parked in a neat row.

You see that, Butch? I said. Now we really got to get out of here.

Shut the fuck up, Rick. They're Hoboken.

Butch. All this profanity. It's making me feel . . . unloved.

Butch ignored me. Opened the screen door.

Yo, Butch, said a voice from deep inside somewhere. Where you been?

I been around, Butch said.

I followed Butch into the dark.

Who's your friend? asked the voice, the owner of which I couldn't make out in the gloom.

Him? said Butch. That's my buddy Rick.

Rick, said the baritone. Please' ta meetcha.

The pleasure is all mine, I said to a hulking shadow that was gradually materializing in the tar-paper dark.

The shadow laughed.

My eyes adjusted. The shadow appeared to be lounging behind a long glass counter. It put out its paw. It looked about six foot five. Bald on top. Three hundred pounds of green checked flannel shirt and made-in-China blue work pants. Offered me a Marlboro. I declined. I did take the paw, though.

Jones, the former shadow said.

Redman, I replied.

Rick Redman? he asked with a raised eyebrow. The Rick Redman?

What other Rick Redman you think I'd bring you? asked Butch.

Gonna teach ol' Rick here to shoot people? Jones asked.

That's the plan, said Butch.

Well come on in, said Jones. Pick your poison.

He nodded to the counter. Beneath the glass was a vast rusting array of ancient weaponry. I recognized a World War II–vintage

German Luger; what I took, from the movies, to be a mammoth Colt .45, though it appeared to be missing the trigger guard and probably some more important parts as well. The rest was just hunks of once-deadly metal, interspersed with some shiny new bits. Some of the new ones were very big, very nasty-looking. One of them I thought I recognized as an Uzi submachine gun. Short. Stubby. Well-worn wooden stock. It spoke violence. I had no idea why I knew what it was. But it attracted me, in a foreshortened stubby well-worn violent sort of way.

I'll take that one, I said.

Gonna start at the top, eh? said Jones.

No he isn't, said Butch. He's kidding. He brought his own.

I'll decide when I'm kidding, I insisted. I want to try that one. I've always wanted to try one of those.

Rick, you are such a fucking liar, said Butch. Two hours ago you didn't even want to touch a pistol.

I just remembered. Summer camp. We had a little Uzi squad. Loved the smell of them. Gun grease in the morning.

Rick, get out the fucking Mauser.

I got out the fucking Mauser.

I placed the box on the counter. Opened it for Jones's inspection. He lifted the pistol carefully out of the box. Turned it over. Hefted it.

Nice, he said.

Yeah, said Butch. I got it off Spirodinov.

Yeah, said Jones. Figures. Not too many of these running around.

So, you call the Bulgarians.

As it should be. Rick, said Jones, step back here. We'll introduce you to your new friend.

The range itself looked just like they do on TV. A row of booths, each with a mammoth set of bright orange ear protectors hanging on the wall. Long alleys running from each booth to a row of hanging targets, clipped onto a slack chain that at the touch of a red button noisily flung them back to the booth for inspection. Black silhouettes on white sheets. Mr. Bad Guy.

Jones put the gun in my hand.

I looked at it closely, as if for the first time. It had a kind of angular, well-worn beauty.

It was love at first heft.

Jones showed me how to hold it. How to point it. Where the trigger was. Took it himself. Planted his feet. Aimed. Plugged the Bad Guy four times. Got him good.

Your turn, he said.

I took the gun. This time it felt very heavy. I planted my feet in imitation of Jones. He corrected my stance. I aimed just like I'd seen him do. He corrected my aim.

In spite of Jones's best efforts, my first three shots vanished like gnats in a hurricane. I braced. I squeezed. I felt the backlash. Backfire. Whatever they called it. Recoil. The Bad Guy didn't stir. No happy gun-holes appeared anywhere on him. Jones pressed the red button, retrieved the target sheet, just to make sure. Not a mark.

I told you, Butch, I said. I'm not cut out for this kind of stuff.

Keep at it, Jones said. You'll get it right. Did you ride a bicycle perfectly the first time you tried?

I don't remember.

Butch rolled his eyes.

Jones gave me a few more pointers. Squeeze the trigger, he said. Slowly. Evenly. Like you're lowering a barbell, feeling the pump.

My fourth shot hit the sheet. Barely. Lower right corner. Missed the Bad Guy completely. But. The mark was there. The magic bullet hole. I'd done it. I'd shot something with a gun. Maybe there was hope for me. Maybe one day I'd be a real man.

It gave me a rush. A big, nasty I-want-to-do-that-again kind of rush.

So I did it again. I did it again and again, Butch and Jones interjecting with advice. And over the course of an hour and a half, the scattered holes in the ghosts at the end of the chain got closer and closer together. Patterns emerged. I began to feel powerful. Sexy. I was alive with the strange joy of blasting apart cardboard people with a high-caliber weapon.

It felt way too good.

Okay, said Jones, when the last Bad Guy had whizzed back to the booth, exhibiting an almost perfect bombing pattern: six clean shots within three inches of the cartoon heart pasted on the Bad Guy's chest. Let's get a beer.

Through a swinging door to the left of the booths was a tiny kitchen. We sat at an Arborite table. That fake-marble top, heavily chipped. The tubular aluminum legs. Chairs to match. The ones that had been there forever. Jones got out the beer.

Butch and Jones jawed. I savored the beer. I savored three more. Jones rummaged around, found an old shoulder holster for me. I wanted to pay for it. And for the lesson. He wouldn't let me.

We were buddies now, it seemed.

Comrades in sidearms.

10.

THE PHONE RANG. At ten. Again. I was pissed. But I hadn't been able to sleep anyway. I was too pumped from the gun lesson. When I tried to stop thinking about that, all I could conjure were visions of the World Series of Poker. Spades. Diamonds. Gold-embossed chips. Should I have folded those Jacks the other night? I had to read Sklansky again. The chapter on implied odds. Just one more time. I wasn't sure I'd ever really gotten it. I wasn't a goddamn math-meister. I was just a failed lawyer with a gambling problem. All right. Okay. A drinking problem, too. So sue me.

I picked up the phone.

Redman, I said.

Good morning, Mr. Redman, said a very particular female voice. I couldn't quite place what made it so particular. But particular it was. Soft, a touch of elegance. Used to getting its way.

This is Louise Chandler, it said.

Ah, Ms. Chandler, I said, shaking my head in a useless attempt to clear it.

I gather you've spoken to Mr. Kennedy?

I have. How can I help you?

Mr. Kennedy has been very kind to me.

He always is.

There was a pause. Perhaps, I thought, she wasn't used to ambiguity.

I'd like to see you today, she said at last, if you have fifteen minutes to spare.

I do. What time would be good for you?

In about ten minutes. I just happen to be in your neighborhood.

Ah, sure, I said, wondering if it was possible to make myself presentable in that amount of time.

Then I'll see you shortly.

Jesus, I thought as I rushed to the bathroom. A little pushy, this one. And how did she get my address? Kennedy wouldn't have been that indiscreet.

I threw on some clothes. Ran my fingers through my frantic hair. Brushed some of my teeth. Grabbed a cold cup of coffee from the kitchen.

In precisely ten minutes there was a knock on the door. A small knock. Decorous. But insistent, somehow. Not to be ignored.

Much like the woman herself, as it turned out. A sweet little package. Green linen skirt. Matching jacket. Demure in style, yet provocative. Underneath the jacket, a white blouse. Tight, but somehow not too revealing. Just enough to make you wonder. Green eyes, hennaed hair. A lightly freckled complexion. An air of self-possession.

She put out a gloved hand.

Louise Chandler, she said, eyeing my disheveled self with something between disdain and curiosity.

Rick Redman, I replied. Sorry for my rumpled condition. Just got up. Perhaps I should come back a little later?

No, no. Please. Come in. Make yourself at home. Would you like something to drink?

No, thank you, I'm fine.

Coffee, I mean. Or tea. Water.

No, thank you.

Before I could steer her elsewhere, Louise Chandler was sitting on the sofa. Zebra skin. Real zebra skin. Melissa had had it covered by the best in the business. To match her jungle motif. The leopard-skin chairs. African masks on the wall. The gazelle-headed fireplace tools.

And there was Louise Chandler. Right in the middle of Melissa.

It just wasn't right. But at that point, neither was inviting Louise into the kitchen or, more to the point, disinviting her from the living room. And the kitchen was the only other place we could go. It was as bad as my bedroom. Worse. Things were growing in there.

My ten minutes hadn't been enough for me to anticipate this . . . conundrum.

I would just have to deal with it.

Louise Chandler gave me a wan smile.

She could see my discomfort. But of course, she'd have no idea what caused it. Probably figured I was some kind of nervous neurotic. An anxiety freak. Cokehead, maybe. Yeah, likely that. I'd lost her business already. Not that that would be such a bad thing. I could play poker . . .

Sure you won't have some coffee? I asked.

I'm fine, she said.

Another uncomfortable pause.

I realized that I was still standing. Towering over this tiny sitting woman. This was impolite, I remembered. Concealing my embarassment with action, however ill-conceived, I went to the kitchen. Made her an uninvited drink. I returned. Handed her the glass. She was too polite to refuse. I took the armchair.

Well, I said to Ms. Chandler, perhaps you could tell me a bit about your, ah, problem. Situation.

My tongue wasn't working. My brain wasn't working. Hell, I wasn't sure my entire central nervous system wasn't shutting down. The central nervous system, I thought. The system that makes you nervous. So that was it.

And it wasn't just the hangover. There was something really wrong. Nothing was making any sense. Who was this strange woman in my living room? Why were small creatures scurrying about in my digestive tract? Why were their nails so sharp?

Louise Chandler sat impassively for a moment. From her vantage, I deduced, she could see into the kitchen. Empty bottles. Chinese takeout cartons.

Sorry about the mess, I said. I wasn't expecting company.

It's all right, she said, without conviction.

How can I help you? I asked.

It's about my sister, she said.

Your sister.

Yes. My sister.

She looked around the living room. In radical contrast to the rest of the house, this room was pristine. Everything left just the way Melissa had designed it. Lived in it. Died in it. Along with the African stuff, the Bauhaus divan. The carefully chosen paintings, abstract, but with something elusively warm in them. The carpet, furiously, elaborately Persian. All of the contrasting styles somehow synergizing into something ineffably peaceful.

It's a nice room, said Ms. Chandler.

Your sister, I said. You were telling me about your sister.

It was bad enough she had invaded Melissa's space. I wasn't going to start chatting about the décor.

She was taken aback, momentarily. Recovered herself, I was relieved to note.

Yes, she replied. Eloise.

Eloise, I said. Louise and Eloise.

Yes, she said with an air of having heard it before. Our parents were, I don't know, odd.

Well, yes. I'm sorry. Didn't mean to cause offense. I mean, George Foreman's sons are all called George. I think there are eight of them. So it could be worse, I guess.

Don't worry, she said. It doesn't bother me anymore.

I gave her what I hoped was a reassuring smile and not a leer. In my condition, I couldn't tell the difference.

Yes, she said. Well. The problem is, I haven't heard from Eloise in a long time.

I waited. I tried to remember the last time I'd talked to my sister.

I know that's not necessarily unusual, she said.

I see, I said. So you're not saying that she's . . . missing?

I'm not sure. I haven't heard from her. I'm not going to pretend that's abnormal. We haven't been close in a long while. But she is my sister. I'm concerned for her. The last telephone number that I had for her is out of service. I'm not saying anything bad has happened to her. I don't know. I'd just like to know that she's . . . all right.

I understand. Well. I'll—we'll need some information.

Of course.

There was another pause. Ms. Chandler smoothed the sleeves of her jacket. Ah, I thought, self-soothing behavior. A sure sign she was bluffing.

Unfortunately, there wasn't anything for her to be bluffing about.

Had to get my mind out of the poker gutter.

Mr. Redman, she said, do you carry a firearm?

Uh, I'm not sure why that's relevant.

Do you?

Do I what?

Carry a firearm.

No, I don't.

That's strange. I thought it was standard procedure in your business.

Well, I do own a gun, I said. The phrase had a novel feel in my mouth. But I don't usually carry it. Anyway, if this is danger work, I get hazard pay.

Oh, don't worry about compensation, Mr. Redman. You'll be taken care of. Oh, and you wanted more information.

She fished around in her tiny handbag. Pulled out a piece of paper, folded many times. But neatly. Folded neatly.

She handed it to me.

I opened it.

Her handwriting was tiny. But clear. At least, it looked as though it would be clear. Once my eyes began to focus.

I have an appointment, she said. I apologize. I must go. Please read that. I've tried to put everything down. But I'm sure you'll have some questions. I'll call you again when I'm free.

Of course, I said. Of course. Please.

I showed her to the front door.

Brendan was just coming up the stairs.

I introduced them. Brendan shuffled his feet. Extended a hand.

A pleasure, he said, without conviction.

Pleased to meet you, said Louise, very properly.

But her eyes lingered a bit on Brendan. Just enough to make me notice.

Well, no harm in that. Brendan was a good-looking guy. Blue eyes. Good jawline. Wavy, dirty-blond hair. Any woman might take a second look. And seeing as how he was gay, he wasn't a threat to my own nascent inappropriate intentions.

Back in the kitchen, I gave Brendan a beer and the download.

I hope it doesn't interfere with the poker schedule, he said.

Yeah, I said. I didn't tell her about that. Wouldn't be good for business. But if she's going to weasel her way into our lives, she'll have to pay for it.

Yeah?

Yeah. If she shows up again, I'll ask for a big retainer.

11.

I WASN'T OPTIMISTIC. Find a sister. How much could we bill for that? A couple grand, maybe? I supposed we could just bill by the hour.

Hated that, though. Had enough of it in the law business. It just encouraged useless effort. Waste. Dishonesty.

I looked at Louise Chandler's tiny handwriting. I crossed and uncrossed my eyes a few times. My vision unblurred a bit. The writing was small but neat. Precise. Scary precise.

Name, Eloise Chandler. Date of birth, June 13, 1970. Description, green eyes, five foot two, slim, pale skin, red hair.

A lot like her sister.

Allergic to sunlight. Ouch. What was that? Lupus? Phone number, no longer working. 702 area code. Last known address, Henderson, Nevada. My, my. Maybe she'd died of lupus. Could you die from lupus? I made a mental note to look it up.

I read the rest aloud to Brendan:

My sister and I were never particularly close. I was four years older. Eloise was always very introverted. Bitter, you might say. She never had many friends. She tended to be easily dominated by larger personalities.

As a result, despite our relative lack of intimacy, I was always very protective of her. Our parents died when we were high school age. We were taken in by an uncle. He was not a nice man. I've always feared that he did something to Eloise. She never said anything of the sort, but then she would not have. Certainly not to me.

Eloise left home when she turned eighteen. I did not blame her. I would have as well, but I was in college, and could not afford to do so. We stayed in touch, however, as sisters do. When she became ill, it seemed to affect her psychologically. She began having less to do with me. She became somewhat reclusive. Eventually she left the city. I do not know where she went initially. I lost track of her for a time. Eventually she settled in Nevada. She wrote to me from there, from time to time, at first. She found a boy she liked. He was a Russian immigrant. He repaired old cars and sold them. That is all that I know about him.

The letters became more sporadic. And then they stopped. I kept writing. My letters were not returned by the post office, but they were not answered either. I did not worry at first. As I said, we were never very close. She had that bitter, independent streak. But as the years went on, I began to be concerned. Finally, I called a local agency in Nevada, and asked them to check at the address I had for her. They told me that she did not live there. That was when I became concerned. I spoke to Mr. Kennedy, who is my personal lawyer. He recommended you.

A bit strange, I said.

Sounds pretty standard to me, said Brendan.

Not the story, I said. The story's as common as bad cheddar cheese. What's strange is why she felt she had to write it down. There isn't anything in there she couldn't have told me in ten minutes. And if she had, I could have asked the obvious questions. How much she was willing to pay, for example. And the writing. Stilted as hell. Not a contraction in the whole thing. 'I could not afford to do so.' Sounds like it was written by the star student in a class of Chinese taking English as a second language. Not that any of that has anything to do with the case. If it is a case.

Okay, Brendan laughed. But you got to figure. We just started The Outfit, and already we have some business. Doesn't matter if it doesn't amount to much.

No, it didn't matter. And it didn't amount to much. But something about it made me uncomfortable.

Maybe it was the past tense.

The whole thing was written in the past tense.

12.

I COULDN'T GET PAST THE IMAGE OF MELISSA ON THE SOFA. Louise Chandler in her space.

There was only one thing to do.

I called Sheila.

One of her crackhead clients had canceled. She could see me right away.

There are advantages to a shrink who specializes in addicts.

I rang the buzzer outside. I smiled at the security camera. I passed inspection. The door buzzed. I took the ancient elevator to the penthouse. I wondered about the etymology of the word. Penthouse. Nothing obvious came to mind. I made a note to look it up.

Sheila shared the penthouse with a couple of other shrinks. There were patients waiting. This was unfortunate. Not because I was uncomfortable. Because they were. My natural inclination was to smile, nod, say hello. You can't do that in a shrink's waiting room. For some reason everyone's embarrassed. Staring intently at the month-old copy of *Time* magazine. I guess they want everyone to think they're normal, well-adjusted folk.

Hey, I always want to say to them, don't worry about it. There's no such thing.

Sheila's door opened. She ushered me in. I sat on my couch. I considered it mine. For the first time I thought of other people sitting there. Sharing their lives and anguish with her.

I didn't like it at all.

I got down to business. Melissa business.

To me, I told Sheila, she's still on that couch. On her back. Mouth open. A line of saliva drooling from the corner of her mouth, forming a pool on the sofa cushion.

I didn't say it in those words. But Sheila understood: I was stuck in the memory.

She nodded sympathetically.

I'd left the living room just like it was, I explained. Her space. Her final resting place. Penultimate resting place. Oh, hell, where she died. Choking on her own vomit. Call me weird, shit, call me neurotic if you want, but I couldn't touch that living room. And I certainly wasn't going to ask anyone else to, or let anyone else, touch it. So there it was. Everything in its designer place. Her cigarettes still on the coffee table, even. The way she made it. The way she lived in it. The way she died in it.

Kind of like a museum.

A natural history museum. Not so natural. A diorama.

Sounds like you won't let yourself grieve, Sheila said.

Yeah, yeah, I said. The eighteen stages of grief. Or twenty. Whatever it is. I know. Well, I don't know, actually. But I don't really want to know. Why does everyone have to deal with shit in the same way? Why can't I have my own way?

Is your own way making you happy?

Oh, please. Does anything make me happy?

Kelley?

Of course. But that's different.

Of course it's different. But that doesn't mean it doesn't matter. And it doesn't have to be the only thing that makes you happy.

Of course it does. I'm a miserable depressive. I guess I'm as happy as a miserable depressive can be. And I mean that in the nicest possible way. Don't get me wrong. You're very helpful. The drugs are very helpful. They really are. But happiness, Jesus. That's for people who do good works. And I'm not the type.

Maybe you could try.

Doing some good works? I've tried. And it only makes me more depressed. All those sad, lonely people? It's really depressing.

You're in quite a state today.

I am. I'm sorry. Can't make much progress when I'm in this mood.

Let's talk about something more concrete, then.

Like what?

Like anything you choose.

Well, speaking of happiness, I met this woman.

Oh dear.

Yes, I know my history isn't promising. But she really seems special.

So did Dorita.

Dorita *was* special. It's just that, I don't know, she needed even more medication than I do.

But you know your real problem.

Of course I do. Idealization. I have to find the perfect woman, never will, perfection is for heaven, not this vale of . . . what is it, sludge? I know, I know. But let me tell you about Louise.

All right. Tell me about Louise.

I told her about my new client. Her legs. Her silky manner.

Are you supposed to be having these kinds of thoughts about a client?

I'm not a shrink, I said. I'm not her lawyer. I'm just an investigator. A helper. I'm not sure there's a code of ethics for helpers.

You don't need to have a code of ethics in order to have ethics.

A good point, I said. Excellent point. I'll give it some consideration. But I haven't done anything, anyway. I'm just telling you how I feel.

All right.

So, I'm having this meeting with Louise, my client. She bends over to reach for a glass. I take a sharp breath. Really. Just like they say in the books. I try to disguise it as a cough. If she notices, she doesn't let on. Anyway, you know how some guys say they're breast men? There's the ass guys? Love that booty? Some guys go for legs. Long, shapely legs. I go for all those things, of course. But at heart I'm a skin guy. Smooth skin sends me. So, when she bent over, her shirt lifted up from her skirt. I saw a few inches of her back. I was sent to the moon.

I see, said Sheila.

Skin that sun-blessed color you can't buy in a tube or a tanning salon. Soft and firm. You don't have to touch it, to know. You can see it. You sure as hell know. That and the curve of it. A curve so pure and gently placed, you had to know it went on endlessly, and just right. All the shapes and valleys just where they should be.

I could feel Sheila's disapproval. But I couldn't stop.

It kills you. It could kill you. Such perfection in a human form. You have to have it. You have to have it or die. You have to have it to know. To know if it really is the perfect embodiment of the female flesh. In which case you'll never let it go. Or that it isn't. Which is a relief, I guess. A relief from the responsibility. The need to have it at all costs. Because if you never had it, never tried it, never found out, everything else you ever touched would suffer from the image of perfection you'd constructed. From that one glimpse of that one part of that one whole you'd sought forever, now and forever past, before you were born, even, the other half of the Platonic egg, you flattered yourself . . .

I looked down. I realized that I'd pulled half the tassels off a throw pillow.

It's all right, Sheila said.

I'll buy you another.

Don't worry. I've got extras.

But still.

As we were saying, said Sheila.

Yeah. Idealization. Am I boring you?

No, she said. But the time's up.

Ah. Saved by the bell.

13.

WE WERE AT FAST VINNIE'S GAME AGAIN, BRENDAN AND ME.
Looking for a challenge. I mean, the field at the World Series is pretty
weak generally, but if you go deep, last into the third, fourth day, you're
going to be playing some of the best players in the world. Some of the
best players in history. So there's no point in warming up with fish.
Fish like cold water. If you're warming up with them, they're usually
on the grill.

The usual crew was there. Won Ton John, Internet Mike, Bennie
Sniffles with the box of tissues, Donny from Hudson County. I was glad
to see Donny: as big a fish as they came. Bluff Daddy, a fat guy from
Brooklyn with a moon face and speckled gray skin. Sort of reminded
you of an uncleaned ashtray. And a guy called Bruno. New guy. Vinnie
told me to watch out for him. He was huge. Not fat huge. Bodybuilder
huge. Impossibly good-looking, in that square-jawed, blue-eyed way.
And with enough arrogance to tell you he was well aware of both. Had
the Nazi-style motorcycle helmet next to him. Oh yes, he was telling
you, you can see me on the Harley—it had to be a Harley, one of the
biggest, loudest and most obnoxiously beautiful of Harleys—rocketing
down the turnpike, all in black, anonymous and massive, stray dollars
from that night's take flying out behind me like the sparks of the hell-
hounds' claws on the blacktop. Oh yes. A walking, talking comic book
hero. A towering heap of intimidation.

The kind of guy, he got run over by a semitrailer one day, you held
a party.

He bought in huge as his shoulders. Banded stacks of hundreds,
ten thousand dollars each. Made a nice handsome pile in front of him.
Made sure he had more money on the table than anyone else. Had to
be that way, for his style to work. I knew the type. Big bets. Very big.
Always putting the question to you: Are you good enough? Do you want
to invest your whole bankroll with that lousy pair? No? Ship it! Ship
those chips over here. Of course, half the time the guy would have air.
Seven, Four off suit. But when you stood up to him, and you'd guessed
wrong, and he had Kings, or two pair, you just lost all your money.
That's what he counted on. Fear.

Those guys were hard to play against. But not impossible.
Everybody has a weakness. Anybody can be exploited.

There are two ways to play against the big-stack bully, the Bruno type of guy. Both ways require that you have a hand, though. You're certainly not going to bluff the guy, because if he re-bluffs you, it's going to be for all your money. The old saying, you can't bluff a bluffer, has far more than a grain of truth in it. So, you wait for a serious hand. Jacks, say. Or a premium drawing hand. King, Queen of hearts. You can flop a flush, a straight, two pair, all sorts of good stuff. And when he shoves his chips at you, you push back over the top. Put him in for all his money.

Since, most of the time, a guy like Bruno is shoving his chips in with less than a monster hand, he'll usually fold. He doesn't want to play a pot with you. He's looking to intimidate you. Shove you off your cards. And since against most guys at the table it works eight times out of ten, maybe nine, he doesn't need to look you up. Take a risk for a lot of chips. He's making lots of money without having to do that.

The other way is the rope-a-dope. You get a monster, a pair of beautiful Aces, you just call. The flop brings another Ace, he bets, you just call again. He keeps betting, you keep calling. What's he got? Ace, King, probably. Or Kings, or Queens, and he thinks you're on a draw. Or air. He'll play air like this. And on the river, there's no flushes on board, no pairs that could make a full house for him. There's a straight out there, but not something he's likely to have. So when he bets again, you come over the top.

Of course, you can't be too obvious about it. You've got to mix it up. The guy's no fool. He'll pick up on it if it's all you do. But since you'll use both of these techniques with big made hands as well as draws, it'll be hard for him to read you. He'll have to keep betting. He doesn't want to give you a free card if you're on the draw.

That's how you play a guy like Bruno.

The problem was, I found out, Bruno was also sick lucky. There are guys like that. You don't want to believe it. You want to think it's all random. The luck evens out in the end. I mean, you do know it. There's no empirical doubt about it. Long term, the cards even out. But somehow, it seemed, Bruno lucked out more than his share.

So, we're at the table a couple hours. Nothing much happening. Bruno's doing his shoving and talking, laughing and dominating the table. With his chips, and with his outsized personality. I'm playing cagey. I'm staying out of his way. I pick up a few small pots from some of the others. Tight, selective, aggressive. Winning poker.

Everyone folds to me. I'm two off the button. I look down. A smooth, shiny black pair of Aces. The Grand Enchilada. The Holy Grail of poker hands.

I throw in three hundred bucks.

Vinnie mucks his hand. If I don't double up soon, he says, somebody's going to get hurt. Won Ton John folds, too. Everybody else folds to Bruno. He's on the button. The best place to be. Last to act in every postflop betting round. He looks at me. Smug. Calls my three hundred.

The blinds fold.

I got you, I'm thinking. I got you this time, big guy.

The flop comes King of clubs, Ten of hearts, Six of hearts.

I don't hesitate. If I hesitate, it'll look like exactly what it is: Hollywood. I'm acting. I'm trying to look weak. As everybody knows from Poker Tells 101, weak means strong, strong means weak. So, seeing as how I don't figure my adversary for more than a two-level thinker, I'm looking to do the reverse tell: fire out a grand without missing a beat. He's got to figure there's a good chance it's a continuation bet: I was going to bet whether the flop hit me or not. I have to back up my preflop aggression. He knows that. Everybody knows that. And this flop looks good to me. Relatively uncoordinated cards. Two hearts, of course. He could have a flush draw. But the chances of Bruno having two more hearts in the hole are relatively small. And anyway, I bet enough that if he calls with the heart draw it's going to be very expensive for him to try to hit it.

I'll take my chances.

Bruno goes into the tank. He looks at his cards. He stares me down. He looks back at his cards.

It's quite an act.

I'm not sure what it means.

Meanwhile, I'm doing my usual thing: staring at a spot on the felt. Immobile. Unreadable.

At least that's the theory.

Bruno starts making little piles of black chips. I try not to salivate too visibly. He pushes out five piles. A five-thousand-dollar raise.

I'm all in, I say instantly.

This is the moment I've been setting up for hours. I know the guy's a good player. I don't let my distaste blind me to his skills. Most of the time, I stay out of his way. But at some point, I've been telling myself all night, I'm going to punish him. I'm going to look in his arrogant face and gloat. It's going to be a very satisfying moment.

I push my whole stack into the middle. Slowly. It's a big stack.

Oh shit, he says with a rueful smile. You got me. I call.

Damn, I think, that was way too gentlemanly.

Ruined the mood.

No hearts, I tell the dealer, who peels off the Ten of spades.

No more Tens, I say, louder. No more Kings, louder still. No hearts! By now I'm yelling. I'm not embarrassed about it. Yet.

The river is . . . the King of clubs.

Bruno shrugs, turns over the King and Eight of hearts. Three goddamn Kings.

You fucking son of a bitch, I mutter.

I fling my now-pathetic Aces across the table. They bounce off the felt, hit the dealer in the chest. He shrugs, picks them up. Gives me a Look. The Look says, Do that again and I'll be dealing you rags the rest of the night.

I know I'm making a fool of myself.

I can't help it.

The dealer starts sweeping the mammoth pile of chips to Bruno.

If you look at it objectively, shit, the guy had fourteen outs. The nine remaining hearts. The two Kings. Three Sixes. Fourteen outs twice: once on the turn, again on the river. Jesus, the chances were almost exactly fifty-fifty. And anyway, that's poker. Shit happens. You get sucked out on.

But I'd had him right where I wanted him. And he got away. The oversized prick. I slammed out the back door into the yard. Lit a cigarette. Cursed the Poker Gods.

The guys inside having a good laugh at my expense.

I didn't care. I was too fucking mad.

14.

THE SECOND TIME I MET THE DISTRACTING MS. CHANDLER was at Bastone's, a pasta joint in Little Italy. I was pretty sure it wasn't her kind of place, but I liked the baked ziti, and I wasn't going to take the chance that my esteemed client was going to invade Melissa's space again.

Bastone's was the kind of place that had a cheap bust of Julius Caesar on the wall, surrounded by five generations of Bastones, stiffly posed in elaborately framed pastel portraits. The even earlier Bastones were on the opposite wall, stiffly posed in black-and-white framed photographs.

All the waiters in the joint were in black tie. On the wainscoting by the table was a doorbell of the early sixties kind, a little brass hubcap with a Bakelite button, presumably installed when the place was new, to allow you to summon a waiter. Hadn't worked since Rich Little was a big act. There seemed to be more wait staff than customers, anyway. The waiters, of course—Luigi and Pasquale and Giorgio and their kin— were lifers. Guys in their seventies and eighties who had worked their way up from busboy in the fifties and sixties. And never looked back.

The Vegas-style surveillance domes in the ceiling were the only modern touch, giving away—as if you hadn't figured it out for yourself—the real provenance of the place, of the clientele. Although the world was changing, it seemed, seeing as how, looking around at the dozen or so customers, none of them appeared to have been born in Palermo or anywhere in the vicinity. Unless you counted the northern hemisphere as the vicinity.

After a bottle of Chianti, it didn't seem important. If it ever had.

Something about the multiple angled mirrors from the corner table I'd finagled gave me a long-distance image of myself from a three-quarter rear view. My, I thought, you're almost handsome, from that perspective. I resolved to sit three-quarters away from all future prospective conquests.

Ms. Chandler's entrance had a way of unsettling things. She arrived with little ceremony but a great deal of impact. She was dressed in red this time. Not an insistent red. More of an autumn, leaf-turning, cooling red. Everything matched: the shoes, the purse, the look in her eye. And everything looked very, very expensive.

Mr. Redman, she said after a pleasantry or two, perhaps you have some initial thoughts?

Thoughts? I asked, turning myself to the three-quarter view. Ah, yes. About your sister. Well, I have to admit you haven't given me a whole lot to go on.

There's only so much I wanted to commit to paper.

Of course, I replied.

There are some other . . . complications.

I see. Well, I'd be happy to hear about them. But first—

Money, she said. You don't have to worry about that.

I'm not worried, I said, pleased that she'd gotten my drift. At least, you seem like a person with resources. But I think we need to make sure that we're on the same page. Now, this seems to be a missing persons case. I gather there are some complications, as you say. But it's still a missing persons case. And frankly, Ms. Chandler, as much as I sympathize, missing persons cases tend to be rather, well, routine, shall we say. And it just strikes me that my, our, rates might be a little more than you would want to be paying, simply to track down your sister.

How do you mean, routine?

What I mean is, almost everybody in this day and age leaves a trail. Used to be called a paper trail. Now it's electronic. Residence, driver's license, credit cards, cell phone records, everything. And all of it's in a computer somewhere. And you say she'd been ill. There are hospital records. Though those are hard to get. Privacy laws and all. But there are outfits that specialize in getting access to all those types of information. They do it very inexpensively. Because they specialize.

She recrossed her legs.

Volume, she said.

Yes, I replied, pondering those legs. Volume.

Well, thank you for that. As a matter of fact, it merely serves to increase my confidence in you. That you would tell me that. Not that it needed any increasing. If Mr. Kennedy recommends you, I know you're good at what you do.

Well, thank you, Ms. Chandler . . .

But you needn't be concerned. I've already tried that route, you see. I've had all the data mined.

Ah, I said. And?

Nothing.

Nothing?

Not a trace of her. Not since she moved to Nevada.

That's very unusual.

So they tell me.

Hmm. Likely she changed her name, then. But her social security number would have brought something up. You did give them her social security number?

Of course.

And your letters weren't returned.

That's right.

Odd.

Yes.

Well, then. I guess we have some work to do. We'd be happy to do our best. Now, please understand that this is just routine, but—

You need a retainer.

She said it with a touch of amusement. The waiter arrived with her cosmopolitan. He had a large black growth like a sleeping rat on the side of his neck. I repressed a double-take. But if Ms. Chandler noticed, she wasn't letting on. She took her drink with the same practiced smoothness that she did everything else.

Um, yes, I said. A retainer.

How much?

In spite of her charms, I didn't really feel like getting tangled up in Ms. Chandler's little family drama. First, it sounded fishy as hell. And even if it wasn't fishy, it was probably going to get nasty. These family things always do. And, skin or no skin, her imperious manner was getting on my nerves. And I had poker to play. So if I was going to do it—if we were going to do it—it was going to have to be profitable.

One thing I need to tell you, I said.

Yes?

I'll be going to Las Vegas shortly. And when I'm there, I'll be playing a good deal of poker. It's the World Series of Poker. So I won't be spending full time on your case.

Mr. Redman, in the first place, I would assume that even if you didn't have this . . . poker thing, you have other clients. I wouldn't expect you to be devoting your every waking hour to my little problem. And the fact that you'll be in Nevada anyway, she laughed a knowing laugh, well, it's rather convenient, isn't it? Which occurred to me when Mr. Kennedy told me you'd be there.

I made a note to tell Kennedy to keep his damn mouth shut.

Ah, I said, as though I'd known it all along. Of course.

I also have business in Nevada, she said.

You do?

Yes. I have some property interests.

I see.

So you will not be surprised if I mysteriously appear.

This seemed to be intended as a joke of sorts. I chuckled appreciatively.

So, she said. The retainer?

Twenty thousand, I said without thinking.

Fine, she replied without hesitation.

Oh my, I thought.

By wire transfer, I said. I'll give you the account information. I pulled over a napkin. Wrote it down.

Still she didn't blink.

Fine, she said, folding the napkin neatly and placing it in her elegant red purse. You'll receive it tomorrow.

Damn, I thought, is this how it works all the time? I could get used to this business.

Well, I said, perhaps we could talk a bit about the details.

Let's do that, said Ms. Chandler.

She put the purse aside. Unbuttoned her jacket. The blouse beneath was silk, airy. Not exactly revealing, but, how to put it? Enticing.

At the next table were a couple of the regulars. Long Henry, given to poetic pronouncements and other non sequiturs, was trying to impress a middle-aged woman in a hippie-style dress that had seen a lot of days and nights in a lot of bars.

I used to be a professor, he said.

What happened? asked the woman.

She was fiddling with something in her macramé bag. After a while I realized it was a dog. Not one of those poofed-up little-old-lady dogs. Some mangy thing with red eyes.

Happened? asked Henry, seeming genuinely confused.

To your job, she said. As a professor.

Oh that, he said vaguely. I don't remember.

Now, about this Russian fellow you mentioned? I asked Ms. Chandler. Were they married?

Are they married?

Sorry. I didn't mean . . . I mean, I didn't mean to assume, imply, I thought perhaps they were divorced. Or perhaps I meant, had they been married? I mean, I didn't mean to say that she may have come to any harm.

Never mind, she said. No, she's never been married. That I know of.

Was she living with him?

Not that I'm aware of. But I don't know.

Still seeing him, last you heard?

Well, I don't really know. She wasn't, isn't, in the habit of talking to me about her personal life. I don't even remember how I know about him, to tell you the truth.

Do you remember his name?

Vladimir, I believe.

Last name?

I'm not sure I ever knew his last name.

Did she ever say they'd broken up or anything?

No. I don't think so.

Okay. Well, normally we'd start with him. But we don't even have a last name. I think somebody's just going to have to go to the last address you have, ask around.

I've already paid somebody to do that.

I understand. I see. Yes. But you pay guys like us for a reason. Maybe we ask a few questions they forgot to ask, or in a different way, if you know what I mean. Ask somebody those guys didn't think of asking. Follow stuff up. Those guys, they run a service. They have a checklist. They do the minimum. They cash your check. If someone's . . . uh . . . trying to lay low, they'll never find them.

All right. I understand.

Okay. Another thing. You mentioned that she'd been ill.

Yes.

And in your note, it said something about being allergic to sunlight?

Yes.

What did you mean by that?

I did not mean anything by that. That is what she told me. To tell you the truth, it has always puzzled me.

I can understand that. It puzzles me, too. I mean, wouldn't you move to England, rather than the desert, if you were allergic to sunlight? But we can do some research. Figure out what she could have been talking about.

I would appreciate that.

By the way, I was curious about one other thing.

Yes?

You asked if I had a gun.

That seems to be a bit of a detour. From the job at hand.

Yes. Maybe. But it made me wonder. I mean, your sister is missing. She's been ill. Nothing you've told me would make me think that there's likely to be any danger in trying to track her down.

Ms. Chandler gazed at me a moment, a small smile at the corners of her mouth. She smoothed her hair. Looked away with a teasing air.

I was just curious, Mr. Redman. I've never dealt with a private investigator before.

I see.

But I like it that you asked. It gives one confidence. That you would notice something like that. Follow it up.

Well, thank you, I said. So, we'll check out that address. Start there. As soon as we get to Las Vegas. I'll check it out. Or one of my associates will.

The one with the pretty face?

The one with . . .

The fellow on the stairs. At your house.

Oh. Yes. Brendan. Probably. Do you have a problem with that?

Oh no, not at all. I assume he knows what he's doing, if he's with you. I'm sure you trained him well.

Oh, sure, I lied. You can count on Brendan.

Ms. Chandler was laughing.

It was rather disconcerting.

15.

MY EYES PEELED OPEN. I looked at my watch. Ten past noon.

I love an early start to the day.

I glanced through the mail. Anything that looked official meant I owed somebody money. I threw it out. Anything colorful, with pictures, was potential entertainment. Catalogs were fun. They could only take you so far out of your world, though. Eventually you had to get up, put on some clothes. Do something.

The phone rang.

Brendan.

Brighton Beach, he said. Six o'clock.

I don't know, I said. I forgot about that.

What do you mean, you don't know?

I pissed off Evgeny. He'll be there, for sure. I'm not sure I'm comfortable going there when Big Daddy's not happy with me.

Don't worry about that. I took care of it.

What do you mean, you took care of it?

I mean it's okay. I talked to the guys about it. He's not pissed.

The guys?

Andrei and Tolya.

What the fuck do they know?

They know. And anyway, you don't want to be a pussy, do you?

It was funny hearing that from Brendan.

Okay, I said. But let's go to the All In Club first. Warm up a bit on some fish.

Good plan. Let's meet at Puffie's.

Where's that? I asked.

Right next to Shoegasm.

Did I hear that right?

Yeah. It's a shoe store on Twenty-seventh.

Must be a good one.

If you like big heels.

I found some less than rotting jeans. I buttoned up a ridiculous Hawaiian shirt. The black one with the pineapples. I threw on my ultra-faded bomber jacket, circa 1942. I'd found it in a vintage shop in Brooklyn. I figured it was thematic. I posed for the mirror. I looked completely ridiculous.

Perfect.

Then I thought about the Mauser. Brighton Beach. Russians. Not to mention that I'd pissed off Evgeny. Let's be prudent. I took off the jacket. Pulled the antique holster over my head. It fit snugly. It felt nice. Safe. Safer, even, with the gun in it.

I put the Mauser in it.

Truth was, it felt a little dangerous. I mean, I'd had one lesson. I get in a gun thing with somebody, something tells me that guy's used his a bit more than me. I'm going to lose. I'm going to die.

Fuck that. It made me feel manly.

Manly was good.

Puffie's was good, too, in a different kind of way. It was one of those old-time New York taverns, dark and warm and the walls plastered with famous people's publicity shots. *Puffie you're the greatest*, scrawled

Desi Arnaz. *Puffie, loved the shepherd's pie,* from Jack Palance. That kind of stuff.

Brendan walked in. I had to suppress a double take. He was decked out in designer chic. Form-fitting black silk shirt, tailored black pants, a Dior belt buckle saying exactly that, Dior, in brass letters at least three inches tall. He had a black leather jacket, too. But it sure didn't come from the same place I got mine. And there I was, in my pseudo Hawaiian biker cowboy dude outfit. We must have been the oddest couple in town.

Brendan got a few looks. He was a handsome guy. Tanned, in great shape. A vague resemblance to Sylvester Stallone, but more refined. He'd had a part in a straight-to-video parody once, playing the Stallone part. Silently. His voice was too high. They'd dubbed in someone who talked like a man. That was about as far as his acting career got. A couple small parts in commercials. The Ant Terminator, dressed up like Schwarzenegger in the movies. Couldn't even see his face. Hasta la vista, vermin, he said. His only spoken line.

Brendan spent a lot of time in the gym toning those tanned muscles. Hired a voice coach to turn him at least into a tenor. That Stallone thing had shaken him up. He wanted to be the perfect manly object. For other men. But the funny thing was, never mind the muscles, he was the biggest wimp on earth. One night he'd wandered into the wrong neighborhood and got chased halfway around Manhattan by a gang of twelve- and thirteen-year-olds. He'd come over to my place in tears. Hid in the basement for three days getting over it.

He'd grown up gay in a rural Midwestern community. That'll do it to you. His only friend had been his sister. That'll make it worse.

Do you really have to flaunt it that much? I asked.

Flaunt what?

The belt buckle, for starters.

That's a Dior, he said defensively.

You're kidding me, I said.

The shirt's Dior, too. Five hundred dollars at Bergdorf's.

Five hundred bucks that didn't come out of your pocket.

Not a chance, he said.

Brendan, for all his fragility, was good at getting older men to buy him expensive stuff. Or maybe it was the fragility that attracted them. The picture of manhood with a shattered heart. I could see how a certain kind of guy would want to take him under his wing, assuage his pain with costly baubles.

I ordered the corned beef and cabbage. Brendan got the house salad, no dressing please.

I gave him the under-the-eyebrows look.

Body fat percentage up a tenth of a point? I said.

I noticed your gut's starting to hang over your belt. Anybody ever tell you that's a little disgusting?

No, I said. I think it makes me kind of cuddly.

Jesus. I think I just lost my appetite. When was the last time you went to the gym?

Um, I don't know, I said. I'll have to get back to you on that.

This was the pact we'd reached. Without ever saying it, we'd agreed to keep it light. We weren't going to excavate any bodies, agonize over the shared ugly past. What would it accomplish? Well, maybe a lot. But neither of us was equipped to deal with it. I'd keep an eye on him, older-brother-like. But he did his thing, I did mine. And we tried to survive.

The corned beef was great. Wet and juicy from the cabbage. I wolfed it down. Brendan's salad looked like mulch. He didn't touch it. I picked up the check. We went across the street.

The All In was a scungy kind of place. They'd rented out the fourth floor of a walk-up, knocked out all the interior walls and blacked out the windows. Tried to cheer it up with peach-colored walls. The walls just got dirty and made it more depressing, but that didn't matter. We didn't go there for the décor. We went to go fishing. And the fishing was good.

We're sitting down and the dealer's saying, I'm in Vegas last week. Guy gave a hooker a five-hundred-dollar chip. She gave him three hundred bucks cash back, and performed services, too.

Everybody laughs.

Eddie the Butcher next to me says, I'll take those odds any day.

Eddie the Butcher was a friendly guy with a red face and a huge mustache. He didn't murder people for a living. Not that kind of butcher. He chopped up pigs and cows. You could smell it on him. He was a good poker player. Mixed it up. Wouldn't get pushed around. But the rest of them were wimps. Mice and fish. Fish and mice. Worse than mice. Don't mice learn from experience? Every hand I played, I opened with a raise. One or two of them would call, every time. Sometimes three or four. If Eddie called or raised, I'd play my usual game. If he didn't, I could already put the money in my pocket. The flop would come. If they checked to me, I'd bet. If I went first, I'd bet. If they bet in front of me, I'd raise. If they called, I'd raise on the turn. If it went to the river, I'd raise big. And almost every time, at some point they'd fold. Didn't matter what cards I had. Or they had. Oh, sure, if one of them flopped a monster, I'd lose some back. But you just can't give somebody the kind of advantage they were handing out. At some point you have to play back. Re-re-raise. Show you mean business. Eddie knew that. The rest of them never picked it up.

Made you wonder. But not for long. Mostly, you just took their money.

Two thousand bucks in three hours. A good chunk to invest in Brighton Beach.

16.

BRIGHTON BEACH WAS NEW YORK CITY THE WAY IT USED TO BE. Rows and rows of narrow houses. Life on the stoop. People in the street, doing nothing. A family-owned store on every corner, boxes outside overflowing with odd fruit. Pomegranates, maybe. Sausages, the fruit of Eastern Europe. Languages not English. Russian, Polish, Yiddish, Ukrainian. A hint of German. But maybe that was the Yiddish.

The game was in a basement. The door was heavy, painted black, windowless. A large brass handle. The old-fashioned kind, with a thumb-push to unlatch it. An old surveillance camera jutted out above it, big and clunky and smiling at us. A surveillance gargoyle. The small painted sign on the door said *Milan Football Club*. On the door frame was a tarnished brass plate. A button.

Butch pulled up in a cab.

This it? he said.

Unless there's another Milan Football Club on this block, I said.

I pushed the button. Butch scanned the street. Brendan stared at the camera.

I thought you weren't supposed to look at the camera, I said.

What? he said.

The camera. I thought you weren't supposed to look at it.

What?

You're an actor, right?

Used to be.

You're not supposed to look at the camera.

Oh, he said. Ah. Ha ha.

The door clicked. I pulled at the handle. It didn't budge. I pulled again. Butch reached around Brendan. Pushed the door. It swung open.

Hey, I said. There's fire regulations. It's supposed to push from the inside.

Yeah, said Butch. Good work.

The staircase was impossibly narrow, brick red. The walls had once been painted white. Now, they wore flecks and stains and droppings that spoke of an indeterminate, depressing oldness.

We went down single file.

It didn't feel safe.

I put my hand on my new old shoulder holster. The Mauser was there. It made me feel better. I thought of thanking Butch.

But that would be wrong. It would just go to his head. Give him an edge. He didn't need any more edges.

At the bottom of the stairs was another door. Brendan was in front. Butch and I stood on the stairs above him. He negotiated with someone we couldn't see.

I heard him mention names. Andrei. Anatoly.

That seemed to do it.

The door opened.

The room was dim in a greenish kind of way. The poker table filled most of it. To the right was a curtain, tattered and worn. It only partly screened from view a small kitchen. In the kitchen was a heavyset woman in slippers and a smock that could only have originated in Soviet eastern Europe. On the counter in the kitchen were a number of large aluminum trays brimming with what appeared to be hearty eastern European grub. Brown, tasteless stuff. Lots of dumplings.

Andrei got up as we came in, nodding to Brendan. Anatoly unlatched his bones from his chair, unfolded himself to a standing position, grinning. Brendan! he exclaimed, leaning his mantis body over the table to extend his hand.

Tolya, said Brendan, shaking it.

I wanted to puke.

The rest of the guys were in a hand. We got a few offside glances. It was hard to tell if they knew who we were. It didn't seem like they cared a whole lot. Which was okay. They paid too much attention, probably they figured you for dead money.

We locked up seats for you, Andrei said. Brendan took the one next to him. Butch and I were at the other end of the table.

Along with the Brothers A., Evgeny was there, as predicted, taking up a lot of space next to Butch. A guy they called Federov, small and wiry with a greasy baseball cap and never said a word. Georgian John. Not the Georgia north of Florida. The other one. Tbilisi, Georgia. Tbilisi John was hairy beyond human imagining. It was hard not to stare. I'd seen hairy knuckles before, but this guy had clumps of fur on his *first* knuckles. And Jimmy Socks, a dark-skinned guy with a goatee and a paunch. He had a friendly air. They called him Jimmy Socks for reasons I never determined. From Bulgaria, he said. Had an electronics business. Or so he said. And Won Ton John.

The dealer was Artie, a scrawny guy with an easy air, tattoos to his earlobes and a t-shirt reading *Bowling for Soup*. I liked Artie. Knew him from the downtown games. Good to see you, he said. I felt the same. It was reassuring to have him there. Made me think maybe the game was legit.

The first hand once we'd sat down, Evgeny and Federov got it on. They raised and re-raised each other until Federov was all in. Evgeny had a few hundred chips left. When they both turned over Jack, Three— one of the worst hands in poker—the joint almost fell apart from the laughing.

Some guys might have thought, great, there's a lot of dead money in this room. But there wasn't. It was a shtick. I'd seen it before. Play a big pot with mediocre, or in this case lousy, hands early on. A little show for the new guys. Make them think you'll raise with anything. Soften the white guys up for later. It's a standard play. It's just that these guys did it even more so. And with a lot of noise.

Whether that hand was an act or not, almost everybody at the table was loose-aggressive to the edge of madness. And a whole table of those kinds of guys is very hard to play against. You have to pick your spots. You can't play way tight. They'll just take the pot when you fold, and fold whenever you bet. They can't lose. So you have to mix it up a bit. Or more than a bit. And you have to get lucky some.

The volatility—variance, in the math-geek poker lingo—in that kind of game is huge. You just have to play well enough that your ups are bigger than your downs.

The Smock Lady shuffled in from the back room with a tureen of dumplings and a stack of paper plates. She didn't ask if anybody wanted any. She just slung the slop on the plates and passed them around. Nobody declined. I assumed it would be rude if I did. So I balanced the plate on my knee, felt the paper go limp with heat and liquid. After a suitable interval I quietly deposited it under my chair. I was quite sure there were rodents, or other beings, in the vicinity that would enjoy the contribution.

My game started out with a cooler. Federov called my raise from the button. Everybody else folded. I had Ace, King, and a King came on the flop. I was pretty confident—for no reason that I could articulate—that Federov had air. I bet out fairly big. He called, and called my turn bet, too, when a Four came. On the river the club Eight came, putting three clubs on board, and I put on the brakes. Everything Federov had done screamed flush draw—there weren't any straight draws out there. So I just put out a blocking bet: a small bet that might look like I was trying to get paid off with a monster, discourage him from firing back at me if he had, say, a small flush, Nine high or something, and was worried that I might have a draw to a bigger one that I'd been semibluffing with—a semibluff being a bet or raise you make when you have a draw to a good hand, but nothing made yet.

Federov thought for a long time. He pulled his greasy cap down over his eyes. He didn't say anything. Gave me time to reflect on how there was something creepy about the guy, tiny and quiet as he was. Couldn't really put my finger on it. His cap said *Big Kicker Gear* on it, in faded yellow on faded green. I had no idea what it meant.

After what seemed like an hour, Federov shrugged, called, flipped over a pair of Fours for a set. My Kings were dead meat. I lost a big pot right off.

It put me in a bad mood.

We sawed it back and forth for a while, Butch, Brendan and me winning our share of pots, losing a few. Seemed like Butch and Brendan were up a decent amount. I was down a bit. Tbilisi John kept up the flow of vodka. I drank my share. Very uncool to refuse. Worse than saying no to dumplings. Speaking of which, I could feel the mess oozing around under my feet. There was nothing I could do. Any effort to clean it up would only draw attention to my lack of cultural sensitivity.

The vodka flew down my throat.

The room grew hazy.

I went on a rush.

God love the poker rush. You hit every draw. Your opponents miss theirs. Every big pair you have holds up. You hit sets with your small pairs. It's a feeling every poker player loves. You can't get enough of it.

And you don't. The rush will stop as quickly as it started

So just because the deck is hitting you upside the head, you can't relax. You have to maximize your profits in the rush. Bruno aside, nobody's really luckier than anyone else in this game—long term, everybody gets hit the same. Good cards. Bad cards. Which is why the politicians who decry the game as gambling have it all wrong. But that's another story. Point is, you have to make as much as you can off your good hands, or good luck, and minimize your losses on the bad. That's what makes a winner.

Before I knew it, I was up sixty-five grand. Most of which was courtesy of Federov. His yellow eyes were sinking deeper into his pointy face. This could be dangerous. I didn't know the guy. Taking a lot of money off a guy you never saw before could be bad for your health, in Brighton Beach. I needed a break. I wanted to get up and leave, actually. But there's an unwritten rule: you get up big against someone, you stick around. Give them a chance to get their money back.

Hey, I said to Federov, don't worry. I'll be back in a couple. Just need to stretch my legs.

Federov didn't say a thing. Didn't even look at me. But Evgeny bailed me out. Hey, he said—actually what he said was more like cxhay, but it's not spellable in non-Cyrillic characters—let's we all take a break.

Yeah, yah, da came the chorus.

There was a door in the back. Outside was a cracked concrete slab of a yard, ten feet below street level. It was like a prison exercise pen. Except a whole lot smaller. There were a couple of old picnic benches. Long-dead plants in tin buckets. And about fifteen years' worth of cigarette butts.

All the Russkies and assorted other lowlifes lit up their black tobacco, chest-burning non-filter working-stiff-from-Leningrad smokes. I tried to be discreet, tapping out my ultralight menthols.

Butch sidled up. I asked him about Federov. He said he didn't know the guy. But I shouldn't worry. He read him for a degenerate. But not a dangerous one. We talked about tendencies and tells. Andrei had a habit of rolling his eyes a bit to Anatoly when he had a big hand. Evgeny wasn't easy to read. He thought any two cards were fabulous, worthy of big laughs and big bets. We knew that already. Maybe he laughed a little harder when he was bluffing. Hard to tell. Federov, forget it. You could plant fire ants in his anus and he still wouldn't change expression. Excuse, he'd say, his first word of the night, go to the moldy john, blast out his colon with heavy-duty toilet bowl cleaner and steel wool and sit right back down at the game. Maybe his eyes would be a bit narrower. Hard to say.

Meanwhile, Brendan was over at the dead ficus tree chatting it up with his new best friends. I wasn't really getting it. I told myself not to worry. Brendan was sort of childlike, in a lot of ways, but he was also a street guy. After he'd fled the Midwest, he'd knocked about enough to learn his way around. He wasn't stupid. He wasn't going to get screwed over by some two-bit Russkie operators. I didn't think.

I worried anyway.

He came over, looking happier than I'd seen him in a while.

Listen, he said, they really do have some work for us, man.

I rolled my eyes.

Butch grunted.

What kind of work? I said.

Some kind of security thing. Make sure something gets delivered.

You've got to be kidding me, I said.

We're riding shotgun on the stagecoach? Butch said.

Yeah, yeah, I know, Brendan said. Sounds stupid. But I don't think it's that. And anyway, we don't have to take it until we get the whole story. And it's in Vegas. The job. And we're going there anyway.

Sounds too good to be true, I said, with a double dose of irony.

It's going to be good, said Brendan. You'll see. This is just the start.

I was afraid of that, I said.

Butch grunted.

Those vodka shots getting to you? I asked him.

A bit, he said.

I looked at his eyes. The correct answer was: a lot.

17

WE WERE BACK AT THE TABLE, and things had gone back to normal, or as normal as things can get at a basement poker table in Brighton Beach full of Russians and other aliens. Cards were dealt. Hands were won and lost. Nobody's stack got much bigger or smaller.

The intercom buzzed. On the tiny vintage black-and-white security monitor there was a massive blurry figure visible, hunched over Sasquatch-like to fit into the tiny space.

Shit, I said to Butch.

Butch grunted.

The Yeti somehow squoze its bulk down the stairs, hammered on the door. The Smock Lady opened it, and in lumbered Bruno, complete with the hearty Bruno smile and an irritating backslapping routine.

Hey, he said to me, didn't know you played this game.

First time, I said.

Be careful, he chuckled.

I nodded at my chip stack, which had grown to over fifty thousand. Bruno nodded back, did a wide-eyed admiration thing.

It was about as convincing as his smile.

What he was really thinking, of course, was how quickly he could suck that stack over to his end of the table.

Unfortunately, the answer was: not long.

Bruno hung around sucking on dumplings for a while, waiting for a seat to open up. When Won Ton John got up to leave, Bruno took his spot. And immediately performed his usual suckout routine. Bruno was the master of the suckout. He would make huge semi-bluffs—bets that technically could not be correct. But the effect they had when you called and he hit his draw more than made up for any mathematical deficiencies. The bets were mathematically incorrect when viewed in a vacuum, but so many people went on tilt with Bruno that the strategy was a huge winner for him. Guys would spew his way ten times the chips they'd lost on the original hand, trying to bully their way back to where they'd started.

Despite my best intentions, I was no exception. On the very first hand after Bruno sat down, I limped in with Queen, Ten. The flop came Ace, King, Jack. I had flopped Broadway, a Ten to Ace straight, the best possible hand at the time. Bruno called my three-times-the-pot raise with, as it turned out, a lousy Queen, Six of hearts: nothing but the third nut flush draw. He called my big turn bet too. Of course, he hit the flush on the river, and I lost a third of my stack. He'd had no business, mathematically, calling either of my bets. But that was Bruno. The Lifetime Luckbox.

After that I lost a succession of small hands to him. It seemed like there was nobody else at the table. Every second hand was Bruno and me heads up. He never lost his fat smile. I let it get to me. It was flat embarrassing. My irritation slowly inflated into rage. I hunched lower and lower in my chair. I cursed.

The final humiliation came when I raised preflop with Ace, Ten suited. The flop came Jack, Jack, Ten, rainbow. I bet, Bruno called. Now, a very good rule of thumb on a paired flop like that one is that if you don't have trips—no Jack in your hand—and someone calls your bet, you're through with the hand. Very few players will call you with anything that doesn't beat you, and you're likely to have to invest a lot more money to see the river. It's just not worth it to continue with the hand for the few times your opponent is setting up a bluff or calling with a smaller pair than yours, or whatever. Long term, you're going to lose big in that situation.

I knew that.

I did it anyway.

The turn came a rag. I bet. Bruno called.

You got a Jack? I asked, feigning amusement.

I don't know, said Bruno, but I sure would like to see another card.

He was playing me for a fool. He was playing me for such a fool that I convinced myself he was telling the truth: pulling the old double reverse bluff thing.

Yes, I am a moron.

Yes, I called his massive bet on the river.

Yes, he had a Jack.

Yes, I was broke.

Yes, I borrowed twenty thousand from Evgeny to keep playing, get my money back from Bruno.

Yes, I lost that too.

Yes, Evgeny is not a guy you want to owe twenty thousand dollars.

Yes, I could blame the vodka.

But I was the guy that drank it.

In the last pathetic hand of my life-threatening night, Bruno made a big raise preflop. I called in position with Ace, Two of diamonds. Normally I hate Ace, Two. It's a sucker's hand. But it was suited, I had position, and if I hit it, I might be able to double through Bruno. Thoughts of revenge, I admit, may have played a role.

Everyone else folded. The flop came Three, Four, Eight, with two diamonds. So I had the nut flush draw, an inside straight draw to a Five, and possibly an overcard with the Ace. Bruno bet out, a continuation bet, of course, like he almost always would do, like I would do, like any decent player would do after having bet preflop. It gave me no new information. I flat called.

The flop was a beautiful Five, making my straight. Bruno bet out. Once again, he could be doing that with anything. Ideally, he had started out with a big pair, Kings or Queens, and was drawing dead. I went all in. He called. Initially I was surprised. I mean, if he had a flush draw, it didn't include the Ace. The board was scary enough that if he only had an overpair, he had to know he was beat. And he'd made a big bet preflop, so it was very likely that he had high cards, and not anything that this board could be hitting big.

It was a pretty big pot by then, though. Maybe he had hit a set on the flop, and was hoping for the board to pair, giving him a full house. That seemed to be the most reasonable conclusion. Or maybe the lower flush draw. It was the kind of risk I'd seen him take before. And seen him hit more than seemed possible.

Well, I was all in. All I could do was wait for the river card.

It was a Jack of spades. Okay. Given the play, unlikely to have hurt me. I turned over my straight.

Bruno smiled.

This was not a good sign.

He turned over . . . Six, Seven off suit. For a bigger straight.

He'd made a big preflop raise out of position with a dog of a hand, bet out on the flop with a gutshot. For the rest of my money.

Evgeny's money, actually.

I felt sick.

How do you like that? Bruno laughed.

Normally, I try to maintain my cool with the Bruno type. Blowing up only gives them more ammunition. The last thing you want to do is encourage a guy like him in his efforts to put you on tilt.

But this was too fucking much.

I mean, it's bad enough to bad beat someone. It's just totally over the top to gloat about it.

How do I like that? I said, leaning towards him, my voice rising with every word. How do I like *that?*

Whoa, said Bruno, his smug smile on full wattage. Slow down, cowboy. I just meant, I bet you weren't expecting to see Six, Seven off, right?

How do I like that? I said. How'd you like to see your balls in a jar, asshole?

Bruno's smile disappeared. He wasn't used to getting talked back at. He got up, knocking over his chair. He lunged at me. Luck was, Evgeny was in between us. He got up to block Bruno. Red-eyed with rage, not recognizing good fortune when it heaved its bulk in front of me, I looped a right hand over Evgeny, connected with a pathetic tap to Bruno's nose. Bruno reached around the fat man, got me a good one over the left eye.

He'd busted open a two-inch cut on my eyebrow. My head was going to hurt like hell later. But if I was going to take a shot, it was a good spot to take it on. I have Cro-Magnon protrusions over my eyes. I could see him wince.

He'd broken his hand.

Which, at the time, seemed like the more important thing.

The guys pulled us apart. Told us to cool down.

Which I did, quickly enough. Just enough to realize that the whole thing was even more embarrassing than losing my whole stack to Bruno in less than two hours. I'd lost my cool. My edge. My look. I'd probably never get invited back to the game. My chance to get my money back from the clown. My best shot at paying back Evgeny before my kneecaps got in the way of some Russkie hireling's baseball bat.

Shit. I'd been doing fine before Bruno got there.

Looking back, the whole thing was pathetically obvious. Bruno showing up stone sober three hours into the game, when everyone else would be seriously diluted. Jesus. He'd poured a pint of dogshit on the sidewalk, and I'd happily stepped right in it.

Evgeny shoved me towards the door.

Hey, Bruno called after me. Don't worry about it. I'll be around. You'll get your shot.

From any number of people that would have been a nice, conciliatory thing to say. From Bruno, it was just another motherfucking insult.

I looked back at Bruno, my boiling blood seeping into my eyeballs and turning the whole scene to crimson. Butch stood up to block my view of the dirtbag. Brendan stayed in his seat. I looked at him, tilted my head up and out. He shrugged.

Okay, I told him with a nod and a shake of the head. You stay. More power to you.

Butch maneuvered around the table to where I was. I could see he was thinking about what to do. He'd started out trying to protect me from myself. But I knew Butch. He was right on the edge.

I could see it at the corners of his mouth. I could see it in his shoulders. And Bruno couldn't help himself.

Hey brotha, he said to Butch, don't you want to stick around? Make some back for your buddy?

Butch turned around.

He was almost as big as Bruno, and had a lot more street in him— fifteen years a New York City cop, taking care of bigger guys than Bruno. Sure, the sick Italian fuck had muscles on top of the muscles all over his chunky irritating self. But they were gym muscles. Bench-press-with-your-iPod muscles.

Butch glared at Bruno.

I'm not your fucking brother, he said.

. Bruno stood up. To stand up to Butch.

All right, all right, enough, shouted Evgeny, heaving himself up again to get between them.

I grabbed Butch.

It's not worth it, man, I said. We'll pick a better spot.

Butch shrugged. It was half an 'okay' shrug, half an 'I'm just doing this for you' shrug.

18.

WE GOT OUTSIDE. I was breathing heavy. So was Butch. The air was hot and wet. I sat on a fire hydrant. It was gray, had lost its red paint in some forgotten eon of history. Somebody, some night back then or some other time, had stolen the valves. It hadn't seen water in decades. It was a ghost of a fire hydrant.

I lit a smoke. I felt like shit.

I hate confrontations. I mean, I don't run away from a good fight. But somehow I always feel like crap afterwards. Embarrassed.

I hung my head. Looked at the sidewalk. It looked like any other sidewalk. Except dirtier. The litter had turned to sludge with the days and the nights and the rain, the shoes and the boots tamping it down and spreading it out towards the gray brick walls of the buildings. I could make out the corner of a pack of Marlboros. The rest was soup.

It looked about like I felt.

Forget about it, I said.

You forget about it.

Hey, it's me that lost the money. I played like a donkey. I deserve what I got.

You know damn well that's not what it's about, said Butch.

What's it about, then?

Respect.

Yeah, I know. But I'm the one got disrespected. Let me deal with it.

Butch gave me a Look. It was a you've-got-to-be-kidding-me-you-don't-really-think-you-can-deal-with-this-on-your-own Look.

I shrugged. Took a deep drag on the smoke. It calmed me down. A bit.

The black door opened. Bruno stepped out.

Oh shit, I said to myself. This is really stupid, Bruno. You could have just stayed inside, let it blow over. Now somebody's going to have to get hurt.

You guys still here? he grinned.

Unfortunately, the first guy that wanted to show he was still here was Butch. He took a run at Bruno. Normally, I'd expect Butch to make short work of the guy—I mean, he had all those street tricks and shit, I thought—but when Butch tripped over some invisible chunk of nothing on the sidewalk on his rush towards the Italian Barrel of Meat and slammed face-first into the sludge, I was reminded, in the vodka haze that was rapidly re-enveloping me, that Butch was drunk as hell. And Bruno wasn't.

It was the poker game all over again.

Butch gathered himself up and gamely reengineered his rush. Bruno stepped sideways just as Butch reached him. Grabbed a shoulder, spun him around. Butch grunted. Bruno slammed a fist into Butch's gut. Butch doubled over. His eyes bulged. He'd gotten it right in the solar plexus. Hard. Unexpectedly. Which meant his breathing was paralyzed.

Temporarily. But enough to make him useless. He might even pass out for a few minutes.

I knew the feeling.

It was not a good feeling.

Butch staggered across the sidewalk, leaned up against a well-traveled Chevy Caprice. Slid to the sidewalk.

Bruno turned to me. Flexed his shoulders, up, down, up, down. Pursed his lips. Started towards me.

This was ridiculous. He must have outweighed me by fifty pounds. Eighty, if you just counted muscle.

I had to have a plan.

Ah, I thought. A plan.

I pulled out the Mauser.

I pointed it at his head.

I pictured Bruno as a piece of cardboard, suspended on a chain.

It was a plan.

It worked.

He got the point.

He stopped.

He put his hands up, movie-style. Put the Bruno Grin on his face.

Hey, Rick, he said. You can't be serious.

As serious as you were five seconds ago.

Okay. You got me. But it was just an argument, right? Now I seen the error of my ways, okay? Put the thing down.

The error of your ways? Where the fuck you learn that one, Bruno? Now you're the one kidding me. This here's the equalizer, I said, waving the Mauser in his face.

Come on. You're not going to use that thing. You don't got it in you.

The Big Bruno Bluff. He couldn't help himself.

On the other hand, he was right. I wasn't about to shoot somebody. Even somebody as big, menacing and irritating as Bruno.

It was just about then that the gun went off.

I could see Bruno's mouth move. I couldn't hear what he said. My ears were ringing. I was stumbling backwards. I saw him go down on his right knee, lean sideways.

He rolled on his side, clutching at his right shoulder.

You sonofabitch, he said.

Oh shit, I said to myself.

To him, I said: Don't worry about it. It's just something I got in me.

I wasn't about to give him the satisfaction of knowing it was an accident.

Funny guy, he groaned.

I do my best, I said.

So now what're you gonna do? You're fucked, you know. Either way, you're fucked. You kill me, you're a murderer. You don't, you're dead.

Clearly you've watched all the right movies. I'm thinking maybe I should hire you for my outfit.

Fuck you, Redman.

Fuck you, too, Bruno.

I placed the gun barrel against his forehead. I seriously thought about pulling the trigger. Murder, sure. But not most foul. Most . . . pleasant, really. Most justifiable.

But to get a jury to buy that? A different story.

I must be the first prospective murderer, I told myself, to actually think about the consequences of his act.

I stepped back.

I kicked him in the shoulder. The one with the bullet in it.

He screamed.

Pardon me? I said. I didn't quite hear you.

I kicked him again.

I was starting to enjoy it.

A bit too much.

This wasn't me. I was in some kind of fugue state. This was some queer, corrupted part of me, gnarled and greased and cramped from decades in the tar pits, let out for a night, a moment. See what I can do? it was saying to the world.

Jesus Christ, I thought. What the fuck am I doing?

The fuck are you doing? said a voice behind me.

I turned to face my interrogator. I was bizarrely calm. Shock, I guess it was. They say it does weird things to you.

Well, let's see, Butch, I said, as though discussing the choice of drapes for the living room. I've committed a criminal act, punishable by up to twenty-five years in prison, last I heard. Now, I probably have a pretty good defense of self-defense, what with you as a witness. But with a jury, you never know. And now that I think of it, I've probably ruined your career in the NYPD. Though that might not be such a bad thing, for any number of reasons. Of course, I've also sent a message to Bruno, and the rest of that crowd, that maybe I'm not a guy to fuck with. All in all, it might be a positive.

Rick, you're an asshole. Let's get the fuck out of here.

It was hard to argue with the sentiment.

I heard the sound of five cylinders. A very distinctive rattle. Five-eighths of a V-8. A fraction only possible in certain parts of the outer boroughs. A gypsy cab turned the corner. A Lincoln with a touch of age on it. A limping front bumper, a dragging rear. Gray with gray spots, where the rust holes were spray-painted over. The driver's-side window held together with masking tape. A hand-lettered cardboard sign taped on the inside of the windshield: *Bernie's Limo Service.*

Perfect.

I flagged it down.

Bruno was back on the sidewalk. Trying to get himself upright against the black wrought iron fence.

Fuck, he moaned softly. Why'd you have to do that?

I don't know, I said. Manifest destiny. Something like that.

Butch was having some problems making his legs work. I hooked him by the armpits, dragged him in the general direction of the cab. I hauled him up, pushed and shoved. He collapsed into the back seat. I got into the front. The driver had to move his copy of the *Post,* his thermos of coffee and several cartons of what looked to be Egyptian cigarettes.

Sorry, I said.

Where you going? he said.

Manhattan.

Where Manhattan? he asked in an unplaceable accent. Romanian, maybe.

Just get the fuck moving, I said.

He gave me a Look. The Look started out as a get-the-fuck-outta-my-cab-you-creep Look, but soon gave way to a shit-this-guy-looks-seriously-deranged-I-better-listen-to-him Look.

I noticed that I still had the Mauser in my hand.

Ah, I said to myself. Yes. The thing could come in handy.

Get you home faster. All sorts of things.

The cab smelled of gun exhaust and fear.

Or maybe that was me.

In any case, it got us home fast.

19.

THE GASH OVER MY LEFT EYE WAS OOZING. Somebody was playing marimbas in the back of my skull. Or steel drums. Something percussive. I recognized the rhythm, but not the tune. I was still wearing my clothes from the previous night. I suspected they were rank, but since my nose was completely blocked with snot and blood, I couldn't tell. I stumbled to the shower, stripped off the rags and threw them in a corner. I eased into the shower. The water was hot. Not pleasant. But necessary.

After a year or two I turned off the water. I stood for a while, fearful of the frigid air outside the frosted glass. This turned out to be a mistake. The immobility, that is. Thoughts intruded. Memories. Thoughts and memories of the night before. Shit. Had I really shot somebody? Why did I do that? Couldn't I get in trouble for such a thing?

Yes, I answered myself. Serious trouble. Trouble of all kinds. Not just the legal kind. Though that was bad enough.

What the hell was I going to do?

I didn't think Sheila would be much help. And I didn't have a lawyer. Other than myself. And I knew what they said about a lawyer who represents himself. Fool for a client and all that.

I called Butch. Maybe, I thought, he'd tell me the whole thing never happened.

He didn't pick up. I left a message. Put down the phone.

I did the only thing left to me.

I panicked.

I threw on some unobtrusive clothes. I dredged an old pair of prescription sunglasses out of the far reaches of a drawer. I put on a pair of fast sneakers. The holster. The Mauser. The leather jacket.

I saw myself in the mirror. I looked like a bit player in a bad Harvey Keitel movie.

What the hell was I doing? Where was I going to run?

I sat back down on the bed.

The phone rang.

Tell me it isn't true, Butch said.

What isn't true?

You didn't really shoot Bruno last night, did you?

I have some kind of recollection to that effect.

Damn. So do I. Shit.

My thought exactly.

Okay. Stay there. I have to make some calls.

I'm not going anywhere, I said.

Good, he replied, and hung up.

I made some coffee. Read the *Times*. Stuff was happening, apparently. There was conflict. Things were beginning, ending. Some things were good, some bad. More bad than good, it seemed.

The phone rang.

The good news is, it's not official, he said.

What does that mean?

He didn't report it.

No cops? No jail?

So far.

Jesus. That's a weight off.

I put the phone on speaker, put it on the counter. I was out of coffee. I figured I'd just pump some hot water through the used grounds. They spilled into the water container. I tried to fix it. Coffee grounds got all over the counter. I left them there. I'd get a cleaning lady. Tomorrow. Sure. Melissa used to take care of that stuff. Sometimes. I'd have to learn to do it myself. I could still learn stuff. Hell, I'd learned how to shoot a gun.

Yeah, well, said Butch. The bad news is, the word is all over. You're not welcome at the game. Any game, actually.

Ah, shit.

Could be worse, man. Could be worse.

Yeah, I know. Of course. Of course. Listen, can you come over? We got to figure out what to do now.

About what? What's done is done. We let it blow over. You'll be back in spades in no time.

Well, money, for one thing. I blew the whole Vegas bankroll.

You what?

Yeah. Not only that, I owe Evgeny twenty grand.

You're not fucking serious.

Yeah. Dead serious, I'd say.

Evgeny's not a guy you want to owe money to.

Don't I know it. Anyway, we got to figure out what to do.

What's with the 'we'?

Come on, Butch.

I looked in the fridge. Maybe there'd be some cold coffee in there. Strangely enough, there wasn't.

All right, said Butch. I'll be over. After I take care of some stuff.

I never put cold coffee in the fridge, I remembered. Or hot coffee, for that matter. But who knew? Stranger things had been found in my fridge.

I'm sure the stuff appreciates your concern, I said.

What stuff? What the fuck are you talking about?

The stuff you're going to take care of.

Oh. Yeah. That stuff. You can count on that.

I tried making the coffee again. This time I half succeeded. It was still full of grounds. But didn't the Turks drink it that way? I drank some down. It was revolting. How did those Turks do it? And anyway, all it did was make me anxious.

More anxious.

I found a bottle of Jack Daniel's. Mirabile dictu. It calmed me down. A bit.

The doorbell rang. It was Brendan. He was all smiles. All our problems were solved, he said.

You've got to be kidding, I said. I just shot a guy.

It's okay, he said. More than okay.

He'd been hanging with the Russkies all night, he said. They hadn't been offended by my assault on Bruno. Quite the contrary. They couldn't stand the meatball either. They admired me for it. I was the kind of guy they could do business with.

Come on, Brendan, I said. You starting on that again?

What do you mean?

You can't do business with those guys. They do business with you.

There's a lot of money involved.

Yes, Brendan. I would imagine there is. Problem is, it's not for us. It's for them. You work for them, you get a wage. It's not a charitable organization. Dedicated to the care and feeding of washed-up lawyers. And carpenter-actors.

Not this deal.

I saw that Brendan was wearing something on his wrist. Something silver, expensive-looking. Looked to have Maltese crosses on it.

The hell is that? I asked.

It's a bracelet. You like it?

I don't really know. Where'd you get it?

At a place.

Brendan, Brendan. They're setting you up. Or me. Using you to set me up.

Why would they want to do that?

How the hell would I know? Because I pissed off Evgeny. For the fun of it. Because they figure I have more money than I actually do. Because they don't like my teeth.

You have nice teeth.

I better. They cost thirty thousand bucks.

You're kidding me.

I'm not. But let's not go there. I'm still making the payments.

There you go. You need the money.

No, I don't.

But I did need the money.

Damn it.

Give me a minute, I said to Brendan.

I went to the bedroom. Took off the jacket, the holster. Lay down on the bed. Tried to be rational. What the fuck to do? Make priorities. Well, shit. There was only one: getting the twenty grand back to Evgeny. This was a guy you paid back quick. You didn't, all sorts of nasty shit happened. But short of a lucky run of cards, the only cash I could get my hands on was . . . Louise Chandler's retainer.

A nice coincidence, I suddenly thought. Hunh. Twenty grand. Were the Gods telling me something? Well, maybe it wasn't the Gods, exactly . . . I took a slug off the Jack Daniel's that I'd wisely thought to bring with me to the bedroom. Yes. Had to be. And anyway, what choice did I have? Hey, I'd use the Chandler money. Stick to easy games till I got it back. Refill the bank account. She wouldn't know the difference.

Jesus. Was I really thinking this? How low had I fallen? I wasn't welcome in any game in town. Wasn't that what Butch had said? How bad could this get?

Before I could give myself the depressing answer to that question, the doorbell rang. Brendan went to get it.

I closed my eyes. Spare me, I said to myself. Spare me anything but sleep.

Yo, Rick, called out Butch's baritone. Get the fuck down here.

Damn, I thought. Had to do it. Wouldn't be polite to leave the guests alone.

I dragged myself downstairs. Butch and Brendan were in the kitchen. They were smiling.

What's with all the goddamn cheer? I said.

Why not? Butch asked.

Well, I said, let's start with the basics. I almost killed a guy last night . . .

Shut up, Rick. We know.

Have some pretzels, I said.

Thanks, man, said Butch. That's more like it.

We munched the stale pretzels from a plastic bag. I passed around the Jack Daniel's. There wasn't much left. I rummaged around for something else. Found an ancient fifth of Cutty Sark. It would have to do.

Camaraderie is a wonderful thing.

So, I returned to the topic, what about this Bruno thing?

Ah. That. Yes. I can see how you might be concerned.

But I told you, said Brendan, it's okay.

That's the problem with you, Brendan. Everything's always okay. Well, this one isn't okay.

Yes it is, he said.

Oh?

Yeah. I was trying to tell you. They said they'd take care of it.

Who said they'd take care of what?

The Russians. The Bruno thing.

Ah, yes. The trusty Russkies. Take care of it. They didn't happen to tell you exactly what they were going to do to take care of it, by any chance, did they?

No.

Did it involve kneecaps?

C'mon, Rick.

Dismemberment?

Stop it.

A long stretch in a dark place with concrete floors? Brawny meatballs serving knuckle food for lunch?

All right, all right.

Then I don't know it's okay, do I?

Once in a while you could maybe take my word for something.

Don't take offense, Brendan. But we're dealing with my life here. Or at least a limb or two. Three, four fingers at a minimum. I'll take your word for something else, how about that? Tell me where there's a good M club.

M club?

Yeah, M, without the S. I need somewhere to go get myself a good flogging. Punish myself. For being such a fucking douchebag.

I'm telling you, Rick, it's going to be okay.

Butch, I said. Can you tell this guy to shut up?

Shut up, Brendan.

There's a meet in Vegas, said Brendan. Thursday. You guys come. You'll see.

Okay, Brendan, I said, that sounds great. We'll go to a meet. That's what I need. We can purge our anxieties. Reach a higher plane of consciousness. Cross the cultural divide.

Where's the beer? said Butch.

It's ten in the morning, Butch, I said. We finished the Jack. Have some Cutty. And anyway, only I start drinking at ten in the morning.

Rick, said Butch.

Yes, Butch?

It's four in the afternoon.

20.

I SPENT SOME MORE TIME IN BED. I wiped the pus from over my eye. I considered my situation. It didn't take long. I summed it up in one sentence.

Life sucked.

I slept. I woke up. Things hadn't gotten any better. I watched some football on TV. I watched a movie. Something with an aging Paul Newman and an awful lot of shadows. It depressed me. I slept some more.

When I woke again, it was the next afternoon. My eyes wouldn't focus. My mouth felt like well-chewed newspapers. My heart was pounding. The pounding obsessed me. Was it real pounding? Or was it my hyperactive hypochondriacal imagination, zoning in on natural phenomena, inventing life-threatening conditions from woodpeckers hammering on trees in neighboring yards? Or was I really going to have a heart attack? Maybe that was good. It might be a lot less painful than other things that were likely about to happen. Get the fucking thing over with. Get into a hospital bed. Soft nurses with powdery skin, administering to my every need. I got lucky, the insurance would pay for long-term care in a plush facility.

It didn't make the fear go away. If it wasn't the heart, it was the other stuff. Either way, I was fucked. I had to do something. Distract myself from the heart thing. Didn't a heart attack involve pains down the left arm? I felt my arm. The arm was okay. Shortness of breath? Well, come to think about it, I definitely had that. I breathed deeply in and out. That gave me a little relief. But not enough.

Damn it, I was dying.

Well, if I'm dying, I thought, I might as well dress for it. I pulled out my best poker hat, the one with *Dead Money* on it. My blackest pair of wraparound shades. A black t-shirt. The holster. The bomber jacket. I looked for the Mauser. Fuck. Where was it? I scrambled through the junk on my bed. Found the Mauser box under four pizza boxes and a well-thumbed copy of *Gambling Theory and Other Topics* by Mason Malmuth. Somehow I'd managed to put the Mauser in its box. I admired the eagle chiseled on the lid. Took out the pistol. Hefted it. Nice heft. I stuffed it into the holster. A pleasing weight against the chest. Pressing against my heart. Slowing it down. Relaxing it.

I hoped I wasn't going to have to go through any metal detectors. It's okay, I told myself. I'm not getting on a plane, and I'm not in high school anymore. I should be all right.

I looked in the mirror.

Damn, I looked dangerous.

Maybe I could fool somebody.

I went to the bank. I took out twenty grand in cash from the Richard R. Redman Client Trust Account. The balance remaining was seven dollars and forty-three cents.

I guess it was an interest-bearing account.

Shit, I thought. I don't just look like a criminal now, I am one. Well, maybe simply withdrawing the money wasn't a crime. Though withdrawing it with intent to . . . aw, hell. It didn't matter. I'd crossed a line. Not a line I'd ever thought I'd cross. Speeding, sure. Even the odd

DWI—never caught at it, though. But embezzlement of client funds? Jesus. This was a whole new me.

Sure, I intended to pay it back.

But that's what they all say.

Like any criminal, though, I figured I'd get away with it. Double my money. Re-deposit. Even if the Bar Association audited the account, the fact that the money was missing for a couple of days, I'd get a slap on the wrist. It was the guys who took it and lost it that got creamed. Right? Sure, I said to myself. Not a problem.

To be honest, I wasn't really that stupid. Unless you measure stupidity by actions. In which case, I was exactly that stupid.

I went outside. I looked up and down the street. It was a quiet, sunny day. Kids were playing stickball in the street. There wasn't an assassin in sight.

I sighed. I went back to the house. Took off the getup. Lay down in bed.

We were off to Vegas soon. I could win the World Series. All this could be history.

There was still hope.

21.

A JOLLY BAND OF SELF-DELUDED POKER ASPIRANTS, we were, heading for Vegas. Indiscretions, misdemeanors, felonies left behind in the vapor trail. The plane ride was giddy. I'd splurged. Used up the last of my frequent flier miles on upgrades. First class. There was something about getting off the ground, all together in that tiny sumptuous world of free cocktails and unrelenting snacks. Something liberating.

Along with the ground, we left the ugliness behind.

Until we got to Vegas, of course. Then another kind of ugliness hit. Like a sack of wet shit. A sack of wet shit with many, many flashing lights. And sequins. Cubic zirconium. And noise. The relentless chime and jangle of the slot machines—the dark matter of Las Vegas. The Eiffel Tower, shrunk and comic-booked. A black, mysterious pyramid that anywhere else might provoke curiosity. Here, it promised . . . more slot machines. Fat people. More fat people. Badly dressed fat people. Badly dressed fat people dragging annoying children. Badly dressed fat people hypnotically playing jangling slots. And old people. Many, many old people. The sad and dying desperation of the fingers feeding slots.

The worst thing about it was, they all seemed to be having a good time.

The whole thing gave me a headache.

That was only my opinion, mind you. Brendan thought it was cool. Better than Times Square, even. He really was a kid, still. In so many ways.

Until later. Later, he was just dead.

Are you still a kid, a wife, when you're dead? Or are you an ex-wife, an ex-kid?

We decided to save some money on the accommodations. We'd rather be off the beaten track anyway. Find some seedy little joint. Just close enough to smell the money. Not so close we'd get swallowed up by the kitsch.

We stopped at a greasy joint along the way. Got some Buffalo wings. Extra hot. With the bleu cheese sauce.

What, I asked, makes blue cheese better if you call it bleu? And shouldn't it be either blue cheese, or fromage bleu? What's with these people? Why not call white bread blanc bread? Red peppers rouge?

Shut up, Rick, said Butch.

We had a couple scotches. Doubles. I loved Las Vegas. You could get a double scotch in a greasy spoon. Almost felt like home. Especially when I heard something that sounded like Russians ranting, two booths down. They were loud and drunk. I turned an ear their way.

Yup, Russian all right.

Jesus, they were everywhere.

On the way out, I glanced at them. See if I recognized anybody. I didn't.

My heart slowed down.

But I knew it was inevitable. They'd be all over the World Series. A few years ago there were maybe four or five Russians around. Serious players, mostly. Guys you had to be careful of only at the poker table. Now it seemed like there were hundreds.

The Brighton Beach guys would be there. I'd wager on it.

If I had any money to wager.

We found a passable motel off the beaten track, but easy cab distance to the Rio. Where the World Series of Poker would be played.

The Dusty Angel was a joint that once had tried too hard and then, some time ago, had given up trying at all. There was a large circular fountain in the middle of the lobby, empty of water. The pennies had all been stolen. Plastic vines dripped from the ceiling around the fountain. Their leaves were covered with dust. Plastic plants really didn't require less maintenance than real ones, I mused. I mean, you didn't have to water them, but you did have to dust them. Well, they weren't dying, anyway. Though they did have a deceased kind of look about them.

Would you like a non-smoking Queen? asked the innocent young lady behind the counter.

Well, I said, perhaps my friends would. But I'd prefer a room.

The girl seemed a nice young thing, timid, freckled and bucktoothed.

She looked at me like I'd grown a dick out of my forehead.

I put my hand to my brow. No dick there.

Ah, then the dick must be me, I concluded.

She wasn't angry. She just hadn't gotten the joke. She patiently explained to me what she'd meant. Non-smoking meant the room. Queen described the bed.

Thank you, I said. That would be fine.

Actually, said Butch, we'd prefer a suite. Three bedrooms. One for each of us. Do you have suites?

She eyed us suspiciously.

Butch smiled his big smile. Brendan smiled his nervous one.

Well, she said, there is the Executive Suite. But it's very expensive.

We asked how much. She told us. It was less than a single room at the Rio.

Expensive is a relative concept.

And you get what you pay for. The grandly named Executive Suite was done up in that motel beige that does its best to cause no offense. Everything had a distinct air of Scotchgard. Brendan's room faced the front parking lot. Butch's faced the rear parking lot. Mine faced . . . the parking lot next door.

Something to be said for symmetry, I guess. Equality. Fraternity.

But there was a big central living room. A wraparound couch. A wide balcony. And a mini-kitchen. It would do.

We unpacked the four boxes of booze we'd picked up at a package store on the way. We were going to need a lot. After a hard day of poker, you needed to celebrate. Or tranquilize. Depending.

And anyway, only a fool, or Gavin Smith, drinks during the game. We'd need to catch up.

I slouched into the beige wraparound. Butch, cop that he was, took the matching armchair, sat up straight. Brendan joined me on the couch, near horizontal.

Brendan was a bit of a duckling that way. I feared this imprinting thing was going to get out of hand.

But, we had a home. We could stay awhile.

Adventure, I said.

Fame, said Butch.

A million bucks, said Brendan.

Let's make a plan, I said.

Let's plan to get drunk, said Butch.

Excellent plan, I said.

I grabbed the glasses. Made us another set of doubles.

Someone had left a yellow and green striped, miniature rubber football between the cushions of the wraparound. I tossed it to Butch. He made a one-handed grab.

Brendan lit up one of his Gitanes. I was going to protest. Gitanes, besides being pretentious as hell anywhere outside of Paris or Amsterdam, stunk up the joint like the house burned down and you're sitting in the water-soaked rubble. But what the hell. I didn't want to be a hypocrite. I was sure the world was full of people who found my ultralight menthols offensive. Several of them had, in fact, identified themselves to me.

I got to tell you, Butch said, I'm not into this chicken-shit preliminary tournament stuff. For me it's the Main Event or it's nothing.

I tried to think of a clever response, but the second double scotch had just done a flanking maneuver on my left frontal lobe, and that's where the wit resides.

I hear you, I said.

It was the best I could do.

I flung the ball out the window into the parking lot below. A gift, I thought, to the local schoolchildren.

A little mitzvah never hurts.

Did they have schoolchildren in Vegas?

Have you caught the cleavage in this town? I said. There's so much around, it kind of stops meaning anything anymore.

I know what you mean, said Butch.

Another hazard I'm spared, said Brendan.

I don't know, said Butch, there's those guys on the trapeze at the Rio, on the way to the elevator. Spandex. Glutes.

To die for, I said.

I wouldn't know, said Brendan.

You're not fooling anyone, I said. But you know, now that I think of it, there's something kind of weird.

What?

Well, you don't really see any openly gay guys in Vegas. At least, not in the mainstream places. It's another of those fifties hangover things, I think. Like drinks with little hats in them. Must be still underground. I mean, all those trapeze guys have to have somewhere to go to unwind, don't they?

There's more than you might think, said Brendan.

I see, I said. You know more than you're letting on.

You'll have to show us, said Butch.

Sure, said Brendan. But I don't know if it's really anything you want to see.

You'd be surprised, I said. But anyway, we're not going anywhere before we qualify for the Main Event. And not before you track down that sister's address, by the way.

Oh shit, he said.

Yeah. Like I said, we got work to do.

22.

THE WORLD SERIES OF POKER STARTED, back in 1970, at Binion's Horseshoe. Binion's is in the old Downtown district, the original Vegas. It's a time machine now, Downtown. You expect Dean Martin to be headlining at the Gold Dust. All the fancy places are on the Strip. The Rio, where the WSOP is held now, is on the Strip, or just off it, depending on how you define the thing. Harrah's, the casino conglomerate that owns the Rio, bought Binion's a few years ago. They took the WSOP and the Horseshoe name and promptly dumped the hotel itself, so I hear, for pocket change. For one last year they held the final table at Binion's, a nod to tradition. But now the whole thing is at the Rio.

I guess that's progress.

The Rio is a massive hulk of a thing, done up in a carnival theme. There's a Masquerade Tower and an Ipanema Tower. Clever. As you walk through the Masquerade Tower, some enormous contraption full of very un-Brazilian-looking guys and gals in Day-Glo pastel suits and ties swings overhead, the performers dancing to a deafening disco medley. There's a sign:

IF ANYONE DOES NOT WISH TO PARTICIPATE IN
BEAD THROWING AND CATCHING, WE HOPE THAT YOU WILL
ENJOY YOURSELVES IN AREAS OF THE CASINO OTHER THAN
THE MASQUERADE VILLAGE.

Unfortunately, despite the fact that we had not the slightest interest in bead throwing and catching, we could not entirely avoid the Masquerade Village, since the long trek to the poker room went right through it. We lowered our heads and scurried through, dodging fearsome pods of pastel-shorted fat persons and their equally lard-laden offspring, terrified of injury by errant bead fling.

We headed for the satellites. You could play in the super-satellites. More expensive to get into, fewer players to beat out. The regular satellites got you a cheap ticket to the supers. A lot of bluffing involved. You started with very few chips, and the blinds—forced bets the first two players make before the cards are dealt—went up fast. The blinds would come around to you every eight or nine hands, fewer as the field thinned out, so when they got high enough you couldn't afford to wait for good cards. You'd get blinded to death. You had to run over the table. Go all in with any decent hand. Hope everyone folded. If not, hope to get lucky. It wasn't real poker. But it took real skill. If you knew the math, which hands to go all in with, which hands to call an all in with, and when, you had a big advantage. It's just that, compared to real poker, your options were extremely limited.

And if you won a hundred-dollar satellite, took your money, bought into a bigger satellite, you only had to beat out nine other players to play the Main Event, for practically nothing. Top ten percent got a seat. If you didn't make it, you could start again.

Or, you could buy straight into the super for a thousand dollars.

I bought in for the grand. Call me impatient.

Shelley was the floor manager in charge of the satellites. She'd been doing it forever. Every year, first thing I'd do is look her up, say hello. It was a good-luck kind of thing. She was in her sixties, maybe. Sharp nose. Bad teeth. I could only assume she had crates of hair spray left over from the fifties in her efficiency apartment; there was no other explanation for the height of her dyed blonde bouffant. Dime-store lipstick, heavily applied. Another crate in the basement. They hadn't made that shade of orange since 1965.

But you had to like her. She was quick on her feet, and always funny. Knew the job. Every once in a while she'd sit and deal a few hands. She dealt like a pro. One of the best. Fast, slick, efficient and accurate. And she knew all the rules, however arcane. And if somebody got out of line, she knew how to bring down the hammer. Ten-minute penalty, she'd say in a pointy voice that went right to the offender's spinal cord, some tourist who'd cursed at a nasty river card. They'd get up, slink away. Nobody messed with her.

You wished she were always at your table.

Hey, Shelley, I said.

Rick Redman, she said with a smile. Tore yourself away from the courtroom?

I'm not doing that anymore, I said.

She raised her eyebrows, pulling over her cash box to take my ten bills, writing my name on the call sheet with her other hand.

Gave it up, I said. Too much stress. Poker now. And investigations.

Investigations, she said. Sounds exotic.

It isn't. Not yet, anyway. Actually, it's not anything, yet.

We have faith, she said, turning to the next guy in line.

While I waited to be called, I wandered about the playing hall. It was ridiculously big. Several football fields big. An enormous web of aluminum pipes slung from the roof, from which dangled innumerable light fixtures, cameras, table number cards, banner ads for sponsors—most ubiquitously a certain brand of beer. A bevy of delectable young things wandered the floor and hallways, hired by the beer company to dress up in identical outfits: skimpy cut-off jeans, tool belt, work boots, white shirt tied up under their breasts. Their sole job appeared to be to hand out souvenir World Series of Poker chips that could be redeemed in the tent out back for a free beer. But only the sponsor's beer. Which sucked.

Also out back was a food tent, where they sold mass-produced burgers and dogs, low cost and surprisingly tasty. And rows of latrines in trailers, shockingly clean. And air-conditioned. Thank the Lord.

They'd thought it out: you'd never really need to leave the joint.

I checked out the beer tent. They had a pool table. Some huge beanbag chairs to doze in. I didn't drink beer, but it was brutally cold in there, which made me want to stay as long as possible.

I hung for a while. Introduced myself to the bartender. Natalya. Was anybody not Russian anymore? Well, she at least was the kind of Russian I could appreciate. Impossibly tall and slim. Strong Slavic chin. Blue eyes, wide and widely set. A regal nose. Not one of those tiny American things trying desperately to hide its function. This was a nose that announced itself.

Hey, I said.

Hey, she replied with a wide smile. Her front teeth crossed just a little, one slightly shorter than the other. Sexy.

We introduced ourselves. I told her I was a dissolute ex-lawyer-sort-of-investigator-quasi-semiprofessional-poker-player kind of guy. She said she was a model. I feigned feigning astonishment. She laughed.

Yes, she said. The beer company hired a bunch of us. We're supposed to go around giving out coupons to everybody. Tell them to come out back for free beers.

Problem is, I said, the beer sucks.

Shh, she said, putting a finger to her lips.

There's nobody else here, I said, looking around the place.

That's 'cause the beer sucks.

I only drink scotch anyway.

Well, she said, leaning forward, if you're really good to me, I might be able to help you.

I could smell her. Lilac and something. Something good.

I considered giving up the World Series. Moving in with Natalya. Being her foot slave.

Unfortunately, I hadn't gotten the offer yet.

Got to get back to the tables, I said. But I'll take you up on that later.

I got a wink in return.

Back in the playing hangar a couple of the warm-up events were going on, and a bunch of satellites. The place was like the biggest, loudest cafeteria you've ever seen—packed with poker tables as far as the eye could see, every seat filled. Herds of kids in baseball caps and tracksuits. Crowds of old-time guys, guys from Idaho and Illinois, Tennessee and Texas, lots of checked shirts and large belt buckles. Here and there an over-painted old lady. Black guys, white guys, a zillion Asian guys. Democracy at its best. You couldn't generalize. If you thought Asian guys with shades played tight, you'd lose a lot of money to Korean Dave. If you thought guys with yarmulkes were bound to call you down with only top pair, Real Estate Sammy would set you straight. If you thought women could be pushed around, High Times Annie would kick your ass.

No, you had to take everyone as an individual. Every player for himself. Risk, reward. Skill, profit. Foolishness, punishment. But not always. Sometimes Joe the grocery store clerk wins the lottery.

It was even more democratic with the Internet qualifiers. The place was littered with the logos of the major Internet poker sites. If the Internet qualifiers didn't already stand out by virtue of their youth and lack of table tricks—the chip-riffling, hard-staring, trash-talking routines so assiduously cultivated by professionals who'd been around a few decades—they were usually bedecked with so many accoutrements of the site on which they qualified—hats, buttons, t-shirts, whatever, stuff they were contractually obliged to flaunt in return for their good luck in winning a seat—you could spot them a mile away.

Generally, though, nondescript is the word to describe, charitably, your average tournament poker player. Baseball caps, many worn backwards, t-shirts and sweatshirts, many stained. Though there's always a minority of serious characters determined to liven up the place. An ancient guy with enormous thick glasses, a scraggly beard and stupendously large ears, rancid teeth. His shirt said *Sin City Casino and Lounge*, with a silhouette of a naked woman, red on black. He was wearing a *CSI: Las Vegas* hat. Don't be fooled: it turns out he plays a good aggressive game. And a guy named Bernie, with a floor-length black raincoat and enormous hat to match, long fingers, splayed at the ends, he hunched over his cards like an arthritic gecko.

Towards the back I spotted some of the stars. Doyle Brunson, the Godfather of poker. You could spot the cowboy hat twenty tables away. I doubted he'd ever missed one of these events. Daniel Negreanu, eating vegetarian out of a takeout container. As though he were sitting in his kitchen. Munch. Glance at hole cards. Munch. Muck cards. Keeping up a patter, too. Probing for information.

A few celebrities. James Woods. Ben Affleck. Some actress. I was sure she was famous. Couldn't remember her name. Jennifer somebody. Tilly. Cleavage to die for. And Lennox Lewis. Former heavyweight champion of the world. He took up a lot of room at the table. Seemed like a nice guy.

Waiters prowled the room. Not enough of them. It could take a half hour before they came back with your drink.

Not a bad thing, that, necessarily.

My name was called.

My table was near the front. Near the exit doors. A constant stream of players, railbirds going by. Just another thing to ignore.

I looked around the table. Nobody I recognized right away. No big-name pros. That was good. Maybe I had a chance. All I had to do was beat nine other players. Last guy standing had an entry to the Main Event.

There was the usual motley crew at the table. A guy with skin-tight pink shorts and a sour expression. Potbelly. Highlighted hair. Kind of like a tanned, gay Chris Farley. A guy with gray hair, tailored shirt. Looked like maybe a podiatrist in from Utah. Guy with a cowboy hat and a leather jacket. I liked the old-school look. Thought about adopting it.

Wasn't like that in the old days, of course. Used to be lots of cowboy hats. Now they looked a little lonely and quaint. I missed the conversations you'd get:

Where ya from?

Tallahassee.

I went broke in Tallahassee. About thirteen years ago, I reckon.

You don't say?

I reflexively assumed that the guy wearing the cowboy hat knew what he was doing. Just like I concluded that the podiatrist wasn't going to last long. Better to avoid succumbing to those clichés, though. Whether someone knows what they're doing is something to be discerned by their bets, their plays, their mannerisms. The cards they play. Do they sit like statues, never raise, always call or fold? Calling Station Alert. Easy money. Bluff them till they drop. The three times all night they raise, get the hell out of the hand. Do they play every second hand for a raise? Maniac Alert. Easy money, but dangerous when lucky. Tread with care. Don't play for draws. Bust them with made hands. Do they act like a maniac one minute, like a rock the next? Beware. Could be a Cowboy.

Ah, if only it were so easy.

This time it wasn't.

I started out tight. Played a hand or two. Stole a pot with a timely bet. Built my stack a bit. Up to eighteen grand. You started with ten.

The guy across from me, Trucker Jerry, went on a rush. He was one of those overcompensating small guys. He'd been at it for a long time. The overcompensating, I mean. You could tell. The poker, too, for sure. Gray hair. Baseball cap. Baggy jeans. Probably couldn't find any small enough to fit him without going to the boys' section. Kept up a constant patter. Handed around a clipping from *Card Player* magazine with his name in it. He'd won some minor event at the Sands a couple months before. The article was one inch long. From page 185.

Way to go, Jerry, we all said. That's awesome.

Jerry's playing loose as hell, but he's getting away with it, because the deck is hitting him upside the head. He's sucking out on ridiculous draws. Beats Kings with his Jack, Ten when a third Ten comes off on the river, giving him trips. Doubles up. Doubles up again when he fills a flush on the turn.

Pretty soon it was eight men out, just me and him left. And he had my stack dominated. He had way more than half the chips on the table. Well. I had to do what I had to do. Pick my spots. Go all in. Get lucky.

I went way aggressive. Picked up some blinds. Got a pair of Nines. Went all in. He called with King, Ten. The Nines held up. Doubled my stack. I could breathe a bit.

I folded a couple of hands.

You have to mix it up a bit. Not get predictable.

I went out back for the smoke break. I was thinking restful thoughts—about how goddamn hot it is in Vegas in the summer, stuff like that. A guy was leaning against the wall rolling a smoke. The string-tie of his drooping sweatpants was pulled tight, looped under a mammoth belly his t-shirt could only partly cover. He had a puffy face, steel wool hair that might have seen shampoo around about the Tet Offensive. The t-shirt displayed forensic evidence of at least six meals, and several encounters with sharp objects.

The t-shirt said *Alive for Pleasure.*

I felt a mammoth paw on my shoulder. I turned around. A huge guy with thick, greasy lips and spiky hair.

I heard about you, he said.

Great, I said.

From Bruno, he said.

Oh shit.

Luiz, he said by way of introduction. This here's Mikey Z.

He nodded at his companion.

Mikey had the acne scar thing going, and a wispy blond mustache. Both of them huge and with black leather. Slightly smaller than Bruno, but the same general type, except ugly. Both of them holding motor-cycle helmets.

How you doin'? Mikey Z. bellowed in a thick voice from the back of the throat, a broad smile working mightily to make itself as insincere as possible.

Doing great, I said. You?

I hear you owe Evgeny some serious money.

Maybe, I said. What's it to you?

Nothing, he said with an unsubtle wink. Just wondering.

We faked some poker chatter. They said they were cleaning up in the side games. Yeah, me too, I lied. I asked them where they were staying. The Bellagio. Of course. If it wasn't the most expensive place in town, it was close. Well, good for them. If they made half of what they claimed to make in the cash games, they could afford it.

Mikey asked me where I was staying.

Dusty Ranger, I said.

What?

The Dusty Ranger, I repeated.

Don't know it, Luiz said.

I didn't think you would, I said.

I headed back to my table.

The smoke tasted black and brackish in my throat. I worried that I hadn't disguised the motel name enough. Last thing I needed was Bruno knowing where I lived.

I got back in time to be dealt the button. I peered at my hole cards. Pair of Tens. Nice.

I raised a grand.

Too much. I was overcompensating.

Jerry re-raised all in.

Damn.

Again? I said.

He grinned at me. Adjusted his aviator shades.

Tens is a good hand. A very good hand. Not a great hand. But a very good one. Especially all in.

But not a monster. Not at all. Even if he didn't have á higher pair—and I didn't think he did—any hand with a Jack, a Queen, a King or an Ace could beat me. Three cards each to make a higher pair. That's twelve cards to beat me. Five cards to come. Five times twelve is . . . whatever the hell it is. A lot.

No. Not a monster.

If I'd been the one gone all in with my Tens, I'd have been very comfortable. You want to be the aggressor. All the books tell you that. It's called fold equity. When you combine the times that your opponent folds to your bet with the times your hand holds up and wins, you'll be an overall winner. But when you're just calling, you've got to have the better hand at showdown every time: that's the only way you can win. What really drove it home was all the times you didn't bet out. You had a hand. Somebody raised big. You flat called. He flipped over his cards.

A monster.

Yes, guys bluff. Guys bluff all the time.

But they're not bluffing all the time.

And with all of your chips at stake, or most of them, or even just a lot of them, you had to be sure. You couldn't be certain, of course. You could never be certain. But you had to be sure enough about it that you wouldn't be second-guessing yourself later.

And you were a hell of a lot more sure when it was you, and not the other guy, putting in the big bet.

I was trying to work through all this shit when I saw Brendan near the door to the smoking area. He was with two guys. Looked like Anatoly and Andrei. Shit, had all of New York City already got here? And wasn't Brendan supposed to be tracking down Eloise? Or at least her last known address?

I pushed it away. I had a hand to play. I called for time. I didn't have to fake anything. There was no more room for deception. I was either folding, or calling him all in. He, on the other hand, might be giving something away. I looked him up and down. Jiggling legs? You could tell by the upper body movement. Usually meant a big hand. None of that from Jerry. Trying too hard to be inconspicuous? That would mean, probably, that he didn't want a call. I didn't see any of that either. Excessive blinking? Usually meant a bluff. But I hadn't gotten a read on his normal blink rate. So the fact that he was, in fact, blinking up a storm didn't do me any good. Could be he did it all the time. And anyway, if he was good, and I had no reason to think otherwise, he could be doing it on purpose. To give me a false read. The reverse tell. Can be very effective.

So, I had to rely on the betting patterns. The cards. The math.

While I was thinking, I glanced towards the bar. There was Brendan again, still with the Russkies. Looked like they were throwing back vodka shots. Shit, I thought, I've got to go straighten the kid out. He can't have already gone to Henderson and back.

I pushed the thought away. I pondered Jerry's play. There wasn't much to go on, this hand. I'd bet. He'd raised. A re-raise to a raise as big as mine was a pretty ballsy play. If it was a bluff, it was a good one. You had to think about what the other guy was thinking. I was thinking that he was thinking that because of my earlier aggressive play, I'd probably raised with less than optimal hands before. He just hadn't had a hand that could beat a bluff, to call me on it with. But then, recently, I'd folded a few in a row. He had to think I was tightening up. Maybe.

On the other hand, the guy himself had played a lot of iffy cards, earlier.

I looked him down some more. He was staring straight ahead. Riffling a small stack of chips. Doing it smoothly.

Nothing to go on.

I glanced back at the exit. Brendan and the Russkies were gone.

It gave me a bad feeling.

But I had a hand to play.

Forget about what he was thinking about me. What'd he been doing? When I thought about it, Jerry hadn't played many hands lately. He'd gotten a lot more selective. I had to give him credit.

On the other hand, he could have been raising with a real hand, but one less than Tens. A crapshoot hand was very likely. Ace, King. Ace, Queen. Something that was less than fifty-fifty to beat my Tens.

I looked at the guy. Black shades. Still staring straight ahead. Not moving. Giving me nothing.

Ah, shit, I thought. Why take a chance here? I still had a lot of chips. Make my stand later. When I was the aggressor.

I folded.

A few more hands went by. Thrusting and feinting. A grand here, a grand there. We were staying about even. I looked down at Ace, King.

How to play it? I go all in, he probably folds. All I get are the blinds. Though the blinds were big. Two and one. Three grand. Not a bad haul.

But. Ace, King. I could try to trap. Get all his chips.

I called.

He bet. Two grand.

Well.

He could have anything. Or nothing. He was good. He was randomizing his bets. So. I had to calculate on the basis that he had at least a slightly better than average hand. And I had a monster. So. It was easy.

I went all in.

He nodded. Flipped over Aces.

Shit on a stick.

The Aces held up.

Better luck next time.

I nursed my disappointment for a minute. Until the vision of Brendan with those fucking Russkies came back to me. Fuck the satellite. What the hell was he doing? I went out back. Didn't see them. It had been a while. I checked out the hamburger joint. Nothing but stained sweatshirts waiting for mustard.

The beer tent.

Natalya was still there.

Hey, I said.

Hey, Ricky! she said.

You're a lucky girl, I said.

Oh? How so? she said, nonchalantly pulling out a scotch glass and a bottle of Johnnie Walker Black. Ice? she asked.

Sure, I said.

She poured me a big one.

So how is it I'm so lucky? she asked.

I only let really good-looking women call me Ricky, I said.

Ah. Then I am indeed very lucky girl.

That dropped 'a' was the first hint of her Russian roots. Other than the name, and the facial features.

I asked had she seen a couple of Russian guys with a tanned, good-looking American guy, mid-thirties, slim waist.

Sure, she said. They played pool for a while. Drank a lot of vodka. Got a little stupid. So I threw them out.

You didn't.

No, I didn't, she said with a laugh. They took off. But they were pretty tanked.

You know those guys? The Russians?

Not really. I've seen them hanging around the last couple of days.

You're sure the American guy went with them?

Sure I'm sure.

Shit, I thought. There's no way the little fucker had checked out the Henderson house.

Damn, I said.

Problem?

Nothing. If you see him, let me know, will ya?

Sure, she said. How'm I going to do that?

Oh. Yeah. Sorry.

I wrote down my cell number on a napkin.

Now, she said, I have the power on you.

So you do, I said. So there's nothing else for it. You've got to give me your number, too.

Oh, Ricky, you are too quick for me. But no, I think you do a little more work before you get my number.

She said it like she didn't mean it. That I could lean over, say just the right funny thing, and her phone number would pop out of her mouth, just like the winning ticket from the slot machine.

But I didn't have time to follow up. I couldn't let this Eloise thing go. Apart from my general obligation to do the job I was hired for, it might be useful to actually do some work for the money I'd misappropriated. If all went well, I'd earn it, and never have to account for it.

I called Brendan's cell. No answer. No surprise there.

Enough. I'd have to check out Henderson myself.

Had to change out of the poker clothes first. Get into some realistic detective getup.

Appearance, like location, is everything.

To get to the exit from the poker area I had to pass through the Poker Lifestyle Exposition. I wasn't at all sure what the Poker Lifestyle consisted of, but whatever it was, I couldn't imagine anyone wanting to pay extra for it.

Best I could tell, the Exposition was an excuse for anyone with anything to sell that was vaguely poker-related to set up a booth and look bored. It was housed in a mammoth room right across from the playing hangar. In the middle of the place one of the Internet poker sites had set up a two-story extravaganza. Downstairs was a comfortable lounge with laptops, where you could play for free on their site. Upstairs they had put a king-size bed on which reposed three girls in hot pants and t-shirts. A bunch of fat, sloppy, badly dressed guys—poker players, in other words— were lined up on a staircase waiting their turn to sit on the end of the bed, their backs to the girls, and get hit with pillows. One of the girls tossed armfuls of feathers into the air while the other two did the hitting. Some guy with a camera was standing against the far wall taking insta-photos that the pillow guys then might have the honor of purchasing.

I guess part of the Poker Lifestyle is getting slammed with pillows by hot babes while somebody takes pictures.

I'd missed that part.

I vowed not to miss it again.

23.

OUTSIDE, THE HEAT WAS SOLID, IMMOVABLE. I trudged through the thermal wall to the cabstand. I was in luck. No line. I got into the first car. It smelled of dust and dry rot. The driver wore a leather cap, covered with badges. They seemed to have something to do with fishing. I wondered where you went fishing in the desert. I asked him. He chuckled, didn't answer. He got me to the Dusty Angel. I asked the fisherman to wait for me while I changed. The Dusty Angel had a cabstand, but it was usually empty.

I changed into some quasi-respectable clothes. Back in the car, I asked the guy if he knew where Henderson was. He chuckled again, pulled the car into the street.

Heading to Henderson. Heading: Henderson. I cursed Brendan. I cursed him some more. If I'd been wearing a sign, it would have said: *I'd rather be playing poker.*

Henderson, I learned later, is a big part of Vegas. Everyone knows where it is. Rich people live in Henderson. I suppose you might call it a suburb. But it just seemed to be more of the same. You looked out your hotel window—if you were lucky enough to be staying at a hotel, and not a motel with a parking-lot view—and beyond the ludicrous excess of the Strip, Vegas just seemed to stretch on forever, or to the mountains if you were looking in that direction. The same, the same and more of the same, sun-blasted adobe and cinder block. It made the idea of separate towns and jurisdictions, boundaries, borders, sort of, I don't know, futile.

Desert housing developments are just like desert golf courses: watered and manicured to absolute perfection. The golf course fairways look like they've been bikini-waxed, as some famous golf commentator once said, and got fired for saying. I thought it was a pretty good line. But golf culture is not big on candor. Honesty, integrity, yes. Speaking your mind? Get back to the caddy shack, buddy. No, forget it. Get off the fucking course, and never show your face here again.

The point being, the greens and fairways are meticulously maintained. The desert climate is inhospitable to pests, to the insects and crabgrasses that bedevil golf courses in more humid climates. The rough consists of vast stretches of desert wasteland. You hit your ball left off the tee, you're not fighting through tall gnarly grass, you're battling rattlesnakes and rocks, cacti and lizards.

Henderson is like the fairway, the highways. Everything is frighteningly new, extensively watered, groomed and pruned. The houses set discreetly back behind rows of palms. Well-constructed houses. Tailored to the weather and the landscape. One might even admire them, if there weren't so damn many of them. Most parts of Vegas, there were rows and rows of identical desert-brown developments, a parody of old suburbia. In the expensive parts of town, the houses were individual, the product of architectural thought. But it was still hard to tell one from another. There was something homogenous about them. Like American cheese. Not the cheese known as American. That's Ohio. But the way that any cheese you can find in America can only reach a certain level of idiosyncrasy. You'll never find a Brie that tastes like a Brie from Brie. Because there's a law in America: you've got to homogenize it.

The Eloise house was like the rest: low-slung, spread out, neutral. As though the house was trying to show up the palm trees, for their ostentatious height and absurdly fecund crowns, their individuality.

The palms, actually, were also an artifact of the Vegas ethos. There hadn't been any palm trees in the desert, originally, when Meyer Lansky scoped it out way back then. Every one of them was planted in Las Vegas from seeds. You wanted a new one, it'd cost you upwards of ten grand. Every house in Henderson had at least a couple.

You can draw your own moral.

I searched for the doorbell. It took a while. I scoured the door frame. Smooth as a cross-corner draw to the side pocket. The door itself. The only interruption was a bas-relief palm tree pasted on the door. A coconut tree. With exactly one coconut. Aha. I pressed the coconut. I heard a chilly chime deep inside the house. Like the air-conditioning was on too high.

There was no response.

The chime died away.

The silent heat returned.

I pressed the thing again. I waited.

This time the door opened.

She was blonde. She had a man's shirt on, the tails tied up in front, revealing a very fine abdomen. And a navel ring.

I didn't object.

I introduced myself. Told her why I was there. Ascertained that a well-trained, tanned and somewhat diffident young man had not preceded me to the address.

She wiped a charming tress from her forehead with the back of her hand. She invited me in.

I was okay with that too.

My fantasies were interrupted, however, by the sight of children's toys scattered about.

They all looked brand new. Like everything else about the place. About the neighborhood. Hell, about Las Vegas.

Must be the desert air, I thought. Preservative.

The central part of the house was an enormous open space. On the left was the kitchen, gleaming with stainless steel fixtures. In the middle, a sunken living room, three sides lined with what I was sure was the latest Roche-Bobois sectional. Some kind of South American rug. Prints, expensively framed, echoing the Latin theme on the walls. The place reeked of paid-for taste. But even so, it wasn't unpleasant. It seemed comfortable. Even inviting.

Kind of you to ask me in, I said to the blonde.

Dani, she said. With an I. D-A-N-I.

Well, thanks, Dani.

I'm from Oklahoma. We're like the Arabs. Never turn away a guest. Would you like a drink?

Politely ignoring how odd the simile sounded in an Oklahoma accent, I professed a preference for scotch, neglecting to add 'and lots of it,' which I regretted when she returned with a thimbleful.

Oh well, I thought. No need to advertise your weaknesses right away. You have children? I inquired.

Three, she said cheerfully. Six, five and two. Girl, girl, boy.

Wow, I said, wondering again at her smooth, tight midsection. That's a handful.

It sure is. But Matt's a lot of help. He works nights, at the casino? So he's always around in the afternoons? Well, usually he is. This week he's off in Reno with the kids? Plus I have Imelda?

She was playing with her navel ring. A new acquisition, I was guessing.

I was happy for her. That she had Imelda.

That's great, I said. What does Matt do at the casino?

He's sort of the high-roller host? He makes sure the big customers are happy?

Ah, kind of a whale handler.

She looked shocked for a second. Then she laughed.

We were co-conspirators now.

Her navel ring bounced most pleasantly.

Well, I said. I don't want to keep you . . .

Oh, please, she said in that darling Okie drawl—puh-lee-as—it's great to see a new face around here. How is it I can help you?

I explained my mission. Not a cop. Nothing serious. Just tracking somebody down for a relative.

I don't expect you knew the former residents, I concluded. But I have to do my job . . .

As a matter of fact, she said, clearly pleased to help, I did meet them.

Oh, great, I said. Them?

Yes, there was a man and a woman?

Do you remember their names?

Well, she drawled, let me think about that . . .

She looked me in the eye as she thought about it. Very strange. Must be a Midwestern thing, I mused.

I looked away.

I guess I don't rightly recall, she said.

I don't suppose they left a forwarding address?

No. Funny you should say that. I asked them, but they said they'd told the post office? I thought it was a little strange. What if a FedEx package or something came?

That is a little odd, I said. Well, can you describe them for me?

She hesitated. Got up. Began gathering up the kids' playthings, putting them in a bright orange toy chest. She did it quickly, in nervous motion. As though they embarrassed her.

Um, she said as she closed the chest, I don't want to be rude, but I was just thinking . . . I don't really know who you are.

Rick Redman, I repeated. I'm sort of a private investigator. I've been hired by the lady's sister to find her.

You did say that, she said. And I don't have any reason to not believe you, sir. But I suppose it's only right that I ask you for some . . . proof, or something? Identification, I guess?

Sure. No problem. Here's my card. And you can talk to a detective in the New York Police Department, I said, pulling out my cell phone. He'll vouch for me.

Oh, no, she said, looking at the nicely embossed card. That's all right. This will do.

Well, thank you. I must say, I love that Midwestern hospitality.

She flashed her prairie smile.

Well, as I was saying, what did they look like?

She was very good-looking, I remember. Kind of slim? Quite tall. Blondish brown hair. I think she had green eyes. Very striking eyes? He was tall, too. But, I don't know, sort of wide, too? Very big. Dark. She did all the talking.

Did they introduce themselves?

Yes, but I'm sorry, like I said, I don't remember the names. Wait a minute. Her name is coming back to me. Lois, or something like that?

Eloise?

Could have been.

Did his name sound Russian? Eastern European?

I'm sorry, I don't know. I don't remember. Yes. I think so.

Is there anything else you remember?

She was dressed very well. Sort of formal? Some kind of Japanese kimono kind of thing? But with a very high collar? She looked like a movie star, actually. At first I thought she was somebody famous. But when I asked if she was an actress or a model, she just laughed.

I see. Anything else you can recall?

I don't know. I can't remember, really.

Anything unusual about them?

Well, she talked kind of strange. Like she was bored. To me, actually, you know, I'm used to . . . she seemed a little rude. And she was wearing sunglasses? That seemed a little strange. Inside the house? And like I said, he didn't say much.

Did they say anything about where they were moving to?

No. I mean, wait. They didn't say they were moving there, but she mentioned something about New York?

New York?

Yes.

Anywhere in particular in New York? New York City?

No, she didn't say any more than that. It was just some kind of offhand comment? To the man, I think. I don't think she said it to me. Something sarcastic about New York.

Are you sure he didn't have some kind of accent?

I don't know. Like I said, he hardly talked. Oh, wait a minute. He did say one thing. Something about a bartender at Binion's? Let me think. Yes. He was talking to her. They were in the basement. I just happened to overhear. I mean, don't get me wrong, please, sir. I don't eavesdrop on folks?

She said it like the thought was poison.

Of course, I said.

But they were talking kind of loud? Like they were having an argument or something? Something about how the fellow owed him money. And he did have some kind of accent.

The man? Or the bartender?

Yes. The man. The bartender wasn't there.

Yes, I understand. Russian?

I'm sure I couldn't say, she giggled.

This bartender, at Binion's. Did he have a name?

Oh dear, let me think. No. But the gentleman mentioned that he was very small? A very small man? I'm afraid he wasn't being very polite about him.

What exactly did he say?

Oh my dear, I'm sure I can't remember exactly what he said? But he was angry. He called him names.

What kind of names?

All sorts of names.

Do you remember any of them?

Spic, I think, was one of them? Oh dear. I don't use those kinds of words.

It's all right, I said. You're just quoting him. Did he say anything else about this bartender?

No. I mean, maybe, but I don't remember anything else. Heavens, I don't even know if I remember as much as I've already told you! Juan? I think maybe the name was Juan? Something like that.

The bartender's name?

Yes. Something like that.

Okay. What about your husband? Did he meet these folks? Might he know anything else?

Oh, Matt? No, I don't think he was here when I met them. But you could ask. He's in Reno for the week, though? With the kids? I could call him for you.

No. That's all right. Perhaps I'll drop by again when he's back.

Sure, she said.

She didn't seem enthusiastic about the idea.

You mentioned FedEx packages?

Right.

Any reason you said that in particular?

Well, yes, sir. They did get a package! I'd forgotten all about it? Funny. I guess you're right. Somehow I remembered it. Without remembering it?

Do you still have it? I asked.

Somewhere . . . she said. Just wait here?

I'm not going anywhere, I said with a smile.

She smiled back. Nice teeth. Very white. Manicured. She dashed off.

I gazed around the room.

Nothing had changed since the last time I'd looked.

She hopped back into the doorway.

Here it is! she said.

She handed me a well-battered FedEx envelope. Eight-by-eleven type. Corners frayed. Addressed to Vladimir Tomaschevsky. Same Henderson address.

Do you mind if I take this? I asked.

She looked doubtful.

So that I can give it to them, I said. When I track them down.

She brightened.

Oh. Okay. That's a good idea.

Well, thank you again, I said.

It's nothin', she said, exaggerating the accent for me a touch.

Coy, I said to myself. That was the word.

I liked coy.

She leaned over. Gave me a kiss on the cheek. I smelled something sweet. Mango. It smelled very good.

In the cab, once I'd recovered from the mango kiss, I thought through the conversation. I wondered about the bartender. Not much to go on: short Hispanic male, that was it. Juan, maybe. Maybe not. Binion's. Not at all clear he had anything to do with anything. But he'd known them. Some vague possibility he knew where they'd gone. New York? Unlikely, if Dani's report was accurate. Why would you move somewhere you despised?

The driver pulled over at a gas station. Told the guy to fill it up. The guy was old and sad and had a rag in his hand. There was nothing I could do about it. I looked at the FedEx envelope. The sender: Fruits of the Desert, Inc., an address in Brighton Beach, New York, New York.

Small world.

I briefly thought about opening the thing. A federal offense, though, I was pretty sure. Not just a Federal Express offense. A you're-going-to-jail-buddy kind of federal offense. Of course, I wasn't a practicing lawyer anymore. I could take more risks. This was the kind of risk one takes for one's clients, wasn't it? That Palomino guy, in L.A., whatever his name was. Detective to the stars. He did all sorts of illegal shit, they said.

Of course, he was in jail.

I put the package up to my ear. Shook it. Like a child on Christmas morning.

Maybe I'd get a clue.

Something sprinkled on my shirt.

Powder.

I looked at the package. One corner was eaten through.

I pinched some of the powder off my shirt. Looked closely. Very fine. Light brown. Odorless, as far as I could tell. Hah. Mysteriously missing woman. Brown powder. Seedy Russians. Hello? Drugs. Kind of went together. Like sewage and shit.

We drove back to the casino, at a dangerously entertaining rate of speed.

24.

THERE WAS A DARK PURPLE VELVET EMPORIUM in the midst of all the slot machines. A circular bar in the middle. Opulent couches around the perimeter. Heavy curtains around the place served to muffle the endless clinking, clanging and pinging of the slot machines. The waitress had long legs to go with the standard-issue cleavage. She poured serious scotch. Her name was Rebecca.

I was in love.

We had decided to make this the default hang. Anybody got lost, discouraged, too fucked-up to play, he'd go to the Velvet Hang. One or the other of us would show up, eventually. Pick up the tab. Provide commiseration. Whatever was needed.

I settled for a dark corner of the bar. Can a circular place have a corner? Well, this one did, I decided. And I was in it.

I called Butch's cell. He'd just wrapped up his satellite. Qualified for the Main Event. Beat me to it. Damn. I'd never hear the end of it.

A couple of investment banker types slid into the soft purple chairs at the table next to me. Expensive haircuts, tailored cargo pants. The whole kit.

So, one of them said, as part of my many fun tasks of last evening, I needed to look up the exchange rate for Panamanian balboas to U.S. dollars in November 2003, which was and remains one-to-one, in case you're interested. On a whim, I looked up the going rate for Honduran lempiras, which are quoted at 18.340 to one. Until then we had been using a rate of 15.426 to one, which I think was a stab at the exchange rate on the date of closing, though it ought to be 15.462 to one, if that's the case. Anyway, I just want to confirm whether we are, as a matter of principle, using the rate at the time of closing, rather than the time of write-off or the time of loss.

You're a nerd, the other guy interrupted.

I am a nerd, said the first guy. Thank you. Are we using the closing rate?

Before I was treated to the answer to this momentous question, Brendan showed up.

I dispensed with the formalities.

The fuck you been? I asked.

What's up with you? he said.

You were supposed to check out that address.

So?

So did you?

Of course I did.

You did?

Sure, he said, his voice faltering.

Butch arrived, a grin of triumph on his face. Brendan got up, greeted him with a hug. A hug of relief, it seemed. As though Butch would protect him. Which wasn't about to happen.

So? I said to Brendan once they'd sat down.

He'd gone to the house, Brendan told us. A guy answered the door. At first Brendan had been taken aback. Not by any prepossessing feature. By the guy's very ordinariness. He was dressed in tan slacks, hiking shoes, a denim shirt. He had a baseball cap on.

Which team? I asked.

He gave me a sour and puzzled look.

The baseball cap. Which team? Never know what might turn out to be important.

He stared into his drink.

I don't know, he said glumly.

You don't know?

Red Sox, I think. Anyway, he was ordinary.

Ordinary in what way? asked Butch.

Brendan gave Butch a similar sour look, this one tinged with abject confusion.

No, said Butch. I mean it. There are different types of ordinary. They can be important.

Brendan stared at Butch.

Sure, he said. I know.

He knew.

So?

He was ordinary, Brendan said, in that really fucking ordinary way.

Ah, said Butch. That kind of ordinary.

Yes. That kind.

Brendan was fiddling with a ring on his left middle finger. A wide brass ring. It had some inscription on it that I couldn't read.

Okay, said Butch.

The rest of Brendan's story was equally rich in detail. He talked to the guy. The guy didn't know anything. The house was ordinary. The neighborhood was ordinary.

I gave Brendan a Look. The Look said, I know you're full of shit, and you know that I know that you're full of shit.

Uh, Brendan, I said. Could you give Butch and me a moment?

Sure, he said. I got a satellite coming up.

No, I said. Just wait for us at the bar.

Okay, he said without enthusiasm. Trudged to the bar.

He never went to the house, I said to Butch.

I know. Did you see how he was playing with that ring?

I went to the house.

Yeah?

Yeah. He hadn't been there. And it wasn't anything like he said.

There's a surprise.

I called Brendan back.

Brendan, I said, it's bad enough you didn't even do your job.

But—he began to protest.

But nothing. I went to the house. You didn't. You didn't even get the address right. Let alone any of the details.

Brendan hung his head.

Brendan, Brendan, I said. It's bad enough you didn't do it. But you lie to us about it? Give us misinformation? We can't operate like that, man.

Yeah, he said. I know. I'm sorry. I'm really sorry.

I rolled my eyes. Butch shrugged.

I brought in the job from the Russians, said Brendan.

Yeah, I said. That's great. Thank you. But let me tell you two things. Three. One, we haven't seen a dime from those guys yet. Two, we don't even know what the fucking job is. If we can even take it. Three, you can be Mr. Rainmaker all you want, but if you have a job to do, you do the job. Or you're out. You got it?

I got it, he mumbled.

And four, I know I said three but it's four, what's with the fucking ring?

What ring?

The fucking ring on your fucking finger, Brendan. You never owned a piece of jewelry in your life. Now you got two. That I know of.

It's just a ring. I liked it.

They're like the pod people, Brendan. They're taking over your body, your mind. They're starting with the clothes, though.

Brendan laughed.

I hadn't really meant it as a joke.

So what the fuck really happened? Butch asked.

I ran into Tolya and Andrei. We had some drinks.

Yeah, I said. I saw. That was my whole fucking point.

Ease up, Rick, said Butch.

I tried to ease up.

They took me to a club, said Brendan. I just sort of forgot about it.

What kind of club? Butch asked.

The kind you told us about? I said. That we might not be interested in?

Yeah, said Brendan. What's wrong with that?

That's what I figured, I said. Listen, there's nothing wrong with that, in itself. Nothing wrong with it. But I mean, I know we're a bunch of dysfunctional poker geeks and all, but business is business, okay? When you got a job, you do the job. Can you handle that?

Sure, sure, said Brendan, doing his staring-at-the-floor thing. I'll go there first thing tomorrow.

Brendan, I raised my voice. I told you. I did it already.

Brendan, Butch said. Next time, just do what you're supposed to do. That's all.

Brendan looked like he was going to throw up.

I felt bad.

Aw, forget it, I said.

No, said Butch, leaning in and putting his face right up to Brendan's. Don't forget it. Get it right. Get it right next time, and every time after that. You fuck up again, we got no more use for you.

Brendan looked like he was going to cry.

Jesus, I thought. Better change the subject before Butch hauls off on him.

Butch, I said, tell us about your satellite.

Ah, he said, the big smile returning. It was a beautiful thing.

He settled back into his chair. He started going through it hand by hand. Then I bluffed, and he folded, then I made a monster lay-down. On and on. Then I looked down at Five, Six off suit . . .

I'd had enough.

Let's not talk poker, I said.

All right, Rick, said Butch. I know my success causes you pain.

Damn right it does, I said.

I told a story about two girls I'd seen the year before, sitting at the slots at four in the morning. I'd been dragging myself by, they asked me for a light, my name. The usual routine. They were cute as hell. The only problem, apart from the fact that I don't do sex for money, was that there was no way either of them was over sixteen.

Man, said Butch, you expect that in El Salvador, but here . . .

Something you'd like to tell us about your last trip to El Salvador? I said.

I'll tell you that story, he said, but . . .

He was looking over my shoulder.

. . . this might not be the time.

I turned around.

A woman in black. Sheath skirt. Tight silk blouse. Jacket cinched at the waist. An air of delicate but assured self-possession.

Shit, I said, it's the client.

She'd seen us. She walked over. She smiled.

I hadn't seen her smile before. Not that way.

She had a fragile kind of beauty. Small-boned. The kind that would ripen and fall away with the years.

For now, it would do just fine.

Hi, I said, standing up and extending a hand.

Hi, she said, taking it.

Her hand was soft. But it held mine with authority. I could smell her. Something with vanilla. Something good.

I had a frisson. This is not appropriate, I told myself. Then I chuckled to myself. Damn, Redman, I said, stop being such a fucking lawyer.

You've been following me? I asked with a smile.

Las Vegas is a small town, she said with a laugh. I told you not to be surprised if I showed up.

You did, I said. I admit it. Please, have a seat.

She looked at Brendan. For a second too long. Or just remembering who he was. She looked warily at Butch. A hint of apprehension in her face. The woman had instincts.

You remember Brendan, I said.

Yes, she said. I do believe I do.

She extended a hand.

And this is my other partner, I said. Butch. Poker player. Friend. Better at the latter. He's all right. Just looks scary. I told you about him. Used to be an NYPD detective. Maybe still is. I don't remember.

I gave her a big grin. To let her know I was kidding.

I didn't know, of course, what I was kidding about.

I don't think you did tell me about him, she said. But I'm pleased to meet you, anyway . . . Butch.

She hesitated at the name. I'd sort of forgotten. What a silly name it was. It's like you're married for years. Your wife isn't really beautiful, or raven-haired, or whatever other thing you were looking for, before you settled for her. She's just who she is. You love her. And her name is Mabel. You don't notice anymore. That's just her name. Butch was just Butch. Of course, he was also six foot five, two-sixty, and black as the bottom of a well. Took some getting used to, for some folks.

Pleased to meet you, he said in his richest, friendliest rumble.

She sat. She smiled at Brendan and Butch.

I've filled Brendan and Butch in, I said. They're my partners, actually. I'm not sure I mentioned that. They come with the package.

Of course, she said. Yes. You said that. Perhaps they can help.

Butch is a cop in New York, I said. Detective, I mean. A very good one.

I think you mentioned that, too, she said.

Yes. And Brendan's my ex-brother-in-law. Sort of.

Brendan laughed. It was okay. We'd had enough to drink.

Louise gave me a questioning look.

My wife, I said. Brendan's her brother. Was her brother. She died. Last year.

She flinched a tiny flinch.

I'm sorry, she said.

Yes, well. I'm sorry, too. It's okay. We've gotten over it.

Brendan looked hurt. Louise Chandler looked calm.

I mean, I said, the passage of time. You know.

I understand, she said. I'm sorry.

Thank you, I said, remembering the protocol.

Well, I said, desperate to change the subject, and having no idea why I'd broached it in the first place, I've shared the details of your case with my colleagues, of course.

Of course, she said.

She looked around for a waiter.

Can I get you something? I asked.

Don't worry about it, she said. I'll just get myself a drink at the bar.

She got up before I had time to protest.

Okay, guys, I said. Try to stay cool.

Butch laughed at me.

Brendan looked confused.

I ignored them both.

Ms. Chandler returned from the bar with a cosmopolitan. She gave me a Look. I'm not sure, the Look said, I can't trust you yet. I don't really know you.

I put on my most innocent face.

It took a while, but I guess I finally passed the visual inspection. She sat down. Sipped her cosmo. Looked good doing it.

We chatted a while. Vegas stories. What to wear in the heat. Butch told a couple of NYPD war stories. I mentioned the Case of the Red Car Door. Yes, she said, she'd remembered it from the papers, when she'd spoken to Kennedy, the first time.

Ah, I thought. My dubious reputation precedes me.

I have a suite at the Wynn, she said out of nowhere. We could have privacy there.

Certainly, I said.

To talk, she said. I'd like to discuss the case in private.

Of course, I said.

I have my car here, she said. We can drive over.

Even better, I said. Save cab fare.

She grimaced slightly.

I wasn't sure what that meant. Perhaps the idea of cabs was strange to her.

She got up. I got up. Butch got up. Brendan got up.

There was a whole lot of getting up going on.

Too much, apparently, for Ms. Louise Chandler.

Mr. Redman, she said.

Yes?

I don't mean to be . . . awkward. But I would prefer this meeting to be just between you and me.

I looked at Butch and Brendan. Butch shrugged, sat back down with a subtle roll of the eyes. Brendan, on the other hand, looked stricken.

But then, when didn't he?

I'll brief you later, I said to Brendan in my most professional one-investigator-to-another voice.

That seemed to mollify him.

My car's a two-seater anyway, Ms. Chandler said.

I noticed that she'd barely touched her drink. I see, I said. But you do understand, I will be sharing everything with my colleagues?

Of course, of course, she said. It's just that . . . I'll be more comfortable.

Inappropriate thoughts flooded my brain.

I felt bad. I have to admit it. I might even have felt badly, had I been in any condition to attend to the grammatical niceties. But I was more in the mood to attend to Ms. Chandler's niceties. And her niceties were very nice indeed. She was a trim little thing. With a tiny waist. There's something about a tiny waist. Your hands around it. What is that thing? I guess it's just the way it makes everything else fit. Or how it's like a handle. You figure, maybe, that with a handle like that . . .

I reined in my thoughts. Unprofessional, I told myself. Highly unprofessional.

25.

Ms. Chandler and I trekked the two miles through endless clanking chiming chunking slots to the front door of the Rio. Outside, she nodded to the valet parking guy.

Yes, ma'am, he said immediately.

I guess she'd made an impression.

We waited no more than two minutes. But it was a long two minutes. She was silent. I felt awkward. I've never been much of a small-talk guy.

When the valet guy tooled up in a Corvette in British Racing Green—my favorite, as it happened—Louise woke from her reverie. Handed him a couple of bills. Smiled a melting smile.

I squoze into the passenger side.

Wow, I said, finding my voice. You can rent one of these?

What makes you think that it's rented?

Kennedy, I said, I mean Jack, I mean John, said you were here on business. Or you did, I guess. I assumed . . .

You don't have to rent it. If you own one.

Damn, I thought. She does like to be in control. And I still didn't have an answer to my question.

She took a right. The top was down. It was hot as hell. But, of course, it was a dry heat.

The desert heat is different. It really is. It's like being slow-baked, instead of deep-fried. It calms you up. Loosens you down. Until you die.

And with the top down, Louise at the wheel, it was awesome.

We flew to the Wynn. The wind was too loud for conversation. Which was helpful.

The valet guy at the Wynn knew her, too.

The place was huge beyond thought. Like most of the newer Vegas monstrosities. And they did their frantic best to make everything appear terribly classy. Lots of designer shops in the vast entrance promenade. Thirty-foot ceilings that bizarrely squashed down to ten or so—or so it seemed—when you entered the gaming area. I pondered why that might be. More space above for floors of rooms, I supposed. But since building heights appeared to be effectively infinite in Las Vegas, that didn't really seem to explain it. More to the point, maybe, they wanted to keep your eyes down, on the games, the machines, the compelling lights and noises, and the near-naked shopgirls stuffing drinks into your face to fuel the urge to spew your hard-earned cash into those selfsame machines or the rigged-in-favor-of-the-house games, which constitute all of the games. Except poker, of course, though only in a specialized sense, because the house still takes a regular and usurious chunk of change from the poker table in the form of a rake, sometimes a piece per player per half hour and sometimes a piece of every pot, a rake that to be a winning player you must overcome by winning more off the other guys than the rake takes off you. Which for an accomplished player isn't that hard, but still. Somebody's getting ripped off. You just better make sure it's not you.

We went to the twenty-fourth floor. We walked several hundred yards to the door of her suite.

Normally, when you're standing in front of the hotel door of an attractive woman, she's getting out her key, you aren't thinking about a business meeting. You have other responses.

I was having them.

Cognitive dissonance. Bodily dissonance. Cognition in dissonant state with bodily reaction.

Her suite could not have been more different from our motel home. The chairs were deep and comfortable. The furnishings elegant and expensive, if a little overdone, impersonal.

Nothing like a change of scenery.

She unbuttoned her jacket. Placed it on the back of a chair. I supposed the gesture was meant to create a sense of informality.

It didn't work.

I sat. She sat. She crossed her legs.

She did it very well.

Leg crossing. There's no official competition. But if there were, Louise would definitely be on the national team.

I didn't know what the lovely Ms. Chandler really wanted. Still less did I know what might impress her. And at the end of the day, I reminded myself, this was business. I could entertain all the fantasies I wanted. About her ambiguous Looks. My irresistible charm. The likelihood of my actually scoring big in the World Series. But really, when you came right down to it, the best cost-benefit wager here was to play on the impression Kennedy had fostered. To keep her as a paying client. Do what we could for her. At least, I mused, for as long as it took to earn the money I'd stolen from her.

I congratulated myself. Damn. From time to time I still had the capacity to think straight. Maybe, just maybe, I could make a living. Afford my daughter's tuition.

Mr. Redman, said Ms. Chandler, interrupting my reverie.

Yes? I responded. I'm sorry. I was thinking about my daughter. She's a freshman in college. Middlebury. I worry about her.

Ms. Chandler smiled. A warm smile. I was mildly shocked. Maybe there was more to her than style. She sat on a gold divan. Brought her legs up to the side. Tilted her head. She looked like a thirties movie star.

Just about as touchable.

I told Ms. Chandler about my trip to Henderson. The mention of a bartender. The description of the couple.

Yes, she said, that's them. She loves those Japanese outfits.

I thought it was Chinese.

You thought wrong.

Of course, I said. I will defer to your judgement on matters of women's clothing.

I suggest that you do.

Concession made. Meanwhile, I'd suggest you defer to me on matters of investigative procedure.

Have I interfered with your procedures?

No indeed. But then, I haven't given you the opportunity. Yet.

I look forward to the chance to do so.

I look forward to giving it to you.

Can I get you a drink? she said, uncoiling herself from the divan.

Scotch. Whatever they have. Make it a double.

She complied.

Oh, I said when she'd rearranged herself. There was something else. Probably not a big deal.

She looked at me with an air of indifferent expectancy.

Apparently some FedEx package had arrived. After she'd moved out. For the boyfriend.

Really?

Yes. I'm sure it's nothing.

You might want to let me be the judge of that.

Of course. Of course. Anyway, I didn't open it. I'm not sure I can. Legally. It's a piece of mail. Addressed to someone else.

To whom?

I told you. The Russian guy. At least, I assume it's him. It was a Russian name.

What name?

I don't remember.

Mr. Redman, she said severely.

I know, I know. It'll come back to me. Don't worry. I mean, who else could it be?

I don't know. It is my understanding that it is your job to ascertain the facts.

Yes. Of course. Anyway. It was old. A little battered. Something was leaking out of the corner. Some brown substance. Granular. I assume some kind of drug.

I see, she said. Mr. Redman, I think I need to see this envelope.

Yes, well. I understand. But there are issues.

Issues?

It's addressed to someone else. It's a piece of mail. Or the equivalent. It's not at all clear that we have any right to open it. That I have a right to give it to anyone. Other than the addressee.

Mr. Redman, she said.

Yes?

I'm paying you a large sum of money.

Actually, I thought, I wasn't entirely sure of that. I had the big retainer, of course, or rather, what was left of it, but I wasn't at all sure how much of it I was earning. Was I on an hourly rate? Contingency? We'd never discussed it. And the last thing I wanted to do was bring it up. Seeing as how I'd effectively embezzled the funds.

Wouldn't be prudent.

At any rate, I said, we can defer this conversation. I've sent it out for testing.

She gave me a sharp look. Began to twist the watch on her wrist. I braced myself for a lecture.

There was a long silence, her eyes on mine.

I began to think maybe a lecture would be preferable.

I took a deep breath.

She arranged herself again. This time she sat a little sideways. The jut of her hip through the black skirt. How flat her stomach was. Every pose was somehow different. How did she do it? Was it practice? Or natural talent? I vowed to ask her. Some day.

I had to break the silence.

I told her more about Eloise's former home. How the house had looked. How it had felt. What Dani had told me of Eloise and her friend.

I left out some details. The soft pneumatic pout of Dani's lips. The seductive lilt of her Oklahoma accent. The question mark at the end of every phrase.

Didn't seem relevant.

I see, she said.

Not much, I said.

Not much, she repeated.

There was another silence. It pulled at me. I felt obliged to fill it. I started telling stories. Poker stories. I didn't have any other kind of stories. None that you would tell a cultivated woman, on just your third encounter.

I told her about Brighton Beach. The Russkies. Fat guys. Skinny pockmarked guys. How endlessly entertaining it all was. I told her about Dinnie the Magician. Charlie Kick-Ass. Evgeny.

She laughed. She leaned forward in her chair. She seemed fascinated by it all.

Tell me about the most outrageous one of all, she said with a tiny tilt of the head.

That's a tough one, I said.

I thought about it.

Well, I don't know if you can say what's most outrageous, I said, but here's a pretty funny one.

Go ahead, she said.

There's a guy, name of Maxie Veinberg, I said. Maxie's the shape of a stuffed sausage. A very, very stuffed sausage. He can't be more than five foot six, must weigh close to three hundred pounds. But his arms and legs aren't fat at all. They're sort of tiny. Thin and delicate. His arms are way short, barely long enough to handle his cards and chips. And his legs aren't even close to strong enough to carry him around. At the casino he uses one of the electric carts. Seeing as he's a big-time whale, the staff is always happy to park it for him, bring it back to the table when he needs it.

So Maxie's a bit of a freak. But he's a good guy. He loves to play, doesn't care about the money. He loves a good joke.

One night, we're playing in the high-limit room at the Borgata, in Atlantic City, and another guy at the table is this big old Texan, with the cowboy hat and all, a mindlessly happy rich guy with a hundred-thousand-dollar stack and an easy way with losing it. I don't remember his name. Tex, probably. So, Tex orders some food, which in the high-limit room you can get delivered to the table, and it takes a long time to come, and he's bitching and whining about it, and meanwhile Maxie's giant chocolate ice cream sundae's arrived, and he's sucking it down like only a fat man can, when Tex's food finally comes, and it looks like greasy fried rice with green over-boiled lasagna piled on top, the most revolting thing you've ever seen short of a rat-mole colony, in one of those crinkly aluminum takeout things, and the waiter puts it down, and Tex plows into it, and Maxie looks up, and totally deadpan and without missing a beat, he says:

That come with a toilet brush?

Louise smiled. I could see she was trying to keep it to a smile. But she couldn't. She started to laugh. She took out a handkerchief. Coughed into it a while. She lifted her head. Looked at me with still-smiling eyes.

I like a man who can tell a story, she said.

Thank you.

I think it speaks well of you.

I thank you again.

As an investigator, I mean. It gives me confidence. If you can tell a story, you can see the story in things.

I hadn't thought of it that way, I said. But perhaps you're right.

She gave me a Look that said, Of course I'm right, you fool. I'm always right. And don't you think for a second that the momentary loss of studied equilibrium your story occasioned is going in any way to give you some kind of advantage in your relations with me. Quite the contrary. I've given you a gift. And now you owe me.

There was a whole lot in that Look.

26.

IN THE CAB, WHICH SMELLED OF OLIVE OIL AND AMBIGUITY, I thought about that last laugh. It'd been a good laugh. A real one. And when she'd unbuttoned that jacket. There was something awfully handsome going on under those elegant clothes.

I called Kelley. I hadn't spoken to her in days. I was worried. I felt guilty. I was a father, I reminded myself. I reminded myself to remind myself. More often.

Kelley didn't answer. I got her voice mail message: Don't leave me a message! Okay. She'd see that I'd called. She didn't need the message on top of it. She'd call when she damn well felt like it.

God, it's awful. When they turn eighteen. Start getting a life of their own. She was twenty. It was getting worse.

We were stopped at a light. To the left, miles of low buildings, russet and ochre in the fading light. The hills beyond turning to a fine powdery ash. It had a pull to it. I thought about the Europeans who'd first seen this stuff. Stumbled up to the Grand Canyon one day. There had to have been a first one. What the hell could he have thought? I reminded myself to look it up.

A mammoth red thing pulled up beside the cab. It looked like a forties Ford. In fact, it was a forties Ford. A '47 half-ton panel truck, to be exact. I recognized it from the abstract arrow design on the side of the engine compartment. Amazing how far a little eclectic information from a misspent childhood can get you. Although, at the end of the day, I wasn't sure what guessing the vintage of this hulking vehicle actually had bought me. It wasn't restored to original condition. It was tricked out. The windows were tinted dark. Huge chrome exhaust pipes snaked out of the hood, raked back past the rear bumper and flared out, like an angry camel's nostrils. The wheel rims were spinning, shimmering, doing their best imitation of the end of the world. Someone told me once you could spend twenty-five grand on rims like that. Each. A hundred grand for a set.

For some reason the thing made me nervous. It was throbbing and pulsing with the growl and shimmy of a classic giant V-8 engine. As though ready to rear up on its hind wheels. Maybe it was pimp associations. Though every two-bit casino manager had a pimped-out set of wheels by now. There just seemed to be something specially ominous about this one.

The cab inched ahead. The Ford's engine gunned and slowed, gunned and slowed. It was loud. Obnoxious. The light was taking forever to turn green. I had an urge to tell the driver to floor it. Run the light. Get the hell out of there.

The cab driver inched forward a bit.

The Beast inched forward, too.

Now I knew I had a problem.

I mean, normally, they do that. Itchy macho guys with big wheels. They want to get off the blocks first. Show you what they have. But I was in a cab, for Chrissakes. An old, belching Chevy Impala. We weren't about to take on Mr. Drag Racer Hot Rod Big Penis in a race to the next red light. There was something about it. I knew. I just knew. It was bad news.

The window of the Beast rolled down.

Shit, I thought. If I dive to the floor and cover my head, and it turns out it's not a guy with an Uzi but some tourist looking for directions to Caesar's Palace, I'm going to look Really Fucking Stupid.

Bruno's fat smiling head leaned out the window of the Beast.

Redman! he called out. On your way back to the *mo*tel?

Fuck me with a spoon, I said to myself, feeling my bladder weaken.

Yeah, Bruno, I said. Maybe I'll see you at the Bellagio later.

Sure, he said, laughing. Later.

The Beast roared, jerked ahead, screamed to the right. Ninety degrees across the road. Directly blocking the cab.

Shit. Retribution. It wasn't going to feel nearly as good taking it as dishing it out.

There wasn't anywhere to go. Which, even if there was, it was clear we weren't going there. The cab driver was paralyzed with fear. He began jabbering at me in some sort of language I not only didn't understand, I had no recollection of ever having heard before. But the import was clear: what the fuck is going on and why did you get me into this? I tried to explain, that there was nothing to worry about, beyond serious blood-letting and violence of the most extreme sort, but he seemed disinclined to listen. He dove across the front seat, wrenched open the passenger-side door, leapt out and ran down the expressway, waving his hands at nobody in particular.

Which was about the amount of time it took Bruno to exit the Beast, grab open the back door of the cab, drag me into the street by my shaking shoulders, and slam me up against the Ford.

Quite a feat, considering his right hand, arm and shoulder were immobilized by a heavy-duty sling and vast swathes of bandage.

Bruno, I said. Let's be reasonable.

Fuckhead, he replied, kneeing me in the groin. You really thought you wouldn't have to pay for that shit?

Well, no, I said, bent over and gasping. I'd be happy to pay for it. Never thought otherwise. The surgery, pain and suffering, whatever. Just that I'm in a temporary cash crunch, right now.

He leveled me with a fist to the chest. It felt just like I'd imagine it would if you were under a car, changing the oil, and the jack collapsed. Two tons of metal on your rib cage.

I slumped to a seated position against the panel truck. I marveled at the fact that I still was conscious. The cab driver was long gone, the distant sound of impatient gamblers honking at the traffic delay providing a comforting backbeat to the scene. I looked up at my certain demise: Bruno with a tire iron.

Redman, he said. I could kill you right here, right now.

You could, I said. But isn't it a little public? You'd be taking some chances.

Sure. You're a smart guy. You figured that out. But I don't have to do it now. I can do it later. Any time. You think I can't?

Of course you can. Yes. You can. Perhaps I can do something for you? To stave off the inevitable?

The what?

My imminent death. My demise. You beating the living shit out of me.

Yeah, he said, lowering the tire iron to his side. Maybe.

The pain in my chest multiplied. Triplified. Breathing was beyond an effort. I was quite certain that I needed medical intention. Attention. Whatever they called it. But what had he said? Maybe.

Yeah, I said. Yeah. Name it. I owe you one.

Okay. We got a deal?

Unfortunately, the lawyer in me took over.

What kind of deal? I said. Let's get the terms straight.

Terms? he said, raising the tire iron again. The terms is, you do what the fuck I say or I beat your brains to yesterday's oatmeal. You got the terms?

I do. Yes. I get the terms, Bruno. Now would it be okay, before we get to the details, if you let me get these broken ribs treated?

Shit, man, he said to some invisibly large presence behind the wheel of the Beast. Luiz? Mikey Z.? Some other meatball? It didn't matter.

We got to take care of Mr. I'm-All-Busted-Up, Bruno said, before he'll take care of business.

Fuck him, said the Interchangeable Meatball Behind the Wheel in an impossibly deep voice from way up and beyond where I sat slumped to the pavement. Take his head off.

Wait, wait, I said weakly, the last vestiges of consciousness rapidly receding, that might not be in your best interest . . .

Nah, I later remembered Bruno saying. Him we'll use.

In my intermittent moments of consciousness during the long Beastly ride to a superior medical facility, as I vaguely recalled later, at least three major orifices were threatening to spew. I addressed them one by one. No, I said, not here. It wouldn't be respectful. And you'll have to pay the owner of the Beast, Basso Profundo presumably, likely to be an insistent fellow, for the cleaning. And you can't afford it. You're just a poor, overused stuff and nonsense of orifices.

I reminded myself to see my personal physician. Get my testosterone checked. See about a testicle transplant.

The emergency staff, when they saw my condition, looked worried, began that scurrying around and barking out stuff that they do on medical shows on TV.

This did not help my state of mind.

The last thing I recalled before they put me under was Bruno telling me that he would be in touch. Tell me what the deal was.

I couldn't wait.

27.

AT SOME HOUR OF SOME DAY SOME TIME THEREAFTER I AWOKE, the world wavy and confused. I was compos mentis enough to know that I just had to wait. The wait was not unpleasant. They had filled me with something good, something that took the fear away.

The room had started to take on something resembling definition—I could see there was a green plastic chair nearby, that there were curtains surrounding me, hung on tubes by metal rings, could hear that someone next door, next curtain, was wheezing—when a scrubbed and cheerful fellow, far too young to inspire confidence, ducked in, clutching a clipboard.

Hi, he said, I'm Dr. Weiss, and you're a very lucky man.

I am? I said. Funny, it doesn't feel that way.

He chuckled. As though we were sharing a private joke. Which we weren't. The result being, he pissed me off.

I tried to repress the urge to tell him as much. Or worse.

You are, he said. You suffered a brief infarction. Fortunately, you were here when it happened. We were able to get you back quickly. As far as we can tell, no permanent damage.

Infarction, I said.

Myocardial infarction. Some people call it a heart attack. Sorry. I didn't mean to get technical on you.

Yeah. I know what a fucking infarction is. But thanks for your concern.

Anger is a natural reaction, he said, relentlessly cheerful.

It's my normal reaction, I said, to almost everything. Don't think anything of it.

He chuckled again. It still pissed me off.

At any rate, he said. Everything looks okay. We're going to let you go home. We'll give you some painkillers. But you need to rest. Take it easy. And call us if you feel anything untoward. Chest pain. Nausea. Shortness of breath. Anything. We think this was just a result of the blow to the chest. Nothing organic. Nothing likely to recur. But we have to be cautious.

We do.

Yes, we do.

Well, thank you, I said. Cautious is my middle name.

This time I got an ironic smile.

Yes, he said. Well. Ms. Cratchett will be by in a few minutes. Some paperwork. Then you'll be free to go.

You're kidding, I said.

No, no. You'll be on your own shortly. She'll give you some instructions. But I'm pretty sure you'll be okay.

That's not what I meant.

Oh?

Nurse Cratchett? Are you fucking kidding me?

No, I'm not kidding, he said, the good humor gone. She'll be by in a few minutes.

Victory at last, I said to myself. I'd wiped the stupid smile off his face.

A few minutes being in hospital time, I was permitted the luxury of wallowing in the sweaty twisted sheets for two hours before the esteemed and horrifically overweight Nurse Cratchett arrived. She was business-like, efficient, and exhibited a not terribly subtle air of contempt that I surmised was not put on just for me. There's a breed of nurses who seem to think that anyone sick or injured must have brought it upon themselves, or, if not, was in any case causing them unwarranted aggravation, aggravation that could have been avoided had you not foolishly stepped in front of the truck that ran that red light at the corner of Flamingo and South Whatever. Nurse Cratchett, untrue to her moniker, was one of them.

That was okay. I just wanted to get the fuck out of there. Which, after twenty minutes of swearing in writing and otherwise that anything that happened to me subsequent to my release was unequivocally, wholly and without question my fault and not that of the hospital, any of its staff or anyone related by commerce, marriage or any other notion of affiliation or salience with the former, I was permitted to do. So long as I agreed to be wheeled to the front door in a humiliating and utterly unnecessary wheelchair.

At which point I was free to hail a cab. Which smelled of camphor and wet bandages.

But maybe that was me.

When I got to the motel, I crawled painfully out of the cab—my chest still felt crushed, my bloodstream sluggish as a mononucleotic toad's—and hobbled to the House of Beige that we called home. On the way, I resisted the urge to look behind me. I felt like a child walking down the stairs to the basement. Frightened and foolish.

In the Executive Suite, as we laughingly still called it, the gang was all there, none the wiser for my near brush with Annihilation by Italian. They'd opened a bottle of Jack Daniel's, brought in a bucket of ice. The ashtray was already overflowing. The Yankees game was on. I staggered to the sectional, fell into it, braved a smile.

Hey guys, I said, I hope I haven't missed out on too much of the fun.

The fun's all over, said Butch, now that you're here.

I ignored the remark. I recounted my recent adventures.

Shit, said Brendan.

Damn, said Butch.

Thanks for your sympathy, I said.

Let's go fuck him up, said Butch.

Come on, man. We want to start one of those endless cycles of vengeance? We're not in West Virginia.

You're such a pussy, man.

You know I'm right.

Thank you.

Yes. I know you're right.

How was the meeting? said Butch.

I just fucking told you, I said. You call that a meeting? More like a near-death experience.

No, Rick, that was a *beating*. I mean the meeting. Before that. Your tête-à-tête with Ms. Greeneyes.

Oh, that. I don't fucking remember. Not very illuminating.

Rick. Please. Get yourself together. Give us the download.

Fuck you, I said.

Rick, don't talk to us like that, said Butch. We're not your girlfriend.

What the hell are you talking about?

Oh, sorry. We forgot. You don't have a girlfriend. Anymore.

Fuck the two of you, I said. And the lizards you rode in on.

I tried to remember, and described as best I could, my conversation with Ms. Chandler. The earlier one with the blonde in Henderson. I told the story in circles. I tried to make them concentric. From time to time I stopped. Short of breath. Sharp pains in my sternum. Aches in my ankle. Must have twisted it when I manfully slumped to the pavement.

Someone, I recalled eventually, was going to have to go check out that bartender.

Well, I guess we know who that's going to be, said Brendan.

That was the deal, as I recall, I replied. Maybe you can make up for the last one.

Sure, he said. I'll go. Which means I'll need some sleep. Night all.

He went the bedroom. Firmly closed the door.

What's sleep got to do with anything? said Butch. It's Vegas, for God's sake.

Seriously, I said. The fuck's up with him?

I don't know, Butch shrugged. The guy's a square bolt in a round world. What do you want?

A square bolt?

Never mind.

Well, I can't argue that he isn't weird.

You know, he takes this Outfit stuff seriously. Really wants to be a part of it.

If that was true, he'd get off his ass and do what he was told.

He's a kid, Rick.

He's thirty-five years old, Butch.

That's what I said. He's just a kid.

Anyway, I knew enough not to ask Brendan what the problem was. Nothing, was the answer. It was always the answer.

We drank some bourbon. The Yankees lost. I didn't care. I was an Expos fan anyway. Which meant, seeing as how they were long defunct, I didn't care about baseball much at all. And I was eating too many corn chips. I'd wake up in the middle of the night, I knew it. Acid reflux. It'd kill me, if the infarction didn't come back and do it first.

I went to the counter. Got another bag of corn chips.

Oh shit, I said. Something I forgot to tell you about.

Tell me about it. But first get me another bourbon.

I got him another bourbon. Hell, I got myself one, too. I began to feel almost normal.

At the house, I said, that woman gave me a FedEx envelope.

She gave you a FedEx envelope.

It was addressed to the Russian guy. At the house.

The sister's house?

Yeah. Wait a minute, I'll show it to you.

Go for it.

If I can remember where I put it.

Rick, you are a miracle of dysfunction.

Gee, Butch, sometimes you're so poetic.

I know, he said. The babes love it.

I'll bet they do. Let me think about it a sec.

You think about it.

Oh, yeah. It's in the freezer.

The freezer?

Yeah, I put it in the freezer. You know, like you put your cash in there. The place burns down, it's the best place for it to survive.

You planning on a fire?

In this dump? Not inconceivable, my man.

So you think this thing is as good as cash?

I don't know. Twenty thousand, maybe. You tell me.

I got the envelope from the freezer. I took advantage of my proximity to the ice tray to refill our glasses. I brought the envelope to Butch. And his bourbon.

See? I said. A corner's torn open a bit. Seems like there's some kind of powder in there. Heroin, I bet. PCP. Something like that. They're into some dope scam.

What makes you think this is related to the sister at all?

Can't be sure, man. But the woman said the guy had an accent. And Louise, Ms. Chandler, told me the boyfriend, whatever, was Russian. Vladimir. Look at the name.

Vladimir Tomaschevsky.

As Russian as they get.

Seems like it.

And when I told Louise Chandler about it, she seemed awfully anxious to get hold of it.

Hold of what?

The envelope.

So? She's the client, isn't she?

Yeah, but I got a weird vibe about it. I told her we'd sent it out for testing.

Testing what?

Check out the powder, Mr. Detective.

Butch lifted the envelope. Took a close look. Gingerly put his finger in the torn corner. Examined it. Touched it to his tongue.

Doesn't look like any dope I know about, he said.

Really?

Really.

Then what is it?

I don't know.

Well, maybe we should find out.

There are ways.

Problem is, there may be some ethical issues involved. I meant to look it up. Haven't got around to it.

To what?

Looking it up. I mean, interference with the mails and all. A federal crime. But does that apply to couriers?

Don't know, he said. Never ran across that one.

Hard to think it wouldn't, though.

Maybe. Anyway, I'll take care of it.

Take care of it?

Take my word for it. I'll take care of it.

Yeah. I figured you could do that.

Butch was good at taking care of things. I could trust him with it. And keep my hands clean. Relatively.

In bed, I lay awake. What was going on with Brendan? Shit, I didn't know. He always acted weird. Hell, I forgot to ask him about his day with the Russkies. Maybe it had something to do with that . . .

I fell asleep. I had a dream. I was naked in the bed. Asleep. I began to wake up. I felt my chest. There was a strange protrusion there. Years ago, I'd noticed a small lump on my sternum. At first it worried me. But then I got used to it. Years went by. It was just there. Part of me. In the dream, it had grown. It was the size of a plum. But hard. Bony. It scared the hell out of me.

I woke up. It was pitch-black. I felt my chest. Nothing there. Nothing but the usual lump.

28.

I GOT UP. I went to the bathroom. There were spots everywhere. On the mirror. In the sink. On the floor. I didn't know if they were real spots or brain spots. Spots generated from my brain. Non-objective spots. Like maybe my whole life. This whole episode. Starting at the Brighton Beach game. Maybe it wasn't happening at all. Could be my whole life was like that, of course. Wasn't there this theory just came out? That in the universe as we know it an infinite number of disembodied brains floating in the ether is more likely to exist than the world we think we actually live in? Or brains in a vat. We could all be brains in a vat.

Shit, I was having an anxiety attack. Heart palpitations. Oh God. Another heart attack. Hard to breathe. Had to keep taking deep ones to calm myself down. Helped with the palpitations. I knew they weren't palpitations. It was called PVC, or something. No, that was plastic pipe. I'd had them for years. Doctor said they were harmless. But they gave my anxiety extra ammunition. Maybe this was something else. Something that just felt the same. But more serious. Another infraction. Infarction.

I could call the Smiling Doctor. But fuck that. I'd see his fatuous grin over the phone. Maybe I could ask Sheila. She'd diagnosed the PVC the first time. Talked me down from it. But she was in New York. She'd do a session on the phone, I knew, but it just wasn't the same. I needed the whole sitting-on-the-couch thing. I needed to see the diplomas on the wall, the comforting rows of books on the shelves. *How to Be an Addict and Not Die, Quite Yet.* Nothing else would work.

I somnambulated to the living room. Butch was on the sectional. Reading *Bluff* magazine. A pile of *Guns & Ammo* next to him. Hell, I thought, maybe Butch can be my shrink. Such a sensitive soul, after all. I didn't tell him that, of course. He was a guy. But he was sitting on a couch, of a sort. And in the circumstances, that was the best I was going to get.

He put down the magazine. Picked up his boots. Black. Police issue. He had a bootblack kit with him. He always did. He started polishing them. I knew this routine. The goal: a mirrored shine. Cops tend to do that. Normally, I'd make fun of him about it. But I wasn't in the mood.

The hell's wrong with that woman? I asked.

Isn't that redundant? he replied.

Of course, I said, oh Wise One, I'm sure you're right. But it doesn't provide much guidance.

I see.

What is it, exactly, that you see?

I see the problem.

Well, then, we have communication. And so, what to do?

I thought the question was, what's wrong with that woman?

I suppose it was, I said.

Well, there is one thing, said Butch.

Which is?

Have you thought about AA?

Alcoholics Anomalous? I went for a while.

And?

Didn't do a thing for me.

No?

I didn't get high. Even once.

That would be a problem, I guess.

You're damn right. The only good thing about AA is that it sounds like Aces.

I got up to make myself a scotch.

But seriously, Rick, generally speaking, women, and I'm not saying all women, but . . .

He bore down on a particularly stubborn dull spot on the toe of his left boot.

But what? Give me the punch line. You're killing me here.

Well, women tend to like men who are, perhaps, a bit more, say, sober than you.

Sober? You mean drunk sober? Or down-at-the-mouth sober?

Drunk sober, Rick. Women like sobriety.

Not the kind of women I like.

That would be another problem, then.

Why would it be a problem?

Well, now that you mention it, I guess it wouldn't.

So there you are. And anyway, Butch, I'm talking about our client. I'm not talking about the, you know, Woman Thing.

Oh. Shit. Well, count me out, then. I wasn't even there.

That was my last shrink session with Butch.

And I wasn't about to pay him two hundred bucks for it.

29.

THE LEFTOVER PAINKILLERS IN MY SYSTEM were communing happily with the scotch. I went back to sleep. My dreams were mud. Entrails. Bloody shoe prints. Cracked vertebrae. Crawling things. I woke up. Looked at my watch. I'd only slept an hour. I could barely lift myself off the pillow. Once off the pillow, I could barely arrange for my legs to reach the floor. Once on the floor, my legs protested avidly, insistently, that they'd done enough work for the month.

My breathing was shallow. Close to terminal.

Rick! called Butch from the living room.

Minute, minute, I said.

You know what time it is?

No, I said, and frankly, I don't give a shit. You got any Demerol?

No.

Percodan?

No.

What the fuck use are you, anyway?

Oh, you'll find out. When it matters.

Sure, I said. Like the way you took care of Bruno.

There was silence from the living room. Oops, I thought. I'd touched a sore spot. Butch took his manhood very, very seriously.

I pulled on a pair of jeans. Slowly. One leg at a time. I suppose that's the normal way to put on jeans. But this was different. After the first leg, I needed a break. I took one.

I heard ice tinkling in the next room.

Make me one too! I called out.

Butch grunted.

I went to work on the other leg.

Maybe, I thought, that's why they call it a leg? In a race? We're just passing the second leg, etcetera. Which was where I was. Just passing the second leg. I felt like passing some other stuff. I tamped down the urge. Too early in the day for carpet cleaning.

I struggled into the living room and located my breakfast bourbon. A good warm slosh and the urge subsided, only to be replaced by the desire to kill someone. Didn't matter who. Just wanted to commit some mayhem.

Butch walked into the living room. He had a gun in his hand.

Hey, man, I said, I was just joking.

You think you're the only one gets to shoot people?

I didn't have any intention of doing that, I said, swallowing another soft-boiled egg of bourbon.

Meet Pandora, he said, extending the firearm in my direction.

She's a handsome lady, I said, trying not to flinch. You pick her up last night? Some cowboy bar in Paradise?

Rick, my man, I never leave home without her. In fact, I never go to bed without her.

You sleep with that thing? Ouch.

Nah. Too obvious, he said, lowering the mammoth weapon. Come here.

He led the way to his bedroom. Lifted up the sheets at the side of the bed. Clamped under the bed frame was a spring-loaded gun rest.

You got to be kidding me, I said.

I am not, he said. Learned this one in the Air Force.

Nobody goin' to fuck with my man in the nighttime.

You said it.

He wasn't smiling.

But I feel naked now, I said.

Ah, Rick, he said. So little faith.

That I can't deny.

I got something for you.

You know how I love a present.

This one isn't new.

Ah, too bad, I said.

Butch opened the drawer next to the bed. Pushed aside the Gideons, pulled out the Mauser in its box, the shoulder holster.

You shouldn't have, I said.

Actually, I thought it was kind of essential.

I get your drift. But how did you get it down here?

Oh, we have our ways, he said.

I suppose you do.

I didn't have to ask who the 'we' was.

Brendan over to Binion's?

What?

Binion's. The bartender. Investigations. What we do. Remember? Did he go?

Um, shit, said Butch. No fucking way. He left early. He was wearing some suit with the wide lapels, pegged pants. He wasn't going on no investigation.

Fuck, I said.

I called Brendan's cell. No answer. No surprise.

Goddamn it, I said. I'm gonna kill that little fucker.

Calm, calm, said Butch. Don't do anything til you got the facts.

He didn't go. Just like the last job. I know it. You know it. Shit, the guy is more dysfunctional even than me. Can't take a piss without a carrot dangled over the urinal.

Preferably uncircumcised.

How do you know that?

I don't. It was a joke.

I eyed him suspiciously. Butch always seemed to know stuff I didn't. Though he never flaunted it. It never came out as obvious. He never taunted you with it. But there was always some stuff in there. Stuff behind the blue wall. That you could only get when you really needed it.

You don't know anything, said Butch. He could have gone. There could be a good reason he didn't. Wait till he gets here.

Brendan was very lucky that I was still disoriented, enervated and crippled. I would have jumped up, found him, swiped him upside his pretty blond head. Did I have to do fucking everything?

Butch, I said. Would you do me a favor?

Sure, Rick, he said, affecting a conciliatory air.

Could you find him and punch the little fucker in the face?

Rick, take it easy.

I'm taking it really fucking easy. I can't take it any fucking easier. At least I'm delegating.

Butch laughed. I couldn't help it. I laughed, too.

All right, I said. Fuck it. I'll go to Binion's.

Have another drink.

I'll take it to go. Work to be done.

All right, Butch sighed. You're right. Go do your thing.

I didn't need any more encouragement. I jumped up, shouted in pain. Sat down again. Got up more gingerly. Headed for the door. Limped down the corridor, down the stairs, burst out the door, was momentarily blinded. There was a cab line this time. Just what I needed. Stand in line with a bevy of Idaho bovines and garishly outfitted New Jersey chuckleheads, the midsummer Vegas sun burning the skin of my eyeballs.

I skirted the line. Limped half a block. Flagged one down. I got in. It smelled of dust and disaster.

Binion's, I told the driver. Take the expressway.

30.

THE CAB DROPPED ME OFF at the end of the covered promenade that the city had constructed over the old Downtown casino strip. Trying to bring back some tourists to the faded old joints. Vegas Downtown is a world away from the Strip. The casinos advertise one-cent slots. The bartenders rarely have change for a hundred. The promenade is littered with souvenir booths selling things like *Scarface* posters. Do you have to fly to Vegas to buy a *Scarface* poster?

Past the promenade the place degenerates into what the Tourist Board doesn't want you to know about. Check-cashing joints, pawn-shops, boarded-up storefronts. Folks who shuffle instead of walk. Whole lot of shuffling going on. A guy in a wheelchair held together with duct tape. He's wearing a Stars and Stripes t-shirt so old the stars are brown. Stark and crumbling single-story Loserville. No shelter from the sun. No shelter.

I headed that way. It felt right.

A guy on the corner was holding a stringless guitar and an empty bottle.

Hey, man, he whispered.

Yeah, I said.

There's a guy around here. Time. He's killing all the old people.

I'll keep a lookout, I said.

Good, he said. Let me know.

I will.

I walked past another guy.

Sir? he said.

Yes? I said with a smile.

I was ready for the standard pitch. For which I'm always a sucker.

He said his name was Larry. He was darkly black and short and muscular. He wore a white t-shirt and jeans, strangely clean. He had an honest face. He asked me to stop and talk. I stopped. He talked.

He told me that he was HIV positive, was on a cocktail of drugs. On his way to New Orleans, he said. He showed me a very old, frayed bus ticket with a complicated itinerary that didn't seem to end up anywhere near the Gulf of Mexico. Looked like a prop he'd used before, a few hundred times. New Orleans by way of Fort Worth. I guess some people don't read the fine print.

Let me guess, Larry, I said. You want money.

No, he said to my surprise, he would never ask for money. We chatted for a while longer. He told me about how he had tried to find shelter in Vegas. A church had turned him away. He'd asked a cop what he could do, and the cop had said, Don't come to Vegas to start with. We don't want you here.

The story went on. I wasn't sure I believed it all, or any of it, but somewhere along the way I said, Only because you didn't ask, Larry. And gave him a hundred-dollar bill. The basic unit of currency at the World Series and other serious poker venues.

Larry was taken aback. He was effusively thankful. Which, by the way, was not the reason I did it. It was embarrassing, actually.

Larry gave me a big hug. He said he loved me. I said, I love you too, Larry. Take care of yourself.

I turned back in the direction of Binion's.

I take no position on the question of karma, although I am tempted, like most of us, to see causal connections where there may not be any. Funny thing was, though, I felt quite certain I'd just bought me some. Karma, that is. The good kind.

Binion's Horseshoe hadn't changed much since I'd been there the year before. Nor perhaps in the preceding thirty years, other than via the inexorable process of decay. It was something of a Museum of Entropy.

My first time at the World Series, I'd gone for a pilgrimage. Binion's! The Mecca of poker! Cradle of the Main Event! Site of the Biggest Game Ever Played! But it sure didn't have the air of a shrine. You expected, well, I'd expected, glitter and flash. Lights. Cameras. Action. Well, the lights were there, but they were rather dim: a lot of bulbs were out. The cameras were confined behind the usual black ceiling globes concealing the security apparatus. And there was plenty of action, but it wasn't like on TV. Of course, nothing ever is, but this was even less so. For one thing, there was the smell. Or smells. They all sort of blended together in a brown, funky fog. One part ambition, four parts desperation. Half perspiration, three-quarters sweat.

On this occasion both of the escalators, and the elevator, were out of order. Made it a workout to get to the Steak House on the top floor. I went by the much-celebrated Wall of Fame—on which hung photographs of revered poker players—and almost missed it. It wasn't much bigger than a kitchen corkboard. Just a small space on a wall in a corridor. The picture frames didn't match. One of them was missing, the little picture hook dangling forlornly out of the wall. The picture of the late Stuey Ungar—by consensus the greatest player ever, and owner of the saddest story—didn't have a nameplate on it. Well, I thought, maybe he needed no introduction.

While I was taking all this in, a double-wide lady on a scooter was explaining it all to her friend, in a voice loud enough to hear at the Golden Nugget across the street. Among other nuggets, the scooter lady was sharing with her pal the fact that all top poker players are cocaine addicts.

Really? her friend said.

I'm telling you, said the big gal, with an air of absolute knowledge. You learn something new every day.

At the Rio sports book, and all the others I'd been to, the games and odds were displayed in twenty-first-century fashion, on mammoth computerized screens. At Binion's, they were written in multicolored Magic Marker on a wall-size whiteboard.

Ah, the good old days.

I asked the poker room manager where I could get some of the famous brisket. He smiled indulgently.

That, he said, was long ago.

I needed a drink. Before I started crying.

At the bar, I thought for a moment I'd stumbled on a black lung convention. The paradigm Rio player is a morbidly obese guy on a rented scooter. The Binion's crowd leans more to the tubercular. Old men with hollow cheeks and days' gray growth of patchy beard. Guys with serious years of serious living on their faces. One guy came up next to me with three beer vouchers, got his three bottles and sucked all three down within a minute and a half. Then he turned to me and asked if I had a spare beer voucher.

I pulled up a stool. I looked around. A tiny pale cadaverous curly-haired thing, arms tattooed with snakes, fumbled with her purse, looking disturbed. Not enough in there for a beer, it seemed. She dropped the purse on the sticky soaked floor and stumbled away. A toothless lady with a rooster neck and several painfully large–looking spikes inserted through her eyebrows and lips was cavorting with three young Mexican guys. They'd hit the jackpot, their faces told you. The snake lady returned, proudly waving at the barkeep a plastic-embossed card. He looked at it carefully, nodded. Gave her a beer. The card, apparently, entitled her to keep drinking forever.

Damn, I thought. How do I get me one of those?

There was a short, dark-skinned man with an Hispanic air washing dishes at the sink behind the bar. He sported a surly manner and bad acne scars. His shirt said *Jose*.

Aha, I said to myself. Could it be? Could detecting be this easy?

I tried to catch Jose's eye. He was wiping some grime onto some beer glasses. He ignored me.

I waved at him.

Another guy came over. His shirt said *Dave*.

Hi, Dave, I said.

Hi, said Dave, expressionless.

I ordered a double scotch. Lots of ice. Drank it fast. Waved Dave over again. It took three tries. He gave me a Look that said, I've got a lousy job and a worse life, give me some shit, please give me some shit, so I can stomp your face and get at least a little satisfaction out of the day.

I didn't give him any shit.

A couple of stools over were two women who had some hard miles on the odometer. Had that hair that's been dyed so much it looks like you could snap it off like a pretzel. One said to the other,

He killed his sister and her baby.

Well, no, said the other, he hit the baby with a sledgehammer, but apparently it lived.

I ordered another drink. When Dave came back with it, I said nothing about the lipstick on the rim of the glass. Instead, I asked him about Jose.

His name isn't Jose, he said.

Oh, I said.

I refrained from objecting that the name appearing over the pocket of Jose's shirt was, in fact, Jose. I was quite sure Dave, or whatever Dave's name was, was aware of that.

Uh, what *is* his name? I asked.

Fucked if I know, said Dave, turning away from me to share his grim personality with the charming ladies.

I figured I needed to take the direct route.

Jose! I called out.

Even if that wasn't his name, I surmised, he must be used to people assuming it was.

He was polishing the grease on the countertop with an oil rag filched from the trash of a long-abandoned gas station.

He looked intensely interested in the work.

Jose! I called out again.

He looked up.

I motioned him over with a nod.

Slowly, reluctantly, he sidled over.

What's your name? I asked, as nicely as I could.

He stared at me blankly.

Cómo se llama? I asked in my awful Spanish accent, trying to curry some cultural favor.

He gave me a small smile that twitched into something resembling contempt.

Harold, he said, without a trace of an Hispanic accent.

Oh, I said. Sorry, your shirt . . .

Yeah, he said. So whaddya want.

It wasn't a question. It was a reflex.

Hey, I said, I didn't mean to offend you—

You didn't offend me, he said definitively.

Uh, okay, I said. Listen, I'm just looking for some folks. I've been hired to look for some folks. Nothing to do with you. Nothing official, you know what I mean. I just heard you, or somebody fitting your description, might know something about these people. They used to live in Henderson. Eloise and, Vladimir, I think.

Harold took a step back. Leaned against the sink. Crossed his arms.

It was enough to tell me I'd found the right guy.

Can't help you, he said.

Yeah, I said. I know. I get it. Listen, would you just indulge me? Meet me for a drink later? My tab. The Golden Nugget. Could be something in it for you. When do you get off?

Harold considered my offer for a moment. Narrowed his eyes. Scratched his left sideburn.

No, he said, stepping up and leaning forward. Too close. Upstairs bar at the Terrible. Two hours.

At what?

Terrible Casino. The upstairs bar.

Well, I thought, that could describe any number of joints around town. But not wanting to further reveal my utter lack of cool, I just nodded my head. I figured I'd ask around about this Terrible place.

Gotcha, I said.

He got back to his rag duty.

I had a couple hours to kill. I was in a casino in Vegas, famous for its poker room.

The choice seemed obvious.

The poker room was as well-worn as the rest of the joint, though the players had a bit less of the cancer ward about them. One guy, a dealer playing in his spare time, was Rio-sized, which is to say, fat beyond human imagining. And there were a couple of the usual Internet kids: a fat boy in a NY Yankees cap and green flannel shirt, jolly and wheezing and stinking; a tall, weedy guy with steel wool red hair wearing a t-shirt that said *Jesus Died for My Space in Heaven.* One young guy said he was a professional, lived at Binion's. Can't beat the price, he said. Twenty-nine bucks a night, at the poker rate.

Forty-nine on weekends, a veteran corrected him.

I guess with overhead that low it's fairly easy to be a professional, of a sort.

There was a stout lady with a mammoth beehive, playing beside her husband, shorter than her and with a heavy Brooklyn accent and the nose to match. They had an extended discussion about Grey Goose martinis, at the conclusion of which the waitress arrived. Her shirt said *Betty.* The husband gave Betty detailed instructions on how to make the martinis.

Betty had to ask a couple questions, make sure she got it right. She didn't seem too happy about it.

We're not usually . . . difficult, the beehive lady said, but this is the one thing we really like.

At our age, we better be having a good time, her husband clarified.

The game was fairly soft. Too small, though. 1–2 no limit. The biggest game they were spreading. I got up fifty bucks or so. Got stuck there. Got bored.

The guy next to me seemed to be awfully nice. Too nice, maybe, to be a poker player. I struck up a conversation with him. He said he was Jim. He was writing a book. I asked him what it was called.

It's called *Nothing Falls*, he said.

Damn, I said. That's good. That's really good.

Thanks, he said. You know, the dealers mostly come out ahead. I mean, think about it. I tip them every time I win a hand. But when I lose one, do they tip me? No sir. So at the end of the night, they're ahead of me.

You've certainly got a point, I said.

Another woman at our table said her name was Alice. She was a middle-aged woman of the frumpy persuasion. Baggy sweater. Stained sweatpants, extra large, to accommodate her oakish thighs. Mousy hair. She looked harmless.

Then she opened her mouth.

Jesus fucking Christ! she shrieked when someone sucked out on her for a flush on the river. Oscar, change the fucking dealer! I can't take this shit! Paul, how many times you gonna do this to me?! Fucking shit on a stick!

She was a terrible player, so she had a number of opportunities to yell at Oscar, the floor guy, and Paul and the other dealers. She couldn't resist pushing her chips around whenever she had half a hand. She'd make a big preflop raise out of position, a pot-sized continuation bet on some raggedy-ass flop. Hey, aggression is good. You can win a lot of money playing aggressive. But it was clear that everyone at the table had her figured out. They'd all just wait for a hand. Any decent hand would do. Top pair was fine. Because she'd be pushing it in with middle pair, bottom pair, a gutshot. Whatever. Every once in a while she'd hit it, of course. Take down a big pot. Nobody would mind. That's what keeps the dead money coming back. Like a golfer who only remembers the one drive he hit straight last Sunday. She'd tell the story a thousand times, how she was playing with Huck Seed at the Bellagio in '97, pushed all in with Four, Three off suit, hit the boat on the river to crack Huck's flush. Eight-thousand-dollar pot. Or ten. Thirteen. She told the story again every time someone new showed up at the table. The pot kept growing.

Seriously, she screamed after being outplayed in yet another hand, I'm going to commit suicide! I'm going home! Fuck this. I have some Percodan. That's it. It's over. I'm not putting up with this again. Fuck this. I'm going to kill myself.

Jim, like I said, was a nice guy. Real sweetheart. Kind of guy who feels your pain. And apparently he'd never played with Alice before. A few hands after the suicide rant, he takes her down for a nice pot. Alice goes into her routine again. I'm going to kill myself! I have some Percodan! She stacks her few remaining chips into a rack. Storms out.

Oh my God, Jim says softly.

Everyone laughs. A hand is dealt. The beehive lady bets out. I call. Jim looks absently down at his cards. Throws in some chips. The four seat folds. A Korean guy named Henry goes all in.

Jim is staring blankly at the TV monitor. A replay of some NBA slam dunk contest is on. Nate Robinson bounces a ball off the backboard, grabs it on the way up, does a three-sixty and slams it down. Everybody cheers. Jim just stares.

The dealer nudges Jim. Your action, he says. Henry's all in.

Jim shakes his head slowly. Sorry, he says. That really disturbed me. I mean, do you really think she's going to go home and kill herself?

Oh my God, Jim, says the dealer, she commits suicide four times a week. Call or fold?

I remembered why I was there. I looked at my watch. Shit. The bartender. I got up from the table. Bid everyone good luck. Cashed out my tiny winnings.

It was a funny thing. I felt like I'd made some friends. That never really happened in the big-time casinos. I mean, you'd meet people. You'd get to know their names. But you knew you were never going to put them on your dinner invitation list.

At Binion's, I wasn't so sure about that. I would have liked to invite the whole table out for steaks, to tell the truth.

Maybe I'd look into that twenty-nine-dollar-room thing.

31.

I FOUND OUT FROM OSCAR THE FLOOR GUY that although there did not exist a Terrible Casino, and there did of course exist a number of terrible casinos, arguably all of them, there was indeed a Terrible's Hotel and Casino, a fact which astounded me perhaps more than all the astonishment contained within the cranium of one or even two eight-year-olds from Akron, Ohio, upon arrival at the famed New York, New York complex, which resembled New York City only in the miniaturized façades of certain Manhattan landmarks and in no other conceivable way but could nevertheless, I could only assume by its enduring popularity, excite in the average relatively undeveloped Midwestern brain a modicum of otherwise ludicrous excitement comparable to my reaction, as noted, to the existence of an entity in Las Vegas known as Terrible's Hotel and Casino.

But enough of that. Fact was, if I were to have a conversation with Scarface, confirm that he was indeed The Guy, or maybe knew who The Guy was, further discover if he was the repository of any Clues, I would have to find this Terrible place, scope out the upstairs bar therein, and await my fate.

Not a problem. I'd endured worse. Even in the last forty-eight hours I'd endured worse. Far worse.

The cabbie, who smelled of Listerine and almond-scented massage oil—I wasn't about to ask—knew what I meant right away. Took me there.

It was pretty terrible, all right. But when you think about it, the amazing thing about these places is that it's not that they're not trying. And it's not that they don't have enough money. The sixteen hideously mammoth chandeliers didn't come free. The potted plants ubiquitous in faux brass sconces cost something. What was amazing was that some-body, somewhere, had decided, had been paid to decide, to purchase live plants that looked exactly like plastic plants.

The elevator lobby had all the charm of a moldering log. They'd designed it with drop-down curved ceiling pieces, intended, I guessed, to be reminiscent of the Guggenheim or some such. But the effect was more like that of meandering Oreo cookies.

The cost of carpeting all of that acreage must have been enormous. And sure, they didn't have the budget of the Bellagio. But some person no doubt holding themselves out as something of an expert consciously chose this design, abstract sworls of dirty oranges and jaundice yellows, splotches of insect green on a dark background of indeterminate murk. Colors that were guaranteed to become filthier and more unattractive with every compulsive gambler's staggering footprint. It was as though someone had dropped a vat of tricolor pasta on the floor circa 1993 and people had been tromping through it ever since.

And they were all like this, every low-rent, upward-striving hotel and motel and conference center in the whole of these United States of America was the same in all relevant respects. Sure, the details differed. Maybe the design professional they hired for the Quality Inn down the road selected a slightly darker shade of beige for the faux Danish lobby furniture. The Red Roof Inn had faux Bauhaus instead. In any case, they all managed to wear the faux like a neon sandwich board.

You say ugly is relative? Okay. You got me. Then the place was, relatively speaking, ugly as hell.

On the upside, once inside it took but four or five queries to discover what my new best friend Harold must have meant by the upstairs bar. I mean, it was a bar. No mistaking it. They served drinks. And access to it was via a staircase. Hence the upstairs bit.

Hah, I said to myself. Not many out there can out-detect old Rick Redman, say what you will about his untrimmed shock of startlingly white hair, his air of utter confusion in the face of anything more complex than a motel receptionist, his inability to resist the charms of anything more attractive than a floor mop.

Ninety or so minutes later, Harold appeared. By that time I was teetering on the edge of thoroughly toasted. I was relieved that Harold had gotten there while I still could speak.

Harold! I said too loudly, stumbling to my feet and offering a hand.

He took it reluctantly.

His hand was rough and greasy. I hadn't been aware that a hand could be both.

Sit down, I said. What're you drinking?

I'll have a beer, he said.

I called over the waitress. She was very large, stuffed into a tiny black miniskirt and bustier. A roll of fat tumbled over the waist of the skirt.

The Bellagio this wasn't.

She was nice enough, though, kind enough to bring Harold his Corona, lime on the side, and my fifth double scotch.

Harold! I said again.

Harold grunted.

Listen, man, I said, I know you don't want to rat on anybody or anything, but it's nothing like that. I was hired by this lady in New York to find her sister. She lives out here. Or used to. Henderson. Big old house. But she doesn't live there anymore. The lady who lives there now remembered her and her boyfriend, or husband, or whatever. She also remembered them talking about a guy looks like you, worked the bar at Binion's. They said he was Hispanic, and I guess you're not, but if your working name is Jose, I was thinking, they could think so. So I thought it might be you. You see? Nothing criminal or anything. Just trying to find this lady's sister.

I am Hispanic, he said.

Oh. Sorry. I just can't seem to get this right . . .

My mother was Irish.

Ah. Well.

What if she doesn't want to get found?

Your mother?

This lady.

Well, I guess she can tell me that when I find her. Meanwhile, her sister's very worried.

He snorted. Took a large hit off the Corona. Squoze some lime into his mouth. Belched.

So how'm I supposed to know if I even know these people? he asked.

I told him what I knew. The slim woman in the Chinese dresses. Japanese. Whatever.

Harold nodded. Sucked on his beer.

I told him what the house looked like.

Harold ordered another beer.

And the guy, I said. Tall, with an accent. Big guy, probably Russian. Name Vladimir. Probably.

I did it for show. I knew damn well he knew who I was talking about.

Harold didn't say anything. Looked at me with hooded eyes.

But he had a tell you couldn't miss from thirty feet.

There's a vein in the throat. I don't know what it's called, maybe it's the jugular. Maybe not. Everybody has one. In scrawny guys like Harold, it's easy to see. And when they get nervous, like when they're on a big bluff, trying to hide something, you can see the thing go crazy. Thump, thump, thump. Elevated heart rate.

I decided not to dick around. With a guy like Harold, the bull rush was the best. My decision was no doubt influenced by the scotch. But that isn't necessarily fatal to an idea.

So you know them.

I said it as a fact, not a question.

I engaged his eyes.

He looked away.

Then I was dead certain.

And he knew that I knew.

Yeah, he said. So?

Now I knew not only that he knew them, but that they and he were involved in something. Not that I cared. But it was information. And information is . . . well, it's information. And that can come in handy when you're, like, looking for a missing person.

Any idea where they are?

Haven't seen them, he said.

Since?

I don't know, six months.

You're sure it was that long?

Yup, he said.

He was a terrible liar.

C'mon, man, I said. I don't care what they're doing, you're doing. I just got to report to the lady. She wants to know is her sister alive.

Yeah. I got it. She's alive.

I sighed. I mean, I hate to be crude. Obvious. Trite. But it was now or it was after another half hour of fencing.

I put two C-notes on the smoked glass table.

He looked at the money. He looked at me.

One thing I knew about myself, I looked harmless.

I'm not that big a tipper, I said.

All right, he said, reaching for the bills.

I snatched them back.

Wait a second. Information first, money later. And the same again if it checks out. Besides, I know where you work.

He looked disappointed. But two hundred bucks was a lot of money to a guy like Harold.

I used to run errands for them, he said.

Ah. Thank you, Harold. You're a good man. But that won't help me find them. Where are they now?

Last I heard, something bad happened.

Shit, I said, really? What kind of bad?

Not hurt bad, money bad. I heard they got ripped off, they ripped somebody off and got caught, something like that.

And?

And they ended up in some trailer park. Out in the desert somewhere.

Can you be a little more vague?

He looked at me blankly.

Any more than that? I mean, east, west, near the city, in Mongolia, what?

I don't know. But I know a guy I can call.

All right, I said. Now we're getting somewhere.

Harold took out his cell phone, got up, left the bar. I took the opportunity to order another drink. It was weak and watery.

I had to get out of the place.

Harold came back.

He says he's not sure, he said. But it's somewhere north of Red Rock.

Somewhere north of Red Rock, I said. Very helpful.

It's out there. Just go to Red Rock. Go north from there. There's only one road.

Okay. You're all right, Harold. And if it checks out, like I said, another two hundred.

That didn't make him look happy.

But then, guys like him, nothing would.

I had downed enough scotch by then that I might have been mistaken, but I could have sworn that I saw, on my unsteady way to the lobby, Bruno and Evgeny shooting craps.

Bruno and Evgeny?

I resisted the urge to get closer, verify the sighting.

I tried to process the information.

I supposed, for a moment, that they could just have run into one another, each having submitted more or less simultaneously to an urge to play craps at the Terrible Bar and Casino, or whatever it was called.

That notion refuted itself.

Then what?

It would not compute.

I resolved to revisit the issue. Once the scotch-flavored fog had dissipated a mite.

32.

WHEN I GOT BACK TO THE ROOM, I called Sheila.

Sheila, I said. Sorry to have to do this by phone. I know you don't approve.

It's not that I don't approve. I just think that it's not as effective. And also, you've been drinking.

I knew enough not to deny it.

Yeah, I know. But I'm in Las Vegas. Not much I can do. About the phone thing, I mean. The drinking, I'm working on.

I understand.

She always understood. It was one of the great things about her.

I'm starting to realize that I never know what other people are really thinking, I said, apropos of nothing.

What about when you're playing poker? I thought you said you could read them. The other players.

Well, that's true. In a limited sense. Often, you know exactly what someone is trying to do. What their cards are. Or at least a probable range of cards. But that's just it. It's probability, really. You can never be one hundred percent sure.

Why would you want to be?

Easy money.

Not in the poker context. In the real world. Why would you want to be sure? Wouldn't that make life a little boring?

Poker, too. It would be just like picking up money off the table.

Let's get back to the real world.

Me?

Yes, even you.

Okay. What about it?

Why would you want to be certain about what others are thinking?

I guess I wouldn't. Too boring. I know, that's what you said. You were right.

Okay, then let's talk about why you said that.

Said what?

That you're beginning to realize that you don't know what others are thinking.

What I was getting at, I guess, is that I've been feeling very alone.

Lonely?

No. Alone. Not quite the same thing. Worse, actually. If you're lonely, you can call up a friend. Go meet somebody in a bar. Whatever.

And if you're alone?

You're just . . . alone.

Nothing to be done?

Nothing to be done.

But are you so sure? That there's nothing to be done?

What could one do?

Well, you'd be right, if the aloneness was something from outside of you. But if it's something inside of you. Within your control.

It doesn't feel that way.

How does it feel?

Frightening.

Yes, but can you put it in words? The feeling of aloneness?

I thought for a while. I lay back on the sectional. I lit a cigarette.

No, I said. I can't.

Then let's make that your homework.

Thinking about how to put it into words?

Putting it into words.

Anyway. It's all a disaster.

How so?

I told her about the poker losses. The twenty grand. The Bruno Episode. Relying on ephemeral promises from known Russian scumbags. Known scumbags who happened to be from Russia. Embezzling Louise's retainer.

Sounds like you've put yourself in a spot, she said.

Yes, I replied. It seems that I have.

I'm sorry. I don't mean to be unhelpful.

You're always helpful.

Well, let's try to figure this out.

Okay.

In terms of the money, the situation, I'm not sure that you and I can do anything about that.

I know, I said. It is what it is.

I hated that phrase. But it seemed awfully apropos.

Yes, she said. But let's see if we can come up with something. A plan, at least. To get you through it.

That would be something, I said.

We batted it back and forth. We ran it up the flagpole. We saluted it. We tried it on for size. We waved the red flag. Or the white one—there was no bull in the room, after all. I woke up. Saw it for what it was. What 'it' was, I wasn't sure.

We decided that I'd do my best.

It was the best we could do.

33.

IN THE MORNING, after four hours of what could only nominally be called sleep, it occurred to me that I still hadn't qualified for the Main Event. It was preying on me. I had enough other shit to deal with. At least if I could qualify, it would take that load off. There was a mega-satellite. I resolved to win it.

I had some time to kill before it started. Thought I'd pay a visit to the beer tent. Natalya might be there.

Rick! she greeted me with her big-boned Slavic smile.

Natalya, I said with a calculatedly sheepish one.

Just happens I have about a half a bottle of that Johnnie Walker back here. Just enough to warm you up.

You are my princess, I said.

She batted her eyes in faux flirtation. I knew it was faux. I was twice her age. She hung out with tattooed guys younger than her. Guys with the vocabulary of a sea snake and an attitude to match. I wasn't her type. I was an amusement. Possibly a distorted sort of father figure. But I sure wasn't a prospect.

Though maybe, I thought, with a little convincing . . .

I sat at the bar. There were the usual number of customers in the tent: none. Good, I thought. We can have a private moment.

So where's your boyfriend? I asked.

My boyfriend?

Yeah, isn't he your boyfriend?

Who?

Whoever your boyfriend is.

Are you trying to make a joke, Rick?

Yeah. Guess it didn't work.

Nope, she said, refilling my glass.

So, I said, you know those guys?

Is this the same joke?

No.

What guys?

Those guys who Brendan left with? The Russian guys?

Andrei and Anatoly? You asked me that before.

Yeah, but you were a little vague.

Sure, I know them.

More than just from around here?

She gave me a sideways look. Who wants to know? she said.

That would be me, I replied.

Ah. I see.

Well?

Sure. It's a community, you know? Young Russian kids.

They don't look all that young to me. Andrei and Anatoly.

Okay, she said.

How do you know them?

Rick, are you interrogating me?

Just making conversation.

Hmmm.

Okay, I said, I'll be straight with you. Brendan is, I don't know, sort of my ward.

Ward?

Like Robin. You know, Batman and Robin?

Oh, yes, she said without conviction.

A bit like that. Anyway, I'm a little worried about him. Hanging with those guys.

Why worried?

I know them from New York. They're sort of, I don't know, gangster types.

Gangsters? Natalya laughed. I don't think so.

What makes you not think so?

They're too stupid. And ugly.

Maybe you got your gangster ideas from the movies. Lots of gangsters are stupid and ugly. Most of them, maybe.

She refilled my scotch. Looked at me with her head at an angle, chin raised, eyelids lowered to half-mast.

I read the signal. I'd gotten as far as I'd get. Might be some more later. Right now, back to the poker room.

Thanks for the drinks, I said.

She handed me a bill. Thirty bucks.

Suddenly I wasn't quite as grateful. But I put forty on the bar. Left her with a smile.

The poker gods weren't with me. I busted out of the satellite early. I decided to check out some cash games. I put my name on the list. Hung around waiting to be called. Watched some of the TV stars play. Hell, I lied to myself, I can play better than them. Or at least as good.

Grandiosity, I heard Sheila's voice say. Watch out for that. There are ups. There are downs. When you exaggerate them, they're destructive. Both of them. Melissa had succumbed to the downs. Others to the ups.

Of course. It was obvious. But like so many things, easier to understand than implement.

They called my name. I sat down at a 5–10 table. Full of tourists. Arrogant Internet geeks. And a couple of gray-faced regulars. Rocco, a super-tight player with slicked-back hair and an air of menace. Louie, a scrawny guy with a long red face with a lot of mileage on it, longer disheveled hair. His t-shirt read *Let All The Earth Fear The Lord.*

I was ready to bust some ass. And for a few hours I did. I stayed sharp. I declined the drinks impressed upon me by the cleavage-enhanced help. I threw my chips in when I saw weakness. I folded when I sensed strength. I was up a couple grand. Okay, I said to myself. Be responsible. Be mature. Cash out. Get the hell out of here with your profit.

I called for the floor person to give me a couple of racks. I needed two, to hold all my chips. I started stacking them into the racks.

The dealer deals me in.

Wait a minute, I'm about to say, I'm leaving.

Before I say it, I peek down at my cards. Ace, Queen. Nice.

Ah, what the hell, I tell myself. I'll play one last hand.

I lean forward again.

One last hand.

The flop comes Ace, Nine, Three. Rainbow. Three different suits. Could hardly ask for better. I got the Aces. No flushes, no straights on board. I bet. Everybody folds, except the quiet guy. Forgot to mention him. The Quiet Guy. He's over on the left. Three seats down from me. He plays solid. Tight. Quiet. Like I said.

He calls.

The turn's a rag. I bet. He calls. What's he calling with? Got to be an Ace, with a weak kicker. Weaker than my Queen, for sure. Ace, King, he would have raised before the flop. He could have something better, of course. Two pair. A set. He could have come in with a pair of Nines, hit the set. But the probability of that was sufficiently low that, in the absence of further information, I had to assume that wasn't the case. For now. I need to keep it in mind, though. Future bets may tell me different.

The river's a Four of clubs. More nothingness. Hah, I think. Got him.

I make one last bet. Two hundred dollars.

He goes all in.

Shit.

Well, I'm thinking. Got to call that. I've only got another hundred, hundred-fifty in front of me. Seven hundred in the pot. Too much to fold. I'm probably winning anyway.

I call.

He turns over Ace, Nine.

Two pair.

Shit.

He pulls in my chips.

I get up to leave.

Wait a minute, says Rocco.

I turn to him.

He points at the racks in my hands.

Those chips are live, he says.

I stare at him.

It dawns on me.

That is the rule.

You can't take chips off the table.

They're in the game.

I'd called all in.

That meant those chips too.

Jesus.

I look at the Quiet Guy. He's staring, impassive, at my chips. I plead with him, with my eyes. Don't stand on the rules, my eyes are saying. Fuck Rocco. You know I only meant to play with the couple hundred on the table.

He doesn't say a thing.

Which doesn't stop the rest of the rabble.

Sure, the chorus goes up. That's the rule. Those chips are in.

I'll call the floor manager, the dealer says.

No, never mind, I say. I play by the rules.

I slowly stack my chips back on the table. The dealer matches the winner's remaining stack with mine. At least I have more than him. I'll get out of there with some money left.

The dealer slides a six-inch pile of my former chips over to the Quiet Guy.

He nods his head. He doesn't gloat. Not visibly, at least. I appreciate that.

I leave.

I head back towards the exit.

Jesus, I think to myself, it's true. Only dead fish swim with the current.

I have no idea what it means.

I pass through the reception area.

The sun is coming through the skylight there.

I stop at one of the velvet-draped bars along the way.

The waitress has some nice cleavage going.

And anyway.

I need a drink.

Hell, I needed five, at least. I found my way to the purple velvet emporium.

I was on my fourth scotch when Bruno sat down, complete with leather outfit, shit-eating grin, and a lighter sling. Seemed he'd taken the bandages off.

Oh, fuck, I said, feeling sudden pain in my gut, my sternum, my right ankle.

His grin grew wider.

That was quite a show, he said.

What?

The chips-in-the-rack show.

Shit. You saw that?

Sure did, he laughed.

Well, thanks for the sympathy.

Why'd you just give it up? I would've called the floor. Said my intent was clear.

I guess you're a better man than me.

I'll buy you a drink, he said.

That'll do, I replied.

As he rumbled over to the bar, I pondered this sudden change in the Bruno dynamic. It seemed like his pounding me into the emergency room had somehow evened the score. I didn't feel the animosity. It seemed like he didn't either.

I wondered if I was losing my edge.

I made a note to look it up.

Bruno came back with a double for me and a bottle of vodka, three extra glasses.

Expecting some company? I asked.

Maybe, he said.

I'm not in the mood for Russians.

Ah, come on. That's the whole point.

Point of what?

What you're going to help me with.

That. Right.

Right.

So, what is it?

Not yet, he said.

It isn't anything yet?

It isn't anything I can tell you about yet.

At which point arrived the three Russians in question: Alexina, Sashina and Ivankina, as they were introduced. All three were tall and slim. Alexina had on a slinky black dress clinging to her curves. Sashina had white plastic boots flaring to her knees. Ivankina had a magnificent pout.

Ah, I said to myself. My lucky day. Russian hookers.

Listen, I said to Bruno, been a long day. I got to get to bed.

Bruno protested. He genuinely seemed to want me to stay, party on down with his skanky friends. But even if I were interested in Russian whores, which I wasn't, I was still steaming from the chip rack incident. I apologized again, stumbled out of the velvet fog.

34.

I FOUND MY WAY TO A QUIETER BAR AROUND THE CORNER. I hadn't even ordered my first drink when I heard my name paged. Mr. Rick Redman, please call the front desk for a message. I was tired. I had no desire to call the front desk. Get involved in more crap. But if someone was paging me, it might be important. Kelley, maybe. Butch. I had to check it out.

I asked the bartender for the house phone. He pulled it out from under the bar. I called the front desk. Redman, I said. I was just paged.

We have a message for you, sir.

Thanks, I said. I think I figured that out.

Actually, sir, ah, one moment. I'm going to connect you to another line.

I pantomimed the bartender for a double Laphroaig, phone to my ear. He appreciated my effort. Brought it over right away.

Mr. Redman? a rumbling voice with a vaguely Southern twist inquired of my ear.

The very one, I said.

I wonder if I may have a word with you, Mr. Redman.

One, I replied. Each additional, fifty cents. Think about it before you agree. It may not sound like much, but it adds up fast.

I had been forewarned about your sense of humor, the voice reverberated, without a touch of amusement.

Such as it is, I said.

Yes, the voice replied. In any case, would you object to a short meeting? In the High Stakes Room.

You buying? I asked.

No.

Okay, we'll go dutch.

I'll be there in a moment, the voice said.

I put down the phone. The bartender had discreetly vanished. I put back a generous mouthful of Laphroaig. You weren't supposed to drink it that way. You were supposed to sip and savor. Ah, well. I was never one for convention.

I wondered what this could be about. An emissary from Her Louiseness? Some Russian goon come to crush my gonads for disrespecting Evgeny? New business? This last I had mixed feelings about. I hoped it could wait till after the tournament.

I took my glass with me to the high-roller lounge. I wasn't a high roller, needless to say. But I had an invitation. And anyway, I'd learned that if you timed your entrance right, got by the heavies at the entrance—they were off having a smoke, whatever—you could wander right in, and once you were ensconced, nobody dared to challenge your presence. Lest they offend one of the casino's better clients.

I liked the bar in there. It had a cushioned edge, on which I could rest my forearms, weary from all that chip riffling. I could look straight ahead, avoiding any unwanted eye contact. I could use my peripheral vision and finely honed hearing—highly developed from ferreting out tells at the poker table—to examine my potential interlocutors—preferably female—before turning to or away from them. Three-quarters away, in the ideal case.

But all of that depended on the bartender. The barkeep was the one person you couldn't avoid, so it was essential that he or she be either silent and discreet, or adequately personable. On this evening, prowling behind the oak and brass was Hugo, a pompous little number with a tiny mustache and a faux French accent. Well, maybe it wasn't faux. I didn't know. But it sounded faux to me. And I wasn't in the mood for it.

Serving tables, in contrast, was Armand. Armand was Swiss, and his accent, and his French, was real. I could practice. Not to mention that he seemed to be a real nice guy.

I chose a corner table. Sank into a deeply comfortable chair, back to the wall. Had to keep an eye out. You never knew when the swarthy assassin might find you out. I asked Armand, in French, for another Laphroaig. He nodded appreciatively. Didn't make any remark about my Québécois accent. Yes, my type of waiter.

There was a Steinway grand in the high-roller lounge. I'd never seen anyone playing it before, but I awoke, after a short reverie, to Debussy. 'La fille aux cheveux de lin.' It wasn't, I was mildly surprised to note, dumbed-down Debussy either, cocktail lounge Debussy, with added trills and stupid rubato. It was pure, concentrated, evanescent impressionism. Real Debussy. Must be a Juilliard student, summer job, I thought.

I was snorkeling my third glass of the smoky single malt when The Voice arrived, fully clothed and looming. It was true to its word: as large as its resonance would have led one to surmise.

It put out a substantial paw, complete with ostentatious ruby class ring. I couldn't make out what class. Working class, I imagined.

John Taylor Esquinasse, it said. Pleased to meet you, Mr. Redman.

The pleasure is mine, I'm sure, I replied, noting the gold collar pin, the cinched waist, the intimidating shoulder span of the former football player not yet wholly gone to seed. It was that, or this was John Gotti. And Gotti was dead. Anyway, I wasn't sure he had ever played football.

Mr. Esquinasse—could only be Louisiana, that name, I mused, yes, that was the accent—interrupted my thought:

May I have a seat? he asked with exaggerated deference.

I'd hate to try to stop you, I said.

He tried to smile. It came out as a grimace of a sort. He took a seat anyway.

Mr. Redman, he reverberated, I should let you know that I'm an attorney.

And I should let you know that I'm judgement-proof. No lawsuit can touch me. I don't have a job. I don't have any money. I lost the house. And if I win the tournament, I promise to dissipate every penny of the prize money within a week. So you can tell whoever she is to fuck off.

I drifted back into myself as the good attorney Esquinasse pondered this. The pianist was playing 'Feux d'artifice.' Subtly drifting black-key arpeggios at marvelous speed. I wanted to be there. In the fireworks. Alone.

Mr. Redman, Mr. Gotti interrupted. Please do not rush to judgement. I do not represent one of your former girlfriends, or wives, if that's what you're thinking.

Actually, I said, I was thinking of my former housekeeper. I think I stiffed her on that last sixty bucks. Felt bad about it, but I had to get out of town. Right away, if you get my drift.

I'm not sure I do. But no matter. I've been hired by a certain individual.

Certain. That's good. Better than the vague kind, anyway.

This certain individual, he went on, ignoring me, wishes me to ask you a question.

All this lead-in for one lousy question?

Mr. Redman, I hope you'll allow me to address the purpose of my visit at some point.

Certainly, certainly. Sorry. I like to amuse myself. Bad habit.

I understand, he said, without a trace of understanding. Well, this is a delicate matter. The person I represent would like to know, sir, whether you would like to meet someone.

Can you be a little more vague?

The last notes of 'Feux d'artifice' faded away. I wanted them back.

Mr. Esquinasse cleared his throat.

The certain person is your daughter.

My daughter? Who the fuck are you, man? If my daughter wants to ask me a question, she'll call me.

Ah, your daughter. I see. Well, sir, this is—how would you—I guess you would say, another daughter. One of which you were, perhaps, unaware.

It took me a moment to assimilate this rather, shall we say, unusual information. I tried to catch Armand's eye. I was going to need a refill. Or three.

Are you serious? I asked His Seriousness.

I am, he intoned superfluously.

I see, I said. A daughter. Another daughter. Well. How interesting.

Yes, sir. I apologize if I've startled you.

Oh, you've startled me, all right. Who the hell are you, anyway? How do I know you're not trying to shake me down or something?

I am, as I said, merely an attorney. An emissary, if you will.

I'm not sure I will. How sure are you of this?

That she is, in fact, your daughter? That is not my purview, sir. I know nothing. I can inform you, though, that my client is quite certain of it indeed.

And who, pray, sir, I asked, adopting his tone, might your client be?

I'm not at liberty to say, sir.

How did I know you were going to say that?

I don't know, sir. I'm sorry, sir.

Stop being so damn sorry. Listen, can I buy you a drink?

I shouldn't, he said, the first crack appearing in his façade.

C'mon, Esquy, I urged. Surely it's not every day you get to tell someone they're an accidental father? Let's . . . celebrate.

Well, sir, you are right about that. That's true. Perhaps I'll have a small glass of scotch.

Armand! A double scotch for my friend! Make it the best!

I turned to my new friend Esquinasse.

Is there a best scotch? I asked him. I mean, what's your preference? I'm partial to Glenlivet.

Glenlivet it is. Armand! Make it Glenlivet!

I slugged down what remained of my Laphroaig. Knew that Armand would know enough to return with a refill along with Esquy's Glenlivet.

Well, Esquy, I said. I guess the obvious question is, are you here to tell me only that I allegedly have this previously undisclosed progeny, or to tell me who she is? Or where, anyway? Or anything at all? How old she is, maybe?

As a matter of fact, sir, I am.

You am what?

Armand arrived with the libations. I sucked at mine greedily. Esquinasse sipped his with the delicacy of the overcompensating brute.

Well, he said, I hate to add to your . . . burden . . . no, that's not the right word . . .

Don't worry about it. Fire away.

Well, she's eighteen years old. And she's here, sir.

She's here? In town?

In the room.

The room? She's staying in the hotel?

This room, sir.

My chest clenched. Jesus. This was just too much. I needed some time to process this new information before being confronted with the object of it. Subject of it. Decide whether to flee. Find a nice warm monastery in Belize. Preferably one where they brewed their own spiritual condiments.

Right in the room? This fucking room?

At the piano, sir.

At the piano? You mean, the pianist?

Yes, sir.

Playing Debussy?

I thought it was Bacharach.

What the . . .

It wasn't the time to lecture the good Mr. Esquinasse on the finer points of music appreciation. And anyway, he clearly hadn't gotten past the grosser points. I got up. My knee knocked over the scotch glass. My shin smacked the edge of the coffee table. I didn't feel a thing. I staggered piano-ward. I strove mightily to clear my head. I straightened my tie. No I didn't. I didn't have a tie. I wasn't a lawyer any more. I tucked in my shirt instead.

The piano hove into view. For the first time I noticed the silence. The musical silence.

She wasn't there.

What a fucking relief. Or something.

I was confused.

I headed back to the table.

Esquinasse was gone. His empty glass graced the table.

My cell phone rang. Louise Chandler. Needed to see me. Seven o'clock. At the Wynn.

All of this was making me very tired.

I dropped back into the chair.

It enveloped me.

35.

I MUST HAVE FALLEN ASLEEP.

When I started awake, God knows how long later, Armand had been replaced by a bubbly pneumatic thing with a relentless smile, who kindly pretended not to notice that I had been, no doubt, for minutes or perhaps hours, snoring up a storm in her tastefully appointed watering spot.

There was no Esquinasse. And no piano music. I staggered to my feet. Wandered to the Velvet. Hoped to find Butch there. Ask him what to do.

The exhausting clamor of the casino intruded, for a time, until—bizarrely—Bob Dylan emerged on the overhead speakers. I didn't recognize the song—rather shocking, given that I thought I'd once owned every disc he'd ever recorded—but the sound, the rhythm, the unmistakable narrative pulse—despite the shrieks of the brain-dead video poker player communing with two loud black hookers at the bar and then the bartender—who tells the guy, Careful, man, of the whores, and with whom the drunk sadly tries to relate by asking how to say who's your daddy in Spanish—razored through.

I'm not a romantic. I mean, I can get in touch with my inner romantic, when the occasion requires, if you know what I mean. But

I'm not a soft fucker, a kneel-down-and-worship-some-guy-I-never-even-met kind of dude, but every day that I'm reminded—which is maybe most days—I thank the Lord God Almighty, if there is one, for sparing Bob Dylan's life from that motorcycle accident in 1966, or whenever it was, and every other stupid self-destructive thing he may ever have done. A master of word and sound of such natural power. The guy can't even read music. He's so—what's the word?—real, I guess, that even his poses—the late-Dylan-Mexican-pencil-mustache-poseur, for example—are flush with undeconstructible meaning, and the rattling age in his voice now only adds poignancy to the gravity.

I guess I'm a fan.

I closed my eyes. Leaned back. Luxuriated in this new ballad. What a treat. I made out the chorus. Stayed in Mississippi, way too long, syllables descending through the scale, stretching out the last three, with the unmistakable Dylan punch at the end of the line. Amazing. New Dylan. As good as the old Dylan. Maybe better. Didn't think it was possible.

The song ended. I breathed deeply. I opened my eyes.

I wasn't alone.

Sitting across from me was an elegant young lady in a burgundy sheath dress. She had long, full brown hair, seductive almond eyes. She had a patrician nose and a scary pair of heels.

Father? she said.

No, I replied involuntarily.

Wait, I amended, I don't mean no, no. I mean, I don't know. I mean, like, no way, man. I mean, what the hell are you talking about?

I'm afraid it's true, Dad, she said, as natural as if she'd been calling me that since birth.

Ah, I said eloquently. Ah. Ah.

I'm sure it comes as a shock, she said, with an air of possession that only worsened my condition.

Uh. Uh. I mean, hi, I ventured.

I'm Madeleine, she said, extending a long slim hand.

I took the hand. She had a soft grip. I understood. A pianist had to protect her fingers.

You play beautifully, I said.

Someone was talking loudly to the bartender. I glanced over. It was a large shadowy thing with a supercilious air, carrying a mean black motorcycle helmet. Oh shit. Could the guy please get out of my life for a minute? Even two? I tried to shrink into the scenery. It didn't work. He sauntered over, with his usual air of insolent entitlement. I glared at him. He gave my putative daughter a leather Italian leer. I felt ill. Jesus, I thought, if this really is my daughter, if she really is as poised and accomplished as she appears, the last thing she needs is exposure to the ugly underbelly of American life, aka my existence. As exemplified by Bruno and the baroque entanglements that seem to have bound us together.

I wasn't sure, on the other hand, that I could prevent it.

This time, at least, I didn't have to. Bruno satisfied himself with the leer, and a wink for me, hulked away. I turned to Madeleine with a sense of relief that I hoped was not obvious.

Was that a friend of yours? she asked.

I wouldn't say that, exactly, I said.

She paused a moment. She looked like she wanted to inquire further. Fortunately, she seemed to think better of it.

I missed you, she said.

I'm sorry?

Growing up. I missed you.

You didn't miss a thing, I was tempted to say. But I held that one back.

I'm sorry, I said instead. If I had known . . .

You didn't. I know.

Um, this is really embarrassing, but to tell you the truth . . .

You don't know who Mom is.

Um, yes. I mean, no. I don't.

It's okay. I knew that too.

I was silent. It was very hard to know what to say. What would be appropriate. What would offend. This wasn't a situation they trained you for in law school. Or, as far as I knew, anywhere else.

I won't burden you, she said.

No, no . . .

Really. It's not necessary. When you're ready. She . . . passed away. You don't have to feel guilty.

I wasn't sure it was guilt I felt. Confusion, certainly. I was totally at sea. Whatever impediments life might throw in my way, I almost never was at a loss for words. For the quick quip, the deft cross-reference. A way out, if need be. And here it was, an eighteen-year-old, obviously bright, articulate, but in any other circumstance not someone who could, or should, render me mute. She was handling this a hell of a lot better than I was. She did, on the other hand, have the advantage of surprise. She'd no doubt prepared herself for this. For months. Years, probably.

I was dying to know, of course. Who her mother was. For the life of me I had no idea. I could see in Madeleine's face no trace of any likely candidate. Eighteen years ago. Nineteen. Or was it twenty? How did that work? Depended on whether she'd just turned eighteen or . . . oh, forget it. In any case it would have been—Jesus. I was married by then. Long married to Melissa. Kelley would have been two years old. Or one. Had to factor in the nine months. Surely this must have been an event worthy of remembrance.

But I didn't have a clue.

On the other hand, I had no doubt. The genetic imperatives made themselves felt. I wasn't going to contest the diagnosis. Request another opinion. Ask for a lie detector test. Or DNA. A DNA test. I couldn't define it, can't define it now. It wasn't a physical resemblance. At least none that I could put a finger on. God knows it wasn't her unnatural air of self-possession. Must have gotten that from her mother, along with the good looks. It wasn't anything I could explain. It was just there. Immediate. Visceral. True. Here was my daughter.

My other daughter.

The question, of course, was:

What to do now?

I shrugged, a half-smiling shrug.

So, I said. I hardly know what to say. I mean, it's wonderful. Wonderful to meet you. You have a sister, you know. A half sister, I guess.

Yes, she said. I know.

How . . .

Mr. Esquinasse has been very helpful. I didn't want to do this without . . . being prepared. I guess I know a lot more than you might think. When I turned eighteen—

Ah, I said. Of course. That's when they let you see the records, isn't it? And you've done your research. And tracked me all the way to here.

I thought eighteen years of waiting was long enough.

Yes, I said. Long enough . . .

Another silence.

In any case, I said, what I meant to say was, you should meet Kelley. Your sister. Soon as possible. Let's all get together.

I'd like that, she said.

There was an awkward pause. One of many to come, I assumed.

There's one question I'd like to ask, she said.

Of course.

It's sort of . . . personal.

I couldn't help smiling. Did it get any more personal than this?
Go ahead, I said.

Well, I was wondering, are you . . . musical?

Oh my God, I thought, if I'd had any doubts . . .

Debussy, I said. Sublime. You play him so beautifully. I was
entranced. Before I knew it was you.

Oh, she said with a slightly startled smile. Oh. That's so . . .

Yes, I said.

Well, I know you're busy . . .

I wondered what gave her that idea.

. . . but here's my cell phone number.

She handed me a card. It was rose-colored, with her name.
Madeleine. Only that. And the phone number.

I wondered if she'd had it made for me.

36.

I WANTED TO CATCH A BIT MORE SLEEP. Give the bones some
healing time. Four hours' sleep isn't even enough for a normal human.
Let alone one in the throes of terminal alcohol syndrome, or whatever
they called it, and deep-in-the-bone bruise, recovering from an infarction. But it was time to meet Louise. And when the client calls, as we
all know, we listen. We hop on up. Put on the uniform. Salute the flag.
Piss in the right pissoir. You piss in the left pissoir, everybody knows:
you're deeply suspect.

I grabbed a cab. It smelled of cardamom and cloves. Very pleasant.
Told him to get me to the Wynn.

The thing about the big, opulent joints like the Wynn and the Bellagio
is that under the elaborate skin they're still Vegas casinos. The fat people
are better dressed. And the slot machines have designer chairs. But a
morbidly obese slot-head in a designer outfit sitting on a fancy chair is
still a morbidly obese slot-head. My opinion, anyway.

When I got to the restaurant, she wasn't there. I used her name with the maître d'. He gave me a knowing look. What he knew, I didn't know. What I did know was that I didn't like the guy. He had that tall, erect, brushed-back-on-the-sides-gray-hair-black-on-top-in-a-dark-suit thing going. With the tan. In other words, a man in an inferior job, with a vast air of superiority.

There is a message for you, Mr. Redman, he said.

And what might that message be? I asked in my most supercilious manner.

I wouldn't know, sir, he said. It's sealed.

I see. Might I then have the pleasure of receiving this sealed message?

At that point Mr. Slick figured out that I was mocking him. His lips pursed, he said not another word. Turned on his heel.

While I was waiting, I sat at the bar, ordered a scotch. A couple of stools down was an old guy in a ratty sweater and a tattered baseball cap. The bartender put three wineglasses in front of him, poured a tasting amount from three bottles. The old guy looked warily at the glasses, picked one up. Took a sip. Stared at the bartender for a while.

All of a sudden it tastes like a horse, he said in a heavy Eastern European accent.

The bartender chuckled nervously. Yes, sir, he said, it does have a touch of earthiness to it.

If by earthy you mean horseshit, said the old man.

Mr. Slick returned to the maître d'ais. I took my scotch on over. He handed me an envelope.

I turned away, tore it open.

> My apologies. I was called away. Please meet me in two
> hours at the bar in the sports and horse betting area of
> the Bellagio.

She didn't seem like the horse-betting type. Tell you the truth, I didn't recall ever seeing a woman in a sports betting joint. At least, not a well-dressed one. But it was next to the poker room, so I couldn't complain. I'd have something to do with the two hours.

Which turned out to be a good thing. I drew a table full of fish. Picked up a couple grand. Got in a good mood.

When I got to the bar next to the poker room, the esteemed Ms. Chandler hadn't arrived. I was starting to get used to it.

But Bob was there. Bob was the bartender. I'd spent many hours in his company, taking a break from the poker tables. He was a back-slapping, stocky guy who knew how to make a guy feel comfortable. He brought me my scotch without my asking.

I used the downtime to think about the nature of fish.

A fish, I mused, is a very well-studied beast. He's been scrupulously observed, both in captivity and in the wild. His habits and peccadilloes assiduously recorded, analyzed and digested by the sharkish poker tax-onomist. He's been broken down into subspecies. There's the Pure Fish: he calls too many hands, and once in the pot is governed primarily by fear. He's afraid to raise, lest someone have a better hand. Afraid to fold, lest he miss some random opportunity down the road. And afraid to call a big bet, because he can't believe you would do that without a monster. This is pure, exquisite Fishdom. You can bluff him whenever you want. You can string him out with smaller bets when you know you have the better hand. And he'll always be in enough hands to spread his wealth around.

Then there's the Calling Station Fish. He doesn't play as many hands as the Pure Fish, but once there, he's not going away. He, too, has never heard of a raise, still less a re-raise. It's call, call, call, fold. Or call, call, call, lose. Oh, my kingdom for a tankful of Calling Station Fish.

The varieties are endless. There's the Bottom Feeder, a guy who's good, but not good enough to win in the bigger games; you can find him every day in the cheesier casinos, feeding off the tourists at the low-limit tables. Usually wearing a tracksuit and well-worn sneakers. The Catfish: a Bottom Feeder with fat lips and a mustache. The Grouper. You never see him without his posse. Can't play unless there's somebody there he can impress with his knowing banter.

And then there's the Maniac. Ah, the Maniac. The Maniac is a dif-ferent sort of fish. A dangerous fish. A fish with a bite. A piranha of a fish: much harder to deal with in groups. The Maniac has never seen a hand he doesn't like. He'll put in a huge preflop raise with Seven, Five off suit. Or King, Three. Or, of course—and here's the bite—with a pair of Aces or Kings. He counts on scaring everybody out of pots a lot of the time. The few times he's got a hand, or flops a monster hand—his Seven, Five draws Four, Six, Eight, three suits, he's got the nut straight, no flushes to compete—are hard to forget. They prey on you. The next time he puts five hundred dollars in the pot on a nondescript flop, you have to ask yourself: did he hit or miss?

So the Maniac, actually, can make a lot of money, on a given night. With the right opposition. Or the right amount of luck. But the Shark, well, the Shark can see the Maniac coming a mile away. The Shark knows what to do with the Maniac.

What, exactly, you ask, does the Shark do with the Maniac?

Well, something needs to be left for the Advanced Course. The one you pay for. Call me when your luck changes.

My reverie was interrupted when a mismatched couple of guys came over from the betting tables, sat at the bar.

The older guy, with wispy dyed-blond hair and pink and green golf slacks, was lecturing his new best friend, a good-looking young black guy with a confident air.

Don't gamble, the old guy said. You gamble, you don't go out with girls. Sex is five minutes, when I was your age. I came before I got in the girl, when I was your age.

Not me, the kid said.

Stop it now, the old guy said. I'm telling you 'cause I like you. You're a good-looking guy. I'm telling you: don't gamble!

Okay, the kid said, giving me the wink and a nod.

The old guy went back to the pony tables.

The kid turned to me, said, Can you believe that? That guy telling me what to do?

Before I could respond, Ms. Chandler appeared.

If she was a fish, she was an Angelfish.

She was dressed in a red sort of mesh thing, a dress I guess it was, with a gray thing on her shoulders that on closer inspection turned out to be the smallest jacket in the world. It had arms all right, but they stopped right after the shoulders. And the rest of it went down to maybe a couple inches below the collarbone. And it had three big buttons. There's no reason I would have known it, but to me it said: high fashion. Had to be. It was too ridiculous to be anything else.

Somehow it made her look good. But then, everything she wore made her look good.

Why this place? I asked.

I like the atmosphere, she said.

I looked across the rail to the sports betting area, surveyed the local fauna. A heady mixture of graying paunchy old men with bifocals and racing forms, and slightly younger paunchy middle-aged guys with bifocals and racing forms. Didn't see the black kid anywhere. Maybe he'd decided to heed the old man's advice.

And also, she said, it is very unlikely that anyone here will overhear us.

I looked the length and breadth of the bar. Her theory seemed to hold water. We were alone. Except for Bob.

Except for Bob, I said. Just kidding, I said. Bob is very discreet. She looked at him, polishing glasses at the far end of the bar. She frowned.

But it was all right. Bob loved to banter when I was there alone, but respectfully kept his distance in the presence of my slinky client. Though I could hear, word for word, the salacious comments I'd get from him once she left. That was the comfort of a good bar, a good bartender. No surprises.

Okay, she said. So. You have some news for me?

I seem to have traced your sister to a trailer park somewhere north of Red Rock. Not positive. But that's the word I got.

The word I got, she said. You know, Mr. Redman, it's curious. How one minute you're talking like a New York lawyer and the next like some low-rent gangster.

Low-rent gangster, I said. You've got a way with a phrase yourself. Thank you.

Truth is, I've been both. Well, the lawyer bit definitely. I was never a gangster. But before the law thing, before law school, before college even, I spent some years.

You spent some years.

Hanging with the less privileged, if you will.

Hanging with the less privileged.

I did that on purpose. See, you can mix the two up in the same sentence.

She smiled. It was a real, warm, genuine smile, it seemed to me.

Progress, I thought. I'm making progress.

Tell me about this trailer park, she said, the smile gone.

I don't know anything about it, yet, I said. I'm heading out there tomorrow. I just hear that's where she is. Maybe she is, maybe she isn't. If she is, maybe she'll be there. Maybe she won't.

Thank you, Mr. Redman. As ever, you inspire confidence.

No misinformation. Only the facts, Ma'am.

Only the facts, she echoed, placing her hand playfully on my knee, and quickly removing it.

It was enough. I was all a-tingle.

But I couldn't let my imagination get away with me. God knew what she'd meant by that. If anything. And anyway, I had work to do. Poker work. Investigation work. Dad work. Couldn't afford to get distracted.

37.

THERE WAS A DROUGHT IN VEGAS, a drought even by desert standards. Rows of wilting blackened cacti, stranded like syphilitic dicks in the sand. I saw a sign for food and fuel, scrambled the rented Mini Cooper on to a dirt road off the highway to Kick-Ass Gas, two unsmiling guys with beards to their belt buckles pumping the gas and sliming my perfectly clean windshield with a rag. They were wearing old-style Western holsters, with big-ass guns in them. This was a first for me. The gunslinging gas station attendant.

I was five miles down the road before I noticed the gas gauge was at half full. I'd paid for a full tank. But turning back to protest seemed not only time-wasting, but possibly suicidal. I stepped on the pedal. Get the fuck there and get the job done.

Then again, I got thirsty. Or cold feet. Which often are the same thing. I spotted a bar with a shed-like air and a couple of motorcycles parked outside. The sign said *Sam's Pizza.*

Inside, the walls were paneled with 1950s rec-room wood. On the wall was a sign:

TODAY'S MENU
TWO CHOICES:
*TAKE IT
*LEAVE IT

There was an old wooden double telephone booth with another sign on it:

No Phone.

The tables were tiny and round, faded red gingham tablecloths covered in thick yellowed plastic. Hanging from the ceiling on each side of the bar were two ridiculous Tyrolean puppets, holding lanterns.

It seemed like just the place.

The bartender looked like Elliott Gould as a young man: pursed-lip smile, equal parts contempt, amusement and anal discomfort. I introduced myself and my needs:

Redman, I said. I'll have a whiskey, double.

Normally I'd ask for scotch. But here the word *whiskey* seemed right.

James, he introduced himself. Gotcha.

He turned and grabbed a bottle. It didn't seem to matter which one.

Pleased to meet you, James, I said.

The only other customers were two girls sporting cutoff denims halfway up their butt cheeks, and a willowy guy with spiky orange hair. One of the girls had the Big Hair and the other was doing the shaved head thing. The shaved-head girl was absurdly elongated. Six foot two if she was an inch, with a long horse's face, and legs so skinny her knees looked like boles on a banyan tree. Big Hair was short and plump and wearing a white mesh shirt tied up under pendulous breasts. The orange hair guy leaned on the bar with an air of calculated detachment.

They were talking about crossword puzzles.

I like the *Times*, said the orange hair guy.

Six-letter word for when Earth Days occur? said Big Hair.

Leap year? said the bald one.

Jesus, Suzy, said Big Hair.

Monday?

At least that one has six letters.

So that's it, right?

These ones are too easy, said the guy.

So what's the answer, smart-ass? said Big Hair, taking an enormous slug off a very large stein of dark beer.

That's not the point, he said, lighting a cigarillo. The point is, life is short. A good crossword puzzle exercises the mind. A lousy one is like watching TV. It's just you waiting for death.

Speak for yourself, said Big Hair.

I know, I know, said the bald one. Decade. It's once every ten years, right?

James, turning back with my drink, leaned over and drawled at me, with a knowing nod at the threesome:

I can't even count to three.

Yes, it was my kind of place.

I hung for a while. Fortified myself for whatever was to come. Why I was worried, I had no idea. Just one of those random foreboding things. I was on my third whiskey when the crossword trio left the joint. I heard the gravel-strewn roar of a badly maintained exhaust system. So it was just me and James. I asked him if he knew of a trailer park near here.

Best-Bilt Homes? he asked.

I don't know. Probably.

It's off the road a bit. I'll show you.

He drew me a map on a napkin. It was only five miles away. But the last two were on a pretty bad dirt road, he warned me.

Okay, I said. I think I can handle it.

You look like the kind of guy can handle it, he said.

Thanks. I'll try not to misplace your confidence.

Front pocket, he said.

What?

Put it in your front pocket. Less likely to lose it.

38.

THE TRAILER WAS ONE OF THOSE LOW-SLUNG NONDESCRIPT things. Someone had taken the trouble to plant a tiny lawn in front. On second look, someone had taken the trouble to plant some grass-colored gravel out front. There was a Buick Electra parked there. I tried to remember when was the last year Buick made an Electra. Somewhere around the Crimean War, I was guessing. I eased the Mini Cooper into the drive. The front door was painted orange. Someone's idea of distinctive, out here in the land of indistinction. I pressed the buzzer. Chimes inside. Tasteful.

I waited a minute. Pressed again.

No answer.

I walked around the side of the trailer. I wanted to be discreet, but the random cacti and scrub offered no cover. I didn't think crawling would work, and anyway, I wasn't about to sacrifice my two-hundred-dollar custom-tailored one hundred percent cotton shirt—a remnant of the big-shot lawyer days—to just any saguaro. No, I'd just have to take my chances on Mrs. Widow-Next-Door-Without-A-Life calling the cops. If she did, I'd just have to feel good about providing her day, her month, her life, a welcome frisson.

The trailers were close together. A dog barking, somewhere. Small and insistent. Otherwise, not a sound. A fence between the trailers, towards the back. Another sign these mobile homes hadn't been mobile for a while.

The fence had a gate. It wasn't locked. I reached over and lifted the latch. Swung it open.

I was sweating like a hog in the insistent sun.

In the backyard was a pool, small but real, scary blue and shimmering. It took up most of the yard. It was a very small yard.

Reclining on a plastic lounge chair was a woman.

I walked over.

She was wearing enormous reflective sunglasses. A floppy cotton hat. And a raincoat.

It looked like a nice raincoat. Long. Down to her ankles. Double-breasted. A nice teal color. Wide collars. Slightly retro. Way too classy, in fact, for the surroundings.

Speaking of the surroundings, she was wearing a raincoat. In the desert.

I stood over her. She didn't move. I couldn't tell, behind the shades, whether she was awake. Hell, I couldn't tell if she was alive.

The coat was buttoned. Her feet were bare. Tanning the feet, I guessed.

I cleared my throat.

Her head lifted an inch.

Excuse me, I said.

Who are you? she asked in a low voice, slurred with recent sleep, or possibly barbiturates. She was strangely calm. As if accustomed to unknown men showing up poolside unannounced. Which contributed to the barbiturate hypothesis.

Rick Redman, I said. I'm an investigator.

I see, she said, shifting herself up another inch.

The raincoat appeared to be sticking to the lawn chair. She tugged at it. The lapels fell open. The view was promising. Pale, freckled skin.

Enough to make me wonder. Whether she had anything on underneath. No evidence of it. Which could be good. Or bad. There was only one way to find out. And this was not the moment to try it.

I averted my eyes. A little late, but I hoped the gesture would curry me favor.

Ms. Eloise, or whoever she was, gazed at me through the shades. Or at least I assumed she was gazing at me through the shades. Hard to tell. Through the shades.

I thought about that expression. Curry favor. What did Indian food have to do with goodwill? I made a note to look it up.

There was something floating in the pool. It looked like a dead rodent. I wasn't sure. The sun was too bright. It kept flickering in the blue, appearing and vanishing. Maybe it was a live rodent.

Maybe it wasn't there at all.

And what, she said at last, might you be investigating?

Well, I said, you, actually.

She gave a short laugh. It seemed to exhaust her last reserves. Her head plummeted back into the comfort of the slatted plastic chair.

Me? she said.

She fished in the pocket of her raincoat. Pulled out a pack of cigarettes. Pulled one out. Lit it with a Zippo.

Mind if I cadge one of those? I asked.

Sharing vices is good for establishing rapport with the subject. It's in the manual.

She tugged her coat around, searched the other pocket. Pulled out a pack of Gitanes, tossed it to me.

You can have these, she said. I don't smoke them.

I got a friend who does, I said, putting the pack in my shirt pocket. Meanwhile, do you mind if I have one of those?

You're a pushy bastard, Mr. Investigator, she said, flinging a Benson & Hedges at me. I'll give you that.

Thank you, I said. I lit the smoke. Took a haul. I almost gagged. They were full strength. No ultralights for this lady. Ah, I said to myself. Instant black lung.

Anyway, I said, once we were each ensconced in our respective cloud of haze, yes, you. If you're who I think you are. And I think you are. Your sister asked me to find you.

Louise? she said, still languorous. You're kidding, right?

Why would I be kidding? I asked.

Listen, Richard—

Rick, I interrupted.

Rick. Ricky. Dick. Listen, you just appeared uninvited in my back-yard. You claim you've been hired to find me. You found me. I gave you a cigarette. Now get the fuck out of here. Okay?

This seemed uncalled-for. But she'd said it in the same calm, slow monotone, and something about the contrast between the words and the voice gave it a gravity hard to resist.

Nevertheless, I gathered up my gumption. Prepared to protest.

Can I just ask you one thing? I said.

She turned her head. I could see in her shades the sharp elliptical reflection of my face. Hey, I thought. Not that bad. Could pass for a pretty handsome guy. If the world were convex.

She nodded. Almost imperceptibly.

Do you mind if I tell your sister where you are? I continued. She seems genuinely concerned.

I got the short sharp laugh again.

I took it as a yes.

So, I said. I can tell her you're all right? Everything's okay?

You can tell her anything you like.

Okay. All right. I guess I've done my job. Is this your place?

She said nothing.

You live here? I insisted.

More silence.

You know, I said, we couldn't find any records of you anywhere. Made it kind of hard to track you down. If you don't mind my asking, did you change your name?

Silence.

Do you have something you need to hide from?

She didn't move an eyelash. Or at least, that was my impression. I couldn't see her eyelashes. Behind the shades.

Uh, I guess that might be kind of personal, I said. I'm sorry. But do you mind if I ask you one last question? Then I'll leave. Promise.

She raised her sunglasses. Turned her gimlet eye to mine. It was more than a little disconcerting. I mean, I love a green-eyed girl. I really do. Add some copper-colored hair, and I'm in instant love. But this eye. This was a splintered eye. It was mostly green, but there was a sliver, a narrow wedge, of red in it. Like a splinter. A splintered eye. For some reason it scared the hell out of me.

Um, I said, please tell me if I'm being intrusive. Again. But I was wondering. Well, I was wondering about, I was wondering, why the raincoat? In the desert. I mean, the shades, of course, make perfect sense. It's the desert. But a raincoat?

She raised that eye again. Her disinterest was growing more palpable by the second.

Have you ever heard of lupus? she asked.

Right, I thought. Allergic to the sun, Louise had said. I'd meant to do some research.

No, I lied.

She lowered the shades.

Well, I hope you're doing well, I said. Your health, I mean. Your sister will want to know.

I'm fine, she said.

Another long silence ensued.

I wasn't going to get anything else out of her. Hey, I'd been paid to find her. I'd found her. What else did I have to do? I wasn't being paid to take on the Cyclops, after all. Or was it the Sphinx? The one with the riddles.

While I was thusly ruminating, Ms. Chandler or some other name, possibly of Russian origin, pulled her raincoat tightly around her promising self, slipped on a pair of brightly colored and clearly designer-designed sandals, and walked languidly to the back door of the trailer she, to all appearances, called home. She turned. Gave me a Look. The Look said: Go away.

I followed the instruction. As I turned the corner, I glanced back. She hadn't moved an inch.

In the car, I reflected on what I'd seen. Not much, given the costume. Kind of odd, that. I mean, if you're allergic to the sun, or whatever it was, why be in the sun at all?

And how far she'd fallen, it seemed. That fancy house in Henderson, to this? There surely was a story to tell.

It was her, though. I didn't have a doubt. The chin. The mouth. The manner. The calves. It was all Louise.

So I'd done it. Found the sister.

Life wasn't all that bad after all, it seemed.

39

ON THE WAY BACK TO TOWN, I called Louise Chandler. Told her I had some news. We should meet, I said. She suggested a baroque little faux bistro on some street I'd never heard of. It was becoming clear that she knew Vegas better than I did. I wasn't sure that this was a good sign.

She was late. I wasn't surprised. I took a stool at the bar and spent the time downing a few glasses of fairly potable wine.

After a suitable half-hour interval, she made her entrance.

She was wearing a black silk dress with a keyhole neckline, the aperture just big enough to allow me to confirm it again: She had curve. She took the stool to my right. I liked that she wasn't averse to sitting at the bar.

After the usual informalities, I came to the point.

I found her, I said.

Yes?

She seemed almost disappointed.

I did.

Where?

Out in the sticks somewhere. North of Red Rock, like I said. A trailer park. Crappy Desert Homes. Bacon in the Sun. Something like that.

Are you serious, Mr. Redman? You don't remember the name of the place?

It'll come back to me. Don't worry. And anyway, I have it written down somewhere.

Somewhere?

Sure. Somewhere. And anyway, I know how to get there.

Mr. Redman, I'm not finding this very reassuring. How many drinks have you had?

Please, call me Rick. And I'm only drinking wine. Better for the digestion.

Is that your first bottle? she asked, nodding towards the half-empty vessel at my left elbow.

I guess it's the second, I said, unwilling, for once, to tell an unnecessary lie. You were late.

Half an hour, she said.

Forty minutes, I cleverly retorted. And anyway, the first one's just a warm-up. Gets me normal.

She looked at me for a while. Thinking, she seemed to be.

I see, she said slowly.

I tried to read her. Couldn't do it. Inscrutable, she was. Hard to scrute.

I was just beginning to wonder why my drinking habits seemed to be of more interest to her than her long-lost sister, when she got back to the topic.

How was she? she asked.

That's hard to say.

What do you mean?

I told her the tale. The pool chair. The hat. The shades. The raincoat.

That seems a bit strange, she said.

A bit, I replied. Yes. Eccentric, at least.

She always liked to be different.

She seems to be succeeding.

Was her . . . friend there?

If he was, she wasn't letting on.

She sank into thought. I sank into my Chardonnay. The waitress came by and lit the little candle in the glass. Once she'd left, Louise bent over and blew it out.

Not in a mood for atmosphere? I asked.

She ignored me. Or didn't hear. She was looking at the bottles neatly tiered behind the bar. Lost in a thought. Or many.

I watched an old couple at the next table. Neither of them had said a word to the other. The old man was folding his napkin into what looked like an origami moose. The lady was staring into her drink.

So, I said to Ms. Chandler after a while. Job over?

I suspect not, she said. I need to think about it.

Ah, thinking, I said. I used to have that luxury.

Sometimes, Mr. Redman, it is appropriate to have feelings.

I'm not sure I follow you. And it's Rick. Please.

Mr. Redman, we may not have been close, Eloise and I. We may be estranged, or whatever is the proper term. But she is my sister. She is family. And what you are telling me causes me concern. There is something wrong. It is obvious, is it not?

Well, I don't know. But I apologize if I seem too frivolous. It's just my way. I understand your concern.

Apology accepted.

And anyway, it depends on what you mean by wrong. She's alive, it appears. She isn't chained in some basement being tortured by a sadistic clown. Or at least she wasn't this afternoon.

Mr. Redman, she said sharply. Please.

Anyway, the place for sure didn't have a basement.

That's enough.

Sorry. Can't help myself. Sorry.

It is all right, Mr. Redman. I'm getting used to your ways.

She said it with a small smile.

I appreciate that, I said. But anyway, I can see what you mean. She's gone from that nice house to a trailer park. Not normally a sign of— what's the word? Progress.

The smile was gone as fast as it had appeared. I wondered whether I had imagined it.

We need to have a plan, she said.

A plan?

Yes. A plan.

How about you plan to go out there and talk to your sister? Ask her if everything's okay. Kiss and make up.

I can't do that.

Why not?

Ms. Chandler inspected the scotch section behind the bar for a while.

There are things I haven't told you, she said.

Oh my, I replied. You shock me. You mean there are . . . secrets?

All right. All right. I know you're not naïve.

Thanks for that.

Of course you knew I wasn't telling you everything.

I had a hunch. But nobody's paying me to follow it up.

It's about Vladimir.

Ah. Then you do know him.

I know his name.

Cherchez l'homme, I said.

I'm afraid of him.

Ah.

He's not a pleasant man, I understand.

Few of us are.

Yes, she replied with a bit too much alacrity. But he is less pleasant than most.

Ms. Chandler, I said. I love your company. The wine is . . . well, it's potable, anyway. But I must admit I would prefer it if you . . . how to put it? . . . got to the point? Saves so much time, you know.

All right, Mr. Redman.

Is there any way I can get you to call me Rick?

No.

All right, then.

Mr. Redman, do you remember the Joel Steinberg case?

Who doesn't?

The man who beat that woman nearly to death, killed their child, and still she clung to him?

Yes, yes. Sort of a Stockholm syndrome thing.

Yes. Well, my fear is that Eloise is involved in that kind of relationship.

She seemed rather self-confident, I said.

Meaning?

Hard to see her being in thrall to someone who's abusing her.

Be that as it may, Mr. Redman—

Rick, please.

I have my reasons.

Such as?

When I first met her friend, he seemed—

Oh, so you have met him?

—very nice. He had a Russian accent, but he dressed very well. He was always talking about this business he was starting. He was very enthusiastic.

What kind of business?

Investments, he said.

What kind of investments?

He didn't say.

Hmm. Kind of like import-export?

What do you mean?

Well, first of all, it doesn't mean anything, investments. All that says is somebody's putting up some money for something. It could be women's shoes. Or truffles from Saudi Arabia. Could be cocaine from Colombia. Same as with import-export. That used to be code for: 'I'm with the CIA, by the way.' Or something of that nature.

Truffles from Saudi Arabia?

Long story. Didn't work. Too much sand.

I think you've lost me.

In the truffles. Sand in the truffles. Couldn't get it out. I suppose we should have figured that might be a problem.

We? You were involved in importing truffles from Saudi Arabia?

I told you, long story. I'll tell it to you sometime. What can I say? I met a guy at a poker game. Armenian. Full of ideas. He was looking for investors.

Investors to import truffles from Saudi Arabia. And you trusted this man?

Trust, but verify, as me and Brezhnev always say. Well, he used to. He's dead. It's just me now. There really were truffles. And they were way cheaper than the Italian. Anyway, see what I mean? Import-export. Never know what it means.

Was there an export part?

Dollars. To an offshore account.

My, Mr. Redman, you do seem to know a lot of things.

It's my curse, I said, contemplating the long lean line of her thigh as she recrossed her legs.

Why is that?

My brain never shuts off. It's always making another connection. Even in my sleep. I have the weirdest dreams . . .

I put my hand lightly on her leg. A little test case.

She let it stay there for a beat or two. Enough to tell me something. I wasn't exactly sure what it was, though.

Perhaps we'll leave your dreams for another day, she said, pulling down her skirt, which, incidentally, or not so incidentally, served to brush my hand away. She reached for her purse.

Ms. Chandler, I protested. We haven't finished talking about Vladimir.

Yes, yes, she said, standing up. But you know enough for now. He's an unsavory character. I want you to find out if Eloise is still with him. And if not, where he is.

You can't just drop by and ask?

No, I can't, she said, heading for the exit.

As she walked away, I thought about how much she hadn't told me. Why she thought Eloise was in thrall to this guy. Stockholm syndrome. That was a prisoner thing. The captive becomes emotionally attached to the captor.

Eloise hadn't looked particularly imprisoned.

No more than anyone else living in a trailer park.

And she was awfully feisty, for someone supposedly susceptible to thralldom.

Louise Chandler swept through the door.

From the rear, she still made a good impression.

40.

THE PHONE RANG. I stuffed a pillow over my head. It didn't do a thing. I'd been spoiled by down pillows. Down pillows muffle sound. Polyester doesn't.

I told the phone to stop.

It wouldn't listen to me.

I rolled over with a groan.

I picked up the phone.

Redman, I gargled.

Daddy!

It was my Kelley. The fog lifted immediately.

How are you, beautiful? I asked.

I'm great, and better yet, I'm here.

Here?

In Las Vegas! With Peter!

You're joking.

Would I tell a joke?

Of course not. What are you doing here?

We came to keep you out of trouble, Daddy, what do you think? And help out with all your exciting investigations.

Strangely enough, I actually do have an investigation going.

Wow. Peter'll be thrilled.

And very useful too, I'm sure.

Does it have anything to do with old movies?

Not that I'm aware of.

'Cause that's where he'd be really helpful.

Okay, if an old movie angle comes up, I'll let you guys know.

Thanks, Dad. Anyway, come on over. I'm going food shopping. We can make a feast.

Sounds good to me. But where are you?

We're at a friend of Peter's house. He loaned it to us. He's in Thailand looking for boys on the beach.

Charming. What's the address?

She gave me the address. I dragged myself out of bed. Avoided the mirror.

On the way, I remembered about Madeleine. Kelley's half sister, I supposed. Kelley would need to know. But then I'd have to explain. And I didn't have an explanation.

Maybe I could do the Redman thing.

Procrastinate.

The place they'd borrowed was a tiny one-story adobe thing on the edge of the desert, in a poor part of town. It was the first time I'd seen that there was a poor part of town. But I guess the help had to live somewhere. Every surface in the place was occupied by kitschy stuff: 1950s girlie ashtrays, lamps in the shape of bulgy propeller-driven airplanes, bright orange plastic dinner plates, neatly stacked. Hundreds of porcelain dolls' heads. The usual desert decor.

I got the stuff, said Kelley, holding up a plastic bag.

I looked in. Oh, nice. Baby bok choy. Fresh ginger and garlic. Fine rice noodles.

Aha, I said. Chinese soup.

It was our favorite thing to make. One of the few things that had nothing but good memories attached.

They have grocery stores in Vegas?

If you know where to look, said Kelley with a knowing wink.

I had no idea what the wink meant.

I minced the garlic. Kelley chopped the ginger. Peter told us about Anna Nicole Smith's autopsy report.

I mixed the ginger and garlic in soy sauce, rice vinegar and sesame oil. I put on the wok. Kelley chopped up some chicken. I sliced some shiitakes and green onions. Peter, reluctantly, soaked the rice noodles. I prepared the bok choy. Heated up some olive oil in the wok.

Okay, olive oil isn't Chinese. So sue me.

I secretly surveyed the kitchen for booze, in the guise of looking for spices. I managed to open enough cabinets to find a bottle of gin. Peter liked gin. He liked to mix ridiculous colorful cocktails with it.

I surreptitiously poured some into my glass of seltzer.

Kelley was no naïf. She knew my proclivities. But I preferred to keep them from her as much as I could. She had enough to deal with.

I heated a gallon of chicken stock in a robin's egg blue cast-iron pot. Kelley stirred the sauce into the wok. Once the cloud of ginger and garlic flavors became almost overwhelming, she added the chicken, stirred it a bit, added the vegetables and just enough Asian chili oil to give the stuff a nice bite.

You know, said Peter, feigning wistfulness. We really should become vegetarians.

You want me to pull the chicken out now? asked Kelley.

You'd have to take all the liquid out, too, I said. It's chicken stock.

Darn it, said Peter. I feel so sad.

What about? I asked.

The poor chickens, he said. I used to have pet chickens, you know.

You did?

Yes, Kelley said. He really did.

Elvis and Baby, said Peter.

Who?

Those were their names. Elvis and Baby. They were really ugly at first. Then they got cute. Then they started eating everything. And I mean *every*thing.

Let's not go there, I said.

And then they got ugly again. Anyway, my point is, you don't think about the poor chicken's soul. You just cut it up and dump it in the pot.

I do so think about chickens' souls, said Kelley.

Not nearly enough, said Peter.

If I promise to think more about chicken souls, can we finish making the soup?

Yes! said Peter. Victory at last. Chicken souls for the soup.

Oh my God, I said. You didn't do all that just to set up that lame pun, did you?

Of course not, said Peter. It just came to me now.

We poured the sizzling contents of the wok into the boiling chicken stock. It roiled. It gave off the heavenly scent of everything good about having children. Family. An anchor in the heaving world.

So, Dadster, Kelley said. How's it going?

I don't know, I said. Bad. Depressing.

Like the time you cut your fingernails too short? Kelley laughed. You complained about that for a week.

We were so worried, said Peter.

The suicide watch, said Kelley.

And the time he cut his thumb slicing onions? said Peter.

Oh my God, said Kelley, that scream.

I called 411, said Peter.

Unfortunately, said Kelley, they had no information.

I took it all with a smile. Your children, of course, know you better than yourself. Which doesn't mean you believe them when they tell you about it.

I thought about the Melissa years. How Kelley kept me alive. Melissa alive. With her humor and good grace. Maybe, I thought, it had a bad side. Allowed me to indulge my depressions, my negativity. Knowing Kelley would always be there to bring me back to reality. Or at least a funny version of it.

We sat on the couch. A piece of plywood on bricks stood in for a coffee table. I put the bowls on the plywood. I put noodles in the bottom of the bowls. Peter ostentatiously ladled out the soup from an enormous mango-colored tureen.

So how's your big case going, Daddy? Kelley asked.

Yeah, Daddy, said Peter, leaning forward. Tell us all about it. Got any pictures we can see? Naked ladies? Mangled bodies? Naked *men*?

It's not so interesting, I laughed. Just a missing persons case. Or something like that.

Oh, you're holding something back, said Peter, I can tell you are. Come on, we're family. You can share. Who's missing?

Somebody's sister.

A sister. Then there has to be a man involved. Tell me there's a man involved. Tell me he's tall and Bulgarian.

Russian, actually. But I don't know if he has a mustache.

Russian. That's okay. He has to have a hairy chest, though.

I'll let you know. If I ever meet him. The Russians I've been dealing with so far, well, I can't tell you if they have a hairy chest. But I'm quite sure they aren't your type.

Ooh, said Peter. Mystery. Tell me more.

I told them about Andrei and Anatoly. How Brendan was being drawn into their world. How worried I was about him. Kelley and Peter knew Brendan, of course. He was Kelley's uncle, now that I thought of it. She liked him.

Daddy, said Peter. What's wrong with you? It's so obvious.

What's so obvious?

There's nothing mysterious about it. They're showing him the town. The other side of town, if you know what I mean.

I don't know, I said. I mean, I know what you mean. And yes, they are. Harmless, I'm sure. But I'm not sure I know much of anything these days.

Daddy! said Kelley. Did you cut yourself again?

Oh, Daddy, said Peter. Introduce me. Don't even introduce me. All I need is to see them. Then I'll know everything.

Okay, I said, laughing, next time I get a chance, I'll point them out. You're family, after all.

Oh, squealed Peter. Thank you, thank you.

He gave me an enormous squishy hug.

I tolerated it. I loved Peter. I really did think of him as family. But I wasn't sure how I felt about big squishy man hugs, in the best of circumstances.

Anyway, I said. I don't blame Brendan. He's doing his thing. He's allowed. He's an adult.

Well . . . said Peter, officially, I guess.

And anyway, nothing I could say would change what he wants to do. He's very willful, you know. In spite of . . . the other things.

What other things?

Oh, come on, I said. This isn't fun. Let's get back to having fun.

We got back to having fun. We ate the soup. Peter stole more than his share of the shiitakes. I took more of the meat. Kelley was happy with the noodles.

Peter was telling a story. I wasn't listening.

I was ruminating. I was thinking about Dani from Oklahoma. The scent of apricots. Matt was out of town, she'd said. Matt and the kids. For a week. Was the week over? There was no way of knowing.

Afterwards, Peter was saying, we had a little party. There were muffins. Somebody said, I want a muffin. I looked at the security guard. Take *him!* I said. He's well baked. *And* available!

You couldn't stop him when he got like this. I went to the kitchen to pour myself a drink.

I'll have a Grey Goose, said Peter, on the rocks, dirty, with, ah, one olive.

Whatever that means, I said. I'll do what I can do.

I know it'll be enough, Daddy, he said.

Peter, said Kelley, it's time to calm down.

Oh dear, he said. I guess you're right.

For some reason I began thinking about Henderson. Dani. How she'd put the children's toys away. Quickly. Nervously. Like she didn't want me to think of her as a mother.

Everything had screamed desire.

Of course, I'd made that mistake before. Wishful thinking. Followed by swift humiliation.

I was willing to risk it though. The navel ring. Those tight abs. But I'd need an excuse, to just show up again. These Midwestern girls, they stand on ceremony. I needed a hook.

Basements, I said, returning with the drinks.

All right, Peter said. Your turn. What about basements?

Seems like everything important's in a basement.

I think you may need to clarify, said Peter.

Yeah, Dadski, said Kelley. What's this all about?

The Brighton Beach game was in a basement, I said.

O-kaaay.

And.

Yeeesss?

I'm sure there are others. Dani said something about a basement.

Who's Danny?

Never mind. Somebody I interviewed.

Sure, Dadster. Anyway. I used to live in the basement.

When you were trying to avoid . . . I started.

You can stop there, she said.

I'm sorry. I know. I'm sorry.

So, she said, what are they? The other basements. Not ours. The others.

I'm quite certain some other basements will turn up, I said.

Funny how they do that, she said.

You're sitting in a bar, said Peter.

Minding your own business, said Kelley.

In walks a basement.

As though it owned the place.

Sits on the stool next to you.

Just shoves right in there.

God, it pisses you off.

They can be so presumptuous.

Those damn basements.

All right, all right, I said. All this basement talk. How did this start?

The one with Danny in it.

That's the one. Well, I was just thinking, when she told me about overhearing Vladimir talk about the bartender?

Dadster, what the hell are you talking about?

She said they were in the basement.

Who?

Eloise and Vladimir. When she overheard them. She said they were in the basement.

Hello? said Kelley. Interpreter, please?

In a minute, said Peter. We need to get to the bottom of this.

Har, I said.

And? asked Kelley.

I never went to the basement. I mean, I didn't have a search warrant or anything. But I could have asked. I don't know. It just seems like maybe there was something there.

Where?

In Henderson.

Henderson's about a thirty-minute cab ride from here.

I think I could do it in twenty-eight. With the right driver.

Dadminton?

Yes, my dear?

Sometimes I think there may yet be hope for you.

You're the sweetest, I said.

Brownie? she asked.

The ones with the Nutella sauce? Peter replied.

Yup.

Ohhhh, baby.

We ate. We laughed.

This was the life.

A life that was ever receding from my grasp.

41.

When I got back to the motel, nobody was there. I lay back on the sectional, closed my eyes. There was something about spending time with Kelley. It took the tension away. I dreamt of dreamier days. Life with Kelley and Melissa. Before Melissa's Monster intervened. Melissa, lovely and evanescent. I hadn't yet discovered what the evanescence meant. That she couldn't face her demons. That she'd needed to anesthetize herself. But Kelley was everywhere, distracting me, making me dance to Frank Sinatra singing 'Chicago.' That toddlin' town. Jokes, pictures, stories. Homemade plays with her friends. Reading silly books to me. As though she were the parent, I the child . . .

Butch shook me awake.

Hunh? I said.

We got a meet, he said.

What meet?

With the Russkies.

Yeah? What about it?

They called.

They called you?

No, they called you. I picked up your cell. You were long gone.

Isn't that an invasion of privacy?

So sue me.

I'll definitely take that option under consideration. What did they say?

It's at some bar called the Shining Mullet or something.

Thanks for your help.

You can't miss it, he said, it's right across from the place that says My Horse Shall Be Called a Horse of Prayer, For All Peoples.

What?

Just a couple doors down from Furry Paws.

What?

Furry Paws Pet Supplies. And, by the way, they have free delivery.

The horse place?

Furry Paws.

Thank God for America.

Amen.

Find me a pet store with free delivery in Bulgaria.

Exactly. Brendan'll meet us there.

Turned out the joint wasn't that far away. We could walk it. Though the distance was magnified by the fact that the hundred-twenty-degree-in-the-shade trek was across acres of parking lot and a four-lane highway. I slogged across the softening asphalt. I bitched. I whined. I caviled. I'd have ululated. If I'd known how.

Butch ignored me.

The place was a cheesy joint that some of the less affluent WSOP players stayed at because you could get a room for sixty bucks a night. In Vegas, as elsewhere, you can reliably estimate the cheese factor from the room rate. If that wasn't enough, you could tell from the waitresses: they were trying way too hard. And not looking too good.

We tracked down Brendan at the bar. He was wearing some kind of zoot suit and a scarf thing that you might have seen on Cary Grant in 1953. I provisionally refrained from comment.

We had some time to kill before the meet, so we checked out the poker room. The Bellagio it wasn't. On the floor next to the manager's booth was an empty blue plastic milk bottle case. The kind you made bookshelves with in college. On the empty crate was taped a crudely hand-lettered cardboard sign that said:

DO NOT REMOVE FROM THE POKER ROOM!

Okay, I said. I'll resist the temptation.

The biggest game going was 1–2 no limit, but Michael the floor man assured us the place was packed with donkeys, and money could be made. That didn't turn out to be entirely accurate. Apart from a couple of frat boys who would call you down with anything but who packed up early to go party, the players were pretty decent. Nevertheless, I managed to hit a good run of cards and pick up a few hundred dollars before trekking back over to the bar.

Three doubles in, the Russkies still hadn't arrived.

We took a table. Brendan was talking about some movie he'd seen. Something about a guy who did a thing, a girl who got involved, shit happening. The girl gets killed. Turns out she was a guy.

Sounds like a piece of shit, I said. The real world isn't like that. And where the fuck are your friends?

But it's based on real events, he said.

Based on real events. Tell you the truth, sometimes I think my life is based on real events. But most of the time I think it isn't. And by the way, where the fuck are your friends?

They'll be here.

That wasn't the question.

Did I ever tell you that you get obnoxious when you drink? he said.

That's assertive of you, I said. You're showing improvement. And no, you haven't. Nor has anyone else. In fact, I am renowned city-wide for the friendliness of my exuberation. I mean inebriation. The exuberosity of my imbibation.

Yeah, Butch interjected. Not just the city, either. Jersey, too.

Even in Jersey, I agreed. They know me well in Asbury Park.

Seaside Heights, said Butch.

Cape May, I interjected. All the way to the bottom. And by the way, I said to Brendan, what's with that suit? You don't wear suits.

And you sure as hell don't wear *that* kind of suit, said Butch.

I have no idea what you guys are talking about, said Brendan.

Uh, the wide lapels? I said.

The tight ankles? said Butch.

Since when do you guys give a shit about what I wear? he said.

It's one thing to hang out with a bunch of Russian scumbags, said Butch. It's another thing to become one.

Fuck you, said Brendan. I'm going out for a smoke.

That reminds me, I said. Here.

I tossed him the crumpled pack of Gitanes.

Since when do you smoke these? he asked.

I don't. That's why I'm giving them to you. I got them from the sister.

The sister?

Eloise.

What . . . he began. Headed outside for his smoke.

We were spared further inanity by the appearance of the Russian Delegation. Evgeny waddled in the lead. For the first time I noticed that, while his torso was almost completely tubular from top to bottom, his extremities, his legs and arms, were tiny sticklike things, like Maxie Veinberg's. I wondered how he kept himself upright. Didn't you need some balance from the extremities? That tightrope walker's pole thing?

Following Evgeny were a couple of guys I hadn't seen before. A skinny fellow with wispy strands of straw-blond hair, a cleft chin and an air of utter imbecility. He had a long Roman/Armenian nose. Might have been handsome if it weren't for the hair, the slack facial expression and the fact that he looked like a child molester. The other guy had gray hair flecked with white, a receding chin, a turtleneck—who the hell wears a turtleneck anymore?—a stocky build and a menacing air. The kind of immovable cubic gentleman who, should the occasion arise, most definitely was not letting you leave the room.

No Andrei.

No Anatoly.

Gentlemen! cried Evgeny in his heartiest bellow. So goood to see you!

He extended a foreshortened appendage.

I took it manfully, shook it respectfully.

He introduced his companions: Ziggie, he said, and Manfred.

Ziggie was the skinny guy. I could see how he got the name. Never a dull moment, I figured, with this guy at the party. Way Ziggie wid it. Manfred, you could see, lived up to his name, too. The Teutonic bulk. The immobility. The immutable talent for following orders.

Evgeny, seated at last, let it be known with a sigh that they didn't have time for dinner. So sorry, he said with an air of genuine regret. Other business. You understand.

It was just fine with me.

Evgeny, I said, can we step aside for a minute? Something I need to talk to you about.

Sure, Rick-ay. Is alone here! Don't be worry!

Ah, okay, I said, recognizing the finality crouching behind Evgeny's jolly tone. I have something for you.

Evgeny gave me his biggest vodka smile, placed his hands on his enormous belly. I had the impression he meant to enlace his fingers. Look patrician. But his hands couldn't reach each other across the expanse.

You man of honor, Rick-ay. I know that.

I am, actually, I said. This is half of it.

I handed him the envelope.

The rest in two weeks, I said.

Is good, he said. Is good.

He handed it to Ziggie. Ziggie, without hesitation, slipped it into the back of his pants.

I'd have preferred somebody to count it in front of me. Avoid any unwarranted accusations, later. But I wasn't about to argue with Evgeny's methods.

Brendan got back from his smoke break.

Sit! Sit! Evgeny said, motioning to the chair next to him. Johnny bring drinks. Johnny!

Brendan sat gingerly in the high-backed chair. Evgeny leaned over with a grin and ruffled his hair. Brendan grimaced, like he was eight years old, enduring the indignities bestowed by a maiden aunt.

Johnny brought straight vodkas for everyone.

So, said Evgeny, we have job for you. Is small job. You do good, bigger job later. Yes?

Sounds good to me, I said. But I need to tell you right out. You know I'm a lawyer, right?

Sure, sure.

My law license is worth a lot to me. I can't be doing anything . . . shady, if you know what I mean. I can't take that kind of chance.

Rick-ay, Rick-ay. I not getting you in trouble. I get you in trouble, what good you are to me?

Okay. I hear you. But I'll have to be the judge of that. When I hear what the job is.

Sure, Rick-ay, Evgeny laughed. You be judge.

We celebrated our new business arrangement with a round or seven of vodka shots and some stuff on some bread that I took for an attempt at focaccia. The waitress made up for her lack of good looks with an excessive application of good cheer.

The business part of the meeting over, we got down to business.

Okay, Rick-ay, said Evgeny, you want job, yes?

Like I said, we'll consider a proposal.

Ah, ha, ha, went Evgeny.

I tried to maintain my seriously businesslike air through the vodka haze.

Okay, Rick-ay, Evgeny said again. Here is job. We haff friend, name Yugo. Yugo is good fellow. We work together. Do jobs. Yugo has job. Needs help. You going to help him, yes? Go see Yugo. He has something for you. Yugo tell you rest. Yugo is good fellow, also smart fellow. He has something for you. Is simple job.

Sounds basic enough, I said. If a little vague.

Though something was telling me there wasn't anything simple about this, at all. There were sure to be several layers to it that I couldn't see, and no doubt never would. Even if I took the job.

Which I more or less had to do. If I'd already paid back Evgeny in full, not to mention replenished Louise's retainer, I could see turning it down, maybe. In the present circumstances, I couldn't. And anyway, I didn't have a plausible reason to say no. I wasn't about to say, Evgeny, you guys are obviously a bunch of scumbag shakedown artists and borderline personality types or quite possibly worse and I'd prefer not to be involved with whatever unsavory scam you may be cooking up with your good friend Yugo. And anyway, wasn't the Yugo the lousiest production automobile ever built? Or was that the Lada? Same car, I think.

No, I couldn't say that.

Wouldn't be prudent.

What's my take? I asked instead.

Rick-ay, Rick-ay, Evgeny said. This not nice question. We take care each other. You do good job, I pay you good. Everybody happy. Yes?

My choice of responses was limited.

Sure, I said.

We understand, Evgeny said, nodding in Brendan's direction, you do some work, some investigation work, some . . . other kind work, that maybe useful for us, yes?

We're available, I said. To do what we can do. For a price commensurate with the task.

Comm . . . ? said Evgeny, leaning back to Manfred, who whispered in his ear. Ah, yes, of course. The pay it's by job. Hard job, the more pay. Yes.

I nodded.

This small job, he said. Small pay. But you do good, we get you next time. Bigger job. You see?

Sure, I said. I understand about client relations.

Evgeny laughed. He laughed so hard he started coughing a deep and horrible cough, a cough that descended very near his bowels. I was afraid. I was not afraid for his health, frankly. I was afraid for my appetite.

He got it under control.

When do I get the details? I asked, carefully ignoring the near-fatal expectory episode.

Evgeny confined himself to a smile. Ziggie picked at a zit on his neck. Manfred crossed his arms. They were very large arms.

You get details tomorrow, Rick-ay, Evgeny said.

Tomorrow. I thought you meant . . . Aw, forget it.

You have problem tomorrow?

Tomorrow's fine, I said. Tomorrow's beautiful. I look forward to working with you.

One of those stupid automatic responses left over from my law firm days, that last. The ironic smiles on all of their faces—even the obviously brain-challenged Ziggie—told me that it sounded just as inane to them as it did to me.

Nevertheless, Ziggie and Manfred nodded together, like mismatched bobble-head toys.

Yes, said Evgeny, near breathless from hauling himself erect. Is good. Is very good.

The delegation wobbled out.

I looked at Brendan.

I can't wait, I said. And by the way, what with all these jobs in Vegas, I don't know when I'm going to have time to play poker.

I'll help you, he said. We're a team.

Ah, I said. Yes.

It'll be good. You'll see.

You keep saying that.

42.

I WOKE UP. I was confused. When I'm confused, I call Sheila. I called Sheila. She had a cancellation. I was shocked. And pleased. Actually, I wasn't shocked. I was just pleased.

Sheila, I said. I have a daughter.

Yes, she said, calmly ignoring my use of her first name.

No. I mean, yes. I mean, another one. I have another daughter.

Ah. Something you've been keeping from me?

I just learned about her myself.

I can't say that surprises me.

No. I mean, yes. It wouldn't. But this isn't a new new one. It's an old one. I mean, she's an old one. I mean, she's eighteen, actually. She just sprung herself on me. Or at least, some beefy guy from Louisiana did.

Oh dear, she said.

Yes. Oh dear indeed. I don't know what quite to do. Quite what to do.

Why do you have to do anything?

Uh, I don't know. Now that you put it that way . . . I suppose I could do nothing. Let the chips fall . . . damn, these poker metaphors are everywhere. But no, really, I mean, first. I have to tell Kelley, don't I? I mean, she has to know, right? And vice versa. She has to know, right? The new one.

Can we give her a name?

Madeleine.

Thank you. Do you want my opinion?

No, I guess I don't. I mean, yes, but I already know what it is. You agree with me. They have to know. Right?

Right.

Okay so far. But then I get to the hard stuff. I mean, she's my daughter, I get that. I don't have a problem with that. But then what to do?

Well, I guess that depends. What about her mother? Does she have a stepfather?

Of course she has a mother. Had a mother. It seems she's deceased. I know I should know who she is. The mother. I haven't had the nerve to press her on that. She said she'll tell me at the right time. Stepfather, I don't know. I hadn't thought of that. Hasn't been any mention of one.

I see.

But it's weird. She seems so . . . poised. Together. It kind of doesn't make sense.

Why doesn't it make sense? Do you think she couldn't have thrived without you?

I paused to think.

Yes, I said. I guess you're right.

It's all about you.

As usual.

She laughed. I laughed.

Speaking of children, I said, Brendan's been acting weird lately.

Isn't he in his thirties?

Sure, sure. But I sort of think of him as a surrogate son. And he doesn't exactly act like an adult.

Okay.

And I have this guilt.

About what?

About nothing. About Brendan. I don't know where it comes from. That I feel responsible for Melissa's death? For not saving her? I don't know. They were incredibly close, you know. And then he disappeared for years. It was just after he came back that she died.

Maybe it's Brendan who feels guilty.

Yes. I think he has a big burden. That's why he can't grow up.

Tell me about this burden.

It's a long tale, I said.

You can start now. Finish some other time.

I compressed the thing as much as I could. His sister, my ex-wife by decease. How she was pursued by some sick fuck their father was in business with. How good old Dad was happy to have his daughter used as bait. How she rejected the Sick Fuck. The fear, the insecurity that built. Brendan being gay in an uptight Midwest backwater. How he framed Brendan and Melissa, in revenge. Accusations of incest. Humiliation. Outrage. Their father's suicide. Their mother committed to an institution. Brendan had thought she was dead. He was wrong. But it didn't make any difference. She was gone. The body was alive. Nothing more. There was no salvation there.

That's quite a childhood, said Sheila.

Makes mine look like Happy Hour.

Yes, she ruminated, ignoring my Freudian choice of simile.

We sank into our respective thoughts. Mine were about the World Series. Day One of the Main Event coming up. Had to get my mind right.

You're not responsible for getting him to grow up, Rick. That's his job. And even if you were, with that kind of history to deal with, there's very little you could do.

Yeah, yeah. But I can't help it. And it turns into anger. Why the hell can't he grow up and let me stop feeling guilty?

All about you.

All about me.

We said it simultaneously. We laughed.

We understood each other.

It was almost like love.

Not that kind. Anyway, not quite. I still had to pay the bill.

On the other hand, I could have been paying two hundred bucks an hour for a hell of a lot less. Had to count my blessings.

That was my mother's expression. Count your blessings.

I didn't cry when she died, you know, I said.

Melissa?

No. My mother.

How did we get to your mother?

I don't know. Free association or something.

Okay. So you didn't cry when she died.

No, I didn't. It was more of a relief, sort of.

Well, she had Alzheimer's, didn't she?

Yeah, that was part of it, I guess. But I wasn't really exposed to the bad parts. My sister took care of her. Sometimes, actually, it was comical.

Comical? That seems a strange word.

Well, for instance. My sister told me one day that my mother had started drinking again. After fourteen years of AA and abstinence. Turned out she'd forgotten that she'd quit.

Sheila was silent. I guess she didn't find it funny. But really, it was hilarious. In that you-either-have-to-laugh-or-you'll-cry kind of way.

You were saying that it was a relief, of a kind, when she died?

Yeah. Or maybe it was more like, gee, great, orphan at last.

Sheila was silent. Careful not to show disapproval.

I'm not making light of it, I said. Really I'm not. That's how I felt. Now, of course, there's lots of guilt. Not least for thinking that awful thought, to start with . . .

The orphan thing? Why is that an awful thought?

I don't know. It sounds kind of cold, doesn't it? Heartless? Unfeeling? I cried when my father died.

You were eight years old.

But still . . .

Rick, you know this. Feelings don't have values attached to them. There's no such thing as a good or a bad feeling, from an ethical point of view.

What if I felt like strangling Brendan?

There was a long pause. I could feel her discomfort. For all her acumen, her experience, her knowledge of my neuroses, she wasn't prepared with an instant response to this one. It was too damn weird.

I was kind of proud of that.

The feeling itself isn't bad, she said at last. The impulse is not good. I wouldn't advise acting on it.

Sound advice, as always. But damn, you shrinks are so amoral. That always bugs me about you. Can't you every once in a while tell me to get on my knees and confess?

You're free to do that if you like.

Yeah, maybe I would, if I was younger.

What does your age have to do with it?

Hurts the knees. All that kneeling.

43.

THEY WERE HOLDING ONE-TABLE SATELLITES to the Main Event in the old poker room, miles away from the tournament itself. The air was stifling with the desperation of guys like me, guys who knew this was their last chance. Guys who were plonking down their last thousand dollars for a last chance to qualify. Well, it wasn't exactly my last grand. But it wasn't exactly mine, either.

Somehow it all came together. Everybody at the table was being crazy aggressive, trying to build a big stack early so they could coast to the endgame, the final two or three players. All I had to do was wait for a big hand or two and pick them off. My Queens held up against Ten, Nine suited to double me up, and I busted out another guy with Kings when he went all in on the flop with an open-ended straight draw. So it didn't take more than an hour before I was heads up with a chatty Vietnamese guy who called himself Spikey Mike. He had a high marine haircut and a brisk little mustache that stuck straight out from his lip. Never stopped talking, in a heavy accent. On and on about how they played down in Mississippi. Not the first place you would have guessed he came from. Okay, he'd say, when Charlie bets out and the other guy calls—you're playing against two Mexicans . . .

I ignored the banter. But he was a good player. Mixed it up a lot. He'd go preflop from a min-raise to a full-pot raise to an all in, three hands in succession, and show you his cards every time. There was no pattern to it, he was telling you. Call or raise at your own risk. A scary guy to play against, because he could bust you any given hand. But how you play against a guy like that is pretty simple. Just play solid.

So we went back and forth for what seemed like a long time. I kept watching the clock. The Main Event was starting in less than an hour. Damn. I wouldn't even have time to take a nap before heading over. Assuming I could even beat this guy.

I have a small chip lead, and look down at a pair of Tens. A great hand heads up. I put in a standard preflop raise. The blinds are 200–400 by this time, so I make it three times the big. Twelve hundred chips. Mike casually calls. So far, I have very little information, since he's been calling my preflop raises about eighty percent of the time. The flop comes Ten, Eight, Jack, which looks good for me. I've hit my set, three Tens. But the flop is all clubs. A monochrome board will slow you down. Needless to say, I don't have any clubs in my hand, since the Ten of clubs is out there, so all Mike needs to beat my set is any club in his hand—the Two would do—and another one to hit on the turn or river. And that's assuming that he doesn't have two clubs in his hand already. Not to mention there are a lot of possible straights and straight draws on that board.

Of course, if the board pairs on the turn or river, it's all moot, because I'll have a full house and his flushes and straights will be worthless. Have to factor that in, too. All in all, it's a tough situation.

Especially when Mike pushes all in.

He does it with an air of confidence. Which can often mean the opposite. But I haven't been able to get a read on the guy. Like I said, he's been randomizing his actions pretty good, and letting me know he was doing it. Trying to get into my head. And it was working.

So I think it through. It takes a long time. I piece together everything that's happened in the hand. Everything I know about the guy. And I figure this. Number one, he could easily be shoving with nothing at all. A pure bluff. He'd shown me a couple of them already. Of course, him knowing that he'd done that makes it much more likely that he has a monster—a made flush or straight—already, and is hoping I'll call figuring he's on another bluff. So I heavily discount the bluff possibility. Much more likely he's on a monster draw. He has a high club, a Nine, or even the Nine of clubs, giving him an open-ended straight flush draw and making him, actually, close to a favorite in the hand. Or, he could just be on any old draw with a pair to back it up. He could have two pair, with a Jack, Ten in the hole. Perfectly plausible. I weigh the likelihood of each of the possible hands, put some tentative numbers on them. Figure that, overall, I'm a favorite here against his probable range of hands.

But that doesn't end the issue. Complicating everything is the fact that calling here and losing means very likely not playing in the Main Event—I'll have a few chips left, but he'll have me dominated. And that's the whole reason I'm here: the Main Event. I'll have to wait a whole year for another shot. Listen to Butch, and Brendan, and everyone else I know, rag on me for twelve months about it. Of course, the reward is commensurate: I win the hand, I'm in. Sign the papers, get my entry tokens, trade them in for a ticket to the Big One. Walk on over to the Amazon Room. Yes.

I call. Spikey Mike turns over the Nine of clubs and some random card, a Four or something. He's got a straight draw *and* a flush draw. Just about the worst scenario for me, other than a pair of Jacks in the hole, the latter a notion so unlikely I hadn't even considered it.

Damn. Waiting for the turn and river cards is going to take seven years off my life. I'm sweating up a flash flood. My heart is going to split open like a piece of firewood under the axe.

The turn is a King of hearts.

I get up. I shake my cramping hands. I give Spikey Mike a conspiratorial smile. He smiles back. He looks calm as a dentist.

I prepare myself for Doom.

The river's the Jack of hearts.

I jump in the air. I stride over to Mike, give him my hand.

It was never in doubt, I say with a smile.

He nods his head. He's taking it well. I admire the guy. He'd played a great game. I just hope for him he has the ten grand to buy in.

Half an hour later, I'm floating down the endless corridors to the Amazon Room.

All was right with the world.

44.

ON MY WAY TO THE MAIN EVENT, I passed the IDEX Convention. The D stood for Dolls, apparently. I'd first noticed it when one of the Scooter People—a gargantuan woman draped in what looked like chintz upholstery—glided by me in the hallway. She had two dolls in the basket of the scooter and one cradled lovingly in her arms. The one in her arms was scarily realistic, too, small and perfect, like some manifestation of evil in a horror film.

According to the ten-foot-high sign in front of the convention room, you could get the IDEX 15th Anniversary Commemorative Doll for only $130. Apparently this was the Very Special LE300 Susie IDEX, and she came with her own IDEX canvas bag and teddy bear. *Very Few Are Left!!* shouted the sign. Events at the 15th Anniversary IDEX Convention included Teddy Bear Jeopardy, and Sculpting Heads with Jack Johnston. Apparently Jack was an icon of the IDEX world, hosting a number of other seminars, including One-of-a-Kind Shoes. You could also enjoy a seminar entitled Sculpting a New-Born Baby with Maryanne Oldenburg, or The Pro's [sic] and Con's [sic] of Vinyl vs. Silicone, among other topics too enthralling to mention.

God Bless America.

I looked at my Main Event ticket. Table 147. Seat 5. Sighed. Here it began. Days of torture. If I was lucky enough to last more than a day. The starting field was more than eight thousand, way too many players to fit into a room even as big as the Amazon Room at the Rio. So they divided the field into four tranches of two thousand or so, to get it down to a manageable size. To survive Day One, I only had to outlast about twelve hundred players. Easier said than done.

At the beginning of any tournament, even more so the Main Event, everybody plays tight. Well, all the decent players play tight. There's always a few maniacs around. Guys willing to bet their whole stack on pocket Tens on the first hand of the tournament. Sometimes they even win that hand. Get to play another one. But the tournament lasts for five long days. Thousands of hands. You've got to be lucky as hell just to get through Day One, playing like that. A few always do. You got eight thousand players. Maybe a couple hundred maniacs. The odds are pretty good a few of the maniacs will ride a rush to Day Two. Like Guatemala Steve, a five-foot guy with a fedora, a huge gambling habit and a taste for drugs to match. He was the chip leader deep into Day One a couple years ago, busted out around two in the morning when one of his mammoth bluffs finally got called and he failed to suck out with Seven, Three off suit.

Hey, he told me later, I'd been up three days playing poker by then.

Three fucking days? I said.

Sure, he said. Every time the blinds went up, I just doubled the Percodan.

Plus, the joint is packed with rich fish, guys who actually pony up the ten grand entry fee and have a gnat's chance to cash. And a gazillion Internet qualifiers. Guys who got in for thirty bucks by beating a field of hundreds, or thousands, online. Either way, you've never seen or heard of them. They could be good. They could suck. You don't know. They could be tight, or loose. Passive or aggressive. You don't know. So, unless you want to crap out early, the first two hours, four, six, of a five-day event, you've got to be cautious. Give it time. Figure them out. The problem is, all the other decent players are doing the same thing. Waiting. Folding. Watching. So it's hard to get a read. And if you happen to get lucky enough to have a premium hand when one of the lunatics goes all in, you still have to fade his outs, avoid the bad beat, the suckout, the nasty five percent draw on the river. If you do, and you double up early, you can relax, stay patient, sit on your stack a bit.

Even if you've been patient, built up your stack a little, survived to later in the day, they move you to another table. You look around. Nine new faces. Nine new players to figure out. Shit. And if they're not new faces, they're Johnny Chan. 'Jesus' Ferguson. Phil Hellmuth. Professionals. World-class professionals. World Champions. Shit.

So you sit for hours. The first day lasts about sixteen. Hours. Some days are longer. Hours of boredom interspersed with occasional moments of terror, somebody said. Exactly right. And when you do get involved in a hand, after all those hours of fold, fold, fold, you'd better have all your poker skills humming. If you don't, and you crap out, you'll have a whole year to beat yourself up about it.

Poker is a game of incomplete information—you don't know the other guys' cards, and much of the skill, of course, is in using the information you do have to narrow the range of hands they can be holding. So you watch, watch, watch, assimilate and wait. There's a hitch, though: too much information can cause mistakes, too. The thing of it is, sometimes your brain, having assimilated not only what's been going on at this table, but what's happened at every other table you've ever played at, subconsciously throws you a zinger. And you've got to recognize it when it does. If you don't, you start overthinking the situation, thinking about all the information you've consciously acquired, you can make a big mistake.

My first year at the WSOP, I'd been watching a video about tells. One of the well-known tells is what's called self-soothing behavior by the psych mob. Somebody's stroking their fingers, rubbing their thighs. It means they're nervous, worried. My opponent that day, two seats to my right, was a tight, fairly sophisticated player, a young guy who was pissing me off with his arrogant air. He was way too good-looking, for one thing. I hate guys like that. He had the backwards baseball cap, the fancy chip-shuffling tricks. Made a point of telling everybody he'd never read a poker book.

So we're halfway through the first day. I haven't changed tables yet, so I've gotten to know the guys around me pretty well. I look down at Ace, Seven of hearts. I'm in late-middle position. The little snot is in the big blind. The table in general has been quite tight. I take a flier and call. The kid checks, so I get to see the flop cheap. It comes Ace, King, Jack, two diamonds. This is a very scary board. It gives me a pair of Aces. The kid may well have an Ace in the hole, too. He's unlikely to have a King or Jack with it, though, or any other decent kicker, because he likely would have raised preflop with those hands. On the other hand, the board is full of straight and flush draws.

The kid bets half the pot. What does it mean? Well, he could be trying to steal the pot, or he's got that weak Ace like mine.

But without thinking it through, I immediately decide he's on a flush draw. Now, with the benefit of hindsight I could say that, maybe, he has a bit of an insecure expression on his face, but I'm not noticing that. My subconscious is simply screaming it at me: flush draw!

But of course I can't be certain that he doesn't have something else entirely: a better Ace, or an even better hand. Two pair, Kings and Jacks. My Ace, Seven is a donkey hand. You want to keep the pot small with a hand like that, not pump it up. So I just call. The turn is a rag, an inconsequential non-diamond. The kid flips a stack of chips into the middle of the felt, again about half the pot.

I have no reason to change my evaluation of his hand. Flush draw. He hasn't hit it yet. I call again. The odds of a diamond hitting on the river are less than four to one, and if my opponent doesn't hit it, I can take down a decent pot without a lot of risk.

The river, sadly, is the Two of diamonds.

The kid thinks for a while, checks.

And here's where I mess it all up. I look at the little shit. I watch him for a while. His right index finger is, almost imperceptibly, rubbing his middle finger. He looks uncomfortable. And I start thinking. Maybe, I think, I was wrong. Maybe he has a pair of Aces, lousy kicker. Maybe he's the one who's afraid of the flush card on the river. Maybe his kicker is better than mine, and maybe, even if I don't have the best hand, I can bet him off his hand by representing the flush.

So I throw in a big bet. Three-quarters of the pot.

The kid starts thinking, and I'm figuring, bingo, he's got to think, I got him. Then, he shrugs, calls, and turns over . . . the Seven and Three of diamonds.

Ugly. So very ugly.

The fact was, you see, I'd had the situation read perfectly. But on the end, I allowed myself to become distracted by other information. But how do you tell the wrong information from the right information? Is your gut right, or your head? The answer to this one, like the answer to all poker questions is: it depends. In that hand, the right information was my subconscious read. The situation on the river was the distraction. It can easily be the other way around. So, it's all about judgement. It's about seeing what's important, and ignoring the underbrush. The problem, of course, is that the underbrush often disguises itself. As, say, a giant redwood.

This year, I vowed, it would be different. And it started out well. Seemed like I had drawn a good table. There were no name players. There was an online qualifier kid—ridiculously young. He had the sweatshirt with the hood, the cargo shorts, the New Balance sneakers, the beginner's goatee, the shades. In other words, he had the whole look down, except: the glasses had a big, gold D&G on the side. Dolce & Gabbana. Designer glasses! Blatantly designer glasses. I wanted to lean over to him, explain the situation. I decided against it.

A couple seats over was a Middle Eastern–looking guy, smooth and well dressed, who quickly established himself as a loose and tricky player—tricky in the bad sense: bad for him. After losing a few pots, he started backing down. He wasn't going to last long. Next to him, a guy with a double chin big enough it could have been eight of them. He never cracked a smile or, as far as I can remember, played a hand. The guy to my left had greased-back hair, a widow's peak, a jutting cleft chin, a big hook nose. He said he was writing a novel, *The Crucifixion of the Swan*. I didn't want to know what it was about. He told me anyway. It was based on real events, he said. Something about an obscure Bolivian anarchist popular with teenage girls. I told him I'd be sure to pick up a copy.

There was one good player at the table, a sick-looking kid—so skinny and pale he could have been in advanced chemo, or maybe terminal anorexia. But he didn't act like it. He was confident, energetic, aggressive.

He wasn't hurt by the fact that twice in early hands he flopped a monster, a full house and then a straight, both times holding King, Jack. So he had a nice big stack to play with right away. I tried to stay out of his way.

I started out well. I played tight-aggressive. I picked some spots to steal smallish pots. I worked my way up to 13,500 chips, a third above the starting stack. The rest of the day went back and forth, nothing fancy either way. So when at the end of the day I'd not only survived but done a bit better than that, I was feeling pretty good. Solid. Safe. Middle of the pack. I looked around. Saw some guys with stone huge stacks. Eighty thousand. Ninety. I didn't worry about them. They wouldn't survive Day Two. The first-day chip leader had never won the World Series. There's a reason for that.

Two aisles away I found Butch, finishing the last hand of the night. He had a respectable stack. Fifteen grand. Good. Score two out of three for The Outfit.

I thought about Brendan. He didn't have it all together, at the best of times. All the hype, all the lead-up, made it worse. He didn't have the temperament to do well in these long events. Too up and down. You had to be calm. Composed. Impervious. Able to take the bad beats and stay focused. Hunker down. Stay on message. Build up that small stack patiently, if you got small-stacked. Play good hands. Play them strong. The luck runs against you, so long as you're still in the tournament, you live with it. You keep on keeping on. In the long run, you do that, you do okay.

You still had to get lucky a few times, though. In the right spots. And luck was something Brendan had never had. Not big luck. Not when it counted. Starting with being born to some awesomely odd parents. Of course, most of us could say that. But his were special that way. And when your life starts out unlucky, you tend to bring your own bad luck with you. Something to which Brendan was no stranger. His hyper-aggressive, take-no-prisoners style could build an awesome stack, when the cards fell his way. But then the cards always seem to start falling wrong. And that's when you have to be able to adjust. Change your style to suit the different circumstances. And Brendan just couldn't adjust. Or rather, his idea of adjusting was to get even more aggressive. Hope to get lucky again.

And as the sage once said: That don't work, son.

Out in the hallway, I saw him holding court with his Russian buddies. He had a big smile for me.

Hey, he said. One-oh-five. You?

Are you kidding me? I said.

Nope. One-oh-five. You?

Thirteen.

Hah! he laughed.

Ya got me, I said. Today.

I know, I know. I took a few risks.

A few?

More than a few. But I'm looking good, man. I'm feeling it.

Great, buddy, I said. That's great. Champagne time. Let's get Butch.

Okay, he said, without enthusiasm.

He was enjoying his moment. Basking in his chip stack with the Russkie boys.

Meet us over at the Hang, I said.

Yeah, sure, he said.

I corralled Butch. He still had his game face on. Serious. Hooded eyes. His shaved head slick with sweat. Needed to take a walk, he said. Shake out the tension. Okay, I said. Meet you there.

It got hot in that joint. Two thousand players. One room. Too much.

Four more days. Even with a couple of off days, this shit was going to take some stamina.

And some smarts.

And a whole lot of luck.

45.

I TOOK A SEAT IN THE VELVET EMPORIUM. Leaned back with a double scotch. Felt good. One day down. End of the long, long day. Still in it. Up a bit. Victory of a sort.

I thought about Madeleine.

You would think that a poor young girl of eighteen, fatherless until moments ago, subject no doubt to all the sturm und drang that adolescent flesh is heir to, that she'd be at least, I don't know, tongue-tied. Have a pimple. Or something. But she wasn't. Didn't. She had deep almond eyes. Long, luxurious hair. And a wit, it seemed.

Most miraculously, she played Debussy like a dream.

And I couldn't take credit for any of it.

She'd probably make a great poker player, I mused. She was preternaturally composed. She was a great musician. Music and math skills are closely related. Math skills are a big advantage in poker. Only question was, did she have the competitive fire? You had to want to crush people. Take their money.

I wanted to ask her about her mother. What had happened. How she'd fared, alone with a child. Why she had never called, tried to get in touch. I used to make lots of money. I could have helped out. Hell, what was I thinking? For all I knew, she'd immediately latched on to some handsome gazzillionaire, poisoned his cold asparagus soup, the one with the tender sprigs of fresh dill suspended on top, the artfully placed dab of sour cream, daily with arsenic for weeks, until he withered away and died, and then lived in queenly comfort thereafter, she and Madeleine.

In fact, I was certain of it.

Butch showed up. Rescued me from my twisted mind. He had a Day One story similar to mine. Hours of boredom, moments of terror. Survival.

That calls for some champagne, I said.

Won't get an argument from me, Butch answered.

An hour and two bottles of Cristal later, there was no sign of Brendan.

I tried his cell phone. No answer.

Butch sent him a text message. No answer.

The poker day was over. The tables were empty. It was too soon for him to have fallen asleep. There was only one conclusion.

He was doing something stupid.

Natalya, I said.

Say what? asked Butch.

Natalya. In the beer tent. He's gone out with the Russkies. She'll know where. Or have a good idea.

My icon of investigation, said Butch. I bow to your superior technique.

As well you should, I said. I'm going to hit the tent.

Butch stood up and bowed. Followed me in mock obeisance.

The tent was empty. The pool tables looked lonely. Damn, the whole place looked bereft. There's not much lonelier than an empty beer tent.

Outside the tent, we saw a guy. He had a plunger in his hand. He was yelling at us. Something about Jesus. I couldn't hear what he was saying. But it didn't seem important.

Nice plunger, I said.

He yelled something at my back. I couldn't hear what it was. It didn't seem important.

I followed an instinct. It was a large and luminous, orange-coloured instinct. A sort of setting-sun instinct. It led me around the back of the tent.

Natalya was there. Having a smoke with some guys. Young guys, sitting on bar stools at a small round table. Guys in denim vests. Guys with tattoos. Guys with piercings. The umbrella that grew through the middle of the table was open, shading them from the stars overhead. They were passing around a joint and a bottle of Tequila. One of them looked up, gave me a blank look. The others ignored us.

Natalya gave me a smile.

Brendan's friend, she said along with the smile.

Yeah, I said. And this is Butch. He's Brendan's friend, too. Coincidentally, he also happens to be my friend.

She laughed. A nice warm laugh. A laugh that wasn't trying to prove anything.

You seen him? I asked. Brendan?

A while ago. He was with the usual—

Andrei?

And Anatoly.

Any idea where they went?

They were talking about going to this club. Give me a second.

I'll give you more than that, I said, you give me half a chance.

Excalibur, she said, ignoring me. Or something like that.

We'll run with that.

You're welcome. And thanks for stopping by.

Oh, sorry, I said. I'm kind of distracted. And next time, I promise, it'll be all about you.

Promises, promises, she said, turning back to her posse of punks.

Excalibur, I said to Butch. Heard of it?

Nope. We can ask the concierge.

What's a concierge for? I responded.

If not for that, I don't know what.

Sammy was at the concierge desk. Sammy was old-school, round and balding and perpetually cracking a joke. He was there to help. To be your best friend. To do all the scut work for you. Make those pesky reservations and phone calls. Tell you some old-time jokes, if that's what you needed.

He proved to be helpful, if a bit taken aback.

Sure, he said, pulling out a street map. It's right here.

He marked an X on the spot. It was in a neighborhood I wasn't familiar with.

But, he continued with a puzzled air, I'm not sure it's exactly the kind of place you . . . you gentlemen . . . would be looking for.

Yeah, yeah, Sammy, I chuckled. I think I know what you mean. I don't know the place. But we're looking for a friend.

A friend who might like that kind of place, he nodded.

Exactly, I said.

He seemed relieved.

Anyway, he said. It can be hard to get in, I understand. I think perhaps it would be best if you . . . dressed appropriately.

Might have to do a little clothes shopping, I said.

Exactly, said Sammy.

What would you say? A little leather? Metal studs? That kind of thing? In that neighborhood, he said.

Okay. Thanks, my man.

I slipped him a twenty. Sammy smoothly, expertly pocketed it. It was as though it hadn't happened. It wasn't something you wanted to flaunt. You were with a friend. Your good friend Sammy.

Money had nothing to do with it.

46.

WE COULDN'T BRING OURSELVES TO GET INTO FULL COSTUME. We did what we could. I bought a cowboy hat at the Caesars mall. I'd wanted one anyway. I had my bomber jacket. That would have to do. Butch had his leather motorcycle jacket. His shiny black boots. Hey, it was a little out of date, but maybe we'd be seen as charmingly retro. Add a little dash of the old YMCA. If not, hell, we could bully our way into the place, we had to.

I'd expected some Vegas-style extravaganza, but the Excalibur turned out to be a one-story concrete block on a sorry-looking street. Not a palm tree in sight, unless you counted the neon one in the window. In which sat, lotus-legged, a neon Arab boy in full cartoon-Arab-boy regalia, brandishing the eponymous sword.

Didn't know King Arthur was an Arab, said Butch.

In Vegas he is, I said. That's why they call it the Magic Kingdom.

That's Disneyland.

Right. Well. You know what I mean.

We knocked.

No answer.

We knocked again.

The door cracked open. A wizened face, long and badly lipsticked, topped by a platinum blonde wig, peered out.

Yes? it said.

Uh, we'd like to come in? I said.

It slammed the door.

Butch didn't take well to being disrespected. And he didn't hesitate to express his displeasure. He stepped back. Crouched sideways to the door. Gave it his best black-booted straight-from-the-hip tae kwon do kick.

The door splintered and dropped in pieces like week-old matzo. Any old matzo.

Which brought out the troops.

Well, the troop.

He was big. He was bald. He was wearing false eyelashes. But that didn't fool me.

He meant business.

He took a swing at Butch. Butch ducked, threw up a blocking right arm. Eyelashes stumbled. Butch crouched, spun, kicked at the back of his knee. Eyelashes crumpled.

Butch walked through the shattered door. I was about to follow, but Eyelashes was too quick getting back up. He slid in front of me. He was too big to get around.

Goddamn it. I wasn't about to be a pussy, call to Butch to come back out and help me. And I hadn't brought the Mauser, the Great Equalizer. I was going to have to dredge up some of the old fighting moves. Damn. This wasn't going to be easy. It'd been at least two decades since I'd been in a serious bar fight. I sure didn't have the muscle tone anymore, after twenty years of drink and dissolution. I'd have to bank on the reflexes. Wait. No. Two bottles of Cristal. Fuck the reflexes. Okay. The surprise factor.

I grabbed him by the balls.

I really did. I had no choice. I had to make a preemptive move.

I'm not saying I enjoyed it. But I grabbed him by the balls.

And squoze.

He froze.

Fear in his eyes.

And? I said.

Okay, he said. It's all right. No problem.

You sure? I asked, giving them a little twitch.

Sure. You got my word.

Was there honor among scumbags? I asked myself.

Well, I answered myself, it's either believe there is, or stand here with a sackful of nuts in my hand all night.

I let go.

He stepped back. Looked about to launch a haymaker at me.

I cocked my head.

You sure you want to do that? I asked.

He hesitated.

And being the hesitator, he lost.

Shit, he said. I'll buy you a beer.

Scotch, I said. Laphroaig. Water back.

You got it, he mumbled.

I'll have a double Dewar's, said Butch from inside the doorway. On the rocks.

He'd been watching the whole thing.

Fuck you, I said.

Larry, said our new best friend, holding out a surprisingly soft but still huge paw.

Rick.

Butch.

Pleased to meet you, said Eyelashes.

I could have sworn he said it with an Oxbridge accent.

He led us down a long, narrow corridor patched, floor, walls and ceiling, in what looked to be carpet factory remainders. The corridor widened into a large room, similarly appointed. By which I mean not appointed at all.

The joint was populated. Larry introduced us around. One blonde, square-shouldered, in a dress closer fitting than its country origins might easily bear. A four-foot-five-inch Asian queen in Hawaiian shirt and pompadour. A guy in a tight-fitting dress and a scowl. You met the face alone, you'd expect her, him, to be on the porch, sporting a shotgun, ordering you off her parched half acre and a mule. And a sick tall blonde masterpiece. Nothing fake about that one. A Nordic pallor skillfully maximized by cheekbones and highlights, ravine-like cleavage and an air of abandon. Gretchen, an Asian transsexual with a thinly disguised paunch and a Hong Kong accent. When you think about it, I mused, if it weren't for his sexual orientation, she'd be washing dishes in a grungy Chinese restaurant.

God Bless America.

From somewhere in back, over the screams of some long-ago Aerosmith hit song, came the cry, Show us your dick!

On the wall was a sign:

RESUSCITATION KIT HERE ⇒

Leaning up against the wall next to the empty resuscitation-kit box was our good friend Brendan. Wearing a tuxedo. In bare feet. Sporting a carnation in his lapel. Looking way too happy.

Brendan, I said. What the fuck. You were supposed to meet us at the Hang.

What the fuck to you. I changed my mind. I'm an adult.

You're not acting like one. You could have told us.

Fuck off.

Listen, man. You're right. You're an adult. You can spend your leisure time any way you like. But maybe you could show your friends some respect?

My friends are here, he said, indicating the assembled degenerates.

What is this shit? Did we do something to you?

Nothing, man, he said, dropping the aggressive pose. Nothing. I just want to live my life.

Okay, I said. Whatever. Live your life. But Day Two is coming up fast.

Forget Day Two.

What, you're going to drop out?

I'm already out, he said with a shrug.

What? said Butch. You said you had a hundred five.

I lied.

I don't believe it, I said.

Believe it. Check the board at the Rio. I busted out the first hand. Set over set.

Aw, Jesus, man, I said. That's a tough beat. You should have told us.

He shook his head, walked away. Started talking to a guy in the corner. The guy was wearing a bikini. He had a tight body. Curves. Slim calves. You'd never have guessed it was a guy. Until you looked at his face. Under a blonde sixties-style flip-up wig was the narrow, sunken face of a forty-five-year-old insurance auditor.

I looked at Butch. I shrugged. He shrugged.

Life tilt, I said.

Yeah, he said.

We stood there for a while. I was feeling stupid and sweaty in my cowboy hat. I wanted to go after him. But what was I going to say? Come back to the motel, Brendan, we'll set up our own cabaret, just for you and your buddies?

I sighed. We headed out. I brushed off the leers of a couple of older guys. Worried that it was only the older guys.

47.

NEXT DAY, BACK AT THE SUITE, around about the fourth scotch, I started thinking about Tori. Jami. No. Something ending in an un-toward *i*.

I wanted to smell that mango again.

The basement angle. Yes. Saying I had to talk to Matt wouldn't work at all. In fact, I had to hope Matt and the kiddies hadn't gotten back from Reno yet. But the basement. Yes. Who knows, I might even find something there.

I got the Mini Cooper out of the lot. It cost me forty minutes and another five bucks. I tried to remember where the house was. Henderson, wasn't it? I trolled around the Vegas suburbs for a while. I was wandering, really, thinking about shit. Basements. Melissa. Why she died. Why people kept dying. Madeleine, on the other hand. Very alive. New. Like a replacement for the dying. Kind of sick, that thought. And by the way, I had the time to let the thought intrude, who the hell was her mother? I should know. I suppose I did know. I suppose I didn't want to think about it. So why was I thinking about it? Because it made me feel like shit. What had I done? Had a fling, apparently, when Kelley was a baby, two years old maybe. And then forgot it completely? How many different people was I disrespecting there, all at once?

I blundered into the right neighborhood.

Funny how the subconscious works.

I found the house.

It looked the same. Preservative, the desert air. I guess that's why you find a lot of old folks out there. Old cars, too. Old lizards.

Tori, or Lori, or Gustavi, answered the door. I smiled.

Sorry to bother you again, I said.

Who are you? she asked, genuinely puzzled, it seemed.

Rick Redman. The investigator? I was here a couple of days ago? Asking about the couple who used to live here?

Oh, she said, and began to giggle. The giggle rose to a snort, a laugh.

Oh dear, I thought. She's stoned.

Sorry, she said, composing herself somewhat. Yes. I remember. Come on in!

Thank you.

She pulled her hand from behind her back. It had a large lit joint in it. She looked at it, at me, sheepishly. Thrust it towards me.

Just a touch, I said, not wanting to be rude. But equally not wanting to be stoned. Dysfunctional. More dysfunctional than normal.

I took a small hit. Handed it back to her.

The taste of her was on it. Strong enough to compete with the powerful taste of first-class weed. My, I thought. She packs an olfactory punch, this one.

I'd never do this if Matt was here, she giggled. He's soooo straight? But it's okay, once in a while, you know?

She asked it like a genuine question. Like she needed my approval.

Sure, I said. Once in a while is great.

Matt wasn't there.

Perhaps there was a God.

She grabbed my arm, hooked it through hers. Walked me into the couch-filled living room. I remembered it. I still liked it. It wasn't just the dope. Though that clearly helped. We sat together on the couch. She leaned my way. I felt very, very relaxed.

Business first, I reminded myself. I wasn't Brendan.

You know, I said, I was remembering our conversation.

She giggled again.

You mentioned that you'd overheard Eloise and her . . . the man with her, Vladimir I guess, talking in the basement. And it occurred to me that I should have asked to see it.

What?

The basement.

The what?

The basement.

The basement? she said absently, handing me the joint again. Sure. Go look. Nothing down there, though.

Thanks, I said, taking another polite hit. Where is it?

Where is what?

The basement.

Oh, that. Downstairs.

I looked at her, trying to figure out if she was joking. I couldn't tell. It didn't matter. I started to laugh. She looked at me, laughed too. We both laughed. We couldn't stop laughing. The whole thing seemed utterly hilarious. Except I couldn't remember what it was that was so funny. Which didn't matter at all.

Especially after she collapsed giggling into my arms.

I held her, the laughter slowly subsiding. I stroked her back. It was a strong back. It curved to a firm and delectable waist. An apricot scent enveloped me. I liked mango better. But this would do. She kissed my neck. Her lips were cool and wet. I closed my eyes.

Uh, Toni, I said.

Dani, she murmured into my neck.

Dani, right. Sorry. Uh, Dani?

Yes, she said, nibbling at my earlobe.

Where's Matt? Your kids?

I had to make sure.

She started giggling again. Lifted herself up. Held my face in her hands. Smiled.

They're still in Reno, she said.

She had exquisite teeth. Her blonde hair was loose.

Ah, I see. Won't be back for a while, then?

Tuesday, she murmured, moving back down to my neck.

I lifted her face. Looked into her eyes. They were green. I'm a sucker for green eyes. Sort of like I'm a sucker for strong-bodied natural blonde Southwestern gals with succulent lips and the scent of apricots who throw themselves into my arms.

We went upstairs.

She put on Sinatra. *Only the Lonely.* How she knew it was my favorite, I have no idea.

Willow Weep for Me.

We lay down together. The bed was huge and soft.

I told her about a book I'd read a long time ago. A book about a machine. I kept confusing it with other things, but the thing I did remember was that the machine, a computer I guess it was, became so complex that inside it grew a whole world of virtual people, a complete society, mirroring our own to the extent that they developed conscious-ness, an idea of God, who was, of course, the creator of the machine. The machine's creator was able to observe, eavesdrop on, his creation, and agonized about his role. His role as God.

It's a great responsibility, being God, I said to Dani as she removed my shirt.

I began to remember why I hated getting stoned.

Are you God? she asked.

Yes. It happens that I am.

That's a relief, she said, feeling for the evidence of my claim.

Mmmph, I said.

I hate the small ones, she mumbled.

I think we're okay.

So I see, she said, having discovered the burgeoning object of conversation.

The laughing started again.

And some other stuff.

I changed my mind about the stoned thing. The only thing dope is good for, I always say, is listening to music and having sex. And there I was. Listening to music and having sex. Taking full advantage.

It was, as they say, satisfactory.

We lounged for a while. I drifted in and out of sleep. She brought us some coffee. We sipped it and laughed.

Jesus, I thought. Could a guy have a life like this?

Not this guy.

Well, I said, I gotta go.

Aww, she said.

Unfortunately, I do. Business to take care of.

She was sweet. Gathered my clothes together. Walked me to the door. We had a good long hug. I reluctantly pulled away. Turned for the car.

Um, didn't you want to see the basement? she asked.

Jesus, I said. I totally forgot.

She laughed. I laughed. We went back into the house. She took me to a door behind the kitchen. Led me down a flight of wooden steps. Led me by the hand.

At the bottom of the stairs she flipped a light switch.

The basement was unfinished. Concrete floor. Bare plywood walls. Drifts of dust on the floor. A rack of tools. Odd-looking tools. Not hammers, pliers, stuff I was used to. Heavy metal objects that looked like tools. A large wooden bench with a mammoth vise bolted to it. The remains of some large piece of machinery. Someone had been taking it apart. There were wrenches on the floor. Pieces of the machine. I didn't recognize it. The machine. What it was. Seemed like it was electrically powered. A large three-pronged plug lay on the floor near an outlet. There were gears. Some kind of conveyor-belt thing angled into the interior. I got down on my knees. Peered inside.

See, said Dani, nothing.

Well, I don't know if this counts exactly as nothing, I said.

Then what is it? she asked with a faux innocent smile.

The remains of a machine.

Is that anything like the remains of a day? she asked.

Something like that.

I just didn't under*stand* that movie? she said enthusiastically. How that woman, I mean, you know . . .

I started to laugh again. She joined in.

Back at the car, I succumbed to a moment of melancholy.

I'd had another piece of something I could never have.

And what else? I'd seen some old metal stuff. I'd got brown stains on my pants. And dust on my shirt. I stopped to brush as much of it off as I could before getting in the car. It stuck to my hands. I slapped and rubbed them together to get rid of it. It stuck around. The hell was this stuff?

Oh well. I could wash up back at the motel. I drove slowly. I felt drained. She'd drained me. Of my vital bodily fluids, as someone somewhere was fond of saying. It was a good drained, though. Like draining a pustule. Or something.

Jesus, I thought. I guess I'm still stoned.

48.

Now, in my former life, as a put-upon partner at a relatively large and hideously confining law firm whose clients consisted mainly of large corporations and their owners and hangers-on, men, and the odd woman, whose idea of a risqué act would be putting down a ten-spot on the Kentucky Derby, I would not have contemplated for a moment doing a job for some highly suspect meatballs from Brighton Beach that very likely involved picking up a brown paper bag of cash— or perhaps something much worse—of unknown provenance from a mysterious guy named Yugo in some outer borough of Las Vegas. In fact, rather than picking up whatever the hell it was, I might well have picked up the phone and called the authorities. Well, probably not. But I certainly would have called in the firm's resident ethics guru, the terminally unsmiling Uptight Bob Shumaker, so that he could listen gravely to the story, ostentatiously consult the relevant passages of the Bar Association's Code of Ethics, read them aloud to me slowly, like I was the slow kid in his third-grade French class, tell me that he would take care of it, and scuttle back to his manicured office to do whatever it is that law firm ethicists do about such things.

But Evgeny had me pegged correctly: a guy with a debt and a drinking habit, too much free time and a short attention span, a guy whose wife had recently died in most unpleasant circumstances, a guy who, if he ever actually cared about the niceties, which was doubtful, cared less so now. A guy who needed some quick cash. Desperately.

I got a call from Manfred. He'd meet me at the motel. In the lobby.

I hoped the two chairs weren't occupied.

Then I remembered.

I'd never told them where I was staying.

Damn these guys.

Manfred was waiting when I got there. He filled his beige chair to cubic capacity. I slouched into mine. I like to slouch. Lower back, I always say. And I do, actually, have a lower back thing. But I also just like to slouch. I spent most of my adolescence slouching. Hell, all of my adolescence. As a matter of fact, I hadn't stopped slouching since. It's a hard habit to give up.

Manfred gave me the details. Yugo lived in some suburb with a name like all the others. Something with a tree in it. He gave me the address. Told me to be careful. Yugo was a little, ah, eccentric.

Sure, I said to myself. Thanks for the tip. I should need to be careful.

Thanks, Butch, I also said to myself. For the gun.

Funny how these things worked. You got a gun, all of a sudden you needed it all the time.

Yugo's place was at the end of a long drive lined with tall cedars closely spaced. Cedars, in the fucking desert? A water-sucking monstrosity of conspicuous magnificence. The road opened onto a circular driveway. Four or five new SUVs were parked haphazardly. The house was a huge square stone thing with pillars and a crenellated top. The windows were tall and narrow. Supposed to look like some kind of castle, I supposed. Fit right into the neighborhood. With all those other castles and cacti.

At any rate, it seemed like Yugo was a pretty successful guy. At whatever he did.

The door was a big solid thing with a large brass knocker. No bell in sight. I used the knocker.

I waited a while.

I knocked again.

I waited some more.

Yes, a muffled voice said.

Is Yugo there? I asked.

Who wants to know? the voice responded.

Rick Redman. I'm here on business.

What kind of business?

A little business for Evgeny.

Hold on, the voice said.

I heard a number of locks being opened.

The door cracked. An eye peered out. Looked me up and down.

The eye opened the door a ways. Let me in. Behind the door there was another door. It was closed. Between the two doors there was barely room for me and the owner of the eye.

He was a small, wizened fellow with an air of imminent demise. His hair was wispy and white. There were large black spots on his forearms and face. He was wearing a Hawaiian shirt several sizes too large. And sandals too big for his feet. As though he'd been shrinking for some time.

Wait here a moment, he said.

He went back through the second door. I heard him lock it behind him.

The space had the dank air of illness. I thought of an underground jail cell. But it was too small for that. There was just enough dim light, coming from a wrought iron chandelier far above, for me to make out a framed scroll visible on the side wall. It conferred upon someone the Grand Order of the Knights of Malta.

What the hell were the Knights of Malta? I made a note to look it up.

If I ever got out of there.

The inside door opened. The cadaver was back.

Come in, he said with a smile that did not have a cheering effect.

I followed him in. He took me down a long hallway. To the sides were elaborately furnished rooms, each as dank and decrepit as the man himself. There was a powerful odor of carpet mold, and very old chicken soup.

He took me to the back of the house. It seemed to take a long time. In the back were a set of French doors. He opened the doors. Ushered me into the backyard.

Where reposed a large swimming pool and, each in a skintight striped Speedo bathing suit distinguished from the others only by color, half a dozen bronzed immensities. Bodybuilders, to all appearances. Oiled and shiny. Getting the sun.

Jerry, said the cadaver to the nearest brute.

Jerry leapt up from his lawn chair. Sir? he said.

Get me a gin and tonic. And Mr. Redman, what will you have?

Scotch. Whatever you have.

We have many things, Mr. Redman. What type of scotch would you like?

You wouldn't happen to have a little Laphroaig handy, would you?

Indeed we would. Jerry?

Jerry scuttled off. If a man that size can scuttle.

I noticed the unmistakable signs of intravenous usage on the cadaver's arms. Not junkie trails. The kind with bandage marks.

Mr. Yugo is not here, Mr. Redman, he said, his voice a phlegm-filled tremble. But he has told me to make you welcome. My name is Isador. Now, if you would share with me the nature of the business you have with Mr. Yugo, I'm quite sure that I can assist.

Mr. Yugo, I said, there's no need for the charade. Evgeny asked me to pick something up. He wouldn't have sent me if I couldn't be trusted. I'd love to share a drink with you, talk about old times, maybe chat up some of your buddies here, Jerry seems like a nice guy. But we don't need to dance.

Jerry is working on his master's thesis in applied geometrics, Yugo said a bit defensively. My friends are not necessarily what you assume.

I make no assumptions, sir, I said graciously. I understand the value of a good education. I myself at one time attended the school of applied philosophy.

Pardon me?

Law school.

Ah, wheezed Mr. Yugo, beginning a laugh that rose to a gurgle that took on the air of a life-threatening expulsion. He turned away and leaned over the arm of his chair. I was about to call out to one of the beefcake boys to assist when Yugo composed himself, sat up again.

I apologize, he said. A spot of the flu.

Sure, I thought, a spot just about the size of a grapefruit-sized lung tumor.

In any case, he wheezed, I enjoy a man with a sense of humor.

Jerry returned with the drinks, two mismatched glasses and a bottle of Beefeater on a tray. My scotch was in a double shot glass. Yugo's gin, presumably but not necessarily and tonic, was in a tumbler the size of a bedside lamp. Jerry stood by with the Beefeater. Each time Yugo sipped the glass a quarter empty, Jerry topped it up. Even if there had been tonic in the tumbler to start with, by the end of the conversation Yugo was drinking pure gin.

I guess, I thought, the dying are entitled to their pleasures.

Despite his decrepitude, Yugo had something of a patrician air. Noblesse oblige, I think they call it somewhere. One was supposed to be grateful for his company. Or maybe it was the other way around. I made a note to look it up.

I smiled politely through some idle chitchat—apparently he had some audacious plan to tear down a bunch of historical buildings in Brooklyn when nobody was looking, and build on the land some highly profitable condos—while I waited for him to get back to the subject of the meeting. Halfway through his liter of gin, he did so.

I don't want to waste your time, Mr. Redman. Though the view is rather pleasant, wouldn't you say?

I didn't know if he was referring to the pool, the shrubbery or the boys, but I nodded my assent.

This, ah, delivery, he said. Is that what Evgeny said? Delivery?

Not in those words. He said you'd have something for me.

Ah, interesting. Not exactly the same thing.

Listen, Yugo, I'd love to debate the finer points of the English language with you all afternoon. But to tell you the truth, I wouldn't. I don't like it here. I'm creeped out by the place. I'm just here to do a job. I'd like to do it and get back to my business.

This is not your business, Mr. Redman?

Mr. Yugo. Seriously, I'm just the messenger. I'm just supposed to . . . get the something. I don't even know if it's a thing. Could be instructions. But I assume you do know, or why would Evgeny have sent me to you? If you're not going to give it to me, whatever it is, if you have a problem with Evgeny, you need to talk to him about it, not me.

Oh, no, no, he said with a not very convincing display of sincerity, I have no problem with Evgeny. We go way back, Mr. Redman, Evgeny and I. We're like brothers. It is just that it is, really, Mr. Redman, there is nothing here for you to pick up. I do not have something for you.

Well then, sir, I said, mocking his tone as much as I dared, perhaps you would not be averse to letting me know where exactly the something is.

If there is a something, it is with Delgado, sir.

Delgado.

Yes, Delgado. You are not familiar with Delgado?

I told you, Mr. Yugo, I'm just the water boy. The real game's not over here.

He gave me a puzzled look.

Never mind, I said. No, I don't know who Delgado is. But if he's the one with the thing, I'd appreciate knowing where he is.

You do not wish to know why it is with Delgado? If there is an it?

No, I don't. And I've had enough with the *Alice in Wonderland* shit. I have a job to do. It's supposed to be a simple job. Get the something from whomever. Point me at Delgado. I go get the something. If I can't, well, I guess that doesn't concern you.

No, I don't suppose it does.

A silence ensued.

Jerry leaned over Yugo, topped up the tumbler. I got a good look at the pecs and abs. Jerry caught me looking, gave me a gnarly smile. I didn't reciprocate. Looked away. Nice pecs, I thought. But the guy could use some dental work.

You'll get the instructions by text message, he said, draining his tumbler of gin for the third time.

I see. Does this really need to be so . . . cloak-and-dagger?

He gave me a Look that said, I despise you and the mangy burro you rode in on.

I got up to take my leave of the charming Mr. Yugo and his consorts.

Oh, and Mr. Redman? he said, his contempt more palpable by the second.

Sir?

I wouldn't take the gun.

I glanced at my left armpit.

Is it that obvious? I asked.

He gave me that Look that your mom, or the traffic cop, gives you when you ask, wide-eyed, what you could possibly have done wrong.

It might go off, he said.

Ah. I see what you mean. Okay. Next time, I'll leave it at home. Wherever that was.

49.

I LEFT YUGO'S WITH A BAD TASTE IN MY MOUTH and a pain in the pit of my gut. I assuaged them both with a couple of scotches at a watering hole I happened to pass by on my way to Red Rock.

Gentlemen's Lunch, it said, but I knew what it meant. I wasn't going to find any gentlemen inside.

A pickup truck was sitting lonely in the lot. Looking for a party that wasn't ever going to start. Hanging from a bent coat hanger sticking up from the hood was the dreariest, dirtiest U.S. flag I'd ever seen. On the back end was a bumper sticker that said Panty Bandit, next to a crude cartoon of pink underwear.

The only other vehicle there was a police cruiser.

Inside the joint, a beefy uniformed member of the local constabulary had his butt poured like a wedge of soft cheese over the stool at the Donkey Kong machine, furiously ramming and jamming the joystick and grunting curses, oblivious to the strippers lounging contemptuously at the bar.

I ordered a scotch. Double. Ice. The strippers ignored me. I ignored them. There was a couple there, talking. Maybe he was the Panty Bandit. He looked like one. He was way short. Jeans, cowboy hat, that stringy overbaked look you get from working outdoors all your life. His wife, or girlfriend, was six inches taller than him, long straight brown hair and missing more than one tooth. Her skin looked like the hide of a buffalo with mange. Reminded me of the line about refusing to live in a place where the average number of adult teeth is fewer than three.

The Panty Bandit and Ms. Toothless turned in my direction, including me in their conversation as if we'd known each other for years.

You know how you can say something on Monday, the Panty Bandit said to me, and it works, and then you say the same thing on Friday, you get punched in the face?

Yeah, I said. Life can be like that.

Damn straight, man.

God, you're such a punk, Joe, Ms. Toothless said. He couldn't tie me up, she said, nodding to me with complete drunken assurance that I knew exactly what she was talking about.

Did you want him to? I asked.

I'm going to have my daddy fuck you, Alice, said Joe.

You won't let me be the child, said Alice. I always have to be the mother.

My question, I think, said Joe with a hiccup, has become obsolete.

I know about it when men have inside jokes, said Alice. It's all about sex.

No, it's all about trying to get sex, said Joe.

I live in a home, Alice said to me.

Really? I said.

No, I mean, I have a backyard. I live with many cats. They fetch. They're doglike. They run in and out.

You know what? said Joe. Never miss a chance to shut up. Because you might learn something.

Do you have to be on the phone with my mother when you say that? said Alice.

I finished my scotch and dragged myself away from the happy couple.

They were my kind of people. But I had work to do.

In the car, I thought of Madeleine. This new-daughter thing was confusing. Hell, everything that was happening was confusing.

So I stepped on the gas. I pushed the Mini Cooper to its considerable limits. There were endless low and craggy hills. Mesas. Gulches and saguaros. Enough saguaros to cover several smallish planets. A dry and deadly landscape filled, you knew, with dry and deadly reptiles, should you be inclined to park the car, go for a stroll.

All the way to Eloise's friendly trailer park. In a half hour flat.

I parked the Mini Cooper some ways from the trailer. I needed any advantage I could get, to get through to this woman. Surprise was an advantage. Almost always.

The dusty sound of unattended children drifted in the desert breeze. The faintly pleasant smell of marginal existence. An old man was sitting on a chair carved out from a fifty-five-gallon drum.

Howdy, he said.

Hi, I replied.

Don't 'member seein' you 'round here, he said, lighting a hand-rolled smoke, spitting out bits of tobacco.

No, I don't suppose you do.

Sit down, he said, nodding to a pile of worn-out tractor tires. Elmer, he said, extending a withered arm, to which was attached a clenched and largely useless thing that might have once been a hand.

I took the thing. Gave it a squeeze.

Rick, I said.

There was something warm about the guy. His gummy smile. His wattled neck. His air of utter calm. This was a guy who'd done his time.

The rest was bonus. He was going to sit on his oilcan. Watch the desiccated world go by. Master of his patch of sand.

He told me he'd been a fisherman, in Maine. Came down here thirty years ago. For the rheumatism.

I lay back among the rubber. I thought about tires burning in blockades. Lebanon. Chicago. Caracas. Prague.

I wasn't there yet. I still had time to do.

What brings you hereabouts? he asked.

Work, I said.

What kinda work, Rick?

I thought about it a minute. Surveying, I could say. Environmental impact study. Census.

Investigation, I said.

Yah, he said with a bigger grin. Jist what're you investigatin'?

Woman down the way, Elmer. Nothing serious. Her sister wants to know is she okay.

Yah. I know which one yer talkin' about.

You do?

Only one here without a man 'r kidlins. Got to be her.

I see.

Maybe ya do, maybe ya don't. Hard tellin' not knowin'.

Okay.

Har, he said, pointing the remaining centimeter of his smoke at me.

Anything you can tell me about her? I asked.

Yah. Lots.

Okay.

No sayin' I'll do it, though.

I see, I said.

Har, he replied.

Twenty bucks for your thoughts?

Might do.

I'll need a receipt, though.

Har, yar, gahhg, he said, descending into a coughing fit of Leviathan proportions.

Don't die on me now, I said, pulling out a twenty-dollar bill and heaving myself up out of my rubber chair enough to toss it on his overalls.

I got a ways yet, he rasped, plugging at his chest with an arthritic fist. Dontcha worry 'bout me.

He pulled out some rolling papers and a pouch of Drum tobacco. I remembered it from my tent and tar paper days. Dark, moist and stringy. Made a rich, long-lasting smoke.

I maintained a respectful silence while he rolled it perfectly smooth and symmetrical, clenched hands and all.

The twenty had vanished.

Yah, he said. Okay, I don't know 'bout that. She's whatcher call a piece a' work.

In what way?

Well, like I toldjer. She lives all by her lonesome in there. But not so bad. Put in that bitty swimmin' pool. Walks around like she's way above us regaller folks.

And?

And ever once in a while, late in the evenin', early in the mornin', you get noise comin' outta that trailer o' hers. Like two cats fuckin' the same bottle.

You don't say?

Yah. Cain't tell you any more'n that. Some funny stuff goin' on there, fer sure. You'd think. I don't know. Next mornin', there she is, scrapin' dirt 'round in front o' the trailer. Wearin' them Jap dresses in the hunnerd degree. Collars up to her chin. Down to the ground. Don't seem like she own a pair a' shorts.

Chinese, actually, I think, I said.

Yah, har, he coughed. Yer a piece a' work yerself, mate. I guess yer knows yer stuff.

I'll take that as a compliment, I said, struggling out of the rubber ensconcement.

Nice talkin' ter ya, the friendly old guy said.

Pleasure's all mine, I said.

I'll be wagerin' so, he said.

I'd meant it. Though I didn't tell him so.

I sauntered down the dirt as nonchalantly as I knew how, over to the Eloise trailer, the one with the mysterious cat noises. She wasn't outside sweeping the dust. There was no sign of anybody, in fact. Anything. I rang the bell. I heard it echo inside. As though the house were empty. Bereft of furniture, rugs or curtains to absorb the sound.

I wondered. Had she flown the coop?

The door opened.

She was wearing a floor-length robe of some Asian dispensation. Wide sleeves. There were animals on it. Fantastical animals. Things with feathers and fur. Japanese, I thought. Or Korean. What had I decided earlier? Chinese? I had an urge to go back to Elmer, correct myself. Cast some doubt on my earlier assertion.

She looked me in the eye. This, too, was a surprise. The first being that she had opened the door at all.

Yes? she said, leaning an arm against the doorpost.

Rick Redman, I said. From the other day. By the pool. I was hoping I could talk to you again. For just a moment.

I know who you are.

Ah. Well, then please excuse the redundant introduction. Might I come in?

Talk away.

Okay. Thank you. But, I mean, would it be an imposition, I mean, too much of an imposition, if we could perhaps sit down somewhere? It's kind of hot out here. For a Canadian boy.

I'd like to say that I was insinuating myself into her home, such as it was, by impersonating a bumbling fool. Unfortunately, I was just being myself.

She regarded me with an impassive gaze. She turned her back. Vanished into the gloom.

I took it as an invitation. Followed. A flimsy folding door on the right. A dim light. I peered in. She was sitting on a chair. A large, over-stuffed Queen Anne number, upholstered in mattress ticking. Or so it looked. Blue and white stripes. Somebody's idea of a statement. I knew about that stuff. From the Melissa days.

It was utterly out of place.

Just like me.

A Queen Anne chair is high, straight-backed. It has large earlike wings at the top. Where one might rest one's weary head, you think. But when you sit in it, you realize that the back is so straight that there is no rest to be had. Very pretty, but impractical.

I took it as a metaphor.

I slumped onto an undersized yellow divan.

I did not take that as a metaphor. But perhaps I should have.

I hastened to tell Eloise that my slumping intended no disrespect. Lower back, I explained.

She waved her hand dismissively.

At least I hoped that's what she meant. For all I knew, she was summoning the executioner.

She wasn't easy to read.

Thank you, I said, taking a leap of faith. Very kind of you, to let me . . .

She waved her hand again.

Okay, I said, let me get to the point, if I may.

I didn't know why I felt the need to formalize my speech for Eloise. Maybe it was the chair. Its throne-like air. Her regal silence. Who knew? Who cared? Whatever the cause, I didn't seem to have any control over it.

In any case, she didn't say anything in response.

As you know, I said, filling the dead air, I've been engaged by your sister, Louise.

Yes, she said in her flat voice, I remember.

Well, I lied, she was greatly relieved to hear that you're all right.

I'm sure, she said, telling me that she was not so sure at all.

But she did have one concern, I said.

I'm sure she did.

She, um, wanted to know about Vladimir.

Really?

Yes.

She lit a cigarette. Benson & Hedges. She lit it very well. Smoothly. With a wooden match. She shook out the match with a practiced flick of the wrist, placed it carefully in an ashtray on the side table next to her. From where I sat, the ashtray looked like a coiled snake.

Perhaps it was.

I see, she said once her little performance was over.

Then she looked at me, raised her eyebrows, laughed. Pulled out another smoke. Tossed it at me. I thanked her, and for the wooden match that followed.

We were bonding.

I guess, I said, she wanted to know how he is, too.

She gave a short, sharp laugh.

How much is my sister paying you, Mr. Redman?

Rick, please. Um, I guess that's confidential.

Well, I'm guessing it's more than cab fare from the Strip.

I think I can reveal that much. Yes. It's more than cab fare from the Strip.

Then she can get her ass out here and ask me herself, can't she.

Well, yes. Actually, I suggested that myself. But she seemed . . . worried.

By 'worried' do you mean 'scared shitless'?

I'm not sure I'd say that.

I'm quite sure you wouldn't. Anyway, she always was a good actress.

Um, but, uh, is there anything that I can say to her for you? A message? How is Vladimir, anyway?

That's none of your fucking business, she said.

My, I thought, it's remarkable how arresting that kind of language is when delivered in a monotone.

And, she continued, you can leave now.

All right, then. I'll do that. And thank you for your hospitality.

I got up to go.

I changed my mind.

By the way, I said. When I was looking to track you down.

She gave me a weary look.

I visited your old house. In Henderson. Talked to the lady there. Nice lady. Dani. From Oklahoma. You remember her?

Eloise looked away. Out the window. At the trailer homes across the way.

She gave me this FedEx package. It was addressed to Vladimir. Guess it got there after you left.

Eloise looked back at me. Her eyelids were slightly lowered. Ever so slightly.

Did you bring it with you? she asked.

Why would I do that?

Did you?

No.

Next time, bring it with you.

How do you know I'll be back?

You'll be back.

Happy to be the recipient of your confidence, I said.

Bring it.

Why should I bring it to you? It's addressed to Vladimir.

I'll give it to Vladimir.

So, you are still seeing him?

Did I say that, Mr. Redman?

Strictly speaking, you didn't. But it was implied.

She didn't say anything. She leaned her head back against the chair. Blew a long skein of smoke to the ceiling.

Just ask him over, I said. Next time I visit. I'll give it to him.

She laughed.

You really are a bit naïve, Mr. Redman.

I am? How is that?

She took a last long draw on her cigarette, stubbed it out in the ashtray. She did it with an air of finality.

Goodbye, Mr. Redman, she said, leaning back and closing her eyes.

Clearly, the interview was over. Again.

Well, I said. Pleasure to see you.

Oh, she said dreamily, eyes still closed, the pleasure was all mine.

I backed my way out the trailer door.

Turning one's back on Eloise Chandler seemed not to be recommended.

50.

I GOT BACK TO THE DUSTY ANGEL WITHOUT SERIOUS INCIDENT. Shit, I thought, maybe my luck's improving.

Sometimes I could be naïve.

I'd only managed to swill down two double scotches when my cell phone did its vibrating thing.

It was Madeleine. We made plans for dinner.

Which reminded me. I'd neglected to tell Kelley about Madeleine. Neglected? Chickened out. Whatever it was, it didn't feel right. I had to make it right. I could tell her and Peter that I'd come over later. After dinner. I could tell Madeleine about Kelley, Kelley about Madeleine. Complete a circle. It would be a novelty, finishing something I'd started. If you could call conceiving Madeleine starting something. Well, what else would you call it? Anyway. Maybe I could even get Madeleine to come over afterwards. Have a family party. Peter loved a party.

I called Kelley and Peter. Made sure they'd be home. Told them I might have a surprise for them. Maybe that way I wouldn't be able to weasel out of it.

I poured myself another scotch. It tasted good.

My phone buzzed. A voice message had appeared. Origin: unknown. A creditor, I figured. I considered deleting it unheard. Then I remembered I had a client. Children. But why would they go directly to voice mail? The phone hadn't rung. And a creditor wouldn't know how to do it. Now that I thought of it, I couldn't think of anyone who could. Well, it was the kind of thing Butch could find out. But why not just call?

Curiosity took over.

There was a voice. I didn't recognize it. Delgado, it said. There followed an address. I didn't recognize the address. But it didn't take more than a question or two at the front desk to find out it was in the sort of neighborhood sane people—and even I—didn't normally feel anxious to visit. Last I'd looked, the crime rate in Las Vegas made it only the thirty-fourth most dangerous city in America. The problem was, about eighty percent of the bad stuff happened in a ten-block radius of the joint in question.

The phone did its vibrating thing. When did I get to be such a popular guy?

I answered the call.

We need to meet, Ms. Chandler said.

Yes, I said. In fact, I have some news for you.

News?

Yes.

What? Tell me.

I can't. Too much to tell you over the phone. Let's get together.

That's what I just said, Mr. Redman.

Yes. I mean, I agree with you. But I have some important business to attend to first. How about later? Say, seven o'clock?

Rick, I really do need to see you.

Rick?

Yes, Rick.

Wow. To what can I ascribe this honor?

I leave that to your imagination, Rick.

I hope you understand that I have a very active imagination.

I'll take my chances. Meet me at the Wynn. My suite.

Certainly.

Call me when you're on your way.

I will do that.

All right, then, she said.

All right, I replied.

I was leaning back, indulging the imagination, as Louise had given me leave to do, when Butch showed up. I gave him the download. We knocked some theories around. None of them fit the evidence. Darwin we weren't.

The fuck is Brendan? I said. He ever come back?

Nope.

Goddamn it.

He's an adult, Rick.

Why do people keep telling me that? Yeah, I know. He's an adult. He can do what he wants. But I got a bad feeling about what he wants.

I hear ya.

It's those fucking Russians. They've got him into something.

You see any of them at Excalibur? I didn't.

No. But I know it's got something to do with them. He's like a teenager. Defying the parental whatever.

Yeah. You know, maybe it's time for an intervention.

An intervention? For what? Too much partying?

You're right. You're right. But let's at least try to track him down. Hope he's straight. Find out what's really going on.

I'm okay with that.

I guess we got to look around. Problem is, Vegas is a damn big place.

Funny you should say that. Seems to me it keeps getting smaller. Everywhere I go, it's the same people. Evgeny, Bruno, Louise. What's up with that?

We're talking about Brendan, Rick. Not your angst-filled life.

Right. Thank you. Thank you for rescuing me from my pathetic self.

You're welcome. Now let's head over to the Rio. Ask around.

I guess that's the place to start.

We took a cab. It smelled of hamburger meat and indefinable cheese. At the Rio we split up, asked around.

As I wandered about the endless corridors, I remarked that there didn't seem to be quite as many enormously fat folk on motorized scooters as I remembered from last time.

Apparently some visionary entrepreneur had started up a business renting these classy-looking three-wheelers to the supposedly handicapped at casinos all over town. Now, I understand that it's dangerous to take a position on whether excessive fondness for deep fried Twinkies and pork rinds should be categorized as a handicap, so I won't, but I did start keeping count of the ratio of morbidly obese people to those who actually seemed to have . . . oops, to non-obese handicapped people riding the things. The count was up to 14–2 in favor of the chubbies. One guy in supersize jeans and t-shirt was particularly memorable. I was just about to add him to the list when I noticed he was actually sitting in a chair, and not on a scooter. I looked again. It was two chairs. One for each leg. At that moment he heaved himself up, hauled over a black plastic trash bin and spewed something black—or dark brown—into it. Tobacco juice? Bile? Roof tar? Impossible to tell.

But it did seem to convey a message.

I just wasn't sure what the message was.

Butch and I met back at the Purple Velvet. Compared notes. Whilst updating my count of the population of lard-asses on wheels, I'd asked around here and there. I assumed Butch had been somewhat more diligent. In either case, the answers were the same.

Nobody had seen Brendan.

It wasn't smelling good.

Listen, man, I said, I've got to go check out this Delgado guy. Can you see what you can do?

Yeah, I know. I'll do it. You don't want me along?

I'll handle it.

Butch gave me a Look that said, I'll take your word for it. But only because I don't want to hurt your feelings.

On the way to the lobby I saw Evgeny and some of his crew playing craps. They were jumping and hollering at every throw of the dice. Well, Evgeny wasn't jumping. Not in his skill set. Ziggie was there. Manfred. Another guy I didn't know. Leather jacket, loose jeans, the tightly shaved scalp to hide the male-pattern balding. A slightly pathetic don't-fuck-with-me swagger. Another guy, with PMS. Pregnant Man Syndrome. Stick legs and a belly the size of an armadillo. A large armadillo. I started to head over, see if Anatoly and Alexei were there.

Evgeny spotted me.

Rick-ay, he called out. Come play! We got hot strick goink!

I was about to go over. Play the obliging confederate. Help keep his strick goink. But then I remembered that I hadn't finished the job yet. First thing Evgeny would ask me. And I didn't feel like explaining.

In fact, I thought, as I picked up the pace towards the lobby, Evgeny's voice fading behind me into the rattle and hum of the slots, I didn't even know if I had an explanation. I'd taken Yugo's word for this Delgado thing. The whole thing could be a ruse.

Self-aggrandizement, I could hear Sheila say. Why the hell would someone want to pull some elaborate ruse on me? I wasn't important enough. Somebody wanted to mess with me, they could just punch me in the chest, like Bruno.

Speaking of which, I'd almost made my escape when the Italian Buffoon himself hove into view.

Redman, he said. I got something I got to talk to you about.

Yeah, well, I'm in a hurry, I said.

No, listen, man. It's important.

As I tried to bull on past him, he stepped sideways, blocking my path.

You're gonna help me with something, remember?

I panicked.

I took a hard right towards the Chinese noodle shop. Ran past the main cage, skidded to the left, took a glance behind. He was after me, all right. Luckily, his physique wasn't tailored for speed.

Neither were my lungs. But desperation can sometimes buy you a couple extra miles an hour. I managed to launch myself down a flight of stairs to the car park, circle out through the garage, approach the taxi stand from the back end.

I flung myself into a cab.

It smelled of pickled onions. And anxiety.

51.

A COUPLE OF MINUTES INTO THE RIDE, once my chest had stopped heaving and the tremble in my legs had subsided, I leaned back and tried to figure out whether the pain in my chest was another heart attack, or merely severe panic. I tried to remember how I'd gotten myself into this bloody mess. Oh, yeah. Money. My fabulous poker career. Which, with all this other shit going on, I was not exactly attending to.

Which might not be such a bad thing. I'd probably just lose what little I had left. Get whacked by the Russkies.

At least I still had my Kelley.

Which reminded me. Before the Delgado message, I'd made a date with Madeleine. Shit. Peter and Kelley afterwards. There was no way I was going to make either of them. And Louise. Shit.

I reached for my cell phone.

It wasn't there.

I'd left it in the room.

I felt naked. Angry. Frustrated. Pissed.

And there wasn't a thing I could do about it.

When I got out of the cab, the street was dark. Nobody in sight. The car took off. I watched the taillights fade to pinpricks in the night. My eyes adjusted. I saw that I was in an industrial-looking area. Loading docks. Trailer trucks. No sidewalk.

I found a street corner. I was in the right place. I looked for a sign, a bit of neon. Some evidence that the joint existed. There was nothing. Not even a number on a building.

A hot wind picked up, took my cowboy hat into the street. I chased it down. My new cowboy boots were pinching my feet. I'd figured I should complete the costume.

I felt a fool.

I was a fool.

I wandered back and forth on the block. Nothing good was going to come of this. It was pissing me off. Worse, it was scaring the shit out of me. I'd blindly followed the directions in an anonymous voice mail to here, the middle of buttfuck nowhere, so I could wander deserted streets in the dark? What kind of dumb shit was I? How long before the gang of creeps appeared, black-masked and ready to disembowel me with blunt objects?

Lucky I hadn't thought to pack the Mauser. It only would have inflamed the mob.

I stared at a brick wall, painted black. Something odd about it. I tried to think what it was. It came to me. Industrial-type enterprises didn't paint themselves black. 'Paint It, Black.' The song began to echo in my head. I could remember the tune, the refrain. I couldn't remember the lyrics. Not optimistic, I was willing to wager. It was early Stones, after all. Something hidden behind a Stones wall, I mused.

I walked the length of the black wall. Back again. Two-thirds down, I saw what I'd missed before. A small brass sign. Above eye height. Inconspicuous. Available to the connoisseur:

Hole in the Wall

My, I thought. A clue.

I felt like a veritable detective.

I scoured the wall around the sign. Yes. There was a door. No doubt about it. But it was flush with the brick, and also black and made of brick. Almost impossible to see in the gloom. And on it, also black, a button. A small mesh screen.

Press the button.

I thought twice about it. Three times, to tell the truth. Maybe more. Curiosity took over.

I pressed the button.

The door swung open.

Sure, I said to myself. They've been watching me. All the time.

I peered in.

A black hole.

Black brick walls. One in front. One on each side. One above. I was surrounded. I looked down. At my feet, a staircase. Also in black. Barely visible.

I took a deep breath. I'd come this far. What was I going to do? Call a cab? Didn't seem feasible. No cell phone. Let alone prudent. If someone had it in for me, they'd come out after me. I might as well go down. Meet my fate.

I descended. The staircase turned and turned. Always another corner you couldn't see around. I could feel my heart, alive in my chest. Talking to me. Fear, it was saying. Feel fear.

Around the final spiral was a six-foot-square space surrounded by more stone walls. A very large man stood in front of me. Very large indeed. He had a padlock hanging from his left ear. Not an earring in the shape of a padlock. A real, live, heavy brass padlock. The earlobe to which it was attached stretched almost to his shoulder.

You couldn't make this shit up.

I thought of turning around. Scampering up the stairs. Running like the wind. Getting the hell out of there.

No, I thought. That would be rude. Not to mention physically challenging.

Behind Gargantua was an enormous door. The door was studded with large bolts. It was painted a glossy black.

Novel color scheme, I thought to myself.

There was a sign on the door:

PERSONS CARRYING RECENTLY SLAUGHTERED LIVESTOCK
WILL BE REFUSED ADMITTANCE

This was reassuring.

Mr. Padlock told me to raise my arms. I hesitated a moment. So he did it for me. Grabbed my elbows and launched them above my head. Held them there for a moment.

I got the message.

He patted me down. Looking for livestock, I surmised. I wasn't nervous. I knew any livestock on my person had been dead for weeks.

Fifty bucks, he said.

Fifty? I asked.

Fifty, he said with a curl of the lip.

I gave him the fifty.

I didn't ask for a receipt. I wasn't going to ask. Evgeny was going to have to take my word for this one.

He opened the door.

Inside, the place was dark. Once my eyes got used to the blue-orange dimness, I discerned yet more stone walls. What looked like railroad spikes embedded in the crumbling mortar here and there. There seemed to be a pattern. I didn't know what it was. On some of the spikes were hung small crepe-paper lamps that shed in blurry pools the little dimly colored light there was. On other spikes, or strung between them, were Devices. Clamps. Chains. Collars. Enormous Vise-Grip-like things. Coils of rubber hose. Black vinyl bodysuits.

Good job, I thought. Definitely set the right tone. And the lighting. Just right. Nothing more disconcerting than a brightly lit S & M club.

It was too early, it appeared. Nobody in the place. Except you and me, I said to myself. I sidled up to the bar. One for the road, I hummed. One more for the road, I corrected myself. 'One for my baby, and one more for the road.' What a genius, that Frank, I mused for the thousandth time. What soul. And I, I was quite certain, possessed such soul. I, among all the pretenders, truly could sing like Sinatra. Could have. If only I'd started my singing career earlier. Earlier than never.

I stumbled on a bar. A real bar. With bar stools. And an enormous illuminated fish tank. Filled with spectacular orange and blue fish. Some were darting about in groups. Schools, I guess they were. The thing was huge. Big enough to hold a school. Of fish, that is. Several of them. Which it did. It was mesmerizing. They were mesmerizing. The schools of fish. I pulled up a stool. I starting singing 'Willow Weep for Me.' Softly. Almost in my head. Maybe it was in my head. If I sang to myself, and there was nobody there to hear . . .

I remembered that I couldn't sing on key.

My reverie was interrupted by a lithe blonde thing in leather and studs.

Coincidence? That she'd come from the back moments after I'd sat down? Of course not. Surveillance cameras. They were everywhere.

She smiled.

I smiled back.

Can I get you something? she asked, in what sounded like an Irish accent.

Eclectic place, this Vegas.

Cranberry and soda, I said.

You sure? she asked.

I'm sure. It's going to be a long night.

She smiled that smile that says, Yes, I know exactly what you mean.

Save the hard stuff for later, I said.

The ambiguity was quite deliberate. And not lost on my new best friend.

Once she slid the drink to me she leaned back, elbows against the counter behind the bar. I appraised her, up and down. Normally I'd do it in sideways glances when her back was turned, when she was distracted. The civilized man's ogle. But the effort seemed superfluous. She was way too all there. Out front. In my face. Coyness would be out of place.

Here, it was all about the meat.

Her feet were narrow and tightly shod in thin flesh-hugging leather boots. Sharply pointed toes and leather lacing. Slim calves. Not trusting myself with the parts between, my eyes skipped to her waist. Exposed. Tight. Muscular. Neatly accented with a thin silver chain.

The chain looked to be, by God, pierced in and out of her flesh. All the way around her body.

Oh my.

What's your name? I asked.

Lucinda. What's yours?

Lucinda! I exclaimed. A name to conjure with.

And yours? she repeated, not giving an inch.

Rick. My name is Rick.

Ah. Of all the—

Right. You got it. Rick.

Oh, I was pleased. I was very, very pleased.

At which point we were rudely interrupted.

Xena! Lucinda cried.

I turned. I stared.

Xena was wearing a skintight black thing on her lower quarters. The way station between hot pants and a G-string. Not such a great idea. For while Xena had a long and shapely set of legs on him, or her, the upper parts, and even more the buttocks of the beast, were sadly pocked and rippled. Six foot three of estrogen supplements and artful plastic surgery. Surgery that hadn't, sadly, managed to eradicate the cellulite. Maybe that was the next procedure.

I wasn't about to tell him, her, about it, though. She was bigger than me.

She took the bar stool next door.

You married, honey? she asked.

Me?

Well, there's nobody else here, is there, honey?

There's Lucinda, I said lamely.

Oh, beat it with a stick, said Xena with a gargantuan smile. You know what I mean.

Yes. I mean, no. I mean, no, I'm not married. Anymore.

Oh honey, let me ease your pain!

It's okay.

It's never okay, honey. There's always some more pain around the corner, waiting to be eased.

I wasn't sure whether that was supposed to be a good thing or a bad thing.

Buy me a drink, Xena commanded. Lucy, I'll have a cosmo.

Lucinda shared with me a mock-exasperated grimace.

Wow, I said. What a coincidence. My girlfriend drinks cosmos.

Girlfriend!? You didn't say you had a girlfriend! Xena pouted.

You didn't ask.

Oh, he's a clever little honey, isn't he, Lucy? Why don't you bring your little girlfriend over, honey? We have toys for everybody to play with. She'd definitely want to play with me, honey. Let me tell you—

She's busy, I said. No. I mean, not right now. Maybe later.

I didn't want to offend.

I needn't have worried. It was clear that Xena didn't give a damn. Xena was Xena. You'd take her as she came. And by God, you'd take her. If you didn't, she'd crush your head in one of those mammoth black fists she carried on the ends of her heavily muscled arms.

So you and the missus been exercising your little libido, darling? she asked.

I refrained from correcting the 'little' part. That would only get me in deeper.

Yes, I said. We have. We do. But I try to keep it on a short leash.

We have lots of those, too.

Lots of what?

Leashes, honey, she said, rolling her eyes.

Oh, great. Thanks. If I need a new one, I'll let you know.

Oh, baby, you can always use a new leash.

I suppose you're right.

I have my own collection, of course.

I'm sure you do. I'm sure it's a very nice collection.

Would you like me to take you for a walk?

No, thanks. I mean, I appreciate the offer. I do. But that's not really my thing.

Then what is your thing, baby? I have many talents.

In addition to walking?

Oh yes, she laughed. *Many* other talents.

I didn't particularly feel like taking a walk with Xena. Or doing any-thing else with Xena, frankly. What I felt like doing was running. Fast. Out the door and far away. Bobbing and weaving. I wasn't getting paid enough for this. Actually, I suddenly realized, for all I knew I wasn't getting paid a goddamn dime for it.

I was spared further humiliation by a ruckus at the door.

Juan! Xena exclaimed.

She leapt off the bar stool and sashayed to the door. Gave a mammoth hug to a small man in a fedora and a long black coat.

Juan? I asked Lucinda.

Delgado, she said. The Big Cheese.

Delgado?

The one and only.

My, my, I said. I've heard of him.

Who hasn't?

Can you introduce me?

I don't think you'll have to worry about that. He takes a personal interest in the customers.

As if on cue, Xena motioned me to come around the bar, to the far corner, where Juan was taking a seat in a large plush vermilion chair. I waved a couple of fingers at her. I needed a minute to fortify myself.

Double Dewar's on the rocks, I said to Lucinda.

She gave me a wry smile. Poured the beverage. An expert twist of the wrist.

I drank it down.

One more, I said. For the road.

She already had the bottle poised.

I took my glass and sauntered over to the maestro's corner. In the time it had taken me to down the first scotch, a small coterie of sycophants had assembled. None of them had quite the presence of Xena, but, at least as far as I could make out in the dimness, they each had their own thing going. A square-shouldered blonde in a skintight silver body stocking. A slim and sophisticated number in a thirties gangster-style pleated suit. A tiny young thing in shredded denim, with a shaved head, an insolent air and various metal objects incising her flesh in awkward places.

There was another fish tank, floating behind the human tableau, even larger than the one behind the bar. Containing bigger beasts. Predominantly blue and orange again. But some were black. An enormous manta ray, slowly propelling itself with graceful swings of its gigantic wings. Like an aquatic eagle in slow motion. I tried to take it all in. It came in flashes. The black and blue, and orange, ocean. Black eyes and champagne. Sideways glances. Faint but discernible duplicity. An oval face. A hint of Asian blood.

The blonde took Delgado's coat. The tiny shredded one took his hat. They hung them on a coatrack. It appeared to be made of bones. Whose or what's, I couldn't tell.

As I approached the cabal, Xena rushed to me, flung a giant paw around my shoulder, guiding me, with disconcerting force, to my audience with The Delgado.

The man was hairless as an egg. Not so much as a stray strand of eyebrow. And there was no mistaking the pink glitter in the eyes. The translucent pallor. Albino, for sure.

No wonder there weren't any lights in the place.

The pink eyes fixed on mine.

His head was a perfectly smooth dome. His lips were full, just short of African. He held an ornate walking stick in his left hand. The power of the man was palpable. It reeked of New Orleans.

I was quickly getting the picture.

Juan, said Xena, I'd like you to meet my new wife.

I looked behind me. No one there. Who could she be referring to?

Rick, she said, this is Juan.

Oh, fuck.

Xena laughed, slapped my back. Nearly pitched me forward onto the floor. A position in which I did not want to find myself. Not on my first introduction to His Hairlessness.

But I got it. It was a joke. Har har.

I tried to think of something clever to say.

I failed.

Pleased to meet you, I ended up saying, as smoothly as I could.

Rick, said Juan. The pleasure is mine, I assure you.

His voice was soft. It exhibited the tranquility of utter assurance. Like that of a born-again zealot.

Have a seat, he said.

Don't mind if I do, I replied, sinking into the sofa.

The sycophants were jockeying for the best places around Delgado. Looking at me. A mixture of curiosity and resentment. Not fond of strangers, I was guessing. Potential competition for attention from His Whiteness.

I take a personal interest in my guests, said Juan.

I appreciate that, I said.

So, what brings you to us?

I wasn't sure about this guy. The whole scene. I figured I'd get to it slowly. Or maybe not at all.

I'd heard it was an interesting place, I said.

He chuckled, as though I'd said something clever. He lifted his cane. Polished the silver head with his left hand.

Indeed it is, he said. Isn't it?

He addressed the question to the cabal. They all indicated their assent. Yes, boss, it sure be interesting.

Just what kind of interesting were you interested in? he asked me.

I don't know, I said. I'm a writer, you see. I like to see things, soak them up. Use them later.

That's funny, said Juan. So do I.

You're a writer, too?

No.

Oh.

The tiny black-eyed one giggled.

Delgado rapped his stick on the floor. They all fell quiet.

No, he said. I speak as a whore.

Pardon me?

I speak as a whore, he repeated.

Funny, I said. You look more like a pimp.

A shocked silence fell upon the minions.

Delgado stopped, stared at me. His eyes were hard and red and white. His large pale lips pursed.

Damn it, I thought to myself, why can't I keep my fucking mouth shut? It's one thing if it costs you your job. But this guy. He looks quite capable of perpetrating an act of decapitation. Or worse.

But he laughed.

Not many white guys have the nerve to talk to me like that, he said.

This new opening was almost irresistible. The guy was whiter than a baby beluga. A hell of a lot whiter than me, anyway. Black albino, it seemed. That's major fucking weird, I thought. But I wasn't about to say so. I'd already taken enough chances.

I just smiled.

Okay, he said. You are?

Name's Redman, I said.

Actually, he said with a chuckle, I knew that, Rick.

So much for my cover. I mean, it could have been a bluff. But it didn't read like one. I figured I had to play it straight.

I'm just here to, ah, get something. For Evgeny. I don't normally dress this way. I needed to get through the door.

He didn't laugh out loud.

I respected that.

I might be able to help you, he said.

I was hoping you would.

Come, he said. Follow Diamond.

Diamond turned out to be the one in the gangster suit. Thin, lithe and goddamn irresistible. If I was being set up, it was going to work. There was nothing I could do about it. The off chance that this was legit, that, better yet, there was the slightest possibility I could have a few minutes of guilt-free passion with this utterly tricked-out object, was more than enough to counterbalance the risk. Whatever risk there was. Which was major, big-time, sick, stupid risk.

My consolation, my rationalization, was, what the hell would they want to do anything to me for, anyway? I was just the water boy.

52.

I WOKE UP SLOWLY. Very slowly. I needed water. For what seemed like hours I subsisted in a half-dream place. There were people feeding me dry things. Things that made the thirst worse. I was grasping for a hose, just out of reach. I desperately needed it. My mouth felt like sand. A whole beachful of sand. Sand and autumn leaves. The sand poured out of my mouth, onto my bare chest. It congealed there, turned color. Orange and red and fuchsia. It crawled along my flesh. Entwined around my wrists, my ankles. Tightened. Inserted small shards of glass. Made me bleed. I wanted to scream. But my mouth was full of sand and dead leaves.

My eyes cleared a bit. There was a gray and green light coming from somewhere, murky and intermittent. There was a locker room smell. Only worse. It had a funky edge. I could taste it, or something else, in the back of my throat.

That wasn't really the problem, though.

The real problem was the iron shackles binding my wrists and ankles. I was attached, it seemed, to some kind of metal contraption that held me in a rather unnatural position, head below my feet. Not only that, but, to all appearances, I was completely naked. In fact, if the numerous aches and throbs that shot through me at random intervals were anything to go by, I was not only shackled, not only naked, but shackled, naked, bruised and battered. I felt a dull ache in the general area of my prostate. A sharp throb when I tried to flex my right wrist. My lips felt swollen. My tongue was drier than a gecko's tail.

All of which was not good.

The situation reeked of not-goodness.

For some reason the phrase

> *Time crawls on winged feet,*
> *here without you,*

kept running through my head. I pondered what it meant.

I had no idea.

I heard a shuffling sound. Or maybe it was a rustling sound. Either way, it scared the hell out of me. It was bad enough that I was shackled, naked, bruised and battered. I didn't particularly want the perpetrator of all this to appear, ready to resume whatever it was that got me in this state. Or maybe it wasn't the perpetrator. But I was not at all sure the alternative would be better. If not the perpetrator, an audience? I wasn't sure I wanted that either. At all.

Foolish, I thought, my brain slowly coming around to the notion that I was awake, or something like it. That this ... situation ... as awful as it was, was not a dream. That I was not only shackled, naked, bruised and battered, but utterly confused. Drugged. Or something. Had been drugged. Or maybe just hung over. Whatever it was, it was making me worry about some pretty tangential issues. Given the circumstances.

Call out, I thought. Call for help.

I restrained myself. God knows what monstrous feet might be doing the shuffling. What nasty wings the rustling.

But then, I pondered, could my situation get worse? Well, yes. But if it was going to get worse, it was going to get worse anyway. So, I thought, in a certain sense, it could only get better.

I always knew that freshman logic course would come in handy some day.

I called out.

It came out more like a gargle.

A very, very dry gargle.

The shuffling and rustling stopped.

It didn't respond.

This was not good.

The shuffling started again. Just the shuffling. Not the rustling. The shuffling went on for a while. Too long, for my taste. It was coming from the left. I turned my head. I turned it an inch. Something was preventing me from turning it any more.

The shuffler appeared. It was carrying a broom. Hence the rustling, I deduced. It hadn't been rustling. More like swishing. Broom swishing. I thought myself very clever.

It was wearing overalls. And a vacant expression. A very, very vacant expression.

I was hoping the expression was a symptom of intellectual deficit, and not depraved indifference.

I cleared my throat.

He didn't move.

I wonder if you wouldn't mind, I said as politely as I could, helping me out of this, uh, contraption.

He didn't move.

Please? I said.

He looked at the ground. He whisked the broom back and forth. Apparently he had found some dirt.

I cleared my throat again.

Sir? I asked.

My voice was recovering a semblance of its former resonance.

He looked up.

Do you speak English? I asked.

His expression didn't change.

Man, this was one tough interview.

Maybe he was deaf.

I screwed up my face. I rattled the shackles. Despite my desperation, I felt more than faintly ridiculous. I mean terrified. Terrified and ridiculous. What I mean to say is, I'm sympathetic to the intellectually challenged and all, but what kind of moron needs a pantomime show to tell him a naked guy shackled to a metal contraption might want to get the hell out of it?

You want to get off of that thing? he asked.

He asked it in a calm, strangely stilted, high-pitched voice.

I took a moment to recover from the shock. Figured the best immediate strategy was to be polite.

Later, I could beat the crap out of him.

I certainly would, I said, but I can't seem to manage the task alone. Might you give me a hand?

Sure, he said in the same flat tone.

As though it was the most ordinary thing in the world.

He came on over. I flinched. Still half expecting the worst.

But it was fine. He undid the restraints. He did it slowly, deliberately. Then he shuffled back to his broom. Back into the other room. The swishing started again.

I slowly crawled off the contraption. It took some time. I was half upside down. Every joint was stiff. Tiny twisted daggers were being tapped artfully into locations carefully selected for maximum pain.

Once I'd finally stumbled to the ground, I looked at my former captor. It was artfully designed. Bolted to the floor. Painted red. Held together with thick black leather bands. The leather old and cracked. The red paint chipped and weathered. Clearly, it had seen a lot of use.

The aches and pains kept insisting on my attention. I tried to stretch. My lower back seized up. I bent over. I looked at my ankles. Red and raw. Matched the wrists. Jesus. I'd have to avoid rolling up my sleeves for a few days.

Speaking of which, I suddenly recalled, I had no sleeves. Nor a shirt to hang them off. Nor any other stitch of clothing.

This was going to be a problem.

I tried to look around. It was hard to move my neck. I turned my whole body to survey the joint.

The place was cracked and crazed with age and neglect. The metal devices, of which my former captor was but one, were sad and lonely in the gray light of morning. I vaguely recalled an air of danger and foreboding from the night before. That was all gone. Now it just looked kind of pathetic.

The gray light of morning.

I was thirsty as a salt lick.

I went next door to visit my new best friend.

He was sweeping the floor.

Uh, listen, I said, you wouldn't happen to know where my clothes are, would you?

He stared at me blankly.

This no longer surprised me. I was getting to know the guy.

No, he said in his flat soprano.

It hit me. Autism. He was autistic. Asperger's, wasn't it? The one where you can hold a job? You might even be good at something? He seemed to be pretty good at sweeping.

Okay, then. Autistic. Time to get literal.

Uh, excuse me? I said.

He looked up.

What's your name?

Bob, he said.

Bob. Perfect. I should have known.

Okay, Bob, I said. Listen, I need some clothes.

Yes.

And I'd like you to help me, Bob. Can you help me find some clothes? Are there any clothes around there? That I could borrow?

He seemed to think for a while.

No, he said.

Damn.

I wandered from room to room. I seemed to know the place. Of course I knew the place, I'd been there all night. But my knowledge had the dreamy, fitful aspect of déjà vu.

I opened some cabinets. I looked under fixtures. I didn't find anything resembling clothing that wasn't made of vinyl or latticed black leather and studs. Nothing that wouldn't frighten any normal cab driver away.

There was only one thing to do.

I promised myself I wouldn't enjoy it.

I found an iron bar on the floor next to what looked like a small trapeze. Something with a handcuff on each end. I picked it up. I hefted it. It weighed enough to do the job. I padded softly back to the big room. Bob had his back to me. The sweeping seemed to take all his concentration. This was good.

I stepped up silently behind him. I raised the bar over my head. I hesitated. Bob, clearly, was an innocent. He'd been good to me, even. He'd undone the shackles.

But damn, I needed to get the hell out of there.

I apologized to Bob. I'm deeply sorry, I said.

I said it to myself.

I brought down the bar.

I pulled back at the last second. I didn't want to hurt the poor guy. Just knock him out a bit.

It worked.

He fell face-first. I checked his pulse. Strong and steady. No problem. I stripped off the overalls. Hauled them on. They seemed to weigh ten pounds. As I figured out how the snaps worked, I looked for a mirror. To see just how stupid I looked. There was no mirror. But there was a mammoth arched wooden door, painted red and covered in what looked to be Inca-style—or Aztec, how would I know the difference?—etchings, burnt in or carved so skillfully they seemed an organic part of the wood. Two mammoth vintage fifties surgical lamps stood on either side of it.

I didn't want to speculate.

I tried the door. It was locked. I wandered about. The place was a warren of narrow hallways and small rooms. In one of the rooms the walls and ceiling were all mirror. I saw myself.

I looked like a reject from a *Hee Haw* casting call. Maybe a junkie. A junkie reject from a *Hee Haw* casting call.

I found the exit door. It led to a door that led to a hallway that led to a door that led to a spiral staircase—yes, I was beginning to remember—at the top of which was a door that opened onto the bracing hundred-ten-degree Las Vegas air. The overalls hung ludicrously heavy on my afflicted bones. I wanted to crumple down onto the sidewalk. Sleep. Rest. Have nothing more to do with it.

I had no clue where I was. But wherever it was, it was civilized enough that a taxi rolled by. I overcame the lethargy, tried to hail a cab. It passed me by. I sat down. I saw another. I didn't have time to stand up. I waved at it. I could feel my desperation. The cab driver could see it, too. He sped away. I staggered to my feet.

About two years later, another one came by. I conjured a confident taxi wave. He stopped. A guy not offended by overalls. Must have been from Oklahoma.

I managed to communicate my destination.

At which point I asked myself how I was going to pay the fare. I thought of asking if he would take a credit card, or a check, but it didn't take me more than five minutes to remember that I didn't have those on me any more than cash.

I shivered. It wasn't the air-conditioning, which didn't seem to be functioning. It came from inside of me. Frostbite of the liver, or something. I put my hands in the pockets of the overalls.

And discovered that they were stuffed with change. Silver. Coins.

The poor fucker's life savings.

No wonder the damn overalls felt so heavy.

Ah, shit, I said to myself.

But at least I could pay for the cab.

The cab smelled of old metal and dust.

Or I thought it did, until I got out at the Dusty Rathole. Where I realized that it was me.

I stopped in the lobby. The floor was moving. Earthquake? I thought. They don't have earthquakes in Las Vegas, do they?

Ah, but it was only me again.

I stumbled to one of the two beige chairs that graced the lobby. The one next to the potted palm. The real one that looked like a fake one.

That one.

53.

I MUST HAVE FALLEN ASLEEP. Hell, I admit it. I did fall asleep.

I shuddered awake.

There wasn't anyone in sight. I had no idea what time it was. I had a vague recollection that someone had shaken me awake earlier. Brendan? Yes. He'd been there. But that was all I had. A thought that he'd been there. A conviction. That I'd talked to him. I had no idea what was said. Except. He was in trouble.

Maybe he was in the suite.

I stumbled out of the chair. Called the room on the house phone. No answer. I negotiated a room key from the disbelieving desk clerk. Headed for what looked like the right hallway. There was an elevator there. I pressed some buttons. My subconscious didn't let me down. Or muscle memory. Maybe it was muscle memory. Was there a difference? One the subset of the other? I got out on a floor. I headed down another hall. I found a room. I opened the door. It took three tries.

Everything was black.

There was nobody there.

I looked at my watch. Six, it said. Morning or evening, I didn't know. Shit.

I staggered to the bathroom. I scrubbed my face with cold water. It didn't do a thing for me.

I went to the bedroom. I fell into bed. I slept. I slept a dark sleep troubled only by dreams of a menacing, predatory sort.

In short, nothing unusual.

54.

I woke up slowly. Very slowly. I looked around. The ancient flip-number bedside clock said 6:23. Morning or evening, I had no idea. Had I slept for twenty-three minutes? Twelve hours and twenty-three minutes? I listened. Nothing. I was still the only one home, it seemed.

And as hard as I tried, I couldn't remember a damn thing about the previous night. At least, nothing after . . . what was her name, Ruby? Diamond. That was it. I remembered Diamond leaning over me. I was lying down. I could see down her gangster suit jacket. She was wearing nothing underneath. She was tiny. Delicious tiny breasts. I had turned my head. Saw another pair of legs. Nice, muscular, naked legs. And something about a door. The red door. Bodies going in and out of it.

And that was all I remembered. Other than some vague thing about a conversation in the lobby. I'd been sitting in the beige chair, next to the fake real palm tree. But I couldn't remember who it was, or what was said, or how I felt about it. Could have been a dream. I didn't know.

I might have been a sick boozehound, but I never had blackouts. I might misremember a name or two; call somebody named Diamond, Ruby; wonder where the ticket stub for the Cardinals game in my jacket pocket came from—having never been to St. Louis in my life—or the rubber bunny with a faint but discernible scent of hashish. But a whole night gone? Never.

This called for commiseration.

I had to call Sheila.

While Sheila's phone rang, while I listened to her interminable voice mail message—if this is urgent, call X, if this is an emergency, call Y;

what the fuck was the difference between urgent and emergent?—I felt somewhere in between. I thought about the etymology of the expression 'placing a call.' Calls used to be placed, I surmised, because you had to call the operator to place it for you. Put the plug in its proper receptacle. Place the plug. Place the call. Hah. I might even be right. But who would care, four hundred years from now? Somebody might care about the phrase, I suppose. Some ridiculously cloistered graduate student studying Twentieth-Century English Anachronisms. But they'd neither know, nor care, that I'd figured it out, here in the Ashcroft, I meant the Stardust, the Dust-Filled Monk, Motel, in Las Vegas, Nevada, at some god-awful time of the day—was there any other kind?—in some god-awful state of drugged inebriation, unsure of anything anymore. Unsure whether I would even live to see the next day.

I called the emergency number. Could she speak to me by phone? It was urgent.

She called back within ten minutes. She had an opening. Not a surprise, but pleasant anyway. More than pleasant. Damn, I began to realize, I was fairly close to what some people might call desperate.

I told Sheila the story. The whole damn thing. Or as much of it as I could remember. Which wasn't all that much.

Oh dear, she said.

She was always sympathetic. No matter how debauched, demented and deluded I got, she never went judgmental on me.

I loved her for that. Not that kind of love, mind you. Don't get me wrong.

If you abuse alcohol long enough, she said, the blackouts will start. Maybe without warning.

Sure, I said. But that extreme? All of a sudden? One night, memory as clear as a—let's be honest—clear as a frog pond, anyway, once you pushed away the lily pads? And then, the next night, nothing? All night, nothing? Blackness? That's never happened to me before. Nothing even close.

Not to mention, she said sympathetically, that whatever happened, it appears, must have been rather . . . memorable.

There's that too. Jesus Christ on a stick.

I haven't heard that one before.

I just made it up. Pretty good, no?

I'll reserve judgement on that one, she said.

I expected you would.

Let's get back on topic.

Okay. I'm easy.

Frankly, from everything you told me, it sounds very much like someone might have slipped you some benzodiazepines.

What's that?

What they call the date rape drug. It's a family of drugs, actually. They incapacitate you, and often affect your memory.

Yeah, I've read about it. But it could have been other things, no? I mean, I don't know anything about all this . . .

Well of course, we don't know. But whether it was that or something else, trauma, alcohol, autonomic repression, there are techniques for recovering lost memory. I assume you want to know what happened?

Damn straight I do.

That's another new expression. For me.

Your sheltered life. It's kind of a common phrase amongst certain denizens of the more cretinous dark corners of society. Places you haven't been to.

I'll let that one go by too, then. Have you spoken to the police about this?

The police? Christ, no. Why would I want to call the police?

It appears that something criminal might have taken place.

Let's just say that if criminal acts took place, I'm not entirely sure I didn't commit one or two myself.

I see. Well, I guess I'm out of my territory there. So, let's get back to the memory loss.

That might be helpful.

Okay, let's try a little exercise.

Fine with me.

Close your eyes.

I closed my eyes.

Picture the last thing you remember of that night.

I tried to picture the last thing I remembered.

I'm not sure, I said, that I consciously, let alone subconsciously, want to remember anything about it. Now that I think about it.

I understand. But shame is not appropriate here. I'm your therapist, not your mother.

Yeah, but aren't I supposed to be confusing the two, or something? Isn't that what that transference thing is supposed to be all about?

Now I know you're joking. Let's get back to the memory, shall we? It's not about what it is. It's about the details. Focusing on the details may bring the memories back. The picture will fill in. If you prefer not to know—

No, no, I said. Let's go on.

Keep going.

There's something about a door.

What about a door?

I don't know. I just know it's . . . a very important . . . thing. Door.

Is it red?

Is it red, did you say?

Yes.

It is, actually. Why would you ask that?

Silence.

Oh, I said.

Yes, she replied.

The Case of the Red Car Door.

We'd talked about it.

The subconscious works in mysterious ways, she said.

Almost as much as you do, I replied.

She laughed. Think about it, she said. Is there a connection?

I'll think about it, I said. Well, actually.

Yes?

The door really was red. The door in the club. I saw it this morning. When I came to.

I see.

Actually, let's go back to this last-night thing.

Okay.

I'm not really sure it was last night.

You're not.

No. I've been sleeping. On and off. And what with that, and the discombobulation and all, I really don't even know. What day it is.

Wednesday.

I see. I'm not sure that helps me.

It will come back to you.

I hope so. You know, this memory stuff, it reminds me.

Of?

Back in the hippie days, when I was homeless and all? Living in a tent in northern Alberta?

Yes?

We had this thing. I don't know where it came from. There was this schizophrenic guy in the group, very nice, very entertaining guy, we didn't know he was psychotic then, he didn't know it, I mean, he knew there was something wrong with him, or maybe he didn't, I don't know, he knew he was different, I mean, he even looked different, he was one of those skinny, ropy muscular guys, with a skeleton head and those awful pustular acne scars, and he knew all sorts of shit that seemed fascinating back then, Zen stuff, and theosophy, and gestalt, and all those wonderful words, and he had this trick.

Yes?

You would be falling asleep, and you would see your hands. Best would be if you put them together, prayer-like, and stared at them as you fell asleep. And then, later, in your dreams, you would glimpse your hands and, *poof,* like some fairy tale, really, I'm not making this up, you'd be there, in your dream. I mean, you're always in your dreams, in a way, but you have no control over them. They go off in their crazy dream directions and you can't do anything about it, you don't even think about doing anything about it. You're at the mercy of that dream logic. But if you do it this way, you're suddenly in control. You're there. You can decide things. You can turn left, instead of right. You can say, Around the bend there'll be a castle, and in the castle . . . Well, I never got to the point that I could control everything—the dream logic resists you—but I could do a lot. Damn. It's funny to think about. It was so cool. Why did I stop doing it? It just went away. Never thought about it. Years ago. Decades. It just faded away. I wonder if I could do it again, now?

What happened to your friend?

Oh, he's still around. I haven't talked to him in ages. But then they came up with the new drugs. Stuff that makes him more normal. He's not nearly as interesting. I sort of lost touch with him. He got married, even. I don't know if he had kids. I hope not.

I put the cell phone on speaker. Went to get some water. I was still thirsty. A thirst that showed no signs of going away.

That's really interesting, she said. I mean that. I'd like to explore that some more, sometime. But right now I think the agenda is to get your memory of that night back.

Last night.

I'm sorry?

I realized that I was at least fifty feet from the phone. There was no way she could hear me. Unless I shouted. Which, I was fairly certain, was not a therapeutically useful act.

I scurried back to the phone. Took it off speaker.

Last night, I repeated. It was just last night. There's something strange about referring to last night as 'that night,' is what I meant.

Um, okay. Yes. We'll call it last night.

Anyway, yeah, I know, get those memories back. But I did have one last confession to make.

Go ahead.

I spent most of those dream episodes looking for girls.

Sheila laughed. Dream girls? she said.

I was way ahead of my time, I smiled.

Sheila got it.

I loved her for that.

Okay, she said. Let's get back to the point.

Yes?

Can we get back to the point?

Oh, yeah. Well. I kind of thought that was on point.

It wasn't. And I'm afraid I have to go now.

Okay.

Actually, I was kind of relieved.

We'll have to get back to retrieving those memories next time.

Maybe I can try on my own.

You can certainly try. Anyway, from everything you've told me, I'm fairly certain that you were dosed with one of the benzodiazepines, or something similar. If that's the case, this technique can be effective.

God, I thought, this is so clinical. I got dosed. I got abused. I got naked-ized. I had to steal a poor debased fucker's overalls and life's savings. Why wasn't I angry? Full of revenge? Heading back there with pistols drawn? And why wasn't Sheila angry? Or at least asking me why I wasn't angry, full of revenge, and heading back there with pistols drawn?

Good, I said. I'll work on the technique.

I paused. I had a thought.

It's weird, I said. Who would have wanted to do that to me?

It sounds like there are a number of candidates.

Yeah. Just kidding. Of course there are.

We'll get back to work as soon as I have an opening.

Thank you, I said.

I paused.

It makes me feel kind of funny, I said.

Of course it does. It's a powerful drug.

No, that's not what I mean.

What do you mean?

Well, I mean, they give that to girls, right?

Usually.

So it makes me feel kind of, I don't know, not gay, exactly. Emasculated, I guess.

We'll discuss that next time, too.

Okay, I said.

I looked at the clock. Actually, we had five minutes left.

We have five minutes left, I said. Actually.

Oh, she said. I'm sorry. You're right.

I could feel her discomfort again. I left it like that.

There was a long silence.

There are a few other things you can do, she said.

Yes?

One thing I didn't mention before. Because I wasn't sure how you'd feel about it.

There's only one way to find out.

Yes. Well, as you're probably aware, if you have a damaged, a repressed memory, it's often very useful to return to the physical location. Where the event occurred. That you can't remember.

Fuck, I said.

What's wrong? she asked quietly, as though afraid of what I was going to say.

Why didn't I think of that before? I asked.

She laughed, a small, discreet laugh. I don't know, she said. But it makes perfect sense that you didn't.

How so?

I think we can assume that something traumatic occurred there.

I'm with you so far.

You would hesitate, your subconscious would hesitate, to go back to the scene of the trauma. Lest it happen again. Or at best, that you be reminded of it.

Of course, I said. I knew that.

I heard her smile.

I smiled in return.

Yes. We understood each other.

55.

WHEN I GOT OFF THE PHONE WITH SHEILA, I took an hour to stare at the wall. Clear my head as best I could. I could try some memory exercises. Find some nerve. Somewhere. I tried my nerves. No nerve there. I inspected my spine. No spine. Spineless. I looked for moxie, balls, chutzpah. None in the vicinity.

I tried the memory tricks. They didn't work. Except. It seemed to me, vaguely but quite certainly, that something had happened behind that red door. But this, of course, was highly suspect. Sheila had planted the idea. She was a great shrink. A forensics expert she wasn't.

I decided to organize what I did remember. Figure out what I had to do.

First thing, I told myself, you have to talk to the client. Keep the client up-to-date. Jesus. We'd had an appointment, hadn't we? And Madeleine? And Kelley. Jesus on a stick. I'd stood them all up. Every one of them. And where the hell was Butch? He was supposed to find Brendan. Had Butch vanished too?

Things were even worse than I thought.

It was almost beyond my ability to deal. But somehow, somewhere, I found a small mother lode of will. Determination. Moxie, even.

I heard the voice of my father. I knew it wasn't his real voice. Even if I'd heard it, at the age of eight, I knew enough to know that I couldn't reproduce it now. But the message? Yes. The message was not only possible, but true. Resonant.

A man does not give up.

That was his truth. Also true, he died with his face in a bowl of minestrone. But that didn't detract from the power of the message. Much.

True to the fiber of my bones, it was.

Do bones have fiber? I asked myself.

I made a note to look it up.

Meanwhile, I made a list.

- Call Louise.
- Apologize.
- Reschedule the meeting.
- Call Madeleine.
- Apologize.
- Reschedule the dinner.
- Call Kelley, apologize.
- Reschedule.
- Call Butch.
- Apologize.
- No. I didn't have anything to apologize to Butch for.
- Call Butch. Find out what's up with Brendan.

I got to work.

I called Louise. She didn't sound pleased. I didn't blame her.

I don't blame you, I said.

I need to see you immediately, she said.

I'll be right over, I replied.

I grabbed a cab to the Wynn. It smelled of cleaning fluid, and unfinished business.

56.

YOU TOLD HER I WAS ASKING AFTER VLADIMIR? Louise shouted. Are you even more of a moron than you act?

She seemed a little upset.

I was a tad surprised hearing this language from the decorous mouth of Ms. Chandler. On the other hand, I was beginning to realize that the Chandler sisters were full of surprises.

I felt like saying, Hummina hummina. But I thought that might give away my dismay.

I'm sorry, I said. I must have misunderstood.

I guess you did, she said, turning her back and walking to the window. She stood there, hands folded in front of her, gazing at the Strip in all its overheated glory.

It was, I had to admit, a very nice back. A tapered thing, gently curving inward to a belted tiny waist. The belt was made of some velvetlike material, a mysterious shade of green. Chameleon green, maybe. I was lost in it for a moment, absorbed in its sort-of-but-not-quite greenness.

She abruptly turned around.

Mr. Redman, she addressed me in a calmer tone.

No more Rick, I guessed. Two steps forward, one step back.

Mr. Redman, I really did not expect to have to give you step-by-step instructions. You presented yourself as a professional.

Yes, I said. Well. But it's hard for me to see how I could have known that you didn't want me to mention that you were asking after her boyfriend.

Mr. Redman, that is preposterous. Since when does an investigator volunteer anything about his client to others, still less the object of the investigation? Isn't that rule number one in the manual?

I was starting to see her point. I made a note to track down a copy of the manual.

Yes. Well, I can only apologize, again. And hope that irreparable harm hasn't been done.

I don't know, she said in a suddenly quiet voice. A voice with a tinge of despair.

There was a long silence. As I waited for her to break it, I poured myself a scotch. I offered her one. She shook her head. She turned her back to me again. I sat back down in the frighteningly comfortable armchair. I looked around the suite. A remarkable job they'd done. The place had an easy air of luxury about it, but somehow avoided the pretension usually found leaching about these kinds of joints.

I have to tell you, Ms. Chandler, I said, unable to restrain myself any longer, I'm beginning to wonder what the hell this is all about.

What it's all about? Why should that concern you, Mr. Redman?

It shouldn't, necessarily. But it depends. If I don't know what I'm doing, I could end up doing something wrong.

Mr. Redman, please. I'm quite certain you are no stranger to that concept.

Yes, well. There's a difference. If I choose to do something wrong, something that some people might consider to be wrong, that's one thing. I'll take the consequences. It's my choice.

And it's your choice to take my money and do what I tell you.

I had a twinge. I didn't have her money anymore. Or much of it. I elided through the twinge.

Sure. You got a point. And I can choose different, too, I said.

Ms. Chandler turned around.

You're so charming when you slip into that goombah thing, she said.

Yeah, thanks.

She was a slippery number, this Louise Chandler. Hard to keep the conversation going in the right direction.

Where was I? I asked.

Something about being a bad boy.

Listen, I said, so far you haven't asked me to do anything questionable, at least to the best of my knowledge. But at the same time, it's obvious that there's a lot of stuff you haven't told me. And I'm not at all sure that what you have told me was, strictly speaking, true.

She glided over, sat on the couch.

And yes, I continued, you're the client, and I guess that's your right. Sort of. Maybe.

I stopped. She got up and got herself a drink. I began to realize that I was in danger of shooting myself in the gonads. I couldn't go too far with this. What if she said fine, you're fired, give me back the retainer?

Shit on a stick.

I can't help thinking, I said to her, that I could do my job better if you shared more information. I mean, maybe I wouldn't have told Eloise—

Mr. Redman, she interrupted, returning with a drink for herself, one for me, I understand what you're saying. And maybe, someday, I'll tell you everything. But I'm sure you've divined by now that these matters are very sensitive. Family matters. I will give you the information you need to do what I ask you to do.

This wasn't going anywhere. Which was just as well.

Besides which, she went on, are you sure that you have given me all of the information that you have acquired?

What do you mean?

You haven't told me much.

I'm not sure there's much to tell. I found your sister. Told you where she is. I haven't found Vladimir. Yet. I will.

Let's try this, she said. Why don't you go back over everything you've done. Fill in all the details.

She had her eyes locked on mine. She wasn't smiling. In fact, her face had taken on a sharp edge. This was a new Louise. Not one I cared too much for.

And this was just what I needed, befogged, in pain and bewildered as I was. A memory contest.

I took a deep breath.

Sit here, she said, indicating next to her on the couch. It seemed a strange request, in the circumstances. But I had no objection. It would be easier to avoid her eyes.

I moved over. Sank into the cushion next to her. Carefully avoided body contact. Didn't know if it was appropriate, at this time. Didn't want to cause offense. I sat back, tried to get my mind right. See through the sand. All right. I'd gone to Dani's house, Eloise's house . . .

Oh shit, I said.

Yes?

I completely forgot.

That's a surprise.

Damn, I said. I don't know why. It just slipped my mind.

I suggest that you share with me whatever this is. This thing that slipped your mind.

I told her about the basement at Dani's house. The odd equipment.

And, she said, you just totally forgot about all this?

No, no. Not exactly. I mean, I haven't seen you since then. And it didn't seem important, really. At least, I can't connect it to anything.

There was a long silence. During which I considered what it might feel like to throw myself off the balcony of the topmost floor of the Wynn Hotel and Casino in Las Vegas, Nevada.

Louise Chandler got up off the couch. Turned to face me. Crossed her arms. Smiled.

Okay, she said. Forget about that. Here is what you'll do. You'll go to that damn trailer park. Incognito. Can you do incognito?

Of course, I said.

It wasn't entirely a lie. Even if I'd never tried it before, it couldn't be that hard.

You'll stake it out. You won't talk to my sister. She won't even know you're there. Are you clear on that?

Yes, yes.

And you'll wait. As long as it takes. Until Vladimir shows up.

I thought of the days and days that might go by. Days and nights away from the poker table.

I thought about asking for a raise.

Not prudent, I concluded.

How do you know he's going to show up? I asked.

I don't, she said. I have no idea. But if he does, I want you to be there. And if she leaves, I want you to follow her. Find out where she goes.

I didn't like this at all. But it didn't look like I had a choice.

Okay, I said. We'll stake it out. But it won't just be me. We'll have to rotate.

That will be fine, she said.

She smiled.

Victory.

57.

NEXT THING, FIND BRENDAN. Unless Butch had already. I had to talk to Butch. I called him. No answer.

I didn't know where to start. Butch always knew what to do next.

I headed for the Rio. The purple velvet bar.

Butch was there. What a fucking relief. Something normal.

Butch, I said.

Rick.

Did you find Brendan?

Not a trace.

Shit.

Yeah.

I don't know what to do.

I think we got to talk to the damn Russkies.

I think you're right. I deputize you. I can't.

Why not?

I got a problem.

We know you got problems.

You're right. Problems. Plural. I've got a lot of fences to mend.

Go mend your fences, Rick. I'll keep looking.

I hate to say it, but maybe you should check the police. Hospitals. Like that.

Thanks, Rick. Hadn't thought of that.

Okay, okay. I'm useless. Just as well I got other stuff I have to take care of.

Don't wear yourself out. Tomorrow's our Day Two.

Shit.

Yeah.

Feels like a week's gone by.

Yeah.

A tall, slim young woman with a singularly confident air strode up.

Shit, I said under my breath.

Hi, Dad, she said.

Butch raised his eyebrows.

We only met yesterday, I said. Do you think that's appropriate?

What? she said.

Calling me Dad.

But you are my dad.

Butch's eyebrows raised further.

To tell you the truth, I said, I only have your word for that, and that Lesquirrel guy's.

She laughed. Folded herself into the empty chair. It reminded me of someone. I couldn't place who. Which reminded me. I still didn't know who the hell her mother was.

Don't worry, she said. We can talk about that later.

I wasn't sure if she'd read my mind, or . . . what was she talking about? I was confused. Better not to let on, though.

I'm really sorry about last night, I said. I got tied up—I almost laughed—I didn't have my cell phone with me . . .

It's okay. I know you're busy.

I appreciate that. Thank you. Listen, let's do it tonight, okay? Eight o'clock. I promise I won't miss it this time.

Okay, she said, and demurely took her leave.

Butch's eyebrows were in danger of reaching the back of his head.

Jesus, he said, what, or should I say who, was that?

Uh, my daughter, Butch. Did you miss that?

You been keeping something from me all these years?

No more than I've been keeping from myself.

Come on, Rick. Give me the download.

Don't worry about that. One of those long-lost-daughter things you read about. I'll tell you later. Anyway, you know just about as much as I do at this point.

Oh, c'mon, man.

Seriously, Butch. Just leave it alone for now, okay?

Whatever you say, man. So, what're these problems you were talking about? Other than the one that just walked away.

I asked you to leave that alone.

Sorry, man. Sorry.

All right. Listen.

I told him the whole miserable story. Delgado, the club, the blackout, the overalls. The dustup with Louise. The complete unexpurgated ugly mess of it. Well, not entirely complete. I left out the part about Kelley and Madeleine.

So let's go back there, he said. Bust up the place. Break some heads. Find some answers.

Violence isn't the answer to every problem, Butch.

Yes it is.

Anyway, if we have to do that, we'll do it. But first I have to try to remember what the hell happened. I mean, what if . . . I don't fucking know. I just can't go back there, guns blazing, when I don't know a damn thing. Besides, wouldn't whoever did it be ready for that?

You want me to call some people?

It's the same thing, Butch. Sure, I'm going to report that I went, voluntarily, to a sick joint like that, woke up naked and can't remember anything? First, they'll laugh their asses off. Second, exactly what is the crime I'm supposed to be reporting?

Yeah.

Yeah.

So we talked poker for a while. He'd had a bad day. Lost in a couple of one-table tournaments. He'd ended up all in with a dour, pockmarked Asian dumpling. Or maybe it was a dour, pockmarked East Indian dumpling. Are Indians Asians? Technically, yes, I guessed. I made a note to look it up. Either way, the guy had a brown boiled matzo of a nose, as Butch described it. You could store your life's savings in the guy's pores. He called Butch's all in with Eight, Seven off suit. A total donkey play. Butch had Aces. Needless to say, Matzo Boy hit a Seven on the flop and an Eight on the river for two pair. Butch sucked it up. Went to the cash games. Lost a pile there too.

It happens. Sometimes the cards don't fall for you. He understood. I understood. Part of the game. He was drinking it off.

I didn't feel like another drink.

That's when I knew something was terribly wrong.

Butch went to take a piss. I ordered a cranberry and soda. I watched a guy at the next table. He was sitting alone. Enormous ears. Balding, fat. Hooked, veiny nose, thick, shiny lips. He looked like your great-uncle Moishe after a two-week bender. He was reading a hefty book. A half smile on his face. He put the book down. I discreetly leaned over to see the title.

How to Succeed with Women.

I ordered a double scotch.

58.

I HAD DINNER WITH MADELEINE in the high-roller lounge. It was hard to act normal. I did my best. She didn't seem to notice anything wrong. Or maybe she was just being polite. We talked about a lot of stuff. It was therapeutic. For me, anyway. I couldn't speak for her.

She wanted to know about her father. I hardly knew where to start. It's not like I was a dad to be proud of. Even back when I was a big-shot lawyer, I was faking it eighty percent of the time. Not that I wasn't good at it. But I never really bought into the 'The Organization is bigger, more important than you' thing. In fact, I loathed it. Not too strong a word.

Anyway, she was bound to find out a few things about dear old Dad that were less than complimentary. To put it mildly. So I decided to give her a little background. Some context to put them in.

Back when I was a big-shot lawyer, I explained, well, a medium-shot lawyer, some people were surprised at my predilection for sleazy joints. Some guys hung out at the Champagne Bar, I liked to go to the Randy Pony. But it wasn't any mystery. I wasn't born a big-shot lawyer. Or a big-shot anything. I was born in a tiny mining town in northern Québec. And I acquired my taste for the low life early. Started going to the Tavern at thirteen, every night but Sunday, with my friend Weasel. The Tavern was a peculiar Québec institution of the time. Women weren't allowed. It was a refuge for the working man. You'd watch the hockey game. Drink draft beer. Play pool. We got pretty good at it, me and Weasel. We'd go in with a quarter or two. You'd play a game for a draft, loser bought the beer, paid for the next game. We'd almost never lose. Drink all night for a quarter.

We'd hang with the guys. Old guys. Working guys. Guys with lines in their faces and grime under their nails. Guys who went to the track. Bet on the ponies. Guys who lived for *Hockey Night in Canada*. Les Canadiens. Jean Béliveau. Yvan Cournoyer. Later, Guy Lafleur. They were our Gods. We didn't care about much else.

To me, it was a warm place. You could count on it. The same guys every night. The same talk. The smooth green surface of the pool table. The same reassuring tilts and slow spots. The weight of the cue in your hand, slightly warped. You'd try to find the same one every night, the one whose warp you'd accustomed yourself to. The draft beer, in tall fluted glasses. You'd put salt in it, watch the bubbles frantically rise. You'd eat beer nuts, pickled eggs, french fries. The best french fries anywhere.

No nasty surprises.

So I guess the rest of my life, I was looking for that place again.

Never found it.

Came close a few times.

The Wolf's Lair was close.

Vinnie's game was close.

I guess everything else I did was part of the same thing.

I'd been looking at the floor. I raised my head. There she was. Jesus, I'd almost forgotten she was there. It was like I'd been talking to myself.

She looked at me. She had a small smile at the corners of her eyes.

I get it, she said.

I hoped it was true.

59.

KELLEY AND PETER WERE WAITING FOR ME AT THE MOTEL. It was disconcerting. I was desperate to let all the secrets out. They were clogging up my soul. The problem was, I didn't even know all the secrets. The drains were going to run slow till I did.

But as soon as I walked in, the anxiety was gone. There she was, my light, my angel. And Peter. The comic relief. Maybe something more.

I wasn't sure yet. My surrogate son, at least in spirit. And this was good. Please, I thought, don't disappoint me.

We drank some wine. At least, Peter and I did. Kelley didn't touch the stuff. I admired her for that. More than admiration. Relief, too. She wasn't going to go down that road. The path her parents took. Her grandparents. Everyone on the goddamn family tree. For once there was someone who wasn't going to succumb to the poisoned fruit.

It wasn't just me. Everyone loved Kelley and Peter. Everyone given the privilege of entering their world. Who couldn't? They were funny, kind and unselfconscious. Well, Kelley was funny, kind and unselfconscious. Peter was funny. Was there anything more you could ask of a human?

But I knew I was in trouble. Their hours were even worse than mine. They had the depraved need to watch pay-per-view movies and DVDs till dawn, commenting and cackling loudly at every line, every amateurish cut and splice. Inured through years of this, I'd simply pass out in the wine-soaked haze of it, my otherwise terrifying dreams most assuredly improved by the atmosphere.

And, most nights, we found time, between screenings, to talk, and live.

Menopause, said Peter. Women becoming obsolete, but convincing themselves that there's something graceful about it.

That's not very charitable, I said. A lot of people find that very difficult to go through.

I took a course, Peter said. Women in cliterature.

There was no slowing him down.

But I figured it was time to tell them about their sister. Kelley's sister. Half sister.

I told them.

They were speechless.

It was a first.

And you don't even know who her mom is? Kelley said at last.

Not yet, I said.

How old did you say she was?

Eighteen.

So that means . . .

Yes, I know. I'm sorry. Can we not go there right now?

Okay, she said.

But she didn't look happy about it.

I let some time go by.

Would you like to meet her? I asked.

Silence.

You'll have to sometime, I said. Might as well be now. She's really nice. You'll like her. She plays the piano.

Oh, well, if she plays the piano . . . , said Peter.

· Okay, said Kelley.

I was a bit surprised. And relieved. We could get this over with. Started. Over with and started.

I called Madeleine. She was excited. Kelley and Peter were not. I endured some frost for a while.

The wine helped it down.

The doorbell rang.

And there she was.

She couldn't have looked more different than Kelley.

And yet, there was something. I could feel it. Kelley could feel it. I could feel Kelley feeling it.

There really wasn't any doubt about it.

After a few minutes of discomfort, things started to roll. Madeleine told a story. About why she'd changed her hair color. A girl at her school, she told us, showed up one day with the same hair color, the same makeup, as Madeleine. That's it, she told herself. I'll have to change everything.

It's like an original Louis Vuitton bag, she said. Once you've seen so many fakes, the real thing doesn't look so good.

Ah, yes. There was no doubt.

She was one of us.

60.

HE HAD AN ODD EXPRESSION ON HIS FACE. Half smile, half grimace. Part puzzlement. That may add up to more than a whole. But death does strange things to people.

He was lying face up. His right arm twisted behind his back. He clutched something in his left hand. I couldn't make out what it was.

He was in black tie. Tuxedo. White ruffled shirt. Bow tie. Bare feet. Clean, though. As though recently shod.

Oh, Brendan, I whispered. What have you done?

Shit happened. Something about a fountain, a knitting needle.

I heard Butch's baritone voice. Turned around. Saw his extra-wide smile. Trying to be reassuring. Succeeding, a bit.

Ricky, Ricky, he said. Come on. Let's go home.

I felt his arm around my shoulder.

I nodded my head slowly.

We flagged a cab. It smelled of sardines and sweat.

61.

SLEEP FOR AN HOUR. Get up. Drink scotch. Take painkillers. Avoid the mirror. Watch TV. Spit at it. Drink some more scotch. Fall asleep for an hour. Wake up. Get up. Same thing again. Shit.

People kept dying.

And it wasn't that Time guy I was warned about. It was something else.

On top of which, it was fucking Day Two of the Fabulous World Series of Poker. How the fuck was I supposed to play poker now?

There was only one way to get through it.

I'd play in honor of Brendan. Hell, I'd win the whole thing for him. Buy him a statue for his grave.

I was angry as hell. I knew it wasn't right to be angry at the dead. It wasn't their fault they were dead. Though in Brendan's case, I wasn't so sure. But it isn't good karma. It's not like they could fight back. Make their argument. But I was sick of everybody dying on me. Melissa. FitzGibbon. FitzGibbon's kid. Brendan. How dare they all? Make me go through all the fucking emotions? I feel bad. Do I feel bad enough? If I don't feel bad enough, should I feel guilty about it? Do I feel guilty enough about it? Was there anything I could have done? Or did I actually help it along? Damn, I'd been mean to Brendan more than once. Did that make me responsible? For whatever he'd done to himself? Or whatever he'd let someone else do to him? There didn't seem to be a third possibility . . .

Ah, fuck it. I shoved it aside. Dragged on some clothes. Put on the cowboy hat and my darkest shades. Got to the Rio. Found my table. There were a bunch of initials there. Johnnie G. Frankie Z. DJ Donnie.

Vinnie V. I thought of getting one. Ricky R. didn't do it. Had to be Ricky P. or something. Wait a minute. Something wrong with that. Smelled of urination. Ah, forget about it.

I tried to watch the table, between naps. A couple, three tight guys. Maybe good. Maybe just tight. Hadn't seen enough to tell. Johnnie G. was an Asian guy in shades, raising and re-raising. Never smiling. Just raking in the pots. Had to be careful with him. An older woman. Big hat, big shades, stack of chips in front of her. Friendly. Too friendly. Watch out. DJ Donnie was a loud-mouthed guy in a brown suede jacket, guessing everyone's cards. Nice Jacks, he'd say, folding another hand he'd called to the end. We were supposed to be impressed. Frankie Z. was a pro I knew from New York. Solid guy till his fifth Budweiser. Then he could get dangerous.

About an hour in, I'm in a pot with DJ Donnie, Mr. Suede. I'm not unhappy about that. The guy is clearly full of himself, not nearly as good as he thinks he is. He has no idea that by telling everybody what he thinks their cards are—on top of the fact that he's usually wrong—he's doing nothing more than giving the better players information about how he thinks. And information, as we all know, is power. And power, as many of us are aware, is money.

I look at my hole cards. Ace, Ten suited. Pretty good starting hand, in late position anyway. If you play it carefully. Can't get carried away with it. I put in a healthy raise. Everyone behind me folds to Mr. Suede. He calls. The flop comes all rags, Eight, Five, Three. Mixed blessing. Didn't hit me, but not likely to have hit him either. I put in a big bet. Try to push him off the pot. He calls. He's wearing shades. He stares me down. I think he's staring me down. But actually, I can't tell. Because of the shades. His shades. My shades. It's a shady sort of deal.

The turn card is the diamond Jack. It does nothing for me. Apart from vague Bob Dylan associations. Or maybe that was the Jack of hearts. The Dylan song. I check. Not the Dylan song. I'll check that later. I check my hand to Mr. Suede. He bets. Three-quarters of the pot. A healthy raise. I glance at him. He's looking contemptuous. He's too good for this crowd, the Look is telling me.

If he's any good, I figure, the Look means he's got something. Somebody with nothing, somebody looking for a fold, would want to be inconspicuous. Shrink to nothingness. Not raise suspicion. Instead, he's staring me down. I think.

Of course, he could be thinking that I'd be thinking that if he had a hand he'd be doing exactly that, but that he was a good player, which he certainly thought he was, and I, therefore, would think he was, of course, that good a player, and that therefore I'd be thinking that he might be doing it on purpose, doing a reverse tell, and . . .

Well, you see how it goes.

But really, I decide, the guy's a fish. So.

I call.

The river card's a Ten.

I see a tiny flinch. He doesn't like that card.

But he bets three thousand anyway.

I know I have him. I absolutely know it.

I shove all my chips in the middle.

Good river card, he says, shaking his head and raising his cards as if to fold.

I push my cards towards the muck.

I'll pay you off, he continues,

just as my cards reach the discard pile,

and throws in the rest of his chips

to call my bet,

turning over an Eight

to match the one on board,

and as I reach to pull my cards from the muck

with my right hand

to flip over my Ten

and with my left reach for the mammoth pot

Frankie Z. says, Hey, wait a minute,

that hand is dead.

That's right, Johnnie G. says, your cards touched the muck, your hand is dead.

And of course, they're right.

I watch my hard-earned stack disappear. Into the sneering pile of chips in front of Mr. Suede.

Well, I thought five minutes later, as I trudged empty-handed down the hallway in search of a scotch, I guess that was a fitting memorial. Somehow.

62

I FOUND BUTCH IN THE PURPLE VELVET SANCTUARY. A giant pineapple-shaped chandelier revolved slowly over my head. I hadn't noticed it before. The thing covered half the ceiling. It had lumps and projections, orange and purple and green. It rotated. How could I have sat here night after night, scotch after scotch, and never noticed the thing?

I fought off the nausea.

Butch had crapped out, too. We traded bad beat stories. Correction. Butch told me a bad beat story. I told him how I'd beaten myself. I lamented an earlier hand, when I'd folded a pair of Nines to an over-sized raise. It had felt like a bluff. But I couldn't bring myself to pull the trigger. Maybe, if I'd called, reraised, shoved, everything would have been different. But hell, the guy hadn't shown his cards. For all I knew, it was a good fold.

I'd never know.

Stupid. To worry about it.

And anyway, there was some relief to it. There was no way I would have lasted anyway. Not now. Not the way things were. Better to have gotten it over with.

I'll take another double, I said to the cleavage with a tray.

You really don't know, I said to Butch, whether it's real or constructed.

Some of it's got to be real. You can see it.

Yeah. You can see those bits. But what's under there? The substructure. Wires and twine? Toothpicks and cotton swabs? Stuffed bunnies?

That's okay. I'm still looking.

We laughed. We watched the cleavage come and go.

Fuck, I said.

Yeah, he replied.

What're we gonna do?

Nothing we can do.

I mean about Brendan.

Same answer. Until we get the autopsy results.

Can't they get there a little quicker? I thought you had connections.

Butch laughed. It had a bitter edge. Just barely, he said. Anyway, it's only been a day, Rick. This shit takes time. Toxicology and all that. I called once already today. I can't be bugging them all the time. All they could tell me so far is, there were traces of blood on the knitting needle.

What the fuck?

Yeah. And it wasn't Brendan's.

I tried to think about what that might mean.

I didn't have a clue.

Fuck, I said. There must be something more they can tell us.

Sure they can. They can tell us he didn't die by shotgun to the head. He didn't soak himself in gasoline and immolate himself in support of the brave freedom fighters of East Timor.

He wasn't big on East Timor.

Not that I'm aware of.

Good point. Meanwhile, we can't just sit here. I'm a little surprised at you, man.

Listen, Rick, I'm using what leverage I have. If they find anything worth telling us about, I'll know it.

What about Andrei and Anatoly? I asked. They following up on them?

Yeah, yeah. I told them about that. No trace of the little fucks. They're involved or not, you gotta expect they skipped town. The cops are better placed than us to track them down.

I guess, I said. Maybe. All right. Damn. What was he doing in a fucking tuxedo?

Uh, Rick, he was in a tux last time we saw him?

Oh, right.

And anyway, who cares? He's gone, man. Whatever happened, we'll find out. One way or another.

Yeah. We will. We owe it to him.

Well, said Butch, no, I don't think we owe him anything. We owe ourselves. Because if we don't.

You're right. Because if we don't. And what the fuck is with that fucking knitting needle?

Butch shrugged.

You know more than you're telling me, don't you?

Yeah. I know all sorts of shit.

Oh, shut up.

I thought about stuff. Random stuff. Random stuff that led to other stuff, that maybe wasn't quite so random. Somebody else's blood. On a knitting needle. Jesus. I had no idea. Must have been some kind of gay thing. Fuck, I didn't know. Might as well have asked me where they buried Jimmy Hoffa.

I'd never gotten used to Brendan being gay. Not because he was gay, but because when I first knew him, a guy I met in a bar, a poker player, a carpenter, a guy unrelated to me by tragedy or marriage, he'd successfully masqueraded as a straight guy. Picked up girls in bars. Acted hurt if they paid more attention to me than him. Damn. It'd really been convincing. A shocker, when he told us.

And Melissa.

I wished she'd go away.

She had gone away, of course. I hadn't told her to. I hadn't wanted her to. And yet, it had been such a relief. And yet, I still wished she hadn't. But the new Melissa. The one still on the couch. I wished she'd go away, for sure.

But she wouldn't. She, the whole thing, was always in my head. My wife, dead on the couch. My daughter weeping. Compared to that, the shock of finding out that Brendan had been hiding in plain sight as a straight guy was nothing. On the other hand, that he turned out to be Melissa's brother was a bit much.

Everything I'd ever thought was suspect.

Well.

More suspect than before.

It was a lesson, though. Taught me to look behind everything. Under every carpet and sheet. Behind every offhand comment. Beyond the obvious.

Who the hell was I fooling? It taught me to keep them double scotches coming.

Butch and I had a few more.

Listen, man, I said. What we can do is, try to figure out where he went. Trace his steps. See what we can find out.

They're already doing that.

Oh, come on, Butch. You know how they'll do it. Remember FitzGibbon? We can be more subtle. Weasel shit out.

Speak for yourself.

Well, I can be more subtle. You can provide the muscle.

Fuck you.

We staggered to another place. Some overstuffed joint. A bad crooner doing a sad imitation of the Sinatra thing. Nobody could do Sinatra. How dare the guy? Worse, how dare Sinatra? How dare Frank die on us?

We had a few more scotches. I saw a blonde, two tables over. The Mediterranean glow was promising. That and the cheekbones.

I sidled over, on my way to the men's room.

Hi, I said eloquently.

Hi, she chirped.

Close up, she was wrinkled. Pumped up. Inflated. Braised, not bronzed.

I felt ill.

Excuse me, I said with exaggerated politesse.

I stumbled to the men's. I heaved. I sat. I pondered on Doom.

Oh well, I thought. Doom comes in many guises. Maybe this year it'll come in the form of busting out of the World Series of Poker in a stupid and humiliating fashion.

Shit, I'd already done that.

I stumbled back to the table.

Butch was passed out. Head on the table.

His cell phone was ringing.

I ignored it.

Put my head on the table.

Passed out.

I had a dream. I was being chased by an enormous guy in a Hawaiian shirt.

Plastered on the front of the shirt was a giant pineapple.

63.

WHILE WE WAITED FOR THE AUTOPSY RESULTS, or the cops to figure out something else, I buried myself in the endless high-stakes cash games. It wasn't the ideal escape. The relentless rhythm of casino life will pound you down. Sometimes you have to get away. I guess that's why they construct the elaborate spas, at the better places. That, and to keep the trophy wives happy. So, eventually I had to find a way to get away from my way of getting away from thinking about Brendan, brooding about my part in it, getting pissed at the cops for moving so slow.

I went for a swim. Maybe it would tire me out. Let me sleep. Twenty laps of serious stroking. By the tenth, I'd gotten into the groove of it. By the fifteenth, my arms, my thighs were aching. On the final two, I was drowning. Halfway through the final lap I gulped down a quart or two of chlorinated filth. How many geezers had pissed in here in the past couple hours? I thought, a bit incongruously given my imminent demise. I panicked. I flailed. I'm sure I even blanched. I saw my life, such as it was, pass before my eyes. It was a disappointing show.

Fortunately, the pool was only four feet deep. Sensibly, I stood up. I was alive. I coughed. I heaved. I wheezed. I made an effort not to vomit in the pool.

Heard that was frowned upon.

By the time I hit the locker room, the endorphins kicked in. A near-death experience will do that to you. I wrapped a towel around my waist. Strutted to the shower stalls. Admired my desiccated biceps on the way. Back at the locker, I occupied myself with my hair. My thick, prematurely white, sexy hair. The gals loved it. I exulted in blow-drying it to a handsome sheen. I noted peripherally the jealousy in the balding locker–room–majority's eyes.

Showered and dressed, I was feeling good. All atingle. Recent events receding fast. To wherever repressed bad things go.

Ready for a nice double scotch.

I made my way to my favorite circular purple velvet bar.

All of which made the fact that Evgeny was there even more disturbing than it had to be.

He and his Russkie pals were taking up more than half the joint. Thoughts of quickly ducking out, hiding in the oyster bar down the way, were immediately skewered when Evgeny spied me.

Rick-ay, Rick-ay, he called out. Come on ofver. I buy you trink!

I couldn't avoid him, this time. I slunk over.

There was only one thing to do. It would have been churlish to do otherwise. Not to mention dangerous.

I looked him in the eye. Evgeny, I said. I fucked up.

Yah, yah. I know. I know everytink. Not to be worry about it. We got it done. You got be careful, guys like that.

This was the last thing I'd expected. Commiseration. Jesus. Maybe there was hope for world peace after all.

Yah, he said, noting my look of bewilderment. Maybe we got other job for you.

Jesus, I said involuntarily, you got to be kidding me.

Rick-ay, Rick-ay. Not to be worry.

Sure, I thought, not to be worry. Next time maybe Rick-ay die.

Here, said Evgeny, handing me a double scotch.

Evgeny ordered up a shovelful of appetizers. Started up a round of Russian folk songs. At least, at first I assumed that's what they were. Judging by the raucous laughter involved, though, I revised my view, figured they must be the Russian equivalent of Irish limericks. Everybody but me joined in, shouting out the apparently hilarious lyrics, spilling vodka shots on the floor. Not a problem there. The waiters were well greased. The shots kept coming. They had a guy there with a mop.

The Russians knew how to keep a party going.

Somebody came up with a bowl full of pickled onions. Evgeny proposed a toast:

To Amerika! he bellowed. To Rick-ay! To friendship of cultures!

I neglected to enlighten him regarding my nationality.

Someone tossed a smoked herring at me. It bounced off the top of my head, splashed into Evgeny's shot glass. Without missing a beat, he raised the glass, poured the herring down his throat. A roar went up.

There were many more toasts. More bawdy Russian songs were sung. I scarfed down some pierogies, to lay some sandbags down against the scotch.

It didn't work. The levee broke.

My back was slapped by several dozen hands. I grabbed the bar, to keep from falling on my face.

A strong pair of hands grabbed my arm. Pulled me away from the bar. Sat me down at a table. My back was to the room. It made me feel insecure. But then, what didn't?

Ricky, said Manfred. We got another job for you.

Job? I said, trying to orient myself to this new notion. Didn't I already do a job? Or not do it? Or whatever?

Another job, Ricky. You want the job?

Sure. Sure. Depends what it is.

This is a big job, Ricky. Much bigger. But you got to do this one right. No fuckup.

Sure, Manfred, I said.

I felt nauseous. The table began to tilt upward, accelerating towards my face. Vaguely, through the relentless blast of bleary Slavic cheer, I realized, as my forehead hit the table, that it was not rising at all. I was falling.

As I descended, I thought, all right, I got the job.
Now all I needed to do was find out what it was.

64.

First, there was another job to do.

Nothing like a good old-fashioned stakeout, I always say.

The Mini Cooper was unavailable, the guy at the garage said. Something about the brakes. The best they could do for us was a Chevy Malibu.

You've got to be kidding me, I said.

No, sir. It's been a very busy day. Unless you want to pay for a premium.

What've you got?

Well, it just so happens that we have a special today, for players in the poker tournament.

Really?

Yes, sir. We have a brand new Shelby Ford. The new model. Hundred-twenty-thousand-dollar car. Two ninety-five for the day. Gas included.

Jesus, I said. That's pretty steep.

Normally it goes for five hundred.

I bet, I said.

You ever drive one of these?

No, I must admit I haven't.

Worth every penny, sir.

I'll take it, I said.

I was never one for resisting temptation.

The paperwork done, I corralled Butch, told him about our good fortune.

What the fuck, he said. Okay. You drive there, I drive back.

All right, I said. Deal.

The Shelby's hood was as long as a donkey's lifetime. It was black, with an unostentatious gold stripe. One might have said it was almost elegant, if a mammoth American muscle car could ever be said to be elegant. They'd tuned the thing to reproduce that early sixties rumble and thrum.

It wasn't really a sports car. It wasn't built to hug the corners like glue, inconceivably fast-moving glue, like a Porsche. No, what it really was, was a straight-ahead machine, a rocket ship. A big black hurtling mass of teenage testosterone.

In short, just the therapy I needed.

We roared past Red Rock Canyon. We sped through miniature, dying adobe villages, so quickly I had no time to get depressed about them. We flew past miles of rolling lizard hills dotted with black, drooping cacti, like old men long past their pollination days. We curled to a stop outside the badly leaning chicken-wire gate to Eloise's trailer park. Parked there.

No need to draw attention to ourselves.

We stopped by to talk to Elmer. Get the twenty-dollar news.

I introduced Butch. Elmer nodded. The practiced nod of the truly unconcerned.

After he pocketed the twenty-dollar bill, Elmer told us a story.

Other night, he says, over t'other trailer thar.

Which one? I asked.

Down thar, he said, indicating a pale blue thing on stilts a hundred yards in the other direction. All on a sudden they's a crowd of guys over there'n. So I gets me up, go over yonder scrubble bush, get me a view. Figured it was a fight, a car accident, or somethin'.

And?

And I look'n over they heads, the gennelemen thar, and right thar, in her doorway, right thar, Dick, across the street thar.

Yes?

She's buck fuckin' naked, Dick.

Who is?

Lady lives in that thar trailer, Dick.

You're kidding me.

I am not, Dick. I wouldn' do that to ya. She's buck fuckin' naked and doin' some kinda dance, kinda swayin' around. She got a bottle in her hand.

Really.

So anyways, 'round about thar the cops showin' up. Guess'n her husban' called 'em or whatnot. They come on over. Put a blanket on her. Calm her down. Get her back in the trailer.

I guess the gentlemen were kind of disappointed.

I dunno 'bout that, Dick. They got a dern good show fer they money.
I guess, I said.

Nothin' ain't nothin' but it's free.

Right, I said.

Elmer chewed a bit. Spat a bit.

Elmer, I said.

Yeah, Dick.

This got anything to do with the other lady? The one I'm interested in?

Nothin' what I know about.

I thought about asking for my twenty dollars back. Decided
against it.

Elmer, I said.

Yeah, Dick.

I loved that turn of phrase. 'Buck fucking naked.'

Say what?

'Buck fucking naked'? I love that.

I don't git what yer gittin' at, Dick.

Ah, forget about it.

Guess I was jest about figurin' to do that, Dick.

Well, Elmer, I said. You have a good one out here.

Ayup, he said, spewing a yard-long skein of black into the dirt. Gots
to say I use-ally do.

Well, that's good, then.

Ayup.

We parked the Shelby off the access road a bit, half concealed
behind a pile of rocks. The damn thing was stupid conspicuous. Hadn't
thought of that. Butch and I took turns in the car, with the air-
conditioning on. There was no way to minimize your carbon footprint,
on a stakeout in the desert in July, sitting in a Shelby Cobra on the
shadeless dirt. If you didn't keep the air on, you'd die. And then, when
the bad guy showed up, you'd be useless dead.

Whichever one of us wasn't in the car hung around as discreetly as
we could, fifty yards or so from Eloise's trailer. There was a stack of
gray rotting plywood out there you could skulk behind. We had to
change places every half hour or so. Too easy to lose your concentration out there in the prickly mirage-inducing haze. Start counting ants.
Never knew when the Bad Guy might show up, give you only a nanosec-

ond's glimpse of his Evilness, during which you had to absorb and process an almost inconceivable amount of information, nearly all of it unreliable, and come to a conclusion about What Action to Take. Which conclusion might well turn out to be irrevocable. Permanent in its consequences. Especially given the surrounding circumstances.

Were there circumstances that did not surround? I made a note to look it up.

I was on my eighth plywood shift. My ass, my lower back, hurt even more than usual. The likelihood that I would later compensate for these difficulties, by means of some otherwise inexplicable heinous act of road rage, well, it was increasing by the minute. I was about to call Butch, tell him to get the hell back here and relieve me before I detonated the explosive device that I did not have, out of spite, or at the very least refuse ever again to pick up the tab at the Wolf's Lair, when a black Chevy Suburban pulled in through the trailer park gate, slowly crunched its way down the dirt road, rolled onto Eloise's green gravel lawn.

A guy got out of the Suburban. There was something seriously wrong with the picture. I mean, he had the right vehicle, but it was the wrong color. It was supposed to be brown, out here. Pale blue, for the adventurous.

And the guy was hooded. He was wearing a hood. The kind of hood they wear in the 'hood. Except this wasn't the 'hood. It was the desert. In July.

Jesus, I whispered to myself. We got something here. But what? The whole thing seemed way overdone. How many lonely little old ladies in neighboring trailers were peering through their curtains, reaching for the phone to call 911?

Not my business.

Lights. Action. Where was the camera? I pulled out the Canon digital. Pushed the zoom to maximum. Snapped a shot of the plates. New York plates. Okay. Job one.

I pulled out the cell phone. Called Butch.

Something's up, I said.

I saw.

Okay. Get out here. Cover me. I'm going to try to get close.

I got you.

Mr. Hood moved quickly. He didn't go to the front door. He

skulked around the side. The left side. Exactly what I'd done, days before. Or was it weeks?

But this guy didn't hesitate, look around.

He knew the place.

I looked back towards the gate. Saw Butch duck behind a trailer five to the right of Eloise's. Okay. Now I had to move. I didn't want to move. I was scared shitless. But I couldn't just sit there. Sure, the old ladies might have called it in already. The trusty constabulary might already be mounting their steeds for an investigative run to the Happy Sunshine Trailer Park and Rest Home. But maybe they weren't. And if they were, it'd be another half hour, minimum, before they got there. And this thing had all the marks of something that could get seriously nasty. Procrastination, unfortunately, did not seem to be an option.

I had to find out what the guy was up to, at least. Louise would expect nothing less.

Damn. Would I feel this way if my client was a pockmarked old fart?

Yes, I decided. I would.

The debate with myself finally over, I slunk out from behind the plywood. I tried to look as normal as possible. Tough to do when you're slinking. I regretted neglecting to put on my mailman costume.

My footsteps on the sand felt loud as gunshots. I saw Butch around the side of the trailer next to Eloise's. He nodded towards the back. I slunk around the left, following the guy's route. Flattened myself against the side of the trailer, right before the gate. Waited a beat or two. Couldn't hear anything. I climbed as carefully as I could over the fence—didn't want the gate squeaking. Peered around the corner. The guy wasn't there. Nowhere to be seen.

Which meant only one thing: he was already inside the house.

The situation took on a sudden urgency.

I crept up to the bedroom window. Given the necessity for speed, I squashed a couple of geraniums on the way. I mean, I think they were geraniums. I really wouldn't know. I'm not a flower guy. What the hell were geraniums doing in the desert, anyway?

I don't know how I knew it was the bedroom window. But my memory is clear as a suburban swimming pool, that I knew it. And, for some reason I can't explain, even now, I also knew what I was about to see.

65.

I PEERED IN THE WINDOW. Just one eye. I was saving the other for the stereophonic view.

Eloise was lying on a big brass bed. Her arms were over her head. Her head was turned away from me. She was mostly naked. The Hooded Man was standing over her. He had something in his hand. It was long and black, with a bulge at the end.

She was moaning.

The Hooded Man reached for something. Oh shit. It was a knife. He stuffed the black thing in his belt. Grabbed her neck with his right hand. Put the knife up to her face.

God, please, no, she said quietly.

Hey! I shouted.

The Hooded Man looked up. Let go of Eloise. She screamed.

What the fuck? he said.

He ran out of the room. Before I could react, he was lunging out the sliding glass doors. His face was masked. He threw himself at me.

I ducked down. Grabbed at his knees. Pulled them towards me. The knees buckled. But he fell forward instead of back. Right on top of me.

I tried to roll to my left. I didn't get far. The guy was heavy. He got to his feet. I tried to stand up, too, got to my knees just in time to get whacked in the left ear by the black thing.

It paralyzed me. Long enough for the guy to rear back for another blow. I tried to duck left to avoid it, but the thing caught me flush on the spine.

My legs gave out. I thudded to the ground like a sandbag tossed from the back of a truck. I watched him turn and run, back around the side of the house. The guy moved fast.

I heard the Suburban start up. Spinning wheels on gravel. The roar of a big V-8 fading down the dirt road.

I lay there for a while. I made an inventory of body parts. Legs: tingling fiercely. Back: sore as hell. Arms: aching. Head: pounding. Genitals: we'd worry about them later. Butch: where the fuck was he?

I sat up. Felt my head. Looked at my hand. No blood, anyway. But my ear was at least double-size already.

I stumbled back to the glass doors.

I invited myself in.

I found the bedroom. Eloise was still on the bed. Her arms were still over her head. I saw why. She was handcuffed, both hands, the handcuff chain looped over the brass rail at the head of the bed.

She had on some black silk thing. It was half torn from her. I got to see more of her than was appropriate in the circumstances.

Eloise, I said, trying to cover her with the bedsheet, are you all right?

She turned her head to me. Her eyes were red. Her mouth hung open. She rattled the cuffs.

You have any tools here? I asked.

The shed, she said blankly, indicating the backyard with her eyes.

I went back out. Butch was there. I pulled him around the side of the trailer.

The fuck you been? I whispered. I almost got killed.

No you didn't, he said. I was watching.

The fuck you were.

I fucking was.

Why didn't you help me?

Happened too fast. Then you went into the trailer. Figured you and the sister wanted a heart-to-heart. So I waited.

You waited.

Yeah. Called in the plate.

And?

Nothing. Rental. We can track it down. But something tells me the guy who rented it doesn't exist.

I wouldn't bet against it.

But I'll run it down anyway.

That's your job.

Yeah.

Protecting my ass doesn't seem to be in your job description.

Fuck you.

Fuck you, too. Wait out here. I got to talk to her some more.

I'll be right here. Covering your ass. Unless I'm back in the car. Getting cool.

I found a pair of pruning shears in the garden shed. Best I could do. They looked pretty strong.

When I got back, she was hunched over, as much as possible given her restraints, sobbing and shaking. I stroked her hair for a few moments.

It's all right, I said. I'll get you out of those in a second.

She nodded.

It took a couple cracks at it, but I broke the cuffs' chain. She still had the shackles on her wrists, but she was freed from the bed frame.

The cops can get those off, I said.

She turned her face to me, streaked with black, and bruised in more than one place.

No cops, she hissed.

Eloise. You got to report this. That guy's maybe on his way to . . . attack someone else.

No, she said, back to her flat voice. No. No.

Listen, I know this is traumatic. But you can't let this guy just get away.

You don't understand, she said.

What don't I understand?

I can take care of it.

I admire your self-assurance, I said. But this is not something you can handle alone.

I'm not alone.

Well, I'm flattered. But I'm not a cop. I can't chase this guy down.

Not you, she said with a hint of contempt.

Oh. You mean Vladimir? Is he here? Looks like he took care of you real well.

She stared at me, silent. Her eyes were hard.

Sorry, I said. That was inappropriate. Let's get you some clothes.

I can get my own clothes, she said, pulling the shreds of black silk around her chest. Please leave.

Jesus, girl, I can't leave you here alone, like this. He could be coming back. If you won't let me call the cops, you at least have to let me stay. A while, at least.

Whatever, she said. Wait in the living room.

I went to the living room. Slumped on the divan. Took one of her Benson & Hedges. Lit it up.

She took a long time.

I thought about what I'd seen. I hadn't gotten much of a look at the guy. Stocky. Maybe five foot nine, ten at the most. Strong. When he'd opened his mouth, I'd noticed his teeth: snaggly on the bottom. One missing on top.

That was about it.

I was kicking myself for waiting so long. What a pussy. She'd been beaten up pretty bad. Bruises on her neck, her ribs, her thighs. There was blood on her mouth. Shit. I could have prevented all that. Or some of it, anyway.

On the other hand, I thought. Lucky the fucker didn't gutshoot me. Or use that knife. It'd looked pretty nasty.

Three smokes later, just when I was about to get worried about her all over again, she appeared.

She was wearing a floor-length embroidered thing. Looked like some kind of eighteenth-century Russian thing, or something. Maybe it was Nepalese. It provided full coverage. She was wearing a very large pair of sunglasses. She'd cleaned up her face, covered the marks with some kind of makeup. If you hadn't known she'd just been brutally assaulted, in the dim of the trailer you might not even notice.

You have to leave, she said calmly.

Do we have to have this argument again? I asked. I absolutely refuse to leave you alone. At least let me call Louise. She can get some help over here.

No, she said sharply. You will not tell Louise about this.

I wondered what the punishment would be, if I transgressed.

I won't be alone anyway, she said, turning her back to me.

Oh. Well, let me at least stay until he gets here.

That's not a good idea, she said, her monotone returned, reinforced with steel.

Damn. This was a woman who meant what she said.

Her hair fell in elegant trails down the dress, gown, whatever it was.

Get out, she said between her teeth.

I got the message. I invited myself out. I retraced my steps, the steps the Hooded Man had taken. I scoured the ground. Nothing of interest, that I could see. But then, I was no forensics expert.

Butch was back at the Shelby. He didn't look happy. I saw why. The passenger-side window was shattered.

I got in the car. The glove box had been rifled.

Lucky it was a rental.

I filled Butch in. We talked about hanging around. See if there really was somebody coming. Had to be Vladimir, right?

Unless, I said.

Unless.

Unless that *was* Vladmir.

Rick.

Butch.

Sometimes you're a bit slow.

Yeah?

Yeah.

Enlighten me.

Vladmir wouldn't need to sneak around the back. Wear a mask.

Well—

Rent a car.

Unless—

And didn't that Toni bloke tell you he was tall?

Oh, yeah, right.

My back hurt like hell. My feet felt numb. And I knew Eloise was watching, to make sure we left. I could feel it. I wouldn't put it past her to be calling Vlad right now, telling him it was me that did it to her. Have him come over and impale me.

Fuck it, I said. Let's get the hell out of here.

No argument from me, said Butch. He pulled the Shelby around.

Shards of safety glass fell on my head from the broken window.

Shit, I said. I don't think I got the optional insurance coverage.

66.

I WOKE UP. Or something like that. My eyes were open. I could feel pain. Real pain in real time. This meant, I concluded, that I was not only awake, but alive. Though I felt ambiguous about both. I considered closing those eyes back up rolling over, going back to the swirling dream from which I had awoken. Something about failure. I'd been a test pilot. Crashed the plane. Somehow survived the impact. They weren't happy with me. Whoever they were.

Going back to dreamland was not an option, though. Too much pain. Too many questions. The best I could do was drag myself through a hot shower, grab a glass of scotch and a few painkillers, watch some vapid television and wait for the head pain to subside.

After the shower, after I'd poured the scotch, scarfed the meds, lain back with the remote for a while, found some weird foreign film, I mused. Musing can help head pain.

I can't believe how far I've come, I contemplated. Was it so long ago that I was reading every volume in the Hardy Boys series? And yet here I am, watching a Japanese film about a man and his pet eel. Without subtitles.

The eel was talking to the guy.

I mused about Eloise. Something was off. How could someone get shackled, trashed, humiliated, beaten up, and then refuse any help? Jesus, she could have got killed. Had to be that Vlad was coming. That she figured he could find the guy. Break his kneecaps.

But how was he supposed to figure out who the guy was, still less find him? I just didn't get it. It was as weird as the guy talking to the eel. But that was a movie. At least, I thought it was. It had a way of drawing you in. Even if you didn't understand Japanese. There was something about the relationship of the man and his eel that was . . . mesmerizing. Much like my reaction to Eloise, I began to think. I'd had a view of more of her than I'd been entitled to. And I was probably out of line to think about it, but it was awfully hard to repress. Long and slim. Smooth as milk. If you ignored the bruises. Breasts . . . well, breasts to conjure with. And tough. I loved a tough woman. And a tough woman with a body like that, well. How could I not at least think about it? Muse awhile.

It was better than musing about Dead Brendan. Or my humiliating night in the basement at the House of Perversion. Well, the morning had been humiliating. I could only guess, in the absence of any but the vaguest recollection, at just how humiliating the night before had been.

I shoved the past into the past. I made the mistake of looking at my cell phone. Two calls from Louise. Damn. My plans were ruined. I'd have to do something.

If I didn't call her back, it'd only nag at me. Sharpen the pain.

I called her. Not without fortifying myself first with a second scotch. It went down well. The heartburn was tolerable. The effect on my mood was immediate, and highly desirable.

I felt almost smooth.

Ms. Chandler, I said. Returning your call.

I haven't heard from you for some time, she said.

Yes. I didn't want to disturb you until I had some news. Shall we meet, for lunch, say?

That would be fine, she said, the coldness in her voice only slightly dissipated.

Your place or mine? I said, and immediately regretted it.

There was a pause. I knew what it meant.

It meant I was a drunken fool given to radically inappropriate behavior at all hours of the day.

Hey, I said to myself, tell me something I didn't know already.

I'll meet you at the Daniel Boulud restaurant at the Wynn, she said. One o'clock. The reservation will be in my name.

Sure, I said.

I had no idea what restaurant she was referring to. But I wasn't about to tell her that. I'd figure it out.

Fine, she said.

See you then, I said with excessive enthusiasm.

She hung up.

I put down the phone.

I considered calling her back. Telling her I wasn't up to this. That my brother-in-law had just died. That I wasn't handling it well. I'd leave out the part about the Russian mob. No sense in burdening her with unnecessary detail.

I didn't do it, of course. A job is a job. You do your job. You do it well. Or as well as you can. That's it. That's all. Nothing more to it.

My father taught me that. Or he would have, had he lived long enough.

At the desk, I asked a gent with a uniform and a pencil mustache about this restaurant at the Wynn.

Oh, you'll enjoy that, sir, he said. One of the finest in the world.

Really?

Everybody says so.

I'd rather be at the Wolf's Lair, I said.

He gave me a puzzled look.

Forget it, I said. Inside joke.

Certainly, sir, he said with a cheery smile.

67.

On the way to the Wynn, I called Butch. No news on the Brendan front.

At least nothing they'll tell me about, he said.

Shit, man, I thought you had some clout down here.

I never said that.

That doesn't mean I couldn't think it.

Anyway, they're just saying they haven't finished the toxicological tests, all that. Nothing to report. I don't think they're shitting me.

Fuck, I said.

Yeah, he replied. I know.

Why don't you go over there? Bang on some walls. Kick some cans.

I'll do that, man. Nothing else, it'll keep me busy. Oh, I do have one thing.

Give it to me.

This one'll get us a long way.

All right, just give it up.

That powder? From the FedEx envelope?

Yeah.

Clay.

What?

Clay. It was clay. Pure clay. Not a drug molecule in sight.

What the fuck?

Yeah.

Why would somebody be FedExing a bunch of clay to somebody?

It's an excellent question, Rick. Maybe you should ask your client that. Or her sister.

I'm meeting her now. The client.

Ah. Good luck.

I appreciate that.

You'll need it.

I won't. My natural charm is all I need.

That and some major surgery.

Say what?

I don't know. Liposuction. Nose job. Face-lift. Dick extension. The works.

You're a funny man.

They say that.

68.

LOUISE WAS DRESSED IN A SLICK BLACK THING that did everything for her charms and nothing for my self-control. The latter having already been reduced from its usual proportion, minimal, to nonexistent by events, which of course included the imbibation of gallons of spirits and dozens of painkillers.

So I was feeling very spiritual, so to speak, by the time Ms. Chandler arrived.

I took her hand. Made an elaborate display of kissing it.

Mr. Redman, she said, I would appreciate it if in future you refrained, before our meetings, from getting quite this inebriated.

Does it really show? I asked, knocking over the chair I was attempting gallantly to pull out for her.

I guess that didn't need a response. It didn't get one.

I retrieved the chair from its prone position. I waved Ms. Chandler into its springy bamboo seat. I deftly pushed it in as she sat.

My timing was perfect. Hah! I'd show her and her 'quite this inebriated.'

The informalities concluded, I told her of the latest adventures at the trailer park. The stakeout. The break-in. The aftermath.

She sat passively through all of this. Hands in her lap. Occasionally smoothing her skirt. Readjusting her purse. At one point she opened the snap, peered in. As if looking for something apropos of the subject.

I paused, to let her find it.

Go on, she said.

As I continued, she extracted from the purse a tube of lipstick and a smooth black saucer-shaped container of face-enhancing chemical mulch. I recognized the brand. Very elegant. Very expensive. Flipped open a tiny mirror. Fixed her makeup.

By the time I'd finished the story, she'd completed her facial ministrations. She looked straight at me. Calm. Passive. Expressionless.

You don't seem terribly upset, I said.

My emotions are my own business, Mr. Redman.

I didn't mean to intrude. We all deal with things in our own way.

Yes.

We spent the next while in our own ways. I knocked off a couple, three, double scotches. Louise, Ms. Chandler, sluiced down an equivalent number of cosmos.

In effect, I guess, we spent the time in the same way.

To break the polar ice, I told her about the tests on the FedEx package contents.

I told you to give that thing to me, she said.

Well, yes. But it wasn't entirely in my control. And anyway, it doesn't seem to have anything to do with anything. Clay?

You will now retrieve the package and deliver it to me, Mr. Redman.

Do you know what it means? I asked. Clay? What could that mean? Was your sister a sculptor? Did she spend any time in Alabama?

That would have been red clay. Not brown.

You're right. I stand corrected. And impressed. Red clay country. Anyway, any ideas?

You're the one I pay to have ideas, Mr. Redman.

I'd had just about enough. I looked her in the eye.

Is there something you're not telling me? I asked. Again?

She looked at me impassively. Then, ever so slowly, a smile crept its way up the sides of her eyes, metastasized to the edges of her mouth. She leaned forward.

Rick, she said softly. I absolutely forbid you from ever questioning my integrity again.

It suddenly occurred to me that my iron maiden was a little tipsy. Maybe more than a little. It was kind of . . . disconcerting. And sexy. At the same time.

Yes, I said. I have been a bad boy. A very bad boy. Perhaps I should be punished.

I put my hand on her knee.

The silk of it.

She didn't pull away.

Victory.

Round one.

I didn't wait for the bell to sound. To begin round two.

I didn't wait for it. I came out swinging.

Ms. Chandler, I said, drawn close by the sweet subtle scent of her. I think it's time we dropped the pretense.

What pretense might that be, Mr. Redman?

The pretense that I don't find you sickeningly attractive.

My, what a felicitous turn of phrase, she said, leaning back away from me.

Ignore the phrase, I said. Let's get to the point.

Oh God, I thought as the words spilled hazardously from my mouth. I'm ruining everything.

I think I'll visit the ladies' room, she said.

Of course, I said, already slotting this episode into its appropriate place in the Top Ten Most Humiliating Things I've Done When Drunk. I was thinking maybe number eight, and fixing to order another double while she was away. Obliterate the memory. Subsume the responsibility. Was that me? Oh, no, that wasn't me, it was the demon drink what done it.

She strode back to the table, far sooner than expected. My new double hadn't even arrived.

She took my hand. She pulled me to a standing position.

Come on, she said.

I followed obediently. God knew where she was taking me. An intervention, probably. She'd been talking to Madeleine. Wait a minute, I remembered, she didn't know Madeleine. Could she somehow know Madeleine?

She hadn't let go of my hand.

She opened the ladies' room door.

It was one of those private-style restrooms. One toilet. Marble walls. Tasteful appointments. And a lockable entrance door.

She locked the door.

Okay, she said.

She sat back on the blue marble sink.

The iron lady opened up.

69.

MY CELL PHONE RANG.

Redman, I said.

Rick.

Yeah, Butch?

We got a problem.

You're telling me?

No, Rick. We got a real problem.

What? The fact that Brendan is dead, I still owe Evgeny ten grand, which I don't have, I'm now a confirmed embezzler, isn't problem enough? I'm sure I've left out a few . . .

I said *we*, Rick.

All right, all right. What's the fucking problem?

Just grab a cab. Come to 1495 Industrial. Right next to the International Pet Grooming Institute.

Is international different from domestic?

What?

Is international pet grooming different from domestic?

Shut the fuck up and get over here. Downstairs on the left. Basement.

Gotcha. Ten minutes.

Make it five.

I grabbed a cab. It smelled of cheese. Feta cheese, I thought. And uncertainty.

70.

SHE WAS LYING FACE UP. I'd never seen her lying any other way. Standing up, there was variety. But when we're talking reclining, this was the way she was. On her back.

She didn't look that different from the last time I'd seen her, actually. Which immediately brought to mind the author of that misfortune. The Hooded Man. Right away there was no doubt in my mind, not the soupçon of a doubt, that he was the perpetrator of this latest outrage.

I didn't see any ropes, but it was clear as high-class gin that she'd been tied up. There were burns on her wrists and ankles, ugly red-brown circles crying pain and abasement. And the echo of them around her neck. Ligature wounds, in the technical literature. She'd been strangled, in other words. Just as before, she was half naked. Whatever she'd been wearing—it was red, palpably silk, and violently shredded—was gathered about her in knots and pieces. Her face was turned away. I couldn't see the expression on it. And I didn't want to.

Butch, I said. They tell you anything?

Nah. They're too busy doing their thing. I'll talk to the Main Man later. He won't hold back.

What makes you so sure?

Don't ask.

Okay. I'm glad someone in the room has faith.

I do what I can, he said. But faith's got nothing to do with it.

Meanwhile, let's go get a drink.

Can't argue with that.

There was a cheesy Irish pub across the street. The Stuck Pig, or some such. We sat at the bar. I ordered a double Dewar's on the rocks. Butch had the same. Safe but effective, I thought, inhaling the first one and calling for a second.

Shit, I said.

Yeah, said Butch. Shit.

What the fuck am I going to say to Louise?

It's all about you, Rick, isn't it.

Fuck yeah. Eloise is dead. What does she care?

Jesus, man. You really mean that?

Of course not. I'm bitter. And scared. You got a problem with that?

Butch didn't say anything. Slugged down his scotch. Waved at Manny, the bartender, for another. I felt a dark, dull stabbing in my chest. My throat tightened. Oh fuck, I thought.

Typhoid fucking Ricky, I said.

Yeah, said Butch. Funny.

But seriously. She's paying us big money to keep tabs on her sister, follow up the Vladimir thing, whatever. And the sister's cold toast. It doesn't look good.

It feels worse than it looks.

My point exactly. I were her, I'd be pissed as hell.

Yeah.

I gazed blankly at the photos of dead celebrities on the wall. Frankie Avalon. Joey DaSilva. Who the hell was Joey DaSilva?

So what are we going to say? I asked.

What's to say, man? We did what we could. He got to her. We're sorry. We're really fucking sorry.

Ain't that a fact.

It has the virtue of being true.

I'm hitting the head, said Butch.

Give it my best.

I'll give it my best.

Okay, I said. That'll have to do.

I rubbed my face. I uncracked my clenched jaw. I tossed back my second double scotch and nodded at Manny for another. I thought about the scene across the street. Melissa on the couch. People kept dying on me. What the fuck was wrong with me? I could have saved Melissa. Brendan. I could have saved Eloise. I could have saved them all. Hell, one of them, at least. I was sure of it. If only I weren't so fucked-up. Just think what I might have figured out, been able to do, if my veins weren't pumping two percent eighteen hours of the day and over-loading my liver with the refuse for the other six while I dreamed of blackness and airplane crashes.

Aw, fuck it, I said out loud. Stop feeling sorry for yourself.

Hey you, said a voice that could only have come from a six-foot-four-inch bear of an over-tanned cop named Rod.

Hunh? I replied.

What were you doing over there? he said.

I thought of saying Where? but that would only piss him off. And he already looked pissed off enough. Not to mention twice my size and packing a big fucking gun in a bulging holster under his left armpit.

I remembered his name, but not why I knew it. He reminded me, in a way I couldn't quite place, of a guy who'd been involved in one of my pro bono criminal cases, back when I was a real lawyer, representing the indigent accused, aka the guilty as hell, ensuring they'd get off with less than they deserved. It wasn't the way to make friends with guys like Rod, if he really was that guy. Which seemed improbable. Seeing as how we were about three thousand miles from Queens.

I knew her, I said.

You knew her, the Bear said with his best cop sneer, the one that says, You're going to lie to me, I know you're going to lie to me, and you know that I know that you're going to lie to me, and you're just like every other lying sonofabitch creep I've ever had the misfortune to come across every stinking night and day in the course of my vastly underpaid line of work, so don't think you're anything special, asshole.

There was a whole lot in that sneer.

Just how well did you know her? he continued, with an air of already knowing the answer.

He's with me, Rod, said Butch, returning from the men's room just in time.

Ah, said the Bear, still looking straight at me, clearly still less than convinced of my bona fides. Let me rephrase, then. In what capacity did you know the deceased, sir?

I'm not sure I'm at liberty to say, I said, with less confidence than I had intended to muster.

Hey, Garcia, he called out to a tall pockmarked colleague lurking by the door, the presence of whom I had failed to note. Jerk-off here says he's not at liberty to say.

Garcia was in the midst of lighting a cigarette, in violation of a large No Smoking sign on the wall right next to his head. He coughed out a guffaw, apparently finding Detective Bear's attempt at humor unbearably effective.

Take it easy, Ferguson, said Butch. His name is Rick. And he's okay. I'll vouch for him. C'mon, let's go talk in private.

Hardiman, said the Bear, whose surname appeared to be Ferguson, you still with the force?

Yeah, I'm still with the force, Butch said, with the air of someone who'd answered the question a few too many times. Got promoted, actually, and now that I think of it, I'd be your superior officer now.

Not in this jurisdiction you ain't, the Bear replied.

It came back to me. Butch and the Bear used to work together in the twenty-eighth precinct, Manhattan. The Bear had apparently relocated to the desert. Work on his tan.

I don't see any crime scene, said Butch, looking around the bar. Rick, do you see any crime scene?

I studied the lively patterns of light refracting through the ice cubes in my glass.

Hey, Butch went on, putting his hand on Ferguson's shoulder. I'm not pulling rank. I know, I know. I don't have any rank to pull. Let's just go in back and talk, okay?

Ferguson the Bear regarded him for a moment, his face betraying a near ineluctable desire to bull his way through the situation—his default mode, I'd already surmised, aided by some vague recollection of a case involving an underage pimp with an abiding affection for glue and the paper bags from which it was nasally dispensed.

But Butch's big brown eyes prevailed.

All right, said Ferguson reluctantly. I'll give you a few minutes.

There were a couple of old pinochle players in the Pig Snout's back room. I'd thought all the pinochle players had died out by then, but I guess a few were hanging on. Though these guys didn't look like they had all that many hands left in them. One desiccated hombre in a drooping ten-gallon cowboy hat was wearing a sagebrush mustache encrusted with at least five years of unexhumed nasal dust.

I slipped Manny twenty bucks to hustle them out of there, and we took up residence.

The room wasn't really a room at all. More like a cubicle, slightly elevated and concealed from the rest of the degenerates in the place by a set of long-faded cigarette-burned vintage 1930s speakeasy-style maroon velvet drapes.

The VIP cubicle.

I was happy to see that Rod didn't stand on department protocol, and ordered a Guinness with a tequila back. I refrained from commenting on the curious libatious juxtaposition. More power to him, I thought.

Mr. Pockmark stayed at the door. I guess they figured me and Butch for an escape risk. Or maybe an excape risk, as I imagined Mr. Pockmark putting it.

After the obligatory pleasantries between Butch and Rod, Rod leaned his chair back against the wall, gave us the download. Slowly. Taking his time. Like a guy having a beer after a hard day pounding the pavement.

She'd been found face up. There were open wounds on her back and buttocks. Looked like lash marks. Cause of death as yet undetermined. But ligature marks on her neck pointed to strangulation. Whatever it was, it hadn't happened across the street. The body had been brought there from somewhere else.

Sexually assaulted? asked Butch.

I'm not the medical examiner, said the Bear, making a show of scratching his crotch, but just between you and me, yeah. Anal.

Shit, I mumbled into my scotch glass. The fucker.

What you say? asked Rod, his chair banging to the linoleum as he leaned forward to give me a hard look.

Damn, I said. I wish I hadn't said that.

No you don't, he said. You're damn happy you did. 'Cause if you didn't, when I found out later you knew something you didn't tell me, I'd be reaming you a new asshole. Maybe two.

In the circumstances, I regarded the remark as being in poor taste.

And you're going to be a damn sight happier, he went on, when you tell me what the hell you meant by that. Or should I say, fucking unhappy as hell if you don't.

Hey, hey, said Butch, calm down, Rod. Rick's going to tell you.

I know he is, he said evenly.

Rod didn't take his eyes off me. His Look was half 'you dumb fuck' and half 'you bought it, now you gonna pay for it.'

I know I have to tell you, I said. I'm going to tell you. But my information comes from a case I'm working on. Very private matter. Very sensitive.

Not as sensitive as your left nut's gonna be when I get through with it, Ricky boy.

Come on, guys, let's take it easy, said Butch. Rick, go to the men's room or something, I got to talk to Rod about something.

I got up real quick. Rod didn't seem too happy about it. Nodded at Mr. Pocky. Pocky followed me to the gents, stood outside the door. I guess that was his specialty. Standing in doorways. He must be in big demand, I thought. Everybody needs a guy to stand in a doorway.

I took my time. I took enough time that Pocky came in to check me out. See if the perp had fled out the two-foot-by-six-inch barred window seven feet above the urinal. Anyway, I gave Butch enough time to soften Rod up. Alert him to the sensitivities. Nothing would come back to us. He'd use what we told him, but he'd take ownership of it.

That was good enough for me. Hell, it had to be. I get an allergic reaction to jail cells. And testicle clamps.

I told Rod the story. Some of it, anyway. I didn't need any nods and winks from Butch to know not to tell him Butch had been at the stakeout. I told him about the Hooded Man. Gave him the best description of the guy I could. Which wasn't much. And the car. Told him we'd already run the plates. Rented. Butch had followed up. Guy who rented it didn't exist.

So, Mr. Rick Redman, said Rod when I'd finished the story. Just how did you come to be staking out the suburban home of the recently deceased, anyway?

Suburban? I said involuntarily.

Rod, Rod, said Butch. Can you give us a ride on that one for now? Just for a while. You know Rick was on a job. The client doesn't know about . . . what happened. The thing across the street. I'm telling you, man, if you guys barge in with this news . . . the client—Butch almost slipped up and said 'she'—ain't gonna give you a thing. You gotta trust me on this one, man. We go to the client, the client trusts us. Trusts Rick. We can get stuff you wouldn't. Whatever there is, anyway. I can tell you for sure the client isn't involved in this. But the client may have . . . some information. I don't know. But you have my word we'll share it with you. Just give us a day or two.

Rod never looked at Butch during this speech. He kept looking directly at me. He stared me down. I played with my scotch. I sucked on an ice cube. Hours went by. Well, minutes, maybe. Or seconds. But they were those hour-type minutes and seconds.

Okay, said Rod.

My toes unclenched.

I remarked to myself that I had been unaware that my toes had been clenched. In fact, I ruminated, I hadn't even been aware that toes could be clenched. The concept of toe clenching was a new one for me. I wondered whether it was a tell. Like tooth clenching. Or riffling your chips with your left hand instead of your right.

Rod turned to Butch. But only 'cause it's you, he said. I'm releasing this guy into your custody.

What do you mean, releasing me? I said. What the fuck did I do?

Material witness, he said. Whatever. I don't need to justify it to you. You'll get plenty of justification later.

Jesus. I hadn't felt such palpable disrespect since the old days with that pompous martinet Warwick, esteemed chairman of my late and wholly unlamented law firm. Hmm, I pondered, was the expression 'pompous martinet' redundant? Are all martinets pompous? I shelved the question for another day.

Anyway, Rod's pronouncement would have to do. I was still a free man.

It was a start.

We went out to flag a cab. In the empty lot next door, sitting on a decaying concrete block, was a dyed blonde in cutoff shorts and a Megadeth t-shirt, her thighs tattooed from the knees up. She had a slight pot belly, and when she smiled you could see the missing molars. She was playing with a raggedy little girl. She was holding one end of a stretchy rubber spider. The kid was trying to pull it away from her mother. It stretched and stretched, snapped back to Mom, sending the little girl into cascades of giggles. They did it over and over.

They looked happier than anyone I'd seen in a long time.

71.

WHY ARE YOU DOING THIS? Sheila asked.

Doing what?

This orgy of self-destruction.

Is an orgy something that you do?

Rick.

Yes, okay. I'll stop being childish.

Silence.

I don't know, I said.

Then let's talk about how you feel.

Feel about what?

Not about. When. How you feel when you're doing these things.

What things?

Rick, please.

Okay, okay. Let me think about it.

Silence.

I don't know, I said at last.

You don't know.

You know what's nice about this motel room?

What?

There aren't any mirrors. The only mirror is on the inside of the closet door. I can keep it closed. Not have to look at myself.

Rick.

Yes?

Can we get back to the question?

What was the question?

How you feel when you're doing these self-destructive things.

What self-destructive things?

Rick, it's your money.

Yes, yes, sorry. You mean, drinking myself sick every night? Shooting people? Getting into debt to known Russian psychopaths?

That kind of thing.

Embezzling client funds? Getting into fights? Messing up every relationship with a woman I've ever had? Having unprotected sex with near strangers? That kind of thing?

That kind of thing.

I don't know.

You don't know.

No, I don't. I really don't. Because when they're happening, I'm just there. It's happening. Stuff is happening. And I may be terrified. I may be confused. I may be riding the endorphin wave. Either way, I eat it up. I need it. There's something in me that just needs it. Whatever it is. The more extreme, the better. The more outrageous, the better. It's like I'm proving something.

What are you proving?

I'm not sure.

Think about it, she said.

I didn't want to think about it. But I pretended to anyway.

I couldn't think of anything.

It seems to me, she said, that anybody in your position would be angry. Furious. Enraged. Somebody drugged you. Left you shackled. Your friend died. Somebody killed your client's sister. But you don't seem to be angry.

No, I'm not angry.

Why not?

I don't know. I guess I've trained myself. Not to go on tilt. Poker tilt, life tilt. Tilting is bad. When you tilt, you lose.

Poker isn't life.

Yes it is.

No it isn't, Rick. In life, if you suppress your emotions, they come back later, in another form. Illness. Anxiety. Depression. Does that sound familiar?

I thought depression and alcoholism were diseases.

They are. Of course. But the things you do can make them worse. Much worse.

I know I'm not perfect, I said. Jesus, I know I don't even come close. My problem isn't that. It's that I can't stop worrying about it. Keeping score. It's like my life is the perpetual World Series of Goodness. Night of laughter and love with Kelley and Peter—home run. Run off to the bar to avoid ambivalence about the direction of my life—two-run double for the Devil in Me. Quit my job—okay, that was a while ago, and it's hard to say who scored on it. Call it a wash. Do they have washes in baseball? A scoreless inning, I guess. Poker metaphors are better. Hit the flush on the river. Folded Aces on the turn. Got my Kings cracked by Seven, Eight suited. Every poker hand has a real-life analogue, contrary to the opinion of certain shrinks of my acquaintance. Fail to save two lives, big suckout, baby. Big suckout.

Rick, you realize what you're doing, don't you?

Yes, I do, actually. Avoidance. I'm supposed to be thinking about what I'm trying to prove.

How you feel about it.

That, too. Exactly. I know, I know. I'm babbling. Free-associating. Trying to eat up the minutes with trivial entertainment so I don't have to face up to the pathetic reality that is my life.

Entertainment?

Okay, okay. A desperate but doomed attempt at entertainment.

She laughed.

It felt good.

But you're right, she said, serious again. Not the pathetic part. The avoidance part.

So let's face up to it, I said. Let's square up to the basket. Let's shoot the ball and see if it goes in.

Rick . . .

Yes, yes. Jesus, I can't stop myself.

Let me try, she said.

Shoot, I said, wincing.

Rick, she said sternly. I want you to stand up.

I stood up.

I want you to walk to the closet door.

I walked to the closet door. I felt oddly relieved. Someone was taking responsibility. Taking my choices away. The choices I didn't know how to make.

Open the door, she said.

I opened the door a foot or so.

It's black in there, I said.

All the way, she said.

I opened the door all the way.

Look in the mirror, she said.

I looked.

What do you see? she asked.

Veins in my nose, I said.

What else?

Three days' growth.

And?

A paunch. Slumped shoulders, narrower than they used to be. A guy who needs a haircut. Badly. A long stain on my shirt that looks like dried blood and probably is. A shirttail hanging out. My right-hand pant leg partly tucked into my sock. Red rings around my wrists.

Yes?

How the hell did that happen?

And?

Blood in my eye?

Blood in your eye?

It's a metaphor.

A metaphor?

Yes, I thought, a metaphor.

Back to that.

72.

BUTCH AND I TRIED TO FIGURE STUFF OUT. We didn't get far.

I got to go tell Louise, I said.

Yup.

The cops won't have found her yet.

Doubt it.

There's no way. There was no record of Eloise under her real name. They won't be able to trace any relatives. Not for a while, anyway.

Yup. You got to tell Louise.

I was afraid you'd agree with me.

Not looking forward to it?

What do you think?

He grunted. For Butch, it was part of the job. And it would have been for me. Sort of. If I hadn't turned Louise into more than a client. Bad enough I'd somehow let the client's sister get killed. The object of my job. But now. Layers. Multicolored layers of guilt. Eons of striations of guilt. Guilt sediment.

I wasn't about to tell Butch about it.

Tell me about the last time, said Butch.

What?

The last time you saw her.

Who?

Eloise, you dumb fuck. Who are we talking about?

Oh. Yeah. What's to tell? I told you already.

Go over it again. Tell me what she looked like. Go back to the trailer. Tell me every damn thing you saw. Every damn word she said. Don't leave anything out. There's always something there. Something you didn't think was important.

Jesus, Butch, who's the detective here?

Me.

Oh. Right.

I went back over it. Every ugly detail. I described how she'd looked. Handcuffed to the bedstead. Face to the wall. Bruises everywhere. Black, blue, yellow.

Wait a minute, said Butch.

What?

What did you just say?

I repeated the thing about the bruises.

Yellow?

Yeah, yellow. But mostly black. And blue. Like they say in the comics.

What's comical, said Butch, is your . . . ah, forget it. How long was it? Between the time you saw the guy go around the house and the time you got there?

I don't know. Five minutes. Ten.

Think about it. Jesus.

Jesus what? What's your fucking point?

Rick, how long do you think a bruise takes to turn yellow?

I don't know. Never thought about it.

I was thinking about it now.

Days, Rick.

Days. Of course.

Meaning . . . ?

Yeah, Butch. I'm not all that stupid. She'd been beat up before. Recently. But not that day.

You got it.

So she knew it was coming.

She knew the guy.

A reasonable assumption. But where does it get us?

We go there. We talk to your Elmer buddy. We talk to the neighbors. We find out who she knew. What they saw.

The cops are doing all that shit.

Maybe.

Of course they are.

All right. You're right. We wait to see what they come up with. If they come up with shit, we do it ourselves. That what you're saying?

I don't like it, I said, but I can't see any other way. We start stepping on their dicks, it's the last time we get anything from them.

Yeah. You got a point. So we wait for them on Eloise. What about Brendan?

Same thing, I guess.

No. We don't wait for them on Brendan. They're not doing anything on Brendan. They're waiting for the Toxicology results. They figure he OD'd or something. Why waste resources on a degenerate?

How do you know that?

Please, Rick.

Okay. We wait on Eloise. Brendan, we find out where he went. We retrace his steps. We shake down some transvestites.

All right, man. You're the boss.

Damn. I like the sound of that.

Butch went to his room. Brought out a pine box. Opened it up. Took out his gun. Started disassembling it on the coffee table.

I smiled. I couldn't help it.

That Pandora's box? I asked.

Butch looked up. Grunted. Went back to cleaning the gun.

73.

YES, IT WAS ALMOST MIDNIGHT. And yes, or no, I had no reason to believe that Louise was the kind of person who stayed up that late.

Much more the early-to-bed type. Overly controlled. Controlling. Whatever. I was quite sure she had a regimen. She was very regimented. Unless spread-eagled on a marble bathroom . . .

I buried the thought. Inappropriate, I told myself, at this time. Anyway, this was an emergency, if ever there was one. Well, sort of. What happened had happened. I'd already procrastinated for hours. But we couldn't risk her finding out from some other source. The cops weren't going to find her. But the news would get out, probably. Vegas had a high murder rate. But this one was kind of sexy. I slapped myself. Inappropriate. Newsworthy, I meant. They'd probably be all over it. Damn. I hadn't thought of that before. It might already be all over the TV. What the fuck was wrong with my brain?

A question that was coming up way too often.

They'd fixed the Mini Cooper, put it back in the lot for me. I went to get it. It was a half-hour exercise. Go down the escalator. Present your ticket to the surly woman at the desk. Watch while she takes three phone calls, chats with her girlfriend at the next computer station. Argue about the five-dollar charge. I play here every day, you say. I'm a regular in the poker room. Wait while she calls the poker room, confirms your bona fides. This time, it works. Save five bucks. Be happy. Wait for the car jockey to bring the Mini. Another ten minutes. Watch the folks from Idaho, sad and swollen and laden with way too many suitcases for a weekend trip. They don't speak to each other. They don't speak at all. The Mini heaves into view. Tip the guy five bucks. Oh well, there went five bucks. It's Vegas. What're you gonna do?

I should've taken a cab.

Louise was ensconced on her couch. Her legs drawn tightly beneath her. A glass of . . . I wasn't sure, something purple, in her hand. Hair nicely put up in an elegant coif. Normal, then. Ah, I recognized it: a martini glass in her hand. Containing, then, presumably . . . a martini. A purple martini.

To what do I owe the pleasure? she asked, about as coldly as a woman can who has recently invited you to ravage her in a public restroom.

I have some stuff I have to tell you, I said, going to the bar and pouring myself a large one.

Yes?

But now that I think of it, I said, settling into the armchair, I may need some assurances first.

What the hell are you talking about, Mr. Redman?

Ah, so it's back to Mr. Redman.

I'm sorry, Rick. Rick. Yes. What the hell are you talking about, Rick?

I need you to believe me. I'm going to tell you some stuff. It's not pleasant.

She gave me the Louise stare. Straight through my skull.

Shit. I should have prepared something. Like running for city council. You don't come to a rally without a speech.

She's dead, I said.

Louise got up quickly. Strode to the window, back erect. Stood staring out at the neon nightmare. A tiny downward tilt of her head.

Louise in mourning.

I assume, she said, I can get the details in the morning paper.

Probably. I mean, I'll tell you everything I know . . .

Don't bother.

I held my tongue. If ever there was a time for tongue holding, this was it.

Slowly, Ms. Louise Chandler turned from the window. Faced me. Black streaks of mascara irrigated her cheeks.

Jesus fuck, Rick, she said.

Yeah. I feel terrible—

Shut up!

Okay. I understand.

Just shut the fuck up. This isn't about you.

I know, I insisted. I know. I'll shut up. Sorry.

I don't want you to say another fucking word, she said.

I nodded.

She went to the bar. Made herself another purple martini. Poured me another generous scotch. Handed it to me. Returned to the couch. Sipped her martini.

The mascara had dried.

We sat in silence for a long, long time. Time enough for her to make us another round of drinks. To smoke an absurd number of cigarettes.

I hadn't known she smoked. Maybe she didn't. But the cigarettes appeared. Some very female long slim things. Maybe they came from the minibar. I smoked some too. What the hell.

There are things you don't know, she said to me at last.

She wasn't looking at me. She was staring at the wall.

I'm aware of that, I said.

Another long silence. I started feeling sleepy. I shook myself, as discreetly as I could. It didn't help. Unbearable. Imagine. Could there be anything more insensitive than falling asleep in the middle of someone's grief?

Tell me something, she said at last. Something else. Nothing to do with . . .

I understand, I said.

Tell me a story, or something.

I thought for a while.

Randomness is important, I said at last.

As Rick Redman might say, she said after a pause, can you be a little more vague?

I can, but I'll try not to be.

Thank you.

What I mean is, we're always looking for patterns.

Yes.

It's a fundamental part of human nature.

Also true, she said, lighting another long thin cigarette.

Which brings me back to poker.

Which doesn't surprise me.

My point being, the ability to detect patterns is central to poker skill. Montana Joe always limps in with a medium pair in early position. You use that information. Next time he limps in early position, you don't decide, okay, Joe has a medium pair for sure. That would be naïve. Joe, of course, limps in early position with other hands as well. But you take your knowledge of his pattern into account. In deciding your action, you increase in your calculation the probability that Joe does, in fact, have a medium pair.

I think I follow you.

It's one small part of the picture. But illustrative.

Yes.

Now, the converse is very important too. Just as important, at least.

The converse?

Not to create patterns of your own. That others can perceive. That allow them to adjust their play to your tendencies.

I see.

So, for example, I'm always going to play a big pair—Aces, Kings,

Queens—in early position. And the abstract, mathematically correct way to play those hands in that position is to raise. But the abstract, mathematically correct way to play does not include the value—did I say value? necessity, I mean—of deception. Confusion. The ability to make your opponent draw false conclusions. Or at least, if your opponent is good enough not to tie himself to uncertain conclusions, not to give him a chance—

Or her.

—him or her a chance to identify your hand with more precision than absolutely necessary.

I see.

So, to get back to the concept, you have to find a way—at least, you have to find a way if you're playing often or for a long period with the same players, good players, who will pick up on your tendencies—to randomize your decisions. So, the point is, in this example, you correlate your decision to some random event. You say, okay, I look down and see a big pair. I'm in early position. Most of the time, I'll raise. Some of the time, I have to just call. Not because, if I raise, my opponent knows I have a big pair—I'll raise with other hands too—but because, if I always raise with them, when I just call, my alert opponent will know with certainty that *I don't have a big pair*.

I see.

So you have to randomize.

Randomize.

Yes. So I decide, say, just for an example, I'm at the World Series, near the ropes. There's always a crowd of people behind the ropes. If, when I look over, the third guy from the left behind the ropes is wearing a black shirt, a predominantly black shirt, I'll call. Otherwise I'll raise.

Interesting.

More than interesting. Foolproof. Even if your opponent knows that you're randomizing, even if he . . . or she . . . knows that you're basing it on shirt colors, which of course they'll have no way of knowing, they'd have to know the specific shirt color, the position of the signal person, and what the signal tells you to do, in order to take advantage of your randomizing scheme.

Okay. I think I get your point. That's very clever.

Well, I didn't make it up myself . . .

In any case, it's very clever, but I guess the question is—

What's it got to do with what happened to Eloise?

Yes.

I have no idea. I forgot. And anyway, I thought I wasn't supposed to go there.

She turned her head away. Shit. I'd said the wrong thing. I hadn't just said the wrong thing, I was supposed to tell her a story; instead, I'd been showing off. I'd babbled on forever. Lost myself in my cleverness. Lost her.

Right, she said at last.

I'm sorry.

But actually, she said slowly, I see the connection.

You do?

I do.

She didn't elaborate. I didn't want to ask. It was so easy to make a mistake.

Okay, she said.

Okay, I repeated.

She took my hand. Pulled me out of the chair. Guided me to the bedroom.

It didn't seem quite right. But I wasn't about to complain.

74.

SHE CLOSED THE BEDROOM DOOR. She turned off the lights. There remained a dim refraction, from the neon, through the windows, along the light lines, to the bedroom door, under the door. From there it diffused through the room. Tiny little photons. Enough of them bouncing, or waving, if it's waving they do, to give me the soft outlines of an exquisite creature removing her clothes. Softly and sadly. And then mine. I didn't have to move. She was performing the ceremony, the ritual. Whatever it was that she thought might cleanse her, me, us, of the thing that had brought me there.

Sometimes they kill the messenger. Sometimes the messenger gets something else.

I was in the bed. We were in the bed. She was beneath me, guiding me, soft and like a dream of it, better than a dream of it.

She slapped me in the face. Hard. Grabbed me by the throat. Nails.

Anger. Jesus. I was scared. This wasn't playing. I slapped her back. Hard. She fell back.

I reached out. To say I was sorry. To comfort her.

She moaned. She arched her back.

She wanted more.

I understood.

I gave her my anger. She gave me hers. Slapping. Kicking. I grabbed her by the wrists. Held her down. Pinned her legs with mine. She growled. Snapped her teeth. I bit her shoulder. Hard. I tasted blood. The thrusting never stopped.

The climax was the end of all climaxes. The end of the world. As I knew it.

I rolled aside. She curled herself around me. Kissed my neck, my lips.

It seemed an odd way to express your grief.

But death does strange things to people.

75.

I TOOK A SHOWER. Made it very hot. Cleared my head with deep, insistent breaths. When I emerged, she was there. Wrapped in a towel. I held her. She held me. We didn't say anything.

There was nothing to say.

I left. She closed the door behind me. Very softly.

The world outside blasted the numbness away. The clangor, the call and response of the neon. The hot west wind. I got the car from the lot. I didn't know how I got there.

I pulled out my phone. It was as automatic as walking. I dialed Butch.

What's up? I asked.

You tell her?

Yes.

She okay?

I guess so.

You okay?

Yeah. Yes. I'll be all right. Just give me the download.

He'd been asking around. Sometimes the asking got a little insistent. Helped with getting the answers. I could hear the pump in his voice. He liked that stuff.

He'd tracked down Brendan's movements to a club.

Not surprised, I said.

Yeah.

What's it called?

Don't know. Just got the address.

Where is it?

He told me. It sounded familiar. Unpleasantly familiar.

Pick you up? I said. Or meet you there?

Naw. I got to follow something else up.

What?

Never mind. If it pans out, you'll hear about it. Either way, we'll hit the club after.

Whatever, man.

You're not going there alone, he said with an edge.

It wasn't a question.

Jesus, man, I said. Last couple times, you got your ass handed to you. I might be better off alone.

Silence.

Sorry, man, I said.

You're not going there alone.

Okay, okay. Call me when, I don't know, when your thing. Whatever. Why can't I go with you on this other thing?

It's a cop thing.

I'd be in the way.

Let's just say your presence wouldn't be appreciated.

Spoil the party atmosphere?

Something like that.

All right. I'll take your word for it. But tell me, man.

What?

This club. It's in a basement? I'll bet it's in a basement.

You'd have to give me three to one.

I figured. Fuck you.

Fuck you too.

I hung up. Turned around. Headed for the club.

76.

IT WASN'T THE HOLE IN THE WALL. Though it might have been described as a hole in the wall. From the outside, anyway.

This wall looked like an ordinary stone wall. The mortar crumbling between the rocks. A small iron gate. A spiral staircase leading down. The stairs were wrought iron. Black. Rusted in places. You swung open the gate. You were careful on the stairs. They were spaced more widely than ordinary stairs. You could easily fall. Get entangled in the twisted metal bars.

This again?

At the bottom was a guy. A very big guy. Another one. Must have been six foot five. He wore a black shirt. Black pants. Leather jacket. He had a bored expression. And a silver tooth.

The guy looked me over.

Turn around, he said.

He didn't say it with any menace, any anger. He didn't say it with much of anything.

I turned around.

He patted me down. He did a good job. I'm not sure how I felt about that.

He didn't find a gun.

I didn't have one.

Shit.

He turned to the door. For the first time I noticed it. It looked solid. Painted black. Crosshatched metal bracing. Huge bronze hinges. There was a small grate in the middle. He bent over. Whispered into it.

The door swung open. He stepped aside. Just enough to let me squeeze by with maximum humility.

Inside, there was a cage. Behind the cage, a counter. Seated at the counter was a woman. She had purple bouffant hair. Pink lipstick. A scarlet bustier. A startling cleavage. And a very deep voice.

Fifty bucks, she rumbled.

Seemed like this was the standard rate in Vegas for entry to places you didn't want to go.

I just gave Mr. Big fifty bucks, I lied. Outside.

She looked at me. She rolled her eyes. She sighed.

Fifty bucks, she repeated.

How much are the drinks? I asked. No, let me guess. Fifty bucks? You're funny, she said, unamused.

I found a fifty in my pockets. Folded the bill in half, lengthwise. Placed it neatly on the counter. Flicked it with my fingernail, shooting it under the grate. It neatly stopped inches in front of her.

Made me feel good about myself. Like maybe I should have made the team.

Second door on the right, she said in the same bored baritone.

I went down a corridor. The walls were too close. The ceiling too low. I could turn around, I said to myself, go back to the motel. Let Brendan rest in peace. The cops can handle it. Write off the fifty. Go to the Wynn. Play in a fat cash game. Win it back, with vigorish.

I kept walking. It was dark enough I had to feel my way. It seemed ten minutes before I found a door. The first door. Unless I'd missed the first door. I could have missed the first door. I looked for a doorknob. Here at the first, or second, door. An aperture. A buzzer to ring. More likely, I thought, a brass knocker. In the shape of a large male member, perhaps.

The door was blank.

I kept walking. The walls seemed even closer. An illusion, though, I figured.

Fear will do that to you.

The corridor suddenly widened. The second door hove into view. You couldn't miss this one. A startling blood red in the unrelenting black. A large brass knocker. In the shape of . . . I wasn't sure. Symmetrical mounds. Buttocks, perhaps. Yes. A puckered aperture between.

An ass knocker.

Jesus.

As I was steeling myself to touch the thing, the door opened. A tall black creature in a yellow vinyl miniskirt, ripped muscles and nipple rings gave me a white-on-white smile.

Welcome, it said.

Thanks, I mumbled.

First time? it asked.

Uh, yeah. Is it that obvious?

Don't be shy. Come on in. We don't bite. Well, not right away.

It laughed. A high-pitched shriek of a laugh.

I'm Heather, it said.

Hi, Heather. I'm Rocco.

Its laugh tinkled.

Inside, they'd done it up in classic . . . antique hospital. There were anatomical charts on the walls. Things from the forties and fifties. Genitalia, the crosscut view. The digestive tract. Unappetizing skin conditions. Didn't want to know. There was a gynecological table against the wall. Stirrups. The top covered in fifties green plastic. On it were artfully placed a too-large speculum, a mock-up vagina and a set of mammaries originally designed, it appeared, to assist in teaching the art of breast examination.

An educational institution.

The hospital green was relentless, relieved only here and there with splashes of yellow. Parachute ceilings in green. Small green lamps. Arched doorways, leading to other green places.

That must have been where everybody was. The other places. Where the fun happened.

There was a bar against the left wall. An oasis.

I headed straight for it.

Hector will be right with you, Heather tinkled.

I pulled up a green velvet stool.

The bar was fully stocked, I was pleased to note. Tier on tier of beautiful bottles, lit green from below. A nice aquatic green. My mouth watered.

Hector appeared. She wore a chain mail halter top. She had a square jaw and a soul patch. She smiled. She winked. I admired her fishnet stockings. She handed me a menu. The menu offered:

- Thermometer
- Turkey baster
- Sewing kit
- Pink duct tape
- Yo-yo
- Fishing rod
- Selection of marbles
- Skull clips
- Mangina
- Disposable diapers
- Cat-woman
- Doggy bag

And that was just the first page.

Uh, how about a scotch? I asked.

We can do that too, she said.

As she poured me the libation, I decided to take the straightforward approach.

I'm kind of new to this, I said.

She looked at me in mock surprise.

Oh, I said. I guess you can tell.

You never know, she said, laughing a friendly laugh.

So, I said. I may have a few questions about the menu.

We're here to assist. In fact, it's my middle name.

Really?

Yes. My full name is Hector I Gonna Assist Yo Ass to Have a Good Time Charlie.

Charlie, I said. An unusual family name.

Hector laughed long and loud, spraying the bar top with whatever pink and green substance it was she'd been ruminating out of a shot glass as we talked.

I asked whether the duct tape came only in pink.

Oh no, she said. We have the full range. Do you prefer black? Many do.

I'm not sure yet. Uh, this yo-yo. What exactly is that for?

A yo-yo, she said with a wink, is anything with a string.

I see. And the marbles?

The string is optional.

Ah.

I finished my scotch. Another one appeared.

Gee, I said, I know I'm setting myself up for big laughs here, but as I said . . . well, what are skull clips?

If you have to ask, darling, she said, a provocative arm on her hip, you don't need them.

I see, I see. And the . . . the sewing kit?

If you need something fixed, it can be almost anything you want it to be.

Ah. Well, could it have, I don't know, a knitting needle in it?

Aha, she laughed. You know more than you're letting on, don't you, darling?

Actually, I don't.

You're a bad boy.

Well, I try. But, if you wouldn't mind just humoring me, I mean, say I ordered the sewing kit. With the knitting needle. I guess what I mean is, what would you do with it? Maybe I'm naïve, but, well, I'm thinking there's probably not a whole lot of your clientele that'll be knitting sweaters tonight, and anyway, to do that you'd need two. Needles.

She laughed a long, appreciative laugh.

Oh, honey, she said. You really do need help, don't you. Or you're a cop or something. Which comes to the same thing.

I laughed what I hoped sounded like a genuine laugh.

A cop I'm not, I said. I'm just curious. Okay, I'll admit it. I'm a writer. I have a scene that I want to set in . . . in a place like this. So, I guess you could say I'm doing research.

Sure, honey, she smiled, not entirely convinced. Poured herself another shot of Day-Glo poison.

The mangina? I asked.

If you pronounce it properly, you won't have to ask.

Okay, you got me. How do you pronounce it?

Man-jyna. Rhymes with . . .

Okay. I get it. And the doggy bag?

For what's left over, she said.

Ah. Well, listen, if you wouldn't mind, do you think I could get a look at that knitting needle? Just curious.

She picked up a wineglass. Began polishing it. Raised her eyebrows. You really don't look the type, she said.

I know. I just want to look at it.

Okay, she said, an edge of doubt flirting with her good cheer.

She went behind the bar. Came back with what looked like a velvet box. About ten inches by two. Some shade of peach, as far as I could make out in the dim colored lights. She opened it. Inside was, well, it didn't look like a knitting needle. More like an awl. She lifted it out of the box, displayed it for me. Yes. A knitting needle all right. Fitted with a wooden handle.

Interesting.

She put it back in the box. Closed it. Put it away.

Thanks, I said.

The novelty of my ignorance had worn off. She turned herself to other things. She sat on a stool at the far corner of the bar. Picked up a book, either reading it or pretending to. I squinted over, trying to make out the title.

A History of Hell.

A few minutes passed. I waved for another drink. She poured it silently. I figured it was time to get to the point. The other point.

Do you know a guy named Brendan? I asked.

Brendan? Hector raised her eyebrows. They were nicely painted on. Don't know any Brendan, she said.

Oh, I said.

She started polishing some wineglasses.

He's a friend of mine, I said. Five-ten or so? Pale? Curly hair to his shoulders? Small diamond earrings?

Could be a few of the fellas, she said, curious now. He have any tattoos?

Not that I know of.

She gave me a sideways glance. Apparently I hadn't given the right answer. If I was looking for a guy in here, I guessed, I should know about his tattoos.

Mind if I look around? I asked.

She didn't answer. Picked up a handset. Whispered into it. Ten seconds later a slick number in a black silk suit and shiny black shoes appeared. Introduced himself.

I'm Randy, he said.

Oh. Well, I'm Canadian. If that helps.

Come with me, he said.

He wasn't smiling.

My body remembered, if I didn't, what had happened last time I'd followed some stranger down a hallway. Adrenaline began firing gob-shots of fear at my stomach, my liver, my kidneys. My knees felt numb.

I went with him anyway.

Yes, Virginia, I am a fool.

I followed him through an archway. Into an alcove. The dank smell of unclean basement carpets, mildewed upholstery. The walls papered with peeling silver paint, patched here and there with aluminum foil. A dangling red lightbulb. A narrow corridor.

We passed a wide door. A small neon sign blinked over it. *Karaoke Bar*, it said. Some familiar chords wafted out. Deep Purple. 'Sweet Child in Time.' I loved that song.

Show us the *dick!* a high-pitched voice called out.

Floor show, said Randy.

The scotch was doing its inexorable work. Was it the scotch? Or just an ordinary déjà vu?

Another room. Lit orange and faded. Ratty couches here and there.

Randy went over to a couch against the wall. Nodded to someone. Nodded at me. One of the guys on the couch looked up. A guy in eyeliner and wig, but definitely a guy. He looked surprised. Nodded at me. Turned back to the guy next to him.

He'll be with you in a minute, Randy said.

Who? I wanted to ask. But it seemed like I was supposed to know.

Randy went away.

I found a spot on a couch. Sat and waited. For what, I didn't have a clue. A guy sat down beside me. Charles, he said. He said it with an English accent. Chaws. He was dressed in pink chenille.

He talked about cock rings. He liked them tight.

We discussed that for a while. He told me about how they could get too tight. Stuck. Couldn't get them off. Cut off your circulation. Danger of gangrene. You could have a purple dick for months. If you survived.

I thanked him for the information. Filed it away. Filed it under Futile.

Chaws had just changed the topic, to anal plugs, when Delgado came over.

I suppose I shouldn't have been surprised.

Rick, he said, extending a pale and welcoming left hand.

Delgado, I said, taking the hand, feeling its blanched, surprising strength, attempting artfully to conceal my shock at his presence.

Rick, he said in his softly menacing manner. What are you doing here?

I don't know. But I'm thinking maybe I should be asking you the same question. Or, maybe, the answer is, I came looking for you.

I see.

He said it with a strangely knowing air. The stranger for the fact that my answer had sounded, to my ears anyway, bizarre.

Now, normally I'm not the paranoid type. I don't see conspiracies dangling off of every curtain rod in every skanky upscale hotel room in these glorious States we call United. But something, Delgado's attitude was telling me, was up. I was as sure as a two-to-three shot in the Derby. Which is to say . . . pretty sure.

How to play it, that was the question.

Not by the book, that was certain. They didn't have a book for this one.

By ear?

Didn't seem appropriate.

By the bye?

That seemed more like it.

I made a note to check the spelling.

Well, Juan, I said.

I assumed we were on a first-name basis by now.

Juan, I said, there's more than one reason, actually.

All right. So let's go talk.

If it's going to be anything like the last talk, I respectfully decline. I'd rather get choked with a cock ring.

Delgado laughed. It was a surprisingly warm, understanding laugh. He put a hand on my shoulder. A surprisingly warm, welcoming hand.

Come on back, he said.

I got up. I followed him. Sucker! I said to myself. Asshole! Worse than a rat in a cage! At least they learn from experience!

The back to which he led me, though, was kind of welcoming. It was all done up in silver and blue. Inviting couches lined the walls. Inviting young ladies lounged about in welcoming clothes, or lack of clothes. I followed Delgado to a cozy corner booth. I was tempted to tell him I didn't make out on the first date. Or the second, for that matter. But that turned out not to be necessary.

You're confused, he said.

He said it authoritatively. It wasn't just an accurate appraisal of my current state of mind, which, of course, it was. It was a pronouncement. Something about my soul. I hadn't thought, for quite some time, about my soul. I wasn't even sure, then or later, then or now, that I had one. That anyone had one. That such a thing existed. Well, chickens, of course, had souls. As for us humans, well, one could, I supposed, in the Delgado haze, define it into existence, somehow. The Sum of All Tendencies, or something. The Sum of All Tendencies towards . . . something, maybe. Eggs, or something.

It's all right, he said. It's all right to be confused.

Juan, I said, fighting through the miasma to establish a beachhead of authority in the conversation. I appreciate your concern. But frankly, man, I'm just here to ask some questions. Do you think you can handle that? Or do I have to wade through an hour of hokum to get there?

Delgado sighed. Tapped his cane twice. A frothing blonde beauty in a silver sheath appeared, hair trimmed little-boy short and wearing a beret that matched the dress.

Lola, a double of the best for my friend, said Delgado in a faux tired tone, and—

Yes, sir, she said, in the most melting tone that a Yes, sir has ever been delivered, and turned heel for the bar.

Delgado spent the time before Lola returned giving me the Look that said, I'm sorry you haven't yet seen the light but I have faith that you soon will. I spent the time eyeing the extravagantly displayed body parts of Lola's sistren-in-flesh, who surrounded us like snipers hanging from the trees in the Forest of Temptation.

The drink helped.

Let's start at the start, I said.

Delgado raised his glass in a silent toast that seemed to say, Yes, let's do that.

What the fuck happened that night? I said.

Ah, said Delgado, that night. I'm tempted to say, what night? But you know that you'd just be wasting my valuable time.

He chuckled.

So?

What happened happened. You got very drunk. Certain inhabitants of the establishment, who may or may not be associated with me, one way or in some other way, gave you what you wanted.

Thank you for the clarification. You are most kind.

The pleasure is all mine, he said, with the air of someone impervious to irony.

And just what was it that I wanted?

Humiliation, he said matter-of-factly. Lola! he called out.

Lola slinked, or perhaps slunk, over with the next round. Like she'd been waiting for her cue. Like a prop in a play. Instead of just bringing the damn drinks. She hovered over Delgado like a silver hummingbird. A silver hummingbird in a beret.

I slugged down half of the new double scotch. At this point it was superfluous.

The whole situation had stopped me dead. Did I want to know any more? If it involved a crime I was here to solve, sure. If it didn't, and I had a fair certainty, not beyond religious conviction, that it didn't, knowing more was just going to make me suffer more. My Tendencies were what they were. If I encountered them again, I'd give them a good dressing-down. Yes. That was it. Give those Tendencies a good talking to.

Brendan, I said.

Brendan?

My ex-brother-in-law. Pale. Curly hair to his shoulders. Small diamond earrings.

Ah. Could be any number of the guys . . .

Fuck you, Delgado, I said. You know damn well who I'm talking about.

I didn't, in fact, have any idea whether he had any idea who I was talking about. But if he didn't, it didn't matter what I said. And if he did, this was the surest way to make him think that I knew that he knew something, and that therefore he'd better come out with it, or . . . I don't know, I'd bring out the heavy artillery, or something, something that I didn't have but that he didn't know that I didn't have.

Call it a bluff.

It worked.

Ah, he said. I think I may know who you mean. But he wasn't Brendan. I think he called himself Ivan.

That's him, I said.

I had no idea whether Brendan had called himself Ivan, but given his blind consortium with the Russkies, there was a truth to the notion that was all too clear. And I was going with the rush.

Called, I said. Why do you say it in the past tense?

Delgado looked at me calmly. I don't know, he said. If you said, *Do you remember Joe, he was wearing a sharkskin suit?* you'd be asking in the past tense, right?

I had to admit he had a point.

A black albino red-eyed pimp-like scumbag with a cane, and a grammatical point to make.

Something to conjure with.

There's more to the present than meets the eye, Delgado said.

I'd had enough.

You know, I said, fuck you. I'm tired of this bullshit New Age

I'm-creepier-than-thou-so-get-down-on-your-knees crap. You're so fucking powerful and wise, you pasty dickhead, gut up and take me on with your own scrawny fists. Leave the posse at home. Okay? Fuck you.

Delgado stood up abruptly.

The adrenaline rush hit. I was ready for some serious action.

He turned away from me, leaned over, performed some hand-waving weirdness.

Oh no, I said, is the Wizard going to appear? Will I be zapped into a locked tower in Mordor?

Delgado straightens up, turns around.

His eyes are blue.

What the fuck? I say.

Lola leans towards Delgado, lifts her lips to his. They engage in a long, writhing, what looks like sick passionate kiss.

My, I'm thinking. I wonder how much you have to tip for the extra service.

He turns to me. His lips are red.

A normal red. It isn't lipstick.

I'm starting to get the picture. I'm starting to get the picture that I ought to start doubting all the pictures of all the things that I've purportedly seen, heard and believed for the last . . . hell, maybe my whole fucking life.

Lola slinks behind Delgado, leans over his shoulder. Begins wiping his face with a tissue. Or something. Something more solvent than a tissue. A hand wipe or something.

Within seconds, the right side of Delgado's face is a stunning, radiant, revelatory . . . normal.

I sat back. Surveyed the scene. Lola's motherly smile. Delgado's half-revealed face. He was still striking-looking. He was still hairless. But he sure wasn't any albino. And he sure wasn't black. And there wasn't anything menacing about him anymore. He still had the full lips. But they were just . . . big white guy lips. Mick Jagger lips.

You're an actor, I said.

I am, he smiled.

Lola, I said, playing the rush. You are, too. And a makeup artist.

She smiled a yes.

Congratulations, I sighed. You're very good.

Thank you, they said simultaneously.

Actually, I meant Lola, I said. But you're good, too . . . What's your real name?

Andy, he said.

I almost did a spit-take with the scotch.

Andy?

Yes.

I can see why you changed it.

You don't have to be mean, he said, dropping the affected speech.

He sounded like a regular guy from Jersey.

I was just doing a job, he said. No offense.

So you say. Last I heard, kidnapping, involuntary imprisonment . . .

I stopped. Andy and Lola, or whoever she was, were clearly having a hard time suppressing their laughter.

I already told you—Andy began.

I know, I said. There was nothing involuntary about it. Says you. Shit. Lola, can you bring me another scotch? Can you stay in character long enough to do that?

Sure, she said in a light and not quite as slinky voice.

And who was the producer of this little . . . spectacle? I asked Andy.

I don't know, actually. I never met the main guy.

Who did you meet?

Whom, he said. Some beefy dude. Called himself Vladimir.

Vladimir.

Yeah.

Shit. I thought about it. I guess I'd left a trail as wide as a semitrailer on a mud road.

Lola returned with my scotch and some more hand wipes. Began removing the rest of Andy's makeup.

How much did you get paid for your . . . performance? I asked him.

We haven't gotten paid yet. Completely.

You haven't.

No. We got some cash up front.

Let me guess. Small unmarked bills.

Hundreds, actually. New ones. Crisp.

Did he tell you why they were doing this?

He said it was a kind of, I don't know, psychological ploy, to get some money from you that you owed. When they got their money, we'd get the rest of ours.

Money I owed? What was this? Maybe a different Vladimir? Someone working for Evgeny? But Evgeny had no reason to believe I wasn't going to pony up. Hell, I was working for the guy. Which reminded me . . .

This wasn't computing.

Can you describe this guy any better?

Not really, man. He always wanted to meet in dark corners. I mean, he was big. Strong-looking guy. Usually had a leather jacket on.

Who doesn't?

Right. He had kind of a square face. Couldn't see his eye color or anything. He usually had a watch cap on. Didn't pick up his hair color either.

Why you? I asked Andy. Did you know this guy, this Vladimir guy with the watch cap?

Lola laughed.

I may just be a marginally employed actor slash waiter, Andy said, but I'm kind of well known in this . . . milieu.

He's a character, said Lola. He knows everybody. Everybody knows him.

So this Delgado thing wasn't just made up for me?

Hell no, he laughed. He's one of my main guys.

So it was easy to get some of the others to play along with you. Like Xena, the bartenders . . .

Are you kidding? Andy laughed. Their whole lives are an act. Like. mine. They loved it.

You know what the difference is between a transvestite and a transsexual? Lola asked.

Anatomy?

No. Some transvestites have implants. Some transsexuals don't, yet. Haven't had the surgery yet. No, the difference is, I take my makeup off when I get home.

That dim lighting again. Lola was actually Larry, or whoever, when she got home? Jesus. Hadn't even occurred to me as a possibility.

So, I said, feigning nonchalance, how did you know what to do? Where I was going to be?

We got text instructions.

Do you have the number they came from?

The number was always concealed. User unknown.

Didn't you worry that you were being asked to do something wrong, something illegal?

Come on, Rick, said Andy, reverting to his husky Delgado voice.

Okay, I said. Stupid question.

I mean, if it turned out somebody was going to actually hurt you . . .

Yeah, yeah. I understand.

I leaned back in the blue and silver sofa. It had a nice enveloping feel. It was going to be hard to get up. The whole scene was way enervating. But there was no way I was going to hang around here with a bunch of bit players who didn't know shit about what was really going on.

You know anything else at all about these guys? I asked. Either of you?

I knew the answer.

The answer was no.

I was going to have to get out of there. Get somewhere quiet. Think shit through. Figure out the next move. Which might well be: get the hell out of town. Get away from all this crazy shit. Not show my face in public for a year. Goddamn. I was banned from the New York games anyway.

I asked some desultory questions about Brendan. They didn't know anything, of course. Brendan was a new guy in the scene. Good-looking guy. Got a lot of attention. One night he stopped showing up. They hadn't heard anything at all.

I got their contact information. Gave them my number. Asked them to call me if they learned anything.

One last question, I said.

Fire away, said Andy.

They were clearly enjoying the attention.

Knitting needles, I said.

Lola got a sneaky smile on her face. His face. Whatever.

You want to know what knitting needles are for? Andy asked with a smile.

Other than knitting.

Sure, he laughed. Well, you know what the prostate is, right?

Yes, I know what the prostate is. I get mine poked once a year by a guy with a rubber glove.

Hah. Well, this is sort of like that. I mean, you know that there's a certain type of guy, woman, it can be women, too, but it's usually guys, who hang around with . . . us, that they have this need for extreme, I don't know . . .

Stimulation, said Lola.

Stimulation, I said.

Right, said Andy.

Don't tell me this, I said.

Yes, he said. All the way up.

Through the . . .

Urethra. Right. To the prostate. Stimulation.

Stimulation.

Right.

That's pretty gross, I said.

Some people might think so, he said with a wink. Some people think it's . . . ecstatic.

Let's not go there. But what I want to know is, I mean, it's weird and all, and I suppose you should sterilize the thing, you could get an infection. But unless you sort of, Jesus, pushed the thing too hard or something, punctured something, there's nothing inherently dangerous about this . . . activity, is there? I mean, it's not going to kill you or anything, is it?

No more than a lot of shit that goes on, said Andy.

Lola laughed.

Like what?

Andy laughed too.

They both gave me a Look that said, That's all you're going to get, buddy.

I got the hell out of there.

I thought about it. Yes. There was something there.

But it wasn't Brendan's blood on the thing.

I had learned a lot. But I didn't feel any closer to the truth.

Yes. Life is like that.

77.

THE SECOND I STEPPED OUTSIDE, I was grabbed from behind, thrown face up against the stone wall. My forehead met an unyielding protrusion. My forehead yielded. Something warm and unpleasant flowed into my mouth. It seemed vaguely familiar. A salty taste. Ah yes. Blood. My own. A gray curtain descended. Scene over.

A new scene opening. Set in the half-world. I felt large, rough hands administering handcuffs. I suspended judgement. It was just happening. Maybe it wasn't so bad. I'd done some bad things, after all, in my day. Deserved a little punishment . . .

A familiar voice growled in my ear as I slumped to the ground.

It was saying something about Downtown.

78.

THEY BANDAGED MY HEAD. Splashed cold water in my face. Woke me up. Shoved me into a room. Took my cell phone. Don't I get a phone call? I asked. They didn't answer. They took my belt, too. My wallet. My shoelaces. I wasn't really a suicide risk. But they probably wouldn't have guessed that, to look at me. I remembered what had met me in the closet mirror, at Sheila's behest. And that was several traumas ago.

They left. Locked the door.

And there I was.

Alone with myself.

I hated that.

I wasn't completely alone, I guess. I had a wooden table to keep me company. Scored and patchy from endless elbows, fingernails, the odd smuggled-in nail file. The table was bolted to the floor. I understood the precaution. I might have tried to off myself by lifting the thing up, hitting myself over the head.

Amazing, how concerned they were for your welfare in these places.

And a chair. There was a chair. One of those gunmetal swiveling things that somebody, somewhere, lo these many eons ago, invented for the express purpose of making persons awaiting interrogation as miserable as humanly possible. Police departments the world over snapped them up. The whole production run, apparently. You never saw them anywhere else.

I would have liked to talk to the guy. Ask him what he was thinking when he included the contoured ass-crack ridge down the middle, the butt-cheek indentations on either side. Did he think asses came in only one size—sumo? I mean, the only conceivable purpose for the design, other than the placid comfort of a Japanese wrestling champion, was to prevent you from shifting your place in the chair, on pain of . . . well, pain.

An ingrate, I was. At least they hadn't strapped me upside down to some ancient, peeling torture device. Of course, they had smashed my head against a rock. But I was sure they'd done it with the best of intentions.

An hour and a half later, I was considering revising my view on that, and longing for the presence of some tied-together shoelaces with which I might end all this misery, thinking, I mean, where was the wet bar? If they were going to leave you alone in this desolate twelve-by-eight-foot dust emporium, the least they could do was lay in a generous supply of spiritual condiments, right?

I was just about to lodge a complaint with management when the door opened. And there, in all his brown-clad lumpy glory, was my very favorite well-tanned former-NYC-now-Las-Vegas detective. Rod.

My standards were pretty low.

Rod closed the door behind him. Gave me a Look of infinite Smug. Here you are, it said. Without your big black cop buddy savior guy. Now, scumbag, I'm going to take you apart. I'll start with the testicles. Work my way up to the more painful parts.

That was a lot of stuff for one Look to contain. But it was all there.

Roddy, I said. So good to see you.

Yeah, said Roddy. Get out of the fucking chair.

What? Why?

'Cause it's my chair, he said.

I wanted to get our little confab off on the right foot. So I got out of the chair.

You can sit on the floor, he said.

I'd rather stand.

Sit on the fucking floor, Redman.

Oh. Yes. Certainly. I'll just sit over here on the floor, I said, sitting on the floor.

Roddy grabbed the chair. Hauled it around to his side of the table. Took a heavy-breathing seat. Looked me in the eye.

You, he said.

Me?

Yeah. You. We got you fourteen ways from Sunday.

I ignored the bizarre metaphor. Well, I didn't ignore it. I tried momentarily to trace the provenance of such a turn of phrase. Fourteen ways from Sunday. I didn't succeed. It was almost as impenetrable as two cats fucking the same . . . whatever it was Elmer had said. Bottle. I made a note to look it up. Both of them up.

You do? I inquired with an utterly sincere air of innocence.

Shut up, said Roddy.

I wasn't aware that I'd been talking, I said.

Yeah, he said. You're smarter than me. Let's see what it buys you.

I have no intention of implying that you're not smarter than me, Rod. I apologize if I have conveyed any such impression. In fact, given your position, both physical and . . . what is it, legal? authoritative? I think it goes without saying that you're way, way smarter than me. Given the circumstances.

Shut the fuck up, Redman.

I shut the fuck up.

Detective Rod scraped his sumo chair, the one that mere moments ago had been my very own sumo chair, across the floor until he was inches from me. I looked up at him with the most winsome pair of eyes I could conjure.

Just how winsome that might have been, hey, let's just say I'm not bragging.

We got you coming, he said, and going. And everywhere in between. You've been all over that woman. And now she's dead. And you know a whole lotta shit you ain't been telling us.

Roddy, Roddy. I have to tell you. And I say it with the utmost sincerity. I really do. I couldn't mean it more sincerely. I don't have any fucking idea what the fuck you're talking about.

As I said it, I braced myself for a physical blow. But it didn't come. I admired Roddy's restraint. I saw his hand, the almost-fist of his right hand, twitch. I observed the pugilistic hunch of his shoulders. But the smack, the swat, the hurling of the ashtray, didn't come.

Well, Roddy said slowly, deliberately, I guess we're just going to have to give you the audiovisual.

He nodded at the mirrored part of the wall that beyond a reasonable doubt concealed a host of his confederates, hunched over recording equipment, cameras and whatever other exciting technological doodads had by now infiltrated the law enforcement community. You could count on them to be way behind the times. But not so way behind that they couldn't surprise you.

The door opened. A miserable minion in a gray overall wheeled in a seven-foot-tall metal stand on which reposed, on various shelves thereof, a gigantic video monitor, a DVD player, a fairly compact desktop computer of the horizontal orientation, and something that looked like a pre-amp/mixing board sort of thing, all of which I had no doubt could be remotely controlled from behind the one-way glass.

I had no idea what Rod was going to show me. But I was fairly sure I didn't want to see it.

The minion came back in with a folding wooden chair.

If anything could have been more uncomfortable than the Police Room Special, this chair was it. The seat was made of wooden slats, spaced too far apart. Designed for maximum buttock discomfort. But it was better than the floor.

We'll dispense with the two-hundred-watt bulb in the face, said Rod. For now.

Much obliged, I said. And thanks for the chair.

You're so very welcome. Now, tell me everything you know about Eloise Wittenburg.

Wittenburg?

That was her name.

Not . . .

What?

Never mind. I thought it was something else.

What?

I don't remember. I guess she must have got married.

Redman.

Yes, officer?

First, cut it with the officer shit. Second, you have one more supposed lapse of memory and I'm going to cut your balls off with a ball-point pen.

Interesting choice of implement, I said. But seriously, Rod, I know you're not going to do that. And you know that I know you're not going to do that. And more important, you gotta understand, I'm a sick alcoholic depressive. Our memories are for shit. Look it up.

Rod took a nail file out of the breast pocket of his lumpy brown jacket. Inspected it, as if wondering if it might not do a better job than the pen.

I'll cut you a little slack, Redman, he said as he scraped some flaking skin off the side of his nose with the file. But only if I think—no, only if I *know*—that you're telling me everything you know. Starting with why you're so fucking interested in this broad.

What makes you think I'm so interested in her?

Rod banged the table so hard the nail file flew halfway across the room. Which, now that I think of it, wasn't very far.

Redman, he yelled, you're not off to a good start. First, you show up to look at the body, way before anybody should have even known about it. That would seem to show a bit of interest.

Uh, Butch called me about it, I said.

Second, he said, ignoring me, we've talked to your buddy Elmer. Seems you'd already been showing a whole lot of interest in her.

Elmer? Elmer talked to you?

Ha-yup, he said, doing a fairly convincing imitation of Elmer's down east drawl.

Didn't strike me as the type of guy would want to be talking to the cops too much.

You'd be surprised. He's a lonely old fart. Likes company.

I guess I could see that.

And then you show up at the fucking Mercury Rising.

The what?

The Mercury Rising Club, asshole.

There you got me, Rod. I swear, I never heard of the place.

Rod gave me the Cop Look, above described.

Having retrieved his nail file, he set to work again at an angry flaking spot on the other side of his nose. Little flecks of skin showered the top of the table. He carefully arranged them into a handsome little flake pile.

I had an urge to vomit.

Hector! Rod called out. Roll the Mercury tape!

Ah, I thought. The long-awaited film presentation.

Rod, I said.

Shut up and watch, Redman.

But, really, I said. Where's the popcorn?

He gave me a Look that said, One more fucking joke and I really will use this nail file to perform some ugly and unnecessary procedure on some extremely sensitive part of your person.

I shut up and watched.

It was grainy black-and-white footage, clearly from a security camera. One that slowly rotated a hundred-eighty degrees and then back, on a cycle of about a minute. Judging by the view, it was mounted on the ceiling in the corner of the room. A darkly lit, stone-walled room containing a number of elaborate contraptions and a fair number of mostly naked men and women. One particularly pale and pudgy specimen was strapped head down on one of the contraptions, which with the benefit of this new view looked very much like an abstract rendering of a gynecologist's examining table.

Now I really needed to puke.

That you, asshole? Rod asked with even more contempt than usual.

I am profoundly sad to say that it is, I said. But I can unequivocally assure you, kind sir, that I did not voluntarily put myself in that position. I was drugged. Put there against my will. And if you don't mind my asking, if anything particularly vile was perpetrated on my person in subsequent frames, I have no recollection of it and don't care to acquire one, so please be so kind as to permit me to close my eyes.

That at least got a laugh out of Rod.

Cut out the lawyer-talk crap, Redman, he said.

I laughed. Too long and too loud. But it felt good.

Hector! Rod called out again. Back it up!

A low, rumbling voice descended from the ceiling.

Rod, it said. You don't have to shout. We can hear you.

Oh yeah, said Rod, lowering his voice. Okay. Back it up to 10:23.

And I wasn't trying to be cute with you, Rod, I said. It wasn't called the Mercury Rising, okay? There was a sign outside—

Shut the fuck up.

Another view appeared. Same camera, slightly different angle. In the shot, a formerly respected New York attorney somewhat down on his luck and engaging in a rather pathetic attempt at a poker and investigation career was to be seen fully naked, in a clear state of arousal, and draped on either side by tall, attractive—or so it seemed; it was hard to make out everything in the grainy dark—women. They approached the apparatus, laughing and talking, and the former attorney could be seen quite voluntarily clambering onto it, slipping   .

out of place several times, to general great hilarity, and being strapped securely down with weathered leather straps. That the straps were weathered leather was not actually discernible on the tape. The attorney filled in that detail. From memory.

The tape stopped. The scene was frozen in front of me. I was sorely tempted to make use of the closing-the-eyes option.

Not voluntary? Rod asked.

Video can be so misleading, I said.

Really?

Yes. Remember Rodney King?

You found that misleading?

Some people did. It takes out a lot of context. Context is everything, you know.

I see.

Listen, Rod. I wasn't lying to you. I have no memory whatsoever about what's going on there. I woke up the next morning, strapped to that thing. I know I had to have been drugged. I mean, look at how I'm stumbling around like an idiot.

Doesn't seem like that's maybe so unusual for you, he said drily.

Touché, I said. Sure. Touché. But I'm telling you, if that was voluntary, it was the voluntary of the guy on acid who jumps off the roof of the Hilton.

Interesting comparison.

Damn it, Rod. You know what I mean.

Maybe I do, dickhead. You like that word better? And, as they say in the commercials, there's more.

I don't want to see any more.

You don't have a choice, asshole. Hector! he shouted. Stopped himself. Lowered the volume. Hector, run it to Thursday 10:35.

The scene had shifted again. The attorney wasn't there any more. A red door was. A large red door studded with bolts and crisscrossed with what looked like black metal bands.

The runes were not visible in the gloom.

There was a small group of people huddled before the door. Three men, heavily muscled. They all wore black leather masks, big silver zippers for mouths. Black leather shorts and thick crossed suspenders, silver-studded gloves. Standard S & M stuff, you might say, you might think. The usual hi-jinks.

But there was something else there. I couldn't point out what in the scene made me sure, but the feeling was very strong.

They weren't having fun.

In the middle of the pack was a smaller person. Naked. Slim. Pale. Unforgettable.

The red door opened. It was dark inside the door. The men began pushing the struggling woman towards the door. At the last second before she vanished, she turned her head towards the camera. A full three-quarters view. They stopped the tape right there.

Oh fuck, I said.

There was nothing else to say.

79.

Rod started reading me my rights.

Forget it, Rod, I said. I'm not saying another fucking word till I get my phone call. Talk to my lawyer. This is really fucked up.

Rod shrugged. No surprise.

Here, he said with a jaundiced smirk. Handed me his cell phone.

I called Butch. He wasn't my lawyer. But who the hell else was I going to call? I didn't even have a lawyer. Unless I counted myself. And they'd taken my cell phone away. So I wouldn't have been able to answer my call . . .

Butch answered. I almost puked with relief.

Butch, I said. They're holding me downtown.

What the fuck?

Yeah, I said. Rod and his buddies.

I told him the situation.

Jesus Christ, Rick, he said. You let them do that to you? Why did you even talk to them?

Never mind that now. Just get me the fuck out of here.

Butch hung up.

Rod left the room.

Before he left, he said one more thing:

She didn't leave that place alive.

For fifteen minutes I stared at the frozen video screen. Tried to convince myself it wasn't her.

It didn't work.

The door opened. A cop so scrawny his pants looked in danger of dropping to the floor handed me my belt, my wallet, my shoelaces. Didn't say a word. Left. Left the door open.

I was a free man.

80.

I'M TRAPPED, I said to Sheila.

In what way?

Every conceivable way, I said.

I related the recent events. Edited for shrinkish consumption, and time constraints.

She got the point.

You have to get back home, she said.

I know. I know. Though that's only part of it. And I can't leave yet. There's still some entrails to be tied up.

Entrails.

My little joke.

I see.

Are there any drugs I can take?

I don't think that's the answer.

Of course not. Of course not. It's just that . . . all of this shit is getting very hard to deal with.

I understand. Let's do our best.

Listen, the thing of it is—

The thing of it.

Is entropy.

Entropy.

We're urban beings, you and I. Everything is always disintegrating. It doesn't matter how desperately we sweep up, paint over, shore up the falling bridges. Dust underneath the bed. Or pay somebody else to do it. It's always falling apart.

A discouraging way of looking at things.

Is there any other way? I mean, in nature it's different. Decay is the order of things. Decay is renewal. The maggot feeds on the corpse. The bird—the man—the starving man, maybe just adventurous, eats the maggot. Not so bad after all! he says. Goes off to propagate the species. Happily goes off. Whistling a happy tune.

I see.

When I was small, I said, I had a terrible fear of shrinking. Shrinking.

Or maybe it was the other way around. I'd get these visions. Visions is the wrong word. The world would recede. Quickly. Like it was vanishing into the wrong end of a telescope. If you know what I mean.

I think I do.

That's what my father said. I didn't believe him.

Why not?

Amazing how perceptive children are, at the youngest age. I don't know how old I was. Five, maybe. But I just knew he was trying to comfort me by that. Didn't have a clue what I was talking about. He wasn't a very sophisticated guy.

Which you knew at the age of five?

I read a lot.

I see.

I mean, some of it is ex post facto, you know? But yeah. I knew.

So what's all this got to do with your current predicament?

Well, it's not going to help it, God knows. I was a weird kid. So the fuck what? Who wasn't? But it explains some stuff. I mean, I have some memories. I don't know if they're true. They may be apocryphal. I'd be in the basement. By myself. And I'd shit my pants. Or puke on the floor. And I'd be afraid to move. Just stand there in it. For hours.

That's horrible.

I thought so.

And . . .

And something about that image explains this need for stimulation. You know?

I understand. Escape from the dark. From the basement.

Nobody's coming to help anyway.

You have to get out of there.

And that kind of leads into why I've always liked sleazy joints, you know, better than classy places. I mean, I'm as happy as the next guy to be pampered and served. But there's always something unreal about it. Like they've mistaken me for some other guy.

Perhaps we should talk about how to get you away from that.

I've got to think about it.
Of course. We'll get back to it next time. If you like.
I wasn't sure I liked.
If there is a next time, I said.
What do you mean?
No, no. Not that. Don't worry. Just a general sense of doom.
Nothing new, then.
And meanwhile, I've got a couple of murders to solve.
I laughed.
I was laughing at myself.
Funny, I said, how small children don't laugh.
What are you saying? Children laugh all the time.
They do?
Yes.
Oh.

81.

BUTCH WAS AT THE VELVET HANG. Impatient as hell.
I had to talk to my shrink, I said.
You can't be fucking serious.
I know it's hard to understand—
It's easy as fuck to understand. You're a self-indulgent asshole.
Thanks for that. I know I can always count on your support.
We got dead bodies here, Rick.
I know, Butch. I know that. Please chill a bit. I'm not dealing with
all of this very well.
Butch bit his tongue. Leaned forward, hands on his knees. Looked
me in the face.
Just give me the lowdown.
Download.
Whatever.
I gave it to him.
He relented. Sat back. Took a slug off his scotch.
All right, he said. We need a plan.
Let's plan.
We have to talk to your friend Louise.

I couldn't agree with you more. But I think it's got to be me, not we.

Why the fuck—

Chill, I said. Trust me on this one. There's stuff that . . . stuff that she'll tell me alone that she won't tell me if you're there.

The corners of Butch's mouth twitched. He pursed his lips. Looked me up and down.

Tell me you didn't.

Okay, I didn't. Let's shut that one down right here.

He sighed. I'll pretend to trust you on this one, he said. But don't think for a second that you're fooling me.

I'm not trying to fool you. And by the way, what happened with your cop thing? Your little thing you had to do?

Didn't pan out.

What was it?

It didn't pan out, Rick. So whatever it was, it doesn't matter.

I hate it when you get all mysterious.

Yeah, but it's really sexy.

Fuck you. Okay. Next, Brendan.

I gave Butch the second download. Told him what I'd learned about the knitting needle.

You fucking went there without me?

I had to, man.

You're such a dickhead.

I know. Sorry.

Whatever. Anyway, I already knew about that knitting needle trick.

You did?

Rick, I've been a cop a long time. We had one where the other guy got too excited. Three hours of surgery to get the thing out. Guy was never the same.

How could that happen? The thing's got a wooden handle on it.

This one didn't.

Why didn't you tell me before?

Good question, Rick. What good would it have done you?

I don't know, but shit, man.

Forget about it.

Well, I hope it was fun while it lasted.

What was?

Whatever he was doing with the thing.

I wouldn't know. But meanwhile, all we got is Brendan had the thing in his hand. And it wasn't his blood on the thing. We got to get the forensics.

Getting the forensics is your department, Butch. I'm still waiting.

I know it is. I been working it. In fact, I should be getting a message any second. Meanwhile, though, they did tell me there's no evidence that the thing was used on Brendan, if you know what I mean. No, whatta ya call it, urethral damage.

Yeah, well, that fits with the blood, doesn't it. It seems to me we match the blood on that thing, bare minimum we got a witness, right?

A witness to something, said Butch, showing little interest.

He checked his cell phone.

Any minute, he said.

All right, I said. And . . .

And you and me, we're going to go down to that club and bang some heads. Those fuckers know a hell of a lot more than they're telling you, Rick. You're too much of a wuss.

I pondered that thought. Not the wuss part. The knowledge part.

Butch was right. There was no chance in hell they'd shared with me everything they knew. Actors, shit. I didn't even know if that part was true.

Okay, I said. But it's too early. These lizards only come out from under their rocks after midnight.

Yeah, yeah. Thanks for the update. You go talk to your lady friend. I'll get the forensics lowdown.

Download.

Right.

Call me, I said.

You can count on me.

I knew that was true.

82.

I COULDN'T FIND LOUISE. This wasn't necessarily bad. Things needed to slow down.

Family time. Yes.

Kelley, Madeleine and Peter had become inseparable.

At least one thing in life was working.

I called them up. Asked them out for dinner. Take my mind off the mud and sludge. And knitting needles.

Kelley recommended a cheery little Italian joint that had seen better days. The sign over the door may once have said *Pappa Giorgio's*, but it could as easily have been *Pop My Weasel*, since only the first and third letters remained.

Ah, I said. My kind of place.

When I arrived, they were already there, together in a red vinyl booth, avidly engaged in a first course. Kelley had a spoon clinging to the curve of her nose, the handle hanging down in front of her mouth. It looked magical, but anyone can do it. I knew the routine. I didn't say anything. Would have spoiled the effect. She was waiting for someone at the next table to react, do a double take. At which point she would casually let the spoon fall into her minestrone.

It worked to perfection. It usually did.

Sorry I'm late, I said. There's a lot of stuff going on.

Dad, she said, I need you to get a grip.

It's hard to find a good grip these days, I replied.

And what's that on your head?

That would be a bandage.

And?

I had an unfortunate encounter with a stone wall.

How are your fingernails?

My fingernails are fine, thanks.

A waiter in a stained white apron appeared, said to Peter, Are you finished, sir?

Peter looked at his empty appetizer plate, a small mound of yellowed gluey substance remaining.

No, he said, I'd like to suck up the mayonnaise first, please. Do you have a straw?

The waiter didn't get the joke. Brought over a straw. Peter played along. Sucked up the mayo, or whatever it was, with a straight face. The waiter took the plate away.

Madeleine, I said, I hope these guys aren't a bit too much for you.

Dad, she said. Get a grip.

I ordered the cavatelli, with a creamy mushroom sauce. My instincts told me not to. I ignored them.

When it arrived, I told myself to reacquaint myself with the power of instinct. It looked like a bowl of slugs. Well, thinner than slugs. Maggots. It wasn't just my mood, black as it was. They really were the shape, and color, of maggots. They weren't al dente enough, mind you, to have the texture of maggots—or what I imagined the texture of maggots to be; I confess that I had never actually eaten a maggot—which only made the experience more horrendous.

Peter had ordered the shrimp scampi. How bad could that be?

How's the shrimp? I asked.

On a scale from one to ten, he said, it's shrimp.

Oh dear, I said.

It's okay. If I can chew it, I'll eat it.

Kelley had ordered a calzone.

Jesus, said Peter, that thing's as big as my father's ass.

So, said Madeleine, who had ordered a discreet but inedible salad, Dad?

Yes, dear?

They tell me you're a little weird.

The joys of having children, I said.

I immediately regretted it. But Madeleine didn't seem to have taken offense.

Is it true that you never even finished high school? she asked.

Uh, yes, I guess. I flunked out of high school. Well, maybe flunked out isn't quite right. I could have gone back and retaken that algebra, the French course. I was homeless for a few years. Well, I don't know if that's really accurate. Though I did live in a tent from time to time, and a tar paper shack in the Arctic. Wait, it wasn't above the Arctic Circle, so that's not exactly it. Anyway, later I became a big-shot lawyer. But you know all that. Didn't your Mr. Esplanade do all the research?

Esquinasse. Sure. But I wanted to hear it from you. Kelley showed me some pictures.

Oh dear.

Yes. You used to be so thin!

Ah, yes. Youth is wasted on the young.

What happened? I mean, it's strange, usually when people are thin, they stay thin, don't they?

Sometimes, I said. For the first thirty years, it wasn't really a matter of choice, or metabolism. I didn't have enough to eat. Most days. And then, once I got a job and stuff, I used to spend two hours a day in the gym, seven days a week. But then you get older. You slow down. You don't change your eating habits. You have no time for the gym.

Dad? said Kelley.

Yes.

Tell the truth.

The truth?

The truth is, said Peter, he drinks about four thousand calories a day and barely moves for days at a time.

I wanted to be shocked and appalled, but they were all laughing. Daddy'd been caught. Again. It was okay.

Peter, I said, you've got personality enough for eight normal people.

I know. I was thinking of signing up to be a personality donor.

I hear the money's good, I said.

But the surgery's excruciating.

That can be a problem.

I'm going out for a smoke, said Peter.

I'll join you, said Kelley.

Kelley didn't smoke. She didn't drink, either. Or have any other known vices, other than a terminally sardonic edge. But she had a fundamentally altruistic nature—when a small child, she always offered her cookies to the other children before she'd have one herself—and couldn't abide the notion of poor Peter out there in the heat smoking by himself.

Or maybe it was just a cue.

I was alone with Madeleine. Clearly, she'd been briefed by Kelley and Peter about her dissolute dad. Though what she knew and what she didn't I had no idea. I probably never would. It's one of the burdens of fatherhood. But there was one thing, of course, that I didn't know, and felt that I had to know.

Do you think it might be time to tell me about your mother? I asked.

Madeleine lowered her eyes. Watched her napkin for a while.

You don't have to tell me now, I said.

No, no. I want to tell you. It's just that . . .

I waited.

It's just that I don't know any more than you do. Probably less.

I waved at the waiter. Held up two fingers for a double.

Um, I'm not sure I understand, I said.

She died in childbirth. I was put up for adoption.

Madeleine kept her head down.

Oh my God, I said. I'm so sorry.

There's nothing to be sorry about, she said, raising her face to mine. It wasn't your fault.

If I'd known—

You didn't. Everything's fine. My adoptive parents are wonderful.

They would have to have been. Look at you.

She smiled through the tears. It means a lot to me, she said.

I'm sure they do.

No, not them. I mean, them, too. But I meant this.

This?

To meet you. Warts and all.

Warts and all, I laughed. Mostly warts.

No, she said.

That was all I needed.

It was nice to have someone around who was invested in me being less than all warts.

Kelley and Peter returned, with a saunter and a flounce, respectively. Distributed knowing looks all around.

I'd been the victim of another piece of theater.

But this one was nonfiction.

Thank you, I said. Thank all of you.

Oh shut up, said Kelley.

Get a grip, said Peter. Tell us about your big case. We're dying to know.

Which one? I asked.

There's more than one?

Oh Jesus, I thought. I hadn't told them about Brendan. Well. I had to now. It would be all right. Kelley and Peter hadn't known him well. It wouldn't hit them so hard.

I told them the story.

Jesus, said Peter.

Oh, Daddy, said Kelley. I'm so sorry.

There wasn't anything I could have done, I lied. I think it was kind of, I don't know, predestined.

I feel bad, said Peter.

Why should you feel bad?

I just brushed off those things you were telling me. Maybe if I hadn't—

Oh, cut it out, guys, I said. We don't even know what happened yet. He could have had a heart attack.

Um, yeah . . . said Peter. But listen, tell us everything about it. Maybe we'll have an idea!

I told them as much as I dared.

Oh, said Peter.

Yes?

Well, that place you're going to check out?

Yes?

See if there's a back room. A hidden room.

More hidden rooms.

Why? I asked.

Um, I know you're a sensitive guy, Dad, he said.

Oh, shut up.

So I'll spare you all the details. But there's a certain kind of crowd— I mean, I'm not part of that crowd, don't get me wrong, but you hear things, you know.

Yes, I think I know.

And, Dad?

What?

Can I come along?

Not a chance, Peter.

Aw, come on. Adventure. Excitement. Tight asses in tight pants.

I'm not going to put my surrogate son in the line of fire, Peter.

The line of fire. That's so . . . sexy.

Oh, for God's sake.

Well, if I can't go, you have to make sure to follow my advice. Look for a back room. All will be revealed.

Peter's flight of fancy actually wasn't implausible. These places were like warrens. And there was the red door . . .

All right, I said. I'll make sure we cover that angle.

I could think of a joke, said Peter.

Please don't.

83.

BUTCH CALLED. I took the phone into the bathroom. Sat on the toilet. I didn't tell him that.

I got some stuff, he said.

Shoot.

No. Meet me at Skully's.

I'm on my way.

I liked Skully's. The bartender was this Mexican kid, short and pudgy with a heavy accent and a stringy mustache. One of those ridiculously friendly guys. Soon as he found out you were from New York, he started up the chitchat about the Knicks and Giants. Of course, if you were from San Diego, he was all of a sudden a Chargers fan. You knew he was trying too hard, but you liked him anyway. He always bought you a drink. You'd always tip him extravagantly. See you again, you'd say when you left. And you knew that somehow you would.

Butch wasn't there yet. I tried not to speculate about his stuff. Could be news. Could be he'd run into a sale on vintage Italian ties. I thought about the Brendan thing. The Eloise thing.

I tried to approach them like poker hands. They were, after all, problems of incomplete information. Just like any poker hand. If you could see your opponents' cards, poker would simply be a mathematical exercise. Compute the probability of winning; compare to the ratio of the bet to the pot. Conclude. No fun at all. At least, not for those of us aspiring to a higher rank than Lance Corporal in the I-am-a-Nerd Army.

In any case, it didn't do me a bit of good. I was as confused as ever.

Butch arrived. He wasn't looking happy. He took a stool.

What's up? I said.

He rubbed his temples with his hands.

He turned to me.

Brendan, he said.

I waited.

Inconclusive.

What the . . . ?

The autopsy was inconclusive.

Jesus Christ. What the hell does that mean?

It means he didn't die of a gunshot wound. Strangulation. Overdose. Shock. Distemper. Bovine encephalitic fever. What the fuck do you think it means?

Is there such a thing as bovine encephalitic fever?

I don't fucking know.

Okay. So.

So we gotta go back to that club. Figure out what you missed.

That would be the idea. And thanks.

Anytime.

I see you got your costume on.

Yup, he said, holding out his feet to show off the shiny boots. You? Where's the hat?

You can count on me, I said, reaching behind my chair and placing the magical sunshade on my head. You got Pandora?

Damn right I do.

Good. We might need her.

You got yours?

Yup.

We slagged down a couple more doubles. Improved the coordination. We flagged down a cab. It smelled of burnt bacon, and anticipation.

We wound down the wrought iron stairs. The mammoth black-clad silver-toothed nonentity at the bottom took one look at Butch, stepped immediately in front of him.

You got a problem? Butch said.

You can't come in here.

Why the fuck not?

You know why not.

Butch paused at that. I had no idea what the guy was talking about. I was not sure Butch did either. Had the guy pegged Butch as a cop, that easily? It wasn't because he was black. I'd seen lots of black guys in these clubs. And women. And every composite in between.

Butch stood up to his full height. I was mildly surprised to note that he was only an inch or so shorter than His Vastness.

Get the fuck out of my way, he said.

His Vastness stared him down. Butch reached into his jacket. Paused.

His Vastness got the message. Stepped aside. Opened the door.

Right this way, gentlemen, he said.

As we walked in, I could see him talking into his neck. Warning the troops, no doubt. That was all right. We were ready for them.

We each paid our fifty bucks. Negotiated the black corridors quickly, to the second door. I remembered the way.

I guess I had some rat in me after all. Or fish. Whatever.

We pressed the anus in the door. The door opened an inch. A sallow face peered out. Butch kicked the door open. The owner of the face pitched backwards onto the floor with a convincing squeak.

Sorry, said Butch, not nearly as convincing.

I went straight to the bar, Butch trailing.

Hector was there. In all her . . . glory wasn't quite the right word.

Hey, I said. Is Delgado here? Andy?

Sure, she said. Back room.

The back room. Check.

Don't you want to stay with me for a drink or two? she asked with a charming pout.

We'll take a couple of doubles to go, I said.

She raised her eyebrows at me, at Butch.

My friend, I said. Butch.

Well, hell-o, Butch, she said, deftly pouring the drinks.

Hi, he said, in a fuck-you tone.

That only seemed to inflame Hector's interest.

Oh, Butch, she said. You do seem so very . . . manly.

Let's go, Rick, Butch said.

We stood up.

We'll see you later, I said to Hector.

Well, I dooo hope so, she said.

We headed for the back room. Or at least the back room that I knew about.

There was a confab going on. A bunch of folks on mushroom chairs around a small round table, talking earnestly.

I recognized Delgado, or Andy. Whatever the fuck his name was. Lola. Randy, the usher from the first time I'd been there. And . . .

Bruno.

What the fuck? I said.

What the double fuck, said Butch.

I was momentarily paralyzed. Circuits overloaded.

Butch strode right up. Stood over the group.

I followed. I didn't want to. I thought about the distance to traverse, back through the silver halls, the vast middle room, the door, the dark snaking corridor, His Vastness at the gate, the spiraling staircase. If we couldn't handle whatever was about to come down, we were seriously fucked.

But it was too late. They were looking up at Butch, with various airs of bemusement. Bruno had spotted me. The mammoth Bruno Grin was spreading across his pompous face.

I had to put on a good show.

I calmly adjusted the cowboy hat on my head. Tilted it slightly forward. Pondered the presence of the Mauser under my left armpit. Ah, yes. The Great Equalizer. So long as someone wasn't packing a Greater one.

The tableau was set. Butch standing, big and menacing. The locals sitting, somewhat cowed, a little bit curious. Bruno smirking.

Bruno, I said. The fuck are you doing here?

The fuck are you doing here? he echoed.

Looking for some information. You got some?

I got some.

Yeah?

Yeah, he said. You're a fuckin' loser. And you still owe me one.

I nodded my head. Pursed my lips. The pace of the conversation was allowing me time to formulate exactly the right response. A rare luxury.

I felt the Mauser under my arm. The power. The jam. The I'll-Say-Whatever-the-Fuck-I-Want.

I scoped the situation. I wasn't stupid. I was just drunk. Shit was falling into place. If nothing else, Bruno knew a lot of shit. Shit that was going to illuminate a lot of other shit. It was like a shit problem. I mean a chess problem. You saw an idea. It wasn't the right idea. You figured that out easily enough. But your brain kept coming back to it. There was something there. You saw another idea. Rook here, knight there. There was something to it. Back to the other idea. Queen here, check. He has only two squares. Unfortunately, they seem to be enough. King here, King there. As long as he has one or the other, the King escapes. But if you took the first idea, combined it with the second idea, reversed the move order, interpolated a bishop move . . . there it fucking was.

You got it.

You loved yourself.

Bruno, I said. You're here, with these particular lowlifes . . .

I gave the lowlifes a quick smile, let them know I meant no disrespect.

We'll take it as a compliment, said Andy. Long as you remember we're high-minded lowlifes.

Noted, I said. So listen, Bruno, you're here with these high-minded lowlifes. Which tells me, call me paranoid, you're involved in some of the shit they've been involved in. Shit I happen to have a particular interest in. So . . .

You're gonna make me tell you.

He turned to Andy and company with the big smile. They smiled back. A touch nervously.

Butch had his hand under his jacket. I shook my head. We weren't there yet.

No, I'm not going to make you do anything, Bruno. I couldn't if I wanted to. I'm going to ask you.

Ask me.

I just did.

He laughed. It was a laughing-in-my-face kind of laugh.

I can make trouble for you, Bruno.

Oh, Ricky, he said. Scare me some more.

You're not the only one that knows shit. And we're in with the cops here. You know who Butch is, don't you?

Bruno looked at Butch. Yeah, he said. He's the cockroach I stepped on the other night.

Butch stepped forward, hand going for Pandora again.

I put a hand on his arm. I had to apply a lot of pressure.

Easy, man, I muttered at him. Let's see where this goes.

Butch relented. But I knew it was only for a moment. If the persuasion mode didn't pan out, he was going for the iron solution.

He's a cockroach who happens to be a cop, I said. Who's in with the locals. Who might be real interested in some of the shit you've been dealing around here.

It was a bluff, of course. I had no idea what shit Bruno was into. I was reasonably sure, on the other hand, that he was into some kind of shit. Wouldn't be natural if he wasn't.

Bruno snorted. Narrowed his eyes. Looked at Butch. Looked at me.

You don't know shit, he said.

Calling my bluff.

This called for some table chatter. I waded deeper into the bull-shit zone.

Bruno, I said. You want to be smart about this. You know some shit. I know it, and you know I know it. So we can get it out of you. Me and Butch here. Maybe you got friends. Maybe we got more important friends.

Then I re-raised.

You want to bet your stack on it?

I let that sink in.

Bruno leaned back. Put his hands behind his head. Looked at Butch again. Stared me down.

It was looking like a standoff.

I'm going to get some drinks, said Lola.

Andy got up, went with her.

Hey, Bruno said after a few hours of the stare-down. Tell you what.

Yeah?

I got an idea.

Care to share it with us?

Tell you what, he said. I'll play you heads up. Winner take all.

Where? Here?

There's a poker room in the back.

Aha. The mysterious back room. Peter had been right. Partly right, anyway. Just not quite the type he'd been thinking of.

Eleven grand, said Butch. Freeze-out. I win, I take the cash and you fuck off. You win, you take the cash and I tell you some shit.

Bruno smiled. His every pore was oozing self-regard. There was no room in his fat head, I was quite certain, for the thought that he might lose a heads up match to me; it was a no-risk deal for him. Just another opportunity to humiliate me.

I had a different view.

You got it, I said. Butch holds the stakes.

My cash is at the cage, he said.

I thought you'd say that. You could go get it. But let's get this thing going. You got something you can put up? It's not like I exactly trust you, fine individual that you are.

Sure, he said, laughing. Whatever you say, cowboy.

He reached into his jacket pocket. I reached for the Mauser. He held up his hand. A key chain. I let go of the grip.

It's out back, he said, tossing the Harley keys to Butch.

I nodded. All right, I said. That'll do. The cash and the truth. Or the bike.

I knew he'd never give up the bike.

Butch had had enough. He leaned over, whispered in my ear. The fuck are you doing? he said.

It's okay, I muttered back. This is just for my ego. And to get him away from that crowd. I lose, we shoot him in the knees. Meanwhile, you get what you can from Andy and his boyfriend.

All right, Redman, Butch nodded. You crazy asshole.

84.

BRUNO LED THE WAY TO THE BACK ROOM. Butch went off to find the theatrical troupe.

Bruno, I said, to be fair, I don't have the cash on me. Not eleven grand.

Don't worry about it, he said. I know you're good for it.

The mind games were starting already. I didn't trust him, he'd trust me. If I'd trusted him, he'd have gone the other way. You want to create all the tension you can.

Careful what you think you know, I said. I just got out of the poker hospital.

You did? he said, feigning amused surprise.

Yeah. It hasn't been a great two weeks.

Shit, sorry to hear that.

Yeah, I thought. About as sorry as he'd feel if his grandmother died. And left him a couple hundred grand.

I'll take the chance, he said.

Meaning he'd take it out of me in body parts, I didn't pay up.

And I knew that I'd known that from the get-go. But that's what keeps you going. The big gamble. And what choice did I have?

Ashley! Bruno called to a small, dexterous dirty-blonde number. You want to deal for us?

Sure, she chirped. But I gotta ax Barry.

Don't worry about Barry, Bruno said. I'll take care of Barry.

Nice to be on top of the world, I thought. I was also thinking, how did he come up with eleven thousand as the stakes? That was just about exactly enough to get me even with Evgeny. Leave a few bucks for the hotel bill.

Coincidence? Or were aliens really poised to take over Fort Knox? And the Pentagon? Had they created those crop circles? Was Bruno an alien? He certainly had that air. And what more deceptive way for them to culminate the master plan for world domination than this—an ostensibly innocent heads up poker game with me, Rick Redman, Putative Private Investigator, Overall Loser?

The question answered itself.

I prepared myself to defend the honor of our planet.

I still gotta ax him, Ashley said.

Barrrry . . . Bruno blasted out in his reverberant baritone. Can Ashley deal for us?

Sure, sure, Barry's voice came from somewhere behind a wall. I'll call in another dealer.

Nice to have pull, I said.

Yeah, Bruno said.

All right, I said. Ashley, can you get us some chips? Twenty-two grand.

Okay, she said, fluttering upstairs like the cuddly bunny she was, or so very much wanted to be.

While we're waiting for the chips, Bruno starts telling me a story about the clubs in L.A. He'd took the Commerce guys for a couple hundred grand, he said. Went to a bar with some guys we know. He tells me about the scene. Some singles party going on at the bar. An enormous woman in pink chenille. Sunken chin and beginner jowls; tiny plump hands and sharpened pointy nails; she looks lost, distressed, out of her element. But it is, of course, her element. Or as much element as she's going to get. The guy, he's got a suit and tie. Who the hell told him to wear a suit and tie? He's got that look on his face. Serious. Self-possessed. I'm no loser, it proclaims.

The fucking loser, says Bruno.

The guy's staring around the place, Bruno goes on. Looking for a friendly face. He knows nobody. Shit, he doesn't have a friend in the world. Except maybe his fat fuck computer geek friend from the software store, that he wouldn't be caught dead with in a place like this, lest the loserosity rub off on him and show up on his Sears sucker jacket. He'll stand there, just like that. For an hour. Or two. Nobody will talk to him. Nobody will come up. No girls will catch his eye. And he'll go home. To his studio apartment. The one with the dartboard on the wall. And play Doom 13 for four, maybe five hours. Drink a few beers. Fall down.

Bruno kind of surprised me with that one. I mean, he really was a shit-heel. But he knew how to tell a story.

Ashley came down with the chips. We went to the back room. The tables were full. A wild 25–50 no limit game, stacks of fifty grand all over the table. A tighter 10–25, chip stacks of maybe ten to thirty. A couple guys playing gin on a kitchen table. Another guy I knew from New York, LSD Dan, and a guy Bruno told me was Moishe the Yid, a notoriously sick gambler, playing red card black card for five grand a pop on a coffee table. Very intense. Couldn't get in the middle of that kind of sick compulsive gambling shit. We had to drag a folding table out of a closet, steal a couple chairs from under the asses of the railbirds. We were paying time, the railbirds were there for the free entertainment, or waiting for a seat in a game; we had the dibs on the chairs.

Bruno stole an extra one. Stacked it on top of the first.

Back bugging you? I asked, with as false an air of innocence as I could muster.

Nah. Just want to intimidate.

That may be the only true thing I've heard you say, ever, I said.

Bruno smiled the smile that he no doubt thought was his enigmatic smile. In reality, it was just a slight variation on the same shit-eating I'm-bigger-better-looking-richer-and-more-successful-at-the-poker-table-than-you'll-ever-be smile that he used for just about every occasion.

I didn't tell him that. Saved it for later.

Ashley deals the cards.

I look down at Queen, Jack.

I toss in three hundred bucks.

Bruno folds.

My, I'm thinking. How un-Bruno-ish. Folding the first hand? Maybe he's going to adjust. Or maybe he just has Seven, Two off? Doesn't want to chip me up right away? Get my confidence up? We'll see.

It goes back and forth. A lot of dodging and weaving. Small pot poker. Neither of us indulging in the power game. No all ins. No ridiculous over-bets. Not even a whole lot of the usual banter.

Bruno seems way serious.

I've never seen him like this.

I'm able to push him out of a few pots, my stack getting bigger, his getting smaller. I can tell he's getting more and more nervous. This is a new Bruno. When he was on a roll, you couldn't touch the guy. But, I was discovering, when things didn't go his way, the cards fell against him for a while, he wasn't invulnerable. And I could take advantage of that.

Poker's like chess, or golf. Or life. You let your emotions rule your actions at your peril.

About an hour into the match, he's in first position and raises. I look down at Jack, Ten of clubs. Hmm. Pretty good hand, heads up. I call. The flop comes King, two rags. No clubs. Bruno bets out about three-quarters of the pot. I look him over.

He's stroking one hand with the other. Very small movement, but discernible. Bruno, self-soothing? This isn't the Bruno I know. But then, who the hell said I'd ever known Bruno?

Now, this kind of self-soothing behavior can be a fairly reliable tell. The guy's nervous. But then you have to figure out, is he nervous because he's bluffing and doesn't want a call, or because he hit a monster, and he's worried you might fold and deprive him of his just deserts? He could have been hit big by the flop. Ace, King or King, Queen would be hands he would raise with in first position, for sure. Or he could have a pair lower than Kings, be nervous that the flop had hit me, and be betting for information. Or he could have Ace, Queen or some such hand, have missed the flop, and be trying to push me out.

Of course, a lot of this thinking is irrelevant: I've got nothing at all, not even a flush draw. In most situations, against most players, I would have, should have, stopped overthinking the hand and just mucked it. But I'd been pushing him around. He was nervous. You have to push every edge, against a strong opponent. I can push him out of one more hand, I'm thinking. I'm feeling it strongly. And it isn't going to cost a big part of my stack to try.

I re-raise him. About two and a half times his bet.

He looks worried. He thinks for a long time.

And calls me.

Okay. He called me. Hand over. Go away, Redman. You took your shot. If he bets the turn or river, fold. If he checks, check behind him. He called. He has a hand. You don't.

And I tell myself all that. But then, when he checks the turn and I check behind him, and the river comes another rag, he checks again.

This is very strange.

There's a lot of money in that pot. He's showing extreme weakness. He still looks nervous as hell. I've got him well covered, so he'll be risking a big part of his remaining stack to call. So . . .

I push in a pot-sized bet. Shove it in. Put it to him. Eat this, I'm saying. All you can eat.

Yes, I am a fool.

Although . . .

He thinks a long, long, long time . . .

Before calling.

And showing Ten, Nine. Off suit.

He thought he might have me, with Ten high?

Inconceivable.

Yet true.

I turn over my crap. My better crap than his.

I knew what had happened. Bruno had convinced himself I was bluffing, and even though he didn't have a hand that could even beat a lot of bluffs, he figured if he did win that hand, his call would seem almost supernatural. It would have totally freaked me out. Put me off my game. So it was a risk he was willing to take.

But it didn't happen.

And Bruno went on tilt.

It was beautiful to see.

I'd never seen Bruno on tilt before. Maybe it was because he rarely got taken for a big pot. He was, after all, a sick good poker player. Maybe the added metaphorical weight of this encounter affected him. I doubted it, though. Despite his earlier demonstration of storytelling prowess, I was fairly sure that Bruno did not know what a metaphor was.

He hunkered down low in his double-high chair. His biceps throbbed. Or at least, some veins in his biceps throbbed. Another novelty. Shit, I thought, is this a tell I'd never picked up before? Or a new one, specific to the occasion?

I watched the veins. Autonomic response. By far the most reliable. Only the most accomplished sociopath could control an autonomic response. It did not escape me, of course, that Bruno might qualify as a highly accomplished sociopath, but on this night, at least, he didn't seem to be fully in control.

It went like that. I'd slow play a monster, King, King with another King on the flop. He'd jam his two pair. I'd call, he'd throw his disgust across the table, muck his second-best hand. Another pile of chips in my corner. I'd jam a pair of Deuces, he'd fold his Jacks. I'd show my hand. He'd steam like a hot turd on a cold sidewalk.

Sometimes it just goes like that.

It was a beautiful thing.

I took his whole stack.

He sat back, eyed me with something on the fine hard edge between homicidal intent and respect.

All right, he said. You win.

I'm okay with that, I said magnanimously.

I counted the chips. Twenty-two thousand, as agreed. My eleven, his eleven. I'd deliberately ignored my stack during the session. You can't let your current situation affect your judgement. Or, well, you can. You should. But not in this situation. I knew any excess thinking or emotion would kill my game. So I just let the chips stack up. Knew I was ahead. That was enough. Once we were done, and only then, I counted them up, racked them up, handed them to Ashley. Took a deep breath.

Bruno tossed two stacks of five grand at me, another grand loose.

Victory. It was sweet.

Survival was better.

Information was best. Information was survival.

Information was everything.

85.

TALK TIME, I said to Bruno.

He took it in stride. Wasn't the bad loser I'd expected.

Shoot, he said. Wait a minute, he interrupted himself. Don't take that literally.

I laughed.

I'm impressed, I said. You know the word 'literally.'

Fuck you, Redman.

I laughed again. He smiled. The genuine smile of the defeated.

It was starting to look like maybe he wasn't such a bad guy after all.

All right, man, I said. Tell me about it.

About what?

Well, for starters, how do you know Andy, Delgado, whatever the fuck his name is?

I get around.

Come on, Bruno. Listen. I already know half of it. Just spill me the other half.

What half do you know?

I told him what I knew.

He laughed. Then you know all you need to know, he said.

No, I don't, I said. I don't know who the fuckers were behind this shit.

Aw, Ricky. I thought you were a smart guy.

I thought I was, too. Till I woke up naked, strapped to a contraption. Then I didn't think I was so smart.

Bruno let out a large laugh.

Then it worked, he said.

Oh, fuck, I said to myself.

So it was you, I said.

Me and Evgeny, Ricky. Guys you don't mess with. C'mon, man. We were fucking with you. You deserved it.

What'd I do to Evgeny?

You don't remember?

I thought about it.

Shit, you mean that little diss? The 'you lose' thing?

Evgeny don't forget, man.

Jesus Christ on a stick. So this whole job thing, the package, Yugo, all that shit.

All part of the game, man. Jesus, you got no idea how hard we were all laughing. It was great for Yugo. Probably added a week to his life.

Oh Christ, I said.

C'mon, man. We're all even up, now.

I guess so. Seems to me you guys are a little more even than me, though.

Fuck, Ricky, you shot me. I still can't even lift my arm over my fucking shoulder. It'll be months before I can do presses.

Yeah, I said. I guess that was kind of mean.

Get a sense of humor, man.

I resolved to take Bruno's sage advice.

Listen, man, I said. You got to be straight with me on the other thing. This is really important.

What other thing?

Brendan.

Oh shit, man, I don't know dick about that.

And if you did, you wouldn't tell me.

Probably not.

But you don't.

I don't, man. Talk to Anatoly. I don't know what the fuck happened.

I'd talk to Anatoly if I could find him.

Can't help you there either, man.

Bruno was finished talking. We could try the kneecap thing, I supposed. But it probably wouldn't be prudent.

I got up to leave.

Ah, Ricky? Bruno said.

What?

That money you just took off me?

Yeah.

I'll take ten grand back now.

What the fuck?

You owe it to Evgeny. I'll give it to him.

You are one sweet motherfucker, I said, handing over the two banded stacks of hundreds.

I shouldered my bag of humiliation, got the hell out of there.

86.

BUTCH WAS AT THE BAR, chatting up Hector. I took a stool next to him.

You learn anything? I asked.

Not much. You?

I told him the latest developments. Some Eloise stuff. Nothing on Brendan. I left out the practical joke stuff. My humiliation. Save that for ten or twelve drinks later.

By the way, I said, any word on Anatoly and Andrei?

Not yet.

Fuck.

Yeah, fuck. They gotta know something.

You would think.

Good reason for them to get the fuck out of town.

Yeah.

We drank for a while in silence. Hector kept a respectable distance. She could see it was a business meeting.

All right, I said, it's time to get to the heart of the matter.

Which is?

The other matter.

The heart in question, I was convinced, resided in Louise. We split the joint. Outside, on the sidewalk, I called her. She answered. I was mildly surprised. I didn't know why. She sounded sad. I thought I knew why.

Can we meet? I asked.

Where?

I'll come there, if it's okay.

Where?

Wherever there is.

Okay, she said. Come here.

Where's here?

I don't know. Give me a second.

I heard some shuffling, muffled talking, faint laughter. I assumed the laughter wasn't hers.

I'm at the funeral home, she said.

What?

I knew you wouldn't get the joke.

You're right, I said. I didn't get the joke. Was that a joke?

I guess it wasn't. I'm trying to cope. Don't worry about it. I'm at a place called the Sirocco. It has something to do with a southwest wind.

I think I knew that. Or Volkswagens. Does it have an address?

I'm sure you can find it.

I'm sure I can.

I closed the phone.

All right, I said to Butch. I got her. I'll get what we need to get.

You are one deluded drunken asshole, he said.

You're probably right, I said. But I wish you'd stop saying it.

It was okay. I'd proven him wrong before.

He headed back to the Strip. I flagged a cab. The driver knew where the Sirocco was.

The cab smelled of bad champagne, and disappointment.

Probably redundant, I thought.

Take me there, I said.

You're the boss, he replied.

If only that were true, I thought. Life might be bearable.

With Louise, I was determined, I was going to be the boss. It was what she seemed to respond to. I knew I had some work to do. I'd always known there was hidden stuff. She'd even said so herself. Before, it hardly mattered. But when there's a murder involved, hidden stuff can start getting a little inconvenient.

At the Sirocco she was ensconced at a red and black bar. The place had a Parisian air. Shiny silver-colored tin ceilings. If vintage, very valuable. If new, very expensive. Black leather chairs and red drapes. Deep carpets. That hushed dark wood thing going. I liked it.

I suggested we move to a corner table. If indiscreet things were going to be said, it was better to say them discreetly.

She uncoiled herself from the bar stool. Her eyes were dark. Perhaps it was the lighting. Maybe something else. She was dressed in black. Black dress, simple and elegant. White pearls. Very classic. A classic mourning outfit.

If I hadn't gotten to know her better, I'd have thought she was very proper.

I pulled my chair close to hers. Leaned forward.

You look beautiful, I said.

She shook her head. No. It wasn't appropriate.

Interesting, considering some other things she'd thought appropriate.

Louise, I said.

She lifted her head. Her eyes were red.

Emotion. So she was capable of it.

Or maybe she'd just been smoking a little reefer.

Louise, I said. I need your help. I spent some time at the police station. And not voluntarily. They suspect me of involvement in this. Or at least knowing more than I do.

How can I help you? she said weakly. She took a small sip of some extravagant-looking pink drink.

You could start by telling me everything you know.

You could start by giving me my money back.

Oh, Jesus, I said. Of course. Of course I'll give you your money back. After what happened—

No, Rick. I don't want my money back. Keep it.

But you just said—

A grieving sister is allowed her little jokes, Mr. Redman.

I wasn't going to argue. I had more important things to talk about. And anyway . . . I didn't have the dough.

So, I said, can you tell me what you know?

About what?

My sympathy for the grieving sister was not too slowly turning to suspicion.

About Eloise, I said. What do you think?

Oh, she said, turning her head away. It was a good simulacrum of someone attempting to hide her tears.

And maybe there were tears. For whom, that might be a question.

You can start with this Vladimir guy, I said. Wouldn't he be suspect number one?

There was a long pause. She took out a long thin cigarette. Lit it. Blew pretty smoke in spiraling rings to the ceiling. Turned to me.

No, she said.

No?

No.

Louise. If you think the answer to that is no, then clearly you know something more than I do. So I'd really appreciate it if you'd share it with me.

Don't be harsh with me, Rick, she said. Her voice was trembling.

Sorry. But you didn't have to spend four hours in a tiny overheated locked room at downtown cop heaven. Maybe I'm a little impatient.

I'm sorry that had to happen, she said, with apparent sincerity.

I wasn't at all sure that it had to happen. But I wasn't going to argue the point.

She sighed. Blew some more pretty smoke around the room.

I don't know, she said.

What don't you know?

I don't even know that it was murder, Rick, she said, turning to look me straight in the eye.

I sat back. Took a large slug off my scotch. Tried to reconcile what I'd just heard with everything I knew.

It didn't compute.

What do you mean? I asked. She was bludgeoned. Bruised. There were ligature marks on her neck. Someone had tried to attack her in her home just a week before. If I hadn't been there, he probably would have killed her right then.

Oh, Rick, she said, shaking her head. Oh, Rick.

I was missing something. I was missing something big.

We were sisters, Rick, she said. Sisters share things.

I thought you weren't close.

You don't have to be close to share some kinds of things.

Like?

She lit another cigarette. Her lighter was platinum, had a blue, insistent flame. It took up too much space in the room.

She didn't answer the question.

Ah, I thought. A test. A game. Fill in the incomplete information.

You know all you need to know, she said quietly.

It sure didn't feel like it.

I ordered another scotch. I borrowed a long thin cigarette from my mysterious friend. Client. Lover. Ex-lover, more likely. I blew smoke rings. Mine were intentional. And thereby not nearly as interesting. I drifted to the half dream state.

I love those minutes between wake and dream, that state of utmost imaginative freedom, the mind making any association it liked, following the mystery trains wherever they led. With never a consequence, except forgetting, or waking. Or both. I have my best ideas then.

And always forget them, seconds later.

This time I didn't.

I sat up straight.

Louise, I said.

Yes, she said languidly.

I . . .

I paused. I had to think about how to go there.

She gave me a sardonic smile. You think you got it? she asked.

I think I do, I said, a bit defensively. Give me a minute.

Her smile dissolved in the cigarette smoke. She drifted away with it.

The other night, I said.

Yes . . .

She drew it out.

When we . . .

Yes.

It could have gone farther. Am I right?

Maybe. If you were man enough.

I ignored the insult. If that was what it was.

You and Eloise weren't so different, were you? I said.

Silence.

In that way, I said.

More silence. She crossed and recrossed her legs. Stubbed out her cigarette. A bit too forcefully.

Louise, I said. I'm just trying to find out what happened to Eloise. Your sister. I know you didn't have anything to do with it . . .

She gave me a jaundiced look.

I guess that goes without saying. So I don't understand why you want to be hostile about it. Unforthcoming. Let's just figure out what happened. Get the guy. Get some closure.

I hate that word.

I do, too. But I couldn't think of anything better.

She sighed. Played with her lighter. Flick, on. Blue flame. Flick, off. Repeat.

Okay, she said. What do you want to know?

Uh, how about . . . everything?

Do you have a few days?

I got what's left of a relatively short lifetime.

All right. Get me a Kiss on the Cheek.

What?

The bartender will understand.

Ah. I get it. Like a Dirty Bomb. A Multiple Orgasm. Like that.

Something like that.

I went to the bar. Flagged down the unctuous barkeep. A Kiss on the Cheek, please, I said, almost without flinching. He nodded, like it was the most natural thing in the world. Some bleary paunchy white-haired guy asking for a kiss on the cheek. I watched him mix some Woodford Reserve, a bourbon I'd never heard of, but apparently essential to the concoction, grenadine, Rose's lime, cranberry juice.

I transported the disgusting swirl back to the table.

Louise wasn't there.

I had a moment of panic. She'd run off. If not to kill herself, at least to transport herself out of my life. Deprive me of vital bits of knowledge. Not to mention those legs. I mean, it's not that I had a vested interest in solving Eloise's murder. Apart from making sure that I wasn't further implicated. But there was something . . . incomplete, about leaving town without knowing what had happened.

My fears, for once, were not justified. Moments later she sauntered back from the ladies' room. I saw her purse, a silver and black thing, Dior it looked like, on her chair. I could have saved myself a few skipped heartbeats if I'd noticed it earlier.

She recomposed herself. Placed her hands neatly in her lap. Gave me an expectant look. The good schoolteacher, here for an interview.

I was thinking, I said.

She said nothing.

When you first saw Brendan. And the second time, too. You looked at him . . . well, not strangely. But longer than seemed natural.

I did?

You did.

Silence.

You knew him, didn't you?

She sighed. Took a graceful, trembling sip of her ridiculous drink.

Not exactly, she said. I'd seen him around.

In those clubs.

She nodded.

Oh man, I said. Show me a cat and I'll tell you it's an armadillo.

Louise raised her eyebrows.

Forget it, I said.

She nodded politely.

I think you were going to say something, I said.

I was?

Yes. I'm quite certain of it. I mean, before you went to the ladies' room.

Oh.

She lit another cigarette. Held it near her mouth, as though pondering whether to take a drag. Her wrist was lightly angled, her fingers gracefully arranged.

It was a pose. A very nice pose.

But the fingers were shaking.

Cigarettes. They were everywhere. They told stories. What people smoked. How they smoked them. Told you a lot about somebody. I remembered a jury selection once . . .

Fuck. I was such a goddamn idiot.

Gitanes.

Eloise knew him, too, I said.

She said nothing.

Sisters share things, I said.

She turned her head away. Took a drag of the cigarette.

Friends, I said. Friends with similar interests. Friends who hang out in the same places.

Yes, she said.

Yes.

Another thing we shared, she said, Eloise and I . . . was a father.

That wouldn't be entirely unusual.

But this father was.

I see.

Unusual. I don't want to go into detail. You don't need to know the details.

Well, I—

It is enough to know that the way in which he was unusual was . . . imposed. On his daughters. Had a great influence. On who they became.

I nodded. It was what I'd been expecting, somehow, all along, I knew now. I couldn't give myself any credit. I hadn't constructed the thought. It had been there, though. Muddling about in the twisted synapses. Looking for the exit door.

They grew up, she said. The daughters. They had lives of their own. But this influence. It never really went away.

So when Vladimir showed up—

Ah, Mr. Redman, she smiled sadly, the great detective.

I shrugged.

Yes. Vladimir. Well, as you may have also discerned, in your haphazard way, Vladimir was, in fact, my husband.

I opened my mouth. I closed my mouth.

Ah, she said. You had not discerned.

I was afraid to respond. Lest I make a further fool of myself. Or, worse, stop the flow.

Yes, she said. That's where it began. When we met, Vladimir and I, it was, how to say, satisfactory. We were from very different backgrounds, of course. He was a working-class Russian immigrant, upwardly striving and all that. Full of plans and schemes. I was, well, I was who I am. But our connection was on a different level.

Let me guess, I said.

Yes, she interrupted. We each had certain . . . predilections. That complemented the other's, very nicely. At least for a time.

Until the time, I'm guessing, that he met your sister.

Louise bit her lip. Fiddled with the snap on her Dior bag.

Not right away, she said. But yes. Once they'd . . . got to know each other.

He found out that she was even more willing than you to . . . indulge his predilections, as you like to say.

Yes, Mr. Redman. Exactly.

What's with the Mr. Redman shit?

Let me tell it my way, Rick. Okay?

Okay. Go ahead. I understand. You need to stay in character.

I said it with a not indiscernible touch of bitterness. Which was not lost on her. She narrowed her eyes. Didn't take it further.

So, I said. Vlad the Impaler runs off with sis to Nevada. For a while you let it go. More power to them. But then she stops writing. You get worried. That part was true, yes?

No. Well, not exactly. Not right away.

Ah.

No, Mr. Redman. Actually, we had a business arrangement, Vlad, Eloise and I. And some others.

A business arrangement.

Yes. You don't need to know the details.

So, Vlad running off with Eloise wasn't, like, a complete break with you. You weren't traumatized?

Traumatized? No. Relieved, actually.

I guess I can see that. He was taking you down paths that were, well, at least potentially, frightening.

Yes.

This business arrangement. What was that about?

You don't need to know.

Maybe not. But these things have a way of becoming relevant.

Silence. Fiddling with a pearl bracelet. I hadn't noticed the bracelet before. Precisely matched the necklace.

Let me take a leap at it, I said.

I leaned back. Closed my eyes. Sipped my scotch. Things began to float. As they floated, they arranged themselves. In patterns. Some were merely aesthetic. Some were analytic. Some made sense. Some didn't. One thing. One thing floated into view. That made perfect sense.

Oh.

Louise, I said.

She opened her own closed eyes.

The package.

Yes?

The FedEx package.

I know what package you meant.

That's a part of it, isn't it.

Maybe.

And the stuff in the basement. The machinery. It all had something to do with this business you had, with Vladimir and Eloise.

Maybe.

Yes.

Yes.

What was it?

You haven't figured it out?

I must admit I haven't. Yes, Virginia, there is a human being. And he's right over here. And he's fallible.

She looked at me long and hard.

Rick, she said at last. I haven't done anything wrong.

I didn't say you had.

But you're implying it.

Well, if you haven't done anything wrong, there's no harm in telling me, is there.

She pulled at the bottom of her dress. Smoothed it along her thighs.

I suppose I have done some wrong things, she said. But not what you're thinking.

I'm not thinking anything. I'm asking.

It was stupid, really. Vladimir, and some friends of his . . .

The Brighton Beach crowd.

Some of them, yes. They had a plan. And they needed financing for it. I provided some of the financing.

I see. This didn't involve truffles, I gather?

She smiled. No, she said, it didn't involve truffles. And it never went anywhere. Which is why I can say I didn't do anything wrong.

I guess you're only guilty of attempted wrongdoing.

Something like that.

Give me a smoke and tell me the bloody story, Louise. What were you going to do, rob a casino? They only do that in the movies.

Sort of.

You're kidding me. You were going to hit a casino?

Not me.

Yeah, yeah. You were just the money. But how naïve could you be?

It was actually a pretty good plan.

I'm sure.

Vladimir got the idea from one of the Russian poker players. He was telling Vladimir that there had been a bit of a scandal at the World Series. That when they counted up all the chips at the end of the day, there were more chips than there were at the beginning.

Somebody was slipping extra chips into their stacks.

You are correct, Mr. Redman. So, they announced that from now on for the Main Event they're going to make unique chips. A special design. You can't confuse them with any other. With security things embedded in them. Like currency.

Sure. I heard about that. Meanwhile, though, they'd have to be totally vigilant. They knew this was happening. They'd be watching every chip. You'd be walking right into a bear trap.

My dear Mr. Redman, our good friends from Brighton Beach may be unscrupulous, but they are not entirely stupid. Of course, they knew that. That was why they were going to avoid the tournaments. Do it in the cash games. All at once. One night only. They needed a big crew. Have someone at as many tables as possible.

I leaned back. Took a sip of my scotch.

Why did you think you could get away with it in the cash games if it wouldn't work in the tournament?

The whole idea was to get in and out fast.

Of course. In a tournament the chips don't turn into money till you cash. You can get up from a cash table any time.

That is right.

Yeah. Just had to wait till the chips circulate a bit. So you're not taking a stack of counterfeits to the window.

That was exactly it. And they would all be coming in, and cashing out, within a short period.

I get it.

Yes.

The machinery in the basement. The clay. You were making chips.

Not me.

Okay, okay. They were making chips.

They were going to. They were trying to. But they never got it right. That's why we never went through with it.

Did you get your money back?

That's why I came here. That's why I hired you. My only contact with the people behind all this was Eloise, and through her, Vladimir. And when the deal broke down, they vanished. After I found out about the house, the one in Henderson, it seemed clear to me—

They were living large. On your money.

I could only assume. He wasn't getting rich repairing vintage cars.

I had a faint recollection of something. It came and went. Some kind of déjà vu thing. Or something.

So you hired me, you came here, to track down Eloise, but more importantly Vladimir. To get your money back.

To try to.

Darling, the Russkies never give you your money back.

I'm learning that.

I sighed.

Why did you have to find Vladimir, anyway? Why not go after the other guys?

You just said it, Rick. I was not going to get anything from them. And I never met them, anyway. I did not even know their last names. Or his, even.

That much was true.

Yes. But with him at least I had some leverage. I knew things—

That you could use against him. Or threaten to, anyway.

She was silent.

Louise, I said.

Yes?

Is this what got Eloise—

No, no. No, Rick. I told you.

She paused. Turned away. Put her face in her hands.

Oh, I said.

Yes, she said without turning back. Her voice was muffled.

Time went by.

There was nothing to say. Unless she was going to say it.

She turned her head slightly towards me. She wanted it, Rick, she said.

Wanted it? Wanted to die?

Wanted to die *that way.* She just kept pushing the limits, goddamn her. Of course, of course, she didn't *consciously* want to die like that. But she kept . . . pushing.

It was going to happen.

It was going to happen.

So that guy, the guy I chased off from her place—

She had hired him, probably.

Oh, Jesus.

Or maybe not. She didn't always have to hire them, of course. There are lots of men who enjoy . . .

She broke down. I leaned over. Put my arms around her. Smelled the peach on her skin. Tasted the salt.

She pushed me away. I have to compose myself, she said.

Of course, I said, ever the gentleman.

She got up. Went to the ladies' room.

I waited twenty minutes.

Twenty minutes was way too long.

I asked a waitress to check the ladies' room. She did. Reported back.

The ladies' room was empty.

She'd gone. She'd fled. She'd told the truth and gone.

I never saw her again.

But that was okay. I'd got what I needed.

87.

I DRAGGED MYSELF OUTSIDE. I looked at my cell phone. Old habits die hard. No calls. I was vaguely disappointed. Vaguely relieved. I thought about calling Sheila. Then I thought better of it. She'd only tell me everything would be all right.

And I wouldn't believe her.

I called Butch. He had some news.

About fucking time, I said.

We met at the Velvet Hang. A valedictory meet.

I gave him the Louise, the Eloise download.

Yeah, he nodded.

You knew?

Not everything. But I just came from downtown. They got the guys.

You're kidding me.

There's surveillance cameras all over that joint, Rick. And everybody in there's a regular. Except you, of course.

Fuck. He'd seen the tape.

Shut up, I said.

Okay.

Keep talking.

Okay. Anyway, you already know. It was guys are into this stuff. It was an accident. Sort of. I mean, they didn't mean to kill her. She kept wanting more.

More, I repeated.

Yeah, more. And, you know the rest. Anyway, they're going to be charged. Not first degree. Manslaughter. Depraved indifference. Whatever.

Goddamn it.

You think they should get off? They friends of yours?

No, no. Fuck off. That's not what I meant. I just meant, goddamn it, I can't believe what a fucking fool I am.

Rick, it's not about you.

Thanks.

You're welcome.

So.

So, Butch repeated.

Any word on Brendan?

Let me get you a drink.

I already have one.

Let me get you another one.

That bad, huh?

Yup.

Butch went to the bar, came back with a bottle of Jack Daniel's.

You want, I can wait till you've had a few more.

No, no. Pour it on.

Funny you should put it that way, he said.

Just get to the fucking point, man.

Okay. Well, the toxicology stuff, the drug part, it's not all in yet. But that doesn't matter.

Why not?

Because it was something else.

Please be so kind as to enlighten me, sir. Before I waste this delicious bottle of bourbon by cracking you over the head with it.

Easy, man.

It's been a long fucking day.

A long fucking week.

Month.

So, he was at this party.

This we knew.

They were playing games.

With knitting needles.

Among other things.

Such as?

Silicone.

Silicone?

Yeah.

Okay . . .

Yeah, apparently there's this thing that some guys do. They get the silicone. They inject it. Sometimes in their dicks, make them bigger. It's called a pumping party.

Ouch.

Yeah. It only lasts a while. Then the body absorbs it, excretes it, whatever. I don't know all the science about it.

And?

And sometimes they put it in their pecs. Whole bunch of it. Makes for fun temporary tits.

Jesus Christ. These guys really know how to have a party.

Yeah. And the thing is, after a while it kind of seeps around, drains out of you or whatever. Goes away. And it's not supposed to hurt you.

Not supposed to.

Except sometimes it does.

Oh shit.

Yeah. So that's what happened.

Brendan.

Yeah.

I can't fucking believe it.

Yeah.

All he was doing was having some fun.

Yup.

And it killed him.

Just like that.

I mean, how? There's all these women with implants, sometimes they bust open, there's claims it causes some autoimmune reactions, not that I ever believed that shit. I mean, they've disproved it, last I heard.

I wouldn't know. But no, that's not it.

It couldn't be. Even if it's true, and even if the reaction could kill you, it would take years.

Yeah. This is different. What happens is, and this is why it took so long for them to figure it out, it's very rare. There was a reason to look for it. The silicone can get in your lungs. Basically, you drown.

Aw, come on. That's just fucking, I don't know, ridiculous. Drowning in fake tits.

Yeah. Stupid.

Stupid.

There was nothing more to say. What the fuck. He died having fun. I guess it wasn't so bad. Worse ways to go, and all that.

We sat in silence. Polished off the bourbon.

But, I said at last.

But what?

It doesn't work for me.

I'll see if they have some Maker's Mark.

Not the bourbon, you moron. The story.

What story? Butch asked.

We were pretty far gone into the corn mash nighttime.

Brendan, I said. This just-having-fun story.

Rick, they did the autopsy. These guys are professionals. I talked to them. I looked at the report. It's pretty damn clear.

There's a problem with it. And it wouldn't show up in an autopsy.

All right, Mr. Investigator. Show me.

I can't show you anything. I just have a feeling.

Oh shit. Not feelings again.

Hey, have some respect. Even guys have feelings, you know.

Specially drunk guys.

Yeah, specially those. But seriously, man, Brendan was like a brother to me.

Yeah. Sorry, man.

I knew him pretty damn well.

Yeah.

And I'm telling you, he didn't play those kinds of games.

What do you mean?

He was all into the being-a-manly-man thing. You know, there are queens, there are transvestites—most of those guys are straight, by the way—

Yes, Rick. I've been around a few blocks a few times.

—transsexuals. There's as many types of gay guy as straight guys. More, probably. And Brendan was one of those guys whose goal in life was to marry a straight guy. A lawyer in a suit and tie. And his way to do it was to be even manlier than the men he wanted, in a strange kind of way. The voice lessons. The gym. He worked really hard on expunging any trace of obvious gay mannerisms. Totally had me fooled, back when he was pretending to be straight.

And your point is?

That's not the kind of guy who wants tits. Temporary or not.

Aw, c'mon, Rick. He's drunk, doing whatever else they're passing around on silver trays with tiny spoons. It's a total scene. He could easily just have done it once, for fun.

You don't know Brendan like I do. This was a really powerful thing in him. This wanting to be just like a straight guy. I don't mean he wanted to be straight. He wasn't a self-loathing gay man. He was fine with it. But anything that was queeny in any way, no fucking way. He wouldn't have anything to do with it.

Okay, let's say we buy that. What does it buy us?

I don't know yet, man. But I know I'm right. And I know, if I'm right, we don't have the whole story yet.

All right, maestro, Butch said. I'll go get a bottle of Maker's Mark. Sharpens the thinking process.

Good plan.

Butch got the bourbon. It was too good to slug down. I sipped it neat. It did that spectacular glowing slide-down-the-throat thing that it did. The slow warm suffusion outward, to the extremities, the very fingertips.

It was some fine shit.

I leaned back. I stared at the glorious pineapple overhead. I let my eyes unfocus to the middle distance. I let my mind wander in the spaces between the molecules that science told us made up the world as we knew it. I contemplated the nature of quarks. Spin. Spin. Spin.

I sat up.

Butch was asleep in his chair.

I kicked his shin.

What the fuck? he started out of his slumber.

And the knitting needle, I said.

We've been through all that.

No we haven't. Not all of it.

Butch sighed. Poured us another round.

All right, he said. Next stunning revelation, please.

Somebody's DNA is on that thing.

Yes.

We don't know whose it is.

Correct.

And we've been assuming—I've been assuming anyway, I bet you have, too, since I found out about what they do with those things—that Brendan must have been . . . using it . . . on somebody. Right?

Kind of fits the evidence.

I don't believe it.

More you don't believe.

That wasn't like him either.

Enlighten me.

Brendan was incredibly fastidious, Butch.

Yeah.

Clothes always pressed. He got his hair cut every week, for Christ's sake. Took two hours in the bathroom every morning to get himself just right for public consumption.

And your point is . . .

And he was incredibly squeamish.

Yeah?

I cut myself in the kitchen once. Slicing garlic. Just a little nick. A little blood. He ran to the bathroom. I think he might even have puked.

Ahhh. I see where you're going.

There's no fucking way he was sticking pointy objects up someone's dick, Butch. He'd rather die.

Good metaphor.

Fuck. Yeah. But I'm right.

Which means?

Something else happened.

And what might that have been?

I leaned back. I drifted upward. Became one with the pineapple.

I sat up.

I don't have a fucking clue, I said.

Butch finished his bourbon. Poured another one.

Okay, he said. I don't know if I buy all this. But I got to take your word for Brendan. You knew him a hell of a lot better than I did.

I did.

So I'll go downtown. Ask some questions. Turn over some rocks. See if I can find some slime.

Okay, man. Good. Trust me. There's something there.

We'll see.

88.

BUTCH WENT DOWNTOWN. I went back to the Executive Suite. I had nothing to do but wait. Everything was slowing down. The world in the beige rooms seemed oddly relaxed. People were dead. Others were gone. There was nothing I could do about it. I started packing my things, slowly, deliberately. I thought about going over to the Bellagio. One last valedictory poker session. But I didn't have the energy. I filled a glass with ice. Rummaged around in the wet bar. Found a bottle of Macallan eighteen-year-old I'd forgotten we had. An unexpected delight. I took it over to the sofa. Poured myself a big one. Turned on the TV. Lay back. Lit a smoke. Drank myself back into a pleasant haze.

The intercom rang. What the fuck. Couldn't a guy get a little rest around here?

I dragged myself over to the door. Pressed the talk button.

Who is it? I said.

A Madeleine for you, sir.

Ah. Send her up.

Kelley and Peter had already left. Back to school. Real life. Something that was fast receding from my grasp. Madeleine had stayed behind. I took that as a good sign. I'd been trying to get up the nerve to ask her to come to New York with me for a while. But I didn't want to interfere with her home life. I still hadn't asked about her adoptive parents. She hadn't volunteered. I figured she'd tell me when she was ready.

She knocked. I opened the door. She looked gorgeous. She made me proud.

I gave her a hug. She pulled away, a bit. That was okay. I was still new to her. I understood.

Come in, come in, I said. It's so great you could come by. I was just packing, but we're staying another day. Taking care of some loose ends. Maybe get a little poker in. Try to feel normal for a day.

She laughed.

It was a nervous laugh.

I sat on the sectional. She sat in the chair, knees pressed together. Purse in her lap.

Something was different.

Everything okay? I asked.

Sure. Everything's fine. Dad?

Yes?

I just wanted to let you know that I'm leaving today.

Okay. I was hoping maybe you could come visit us. In New York. But it doesn't have to be now. I know you probably have school and stuff coming up.

Yes, she said.

Silence.

So, I said. Do you want to make a plan? I can fly you out. Show you the neighborhood. We could get Kelley and Peter to come, too. Have a big family reunion. Just let me know when you can come.

That's kind of what I wanted to talk to you about, she said, looking at her lap.

What do you mean? I asked.

The phone rang. I ignored it.

Those tiny claws were scrambling about in my gut again.

I don't really know how to say this, she said.

Then just say it.

Well, Dad, it was really, really nice to . . . to meet you. You know. I always wanted to know who my father was and all.

I'm so thrilled to get to know you, too, I said, mustering up some false cheer.

I knew what was coming.

The phone rang again. I ignored it some more. I poured myself another mammoth Macallan. I could feel her eyes on me. I could feel her disapproval.

Dad, maybe someday I'll come and visit. And I really, really appreciate the offer. But right now . . .

I waited.

Right now I just have to figure some stuff out.

I see.

Get back home. Think about things.

I see.

I hope you understand.

I understand, I said.

I didn't want to understand. I wanted to scream. For God's sake, I wanted to shout. Haven't I lost enough people yet?

Okay, she said. I'm glad you understand. I'm . . . It's hard.

I know. It's not an easy situation.

Okay, then, she said, getting up.

That was it.

I walked her to the door. I gave her the biggest hug in my repertoire. Her arms stayed at her side.

She left. I closed the door quietly.

I went into the bedroom.

And cried.

The phone rang again. I ignored it. I wanted the world to go away. Leave me the fuck alone.

But it kept on ringing. Goddamn it. On the third ring back, I gave in. I picked it up.

I think you better get down here, said Butch.

Down where?

Downtown. The station.

Oh, yeah?

Yeah. You were right.

Now there's a shock.

Just get down here.

Everything got fast again. I grabbed a cab. It smelled of rancid butter, and irresolution.

When I got downtown, they were waiting for me. The mottle-faced guy at the desk said, You that Redman guy? I said yes, and he nodded at a freckly red-haired kid with enormous hands and a uniform two sizes too large. The kid motioned me to follow him through a thick steel door, down a narrow corridor. Another well-secured door opened into the control room. The room behind the one-way glass.

Crammed into the ten-by-twelve room were Rod, Butch, three technicians and two uniforms. Through the one-way window I could see my favorite police-issue gunmetal chair, occupied by a mammoth gentleman with a buzz cut and a sour demeanor. Across from him a detective was taking notes. On either side of the window were video monitors, on each of which appeared a similar scene: beefy guy, gunmetal chair, wooden table, badly dressed detective. Why did they all have to wear those ties? The ones that were two inches too wide and five inches too short?

Butch motioned me over to the counter at which he and Rod had been huddled together, wearing headphones and flicking switches, evidently tuning from one audio feed to another, keeping track of the simultaneous interrogations.

The guys from the video? I asked.

Yup, said Butch.

I looked at the left-hand monitor. The guy in the chair had a lumpy dumpling face, brush cut, shaved high in the back.

I know that guy, I said.

You do, said Butch.

I know I do. Who the fuck is he?

Vitaly, said Butch. From Vinnie's game.

You're shitting me. Damn. You're right.

I know I'm right. And the guy in the window is none other than our main man.

Don't tell me. Vladimir?

The only one. The one and only.

Wow. And the third guy?

Him we don't know. Or didn't before tonight. Some guy named Arthur. Artie. Artie Schwarz.

You're shitting me.

Believe it or not.

Sounds like a bandleader from the forties.

Yeah, well, that was some band he was playing in.

Okay. I take your word for it.

Jesus Christ on a stick, I said.

I was looking at the fourth monitor.

What? said Butch and Rod together.

That's fucking Jerry.

Who? said Rod. Who's Jerry?

That guy on the monitor on the left, I said.

What's this? said Rod, your fucking high school reunion?

I saw him at Yugo's, I said, ignoring the gibe. No doubt about it. That's the guy who was serving the drinks.

Yugo? said Rod, laughing.

Yeah, I said. What's so funny?

Isador Yuganovich?

Isador? I said. Shit, that rings a bell.

Yuganovich is a pimp, Ricky boy, said Rod. Supplies big boys all over town. Fun and games boys.

Shit, I said. I thought they were for him.

He look like he was in shape for boning muscleboys? Rod laughed.

I guess not, I said.

Butch gave me a look.

I ignored him.

So what've we got? I asked. Sounds like there's some confessing going on.

We got everything, Rick. They're just wrapping up. Let's get a coffee and give you the lowdown.

Download.

Down load.

We found some plastic chairs and an empty office. The red-haired kid brought in something wan and scalding in flimsy plastic cups. Rod came in after him. Pulled up a plastic milk carton to sit on.

Respect.

The DNA from the needle, Rod said, matched this Artie guy. Only that wasn't the name we had for him. Oleg Kuryashin, we had him down for. Check kiting. Small-time fraud artist. One arrest for assault. Here, anyway. Haven't got the stuff back yet from other states. Then we got lucky, I guess. Got a report about some gunshots, a parking lot on Industrial. These four jokers were playing shoot 'em up down there. We got Artie, but the other three got away. The guy was tighter than a flea's asshole when we got him here. But that didn't last long. He didn't like the tapes as much as you did, Redman.

No accounting for taste, I said.

Yeah. Anyway, he gave up the other three clowns easy enough, once he saw the position he was in. So we rounded up the goons, and when we got them all down here we did the four-way. Like you saw. Our guys have transmitters in their ears. So we can feed each of them stuff we're getting from the other two. Keep the whole circus rolling nice and smooth.

Nice, I said.

We like to think we know what we're doing. Anyway, your buddy Butch here told me he'd given you the lowdown on our original read. That it was an accident. The fun and games got out of hand, whatever. That you had some doubts. And I got to tell you, what he told us really helped us out. We owe you some thanks.

And an apology, maybe?

No fucking way. So, like you thought, turned out it wasn't so simple. This Brendan kid comes off a little better once you know the whole story.

I could see Rod liked to meander around to the point in his own way, so I just kept quiet and listened.

So after we got the word from Butch here, we're going back over the tapes, Rod continued. Frame by frame, like. Make sure we didn't miss anything. Another perp maybe. A witness we can use. Whatever. And then we got this. Butch, you got that thing?

Here, said Butch, pulling an eight-by-ten black-and-white from a brown envelope and handing it to me.

Look at the upper right, said Rod.

The image was dark, out of focus. But I recognized it. It was a still shot from the same video surveillance camera footage Rod had been so kind as to show me earlier. You could see the red door on the left. It was half open. People going through the door. It wasn't as clear as what I'd seen on the film, but I didn't have any doubt it was part of the same sequence.

Upper right, Rod repeated. Here.

He drew a circle with a black felt pen.

I brought the photo up close to my face. The blacks and grays formed sworls and protrusions, blanks and waves. At first it seemed totally abstract. Like an Ansel Adams black-and-white of a canyon at sunset. But slowly the shadows and shades resolved themselves into a figure. A man, probably. In the midst of turning towards the red door.

He was wearing a tuxedo. And no shoes.

Shit, I said.

Yeah, said Butch.

Yup, said Rod. Turns out your friend Brendan knew Ms. Wittenburg rather well.

Eloise, I said.

Whatever.

It hit me.

Well enough to visit her at home, I said.

What's that? said Rod.

The Gitanes. Butch, you remember that pack of smokes I gave Brendan? I told him I'd gotten them from Eloise.

Yeah, said Butch. And he acted weird about it.

That's why he didn't go to the Henderson house. Why would he need to? He knew where she was all along.

There was a long pause while this sank in.

Yeah, said Rod. It makes sense. This community, whatever you call it. These types who are into this stuff, they're a tight group. Small world. Smaller even than most.

I'm learning, I said.

So anyway, Butch said. It turns out Brendan was really worried about Eloise. She was doing sicker and sicker shit. Dangerous shit.

I know, I said. Louise talked about it.

So there he was, at the club, and these guys are dragging her into the room, and of course she's into it. It's her thing. It's exactly what she wants. But Brendan's scared, he wants to make sure she's okay. So he goes back there with them.

Which at first, Rod said, was okay with these guys. The more the merrier, or whatever. Like I said, it's a tight thing they got going.

Everybody has their thing. Nobody's judging nobody. Nobody gets in anybody's way. Brendan wants to watch, they're okay with that.

He's one of them, I said.

There's a bunch of other people in there already, said Butch.

Yeah, it's a big space. All decked out in chains and clamps and rubber suits and shit. So anyway, these guys start doing their thing with Eloise, and she's totally into it, she's wanting more, and . . . shit, I figure you don't want to know all the details, right?

Damn right I don't, I said.

So anyway. At some point to Brendan it starts looking really scary, like they're really going to kill her. And he doesn't know what to do. I mean, call for help? I don't think so.

I see where it's going, I said.

Yeah, said Butch. He grabs the knitting needle thing. I guess some guys are doing that thing that they do, or they've already done it, and the thing's lying around, and he grabs it, it's the only thing he can find, and he stabs Artie, Oleg, whoever the fuck he is, in the neck with it.

Not too fucking smart, said Rod.

Not too fucking smart, I said.

Yeah. So of course Artie and his buddies go apeshit. Grab Brendan, hold him down, tie him up, whatever. There were bruises on his wrists. They clear everybody else out of the room.

Oh fuck, I said. But I thought—Butch told me the cause of death was this silicone thing.

Well, yeah. That's what they wanted you to think. And it's what we did think. I guess the thing is pretty well known in these circles. So they used it. They pumped a bunch of it right into his lungs.

Jesus fucking Christ.

Yeah. Some ugly shit there.

I put my head on the table. I felt sick.

And Eloise, said Butch.

I lifted my head. Eloise.

Yeah, said Rod. Well, she didn't get that all night. She tells them Brendan was just some nutcase, a stalker. They believe her enough they let her go. But somehow they find out different, send Jerry out to her place, take care of her.

Shit, I said. The teeth.

The teeth?

Yeah. That's all I saw of him in that mask. The shitty teeth. I didn't put it together. I noticed his teeth at Yugo's.

Yeah, well, you wouldn't have been thinking in that direction.

Fuck no.

So anyway you cowboys fuck that one up, just before Vladmir gets there.

Christ, I can't believe it, I said.

What now?

I was right about something.

Congratulations, said Rod. So next night they go to the club, her and Vladmir. He's going to take care of these guys.

Real smart, said Butch.

Yeah, said Rod. There's a whole room full of them and one of him. I mean, the guy's big, he's a mean sonofabitch, but those ain't good odds. So they grab Eloise in the ruckus, get him out of there.

And . . .

Yeah.

So tonight Vlad tracks them down again, chases them to the parking lot.

Got to give it to the guy, said Butch.

The guy don't give up, said Rod.

Doesn't talk easy either, said Butch.

Took a while to get him going, said Rod. Had to have him listen in to what those other clowns were saying about him. Honor among meatballs, I said.

Something like that, said Rod.

So that's the whole fucking story?

We're pretty sure it is. That's what we got. It fits everything we know. Nothing any of those fucks is saying changes anything much.

Aw Jesus, I said.

Sorry, said Rod.

Silence. The coffee got cold. It didn't improve the taste.

So how did they get Brendan's body to the casino? Dump it there without anyone seeing?

I was hoping you wouldn't ask that, Rick, said Rod.

What do you mean?

Butch looked away.

It can't get any worse, I said. Just lay it on me.

Well . . . shit, I'll just tell you. He was still alive.

Still alive?

Yeah. I mean, it kind of makes it worse. He's suffocating with this shit in his lungs. But slowly. He's still conscious. They drive him over to the casino. We got it on tape, from the security cameras. They drive up in this panel truck. Push him out. He staggers in the door. Collapses. By the time you get there, of course, he's gone.

Christ on a stick, I said.

Yeah.

I got up, walked around a bit. Thought about Brendan, desperate for air. Those sick fucks.

Something else was bothering me.

Panel truck? I said.

Yeah.

What did it look like?

Kind of a hot rod thing. Not exactly inconspicuous.

Fuck. A guy who fixed up old cars. An impossibly deep voice.

Was it red? I asked.

The tapes are black-and-white. Could have been.

An old one, from the forties?

Yeah. Looked like it.

Big chrome exhaust pipes from the engine compartment flaring out the back?

Yeah. How the hell'd you know that?

I can't fucking believe it.

What's up with this, man? asked Butch.

When Bruno punched me out, on the expressway?

Yeah.

That was the truck.

You're shitting me.

No. That was the truck. And when you put the speaker on in there, Rod? That way deep voice? I knew I'd heard it before. The guy driving the truck. It was Vladimir.

Whoa, said Butch. Are you serious? So Bruno's mixed up in this, too?

Mixed up, I don't know. In the Eloise thing, Brendan, I don't think so. I really don't think so. But he sure as hell knows those Russian guys.

I must have seen him five, six times hanging around with Evgeny and those. And now Vladimir. Hah.

What?

Explains why he told Delgado, I mean Andy, that his name was Vladimir.

A little private joke.

Yeah.

The fucking shit-heel.

I don't know, Butch. Yeah, he's a shit-heel. Doesn't pick his friends very well. But when we played that heads up, I don't know, I kind of started to like the guy.

No accounting for taste.

Luckily, said Rod, we don't rely on your taste in meatballs to make decisions around here. We'll pull him in.

Yeah, I said. I guess you should.

I shook my head. There was only so much I could take in.

Rod went back to the control room. Butch and I sat in silence. I played with my cup of cold coffee. He leaned back and closed his eyes.

Fucking Brendan, I said after a while.

Yeah.

The problem, I said, was built into him. He could just never fit in. He always wanted to fit in. He had this kind of desperation.

Yeah, I know.

And in the end, what happens? He breaks the cardinal rule, the unwritten laws of the group. He interferes with the natural order of things. And pays the price. For not getting it. Not fitting in.

What rule?

You don't bring a priest to an orgy.

Jesus.

Him neither.

I need a drink, said Butch.

I'm with you, I said.

89.

NEXT MORNING, before the flight, I got a call from Rod. They'd brought in Bruno. He was very cooperative. Seemed like he knew about the chip scam. But they weren't going to hang anything on him for that. And he didn't know anything about the Eloise thing. I mean, he knew about her, from Vladimir. But he didn't know anything about what happened to her. Or Brendan either.

They believed him.

I was relieved. It didn't make any sense, but I was. I'd had enough. I wasn't going to think about it anymore. Tempt the fools.

I had a few hours to kill. Figured I'd make one last pilgrimage to Binion's. God knows what they'd do to it now. Might even raze it to the ground, build some Megalopolis in its place. Eighty-six floors of dancing cleavage and slot machines.

The cab smelled of cheap cigar smoke, and nostalgia.

I told him to let me off a couple of blocks south of the Promenade. I'd take a last stroll through Loserville. Never know who you might meet.

I stopped at a boarded-up storefront to light a smoke. I tried to imagine how it looked thirty years ago. A hat shop, I decided. Fedoras. Umbrellas. Forget the umbrellas. This was the desert. Lots of fedoras.

A hard hand clapped me on the shoulder.

I turned around.

The face looked familiar.

Can I help you? I asked.

You took my money, it said.

I did?

You took my money.

Oh shit. The flat intonation. The awkward stance. The blank stare.

Yes, I said. I did. I took your money. And I'll give it back. Right now. And I'm sorry I hit you, too.

You took my money, he said.

I took your money. Yes.

I scrambled about in my pockets. How much had it been? I didn't have a clue. The cab had been about fifteen. I'd left the rest in a pile on the bedside table, for the maids. Probably about twenty.

And then he'd have to buy some new overalls.

I found forty-nine amongst the crumpled bills in my pockets. Handed it to him.

You took my money, he said, turning away and walking south.

Good delivery, I thought. Not much range.

I nodded after him. You're welcome, I said.

I turned towards Binion's. I had a hundred dollars left. I'd stashed it in my boot.

I felt lucky.

ACKNOWLEDGEMENTS

Thanks to my muse, Carol Polizzi, for invaluable suggestions and moral support. Thanks to Lana, Max and Tess for infinite inspiration and mostly for being themselves. Thanks to Tristan for being so cute. Thanks to Carol Weiss for inspiration, moral support and not having me institutionalized, yet. Thanks to Nick Garrison for having such a cool noir name and for being a fabulous editor. Thanks to Danny Otten for the inspiration and for being the funniest surrogate half stepson on earth and for knowing everything there is to know about cheesy movies.

Thanks to Dan Bush for being such a poker inspiration and teaching me lots of big words like *sesquipedelian*. Well, thanks to Dan for inspiring me to look up the word *sesquipedelian*, and showing me by example how not to play poker. No, seriously folks, thanks to Dan for being such a good friend and failing to live up to his patrynomic and for being a, well, adequate poker player and pointing out in an earlier draft that T,9,8,6,5 doesn't make a straight. And thanks to the whole lot of them for putting up with me.

Once a high-school dropout, GRANT McCREA went on to become an internationally regarded litigator. *Euromoney Guide* named him one of the world's leading litigation lawyers. Now semi-retired from the practice of law, he writes, plays poker and tries, with varying success, to stay out of trouble. Originally from Montreal, he now lives in New York City.